PUZZLE

WHITE HOUSE MEN 6

NORA PHOENIX

Puzzle (White House Men Series 6) by Nora Phoenix

Copyright ©2021 Nora Phoenix

Cover design: Vicki Brostenianc www.vickibrostenianc.com

Model: Steven L.

Photographer: Eric McKinney

Editing and proofreading: Tanja Ongkiehong

Betareaders: Amanda, Layla, Nonny, Tania, and Vicki

All rights reserved. No part of this story may be used, reproduced, or transmitted in any form by any means without the written permission of the copyright holder, except in case of brief quotations and embodied within critical reviews and articles.

This is a work of fiction. Names, characters, places, and incidents either are the products of the author's imagination or are used fictitiously. Any resemblance to actual persons, living or dead, businesses, companies, events, or locales is entirely coincidental. The use of any real company and/or product names is for literary effect only. All other trademarks and copyrights are the property of their respective owners.

This book contains sexually explicit material which is suitable only for mature readers.

www.noraphoenix.com

CONNECT WITH NORA

Connect with me on social media:
- Hang out in my FB group Nora's Nook
- Follow me on Instagram
- Follow me on Twitter
- Follow me on Bookbub
- Sign up for my newsletter
- Become my patron on Patreon

Check out more of Nora's books:
- No Shame series
- Perfect Hands series
- Irresistible Omegas series
- White House Men series
- Ignite series
- Ballsy Boys series
- Kinky Boys series

And for an overview of all my books and audio books, head over to my website!

PUBLISHER'S NOTE

This is a fictional series, set in the White House as it exists in reality, though obviously with a fictional president and staff. Any resemblance to real people, living or dead, is a pure coincidence.

I've tried to be as accurate as possible in portraying the inner workings of the White House as well as the several federal agencies, but for the sake of clarity and suspense, I've taken some liberties. I've included a list of all the terms used.

OVERVIEW OF CHARACTERS

Some names might be a slight spoiler, so only refer to this list of you've forgotten who someone is! This list only contains important names from this book, not characters you'll only encounter once or from the other books.

Agent Sheehan: FBI Special Agent in Charge on the assassination investigation
Amzi: domestic affairs advisor to President Shafer
Annabeth Markinson: widow to President Markinson
Asher Wylie: Secret Service agent, Milan and Denali's boyfriend
Barry: FBI Assistant Special Agent in Charge on the assassination investigation
Basil King: Mrs. Markinson's step-nephew, co-owner of Kingmakers
Branson Grove: CIA analyst, point person for the investigation (aka "Spookybigdick")
Calix Musgrove: chief of staff to President Shafer, Rhett's boyfriend

Christopher Hales: one of the "fossils" President Markinson appointed to key Secret Service positions
Corey: forensic accountant with the FBI
Coulson Padman: FBI Assistant Special Agent in Charge on the assassination investigation, Seth's boyfriend
Delano (Del) Shafer: president
Denali Weiss: server in the residence, Milan and Asher's boyfriend
Diane: Secret Service agent, head of Mrs. Markinson's detail
Director Heeder: CIA Director
Director Huebner: FBI Director
Donnie Smith: security guard at Baltimore Convention Center (killed)
Ella Yung: National Security Advisor
Governor Winkelmann (R-NC): Markinson's opponent in first presidential campaign
Gulat Babur: suicide bomber who killed the president
Hamza Bashir: leader of Al Saalihin
Henley Platt: reporter, Levar's boyfriend
(Senator) Joanna Riggs (D-NY): vice presidential candidate
Jon Brooks: owner of Brooks Construction and Demolition, former boss of Wesley Quirk
Kennedy (Kenn) Shafer: President's Shafer's son
Laurence Paskewich: former federal prison guard who used to work for Kingmakers
Levar Cousins: White House press secretary, Henley's boyfriend
Lisandra James: Secret Service Director
Matthew: Calix's deceased husband
Max: President Shafer's secretary
Milan Bradbury: the first lady's brother, Asher and Denali's boyfriend
Mrs. Morelli: runs the informal kitchen in the residence

Muhammad Bhat: thwarted suicide bomber
Naomi Beckingham: woman who applied for a job with Christopher Hales and hacked his laptop
Officer Abramson: young cop from the Baltimore PD impound lot
Regina King: President Markinson's ex-lover, Mrs. Markinson' step-niece, sister of Basil King
Rhett Foles: White House photographer, Calix's boyfriend, and Levar's roommate/best friend
Rogue: the First Dog
Ryder Treese: forensic accountant with the CIA
Sarah Bradbury Shafer : First Lady
Seth Rodecker: Secret Service agent, Coulson's boyfriend
Steve Duron: Kingmakers employee
Warrick Duvall: law professor and Kenn Shafer's tutor
Wesley Quirk: Baltimore PD cop who's suspected of involvement in the assassination
William (Bill) Markinson: former president (assassinated)

LIST OF TERMS USED

Air Force One: the president's plane, a special Boeing 747
ATF - Bureau for Alcohol Tobacco and Firearms
ASAC - Assistant Special Agent in Charge
Camp David: the secondary residence of the president, situated in a remote area in Maryland
CAT - Counter Assault Team, part of the Secret Service
Chief of Staff - the right hand of the President, basically the CEO of the West Wing. Other high government officials often have a chief of staff as well, including the vice president and the First Lady.
CIA - Central Intelligence Agency
DoD - Department of Defense
DoJ - Department of Justice
East Wing - a building adjacent to the White House where offices are located, including that of the First Lady and her staff
EEOB - Eisenhower Executive Office Building, where the offices of the vice president and his staff are located. The vice president himself also has an office in the West Wing.
FBI - Federal Bureau of Investigations

HUMINT - Human Intelligence (intelligence learned through direct human contact)

JTTF - Joint Terrorism Task Force

Marine One: the president's helicopter

NCTC - National Counter Terrorism Center

NSA - National Security Agency

NYPD - New York Police Department

OEOB - Old Executive Office Building

PIAD - Protective Intelligence and Assessment Division, part of the Secret Service

Residence - the part of the White House where the first family lives

SAC - Special Agent in Charge

Secret Service - the agency that protects the President of the United States, as well as the First Lady, the vice president and multiple other dignitaries

SIGINT - Signals Intelligence (intelligence learned through picking up digital signals, eg phone calls, emails, etc.)

West Wing - the building where the president and his staff work, which includes the Oval Office. Technically, this is not part of the White House, but is an adjacent building

White House - technically, the White House includes several public meeting rooms like the State Room and the East Room, as well as the personal living quarters of the president and his/her family

WHMU: White House Medical Unit

1

In the background, phones were ringing, and people were talking, the occasional burst of laughter drifting into his office, but Ryder was focused on his work. Sipping his coffee, he was going through the spreadsheets he'd created the day before, as always double-checking for potential errors.

His office was small, and considering it was set up for two people, he'd probably have to share it at some point, but he loved it. The window was in the perfect spot, allowing for natural light but not causing any glare on his screen, and his room was located all the way at the end of a long hallway, minimizing the number of people who dropped in randomly.

The only person who stopped by all the time was Branson, and judging by the rapidly approaching footsteps, he was about to pop in for his good-morning check-in. In the four weeks since he'd worked for the CIA, Ryder hadn't been able to dissuade the man from that habit, no matter how clearly he communicated his annoyance.

Ryder was by nature and temperament a patient and

peaceful man, but if Branson called him Ry one more time, he'd bash him over the head with his keyboard. Well, maybe not with his keyboard. He'd need that to do his job. The heavy brass lamp on his desk, then. It looked plenty sturdy to do some damage, though Branson's head seemed so thick it probably wouldn't even make a dent.

"Good morning, Ry...der," Branson said, flashing that irritatingly sunny smile of his. "You look like you're plotting murder."

As much as he disliked him, Ryder had to admit that Branson Grove was damn good at reading people. He'd unfailingly called him Ry when he walked in since Ryder had started working here, but one look at Ryder's face today had him changing course. Fascinating how the man seemed to sense he'd reached the end of Ryder's patience.

"Good morning," he said, biting back a sigh.

"Donut?"

Branson held out a Dunkin' Donuts box, flipping it open. He had Boston Kreme donuts. Branson wasn't playing fair, was he? It hadn't taken him long to discover Ryder's weakness for sugary treats, especially if they contained chocolate. Every time Ryder had wanted to throttle him, Branson had averted his intentions by offering snacks. Between that and his brown puppy eyes, Ryder had a hard time holding on to his irritation.

That Branson was way too good looking didn't help either. His checkered dress shirt was molded tightly around his muscles, showing off the perfect lines of his biceps and chest. And Ryder had no doubt that the man had a six-pack hidden underneath. He looked like a classic jock, one of those annoying, overly muscled assholes who had tried to make Ryder's life hell in high school. Not that they'd ever succeeded. Ryder simply hadn't cared enough about their opinion to let their stupid remarks get to him, and once they'd realized that, they'd quickly moved on to another victim. In other words, Branson Grove was hot as fuck. Ryder wasn't sure of Branson's sexual orientation, though. Not that it mattered.

"I'll take one. Thank you," he added, if only because his parents had instilled manners in him. He'd had to force himself to use them with Branson, but he'd made his folks proud so far. Then again, he always had...and it hadn't been hard.

"My pleasure."

God, Branson was so...happy. In itself annoying, but especially at eight in the morning, when Ryder was still working on his first cup of coffee. He needed at least two to be fully awake, three before anyone should even attempt a conversation. Couldn't a man wake up in peace anymore?

Branson magically made a napkin appear and handed it to Ryder, who took it and used it to take his donut out of the box. He set it on his desk, then turned back to his screen.

"Don't forget to eat it."

He frowned at Branson. "What?"

Branson gestured at the donut. "Make sure you actually eat it."

"Of course I will."

"You mean, like two days ago, when you finally realized you were hungry at three p.m.?"

Ryder's cheeks heated. "I was focused on my work."

Branson's smile was gentle. "I know. Just make sure you eat it sooner, okay? You get grumpy when you haven't eaten."

"Hangry." Ryder cleared his throat. "The correct term is hangry."

"I'm not worried about labeling it correctly as much as I am about preventing it. For both our sakes."

Ryder didn't look at him. Even more annoying than Branson's stubborn cheerfulness was the fact that he was often right. Frustratingly often. "I will."

"Good. Let me catch up on my email and study the reports from the night shift, and then I'll check in with you, and we can talk about where we're at." Branson checked his watch. "Nine okay for you?"

"Yes, thank you."

That would allow him time to finish the brief for the legal team on the access he needed from the Central Bank of the United Arab Emirates. Once that was done, he'd call Corey, the FBI's forensic accountant, to hear about his progress.

Branson must have left at some point, though Ryder hadn't noticed, too immersed in his work. After double-checking his report for Legal, he sent it off. There, done. His eyes fell on the donut, still sitting on his desk. It would have to wait a little longer. He could hardly eat while on the phone with Corey.

"Gimme one sec," Corey said as he picked up the phone.

"Sure."

The rapid *clack-clack-clack* of a keyboard made him smile. Ryder had switched the standard-issued keyboard for his own—with the approval of his supervisor, obviously. He preferred the mechanical keyboards that had a distinct *clack* whenever you pressed a key over the quiet ones that were common here, especially when putting in numbers on the numeric keypad. His brain somehow kept track of the sounds, knowing when he messed up. He wasn't even sure if he heard it was the wrong sound, if the rhythm was off somehow, or what it was, but he'd know before he even looked at the screen. Apparently, Corey was the same.

"Okay, I'm ready," Corey said. "Sorry, I was entering tax return numbers and didn't want to have to start over."

"No problem. Just wanted to check in with you to see if you had any news."

"I do." Papers rustled. "The IRS has sent Kingmakers the official notice that they're being audited. The good news was that Kingmakers' last tax return actually had some unexplained irregularities and differences compared to previous years, so the IRS didn't have to search for an excuse."

"Good. Less chance of them getting suspicious."

"Are you familiar with how the IRS audit process works?"

Ryder smiled, even though Corey couldn't see it. "I worked for the IRS as an auditor and later a forensic accountant, so yes, I know all the ins and outs. Who are you working with?"

"Marcia Lopez."

"Oh, she's the best. I worked with her on several cases. She's one of my mentors, actually, and the person who recommended me to the CIA."

"I've found her extremely pleasant and professional to work with, so that matches my experiences."

"Anything else?"

"Yes. I've gotten access to Kingmakers' bank accounts and credit card statements over the last ten years. I've only started to go through them in detail, but I did flag all travel expenses to the Middle East in that time period. Since much of their work was for the US government in Iraq and Afghanistan, there could be a legitimate reason for visits to countries like Bahrain, Qatar, Pakistan, and the UAE, but I've compiled a list of all expenses and dates. That way, you can cross-reference with whatever you find on Hamza Bashir and Al Saalihin. I'll send it to you in a minute."

"Perfect. I look forward to that list. We're especially interested in anything that involves Qatar, Oman, and the UAE, specifically Dubai and Abu Dhabi."

"Oman? I wasn't aware the investigation had links there."

"As of now, we don't, but it's a quick drive from Dubai across the border into Oman, and on that side of the country, Oman consists of nothing but desert, so quite easy to do business with no one noticing."

He was merely repeating what Branson had told him, of course. He'd done his due diligence and had performed a thorough orientation on the area, talking to several specialists and analysts to get a good picture, but Branson's knowledge was encyclopedic. Then again, he was also fluent in Arabic, which made it easy for him to use different sources than English ones. Ryder had tried to learn French once upon a time, but his brain didn't do well with languages.

"Gotcha. I'll pay specific attention to those."

"I'll also send you a list of the critical transactions so you can look for those on your end."

Together, Branson and Ryder had made an overview of all suspicious big transactions, like the payment for the assassination, payments to the bombers' families, and more. It would help both Corey and Ryder in knowing what time periods to focus on initially.

"That'd be helpful. That was it for me. Anything else?" Corey asked.

"Nope, all set. Next week, same time? We can always reach out if something comes up."

"Sounds good to me. Talk to you later," Corey said, then ended the call.

God, Ryder loved working with people who were as task-oriented as he was. Corey didn't chitchat, didn't need to talk about the weather or sports or any of that shit. They both got to the point, exchanged information, and bam, done. It would save so much time if everyone were that efficient.

A ding alerted him to a new email. Corey had sent over the promised list of dates and expenses. Ryder inspected them, going slow to allow his brain time to match them to whatever information it had already stored. He'd feed the information to his software, which would automatically look for patterns, conflicts, and matching data, but his initial review often revealed the first anomalies.

He focused on expenses from 2014. The Pride Bombing had been in 2015, so the year before would have been a crucial period for preparation. Basil King and Kurt Barrow, the owners of Kingmakers, had purchased plane tickets from Washington DC to Dubai with Emirates for a trip in September 2014.

He checked all expenses in that month. They'd reserved two rooms in the Jumeira Beach Hotel, and a quick check showed that it was close to the Palm Jumeira, the famous island in the shape of a palm tree. Dutch water engineering at its finest, since it had been two Dutch firms who had reclaimed that land from the sea. Ryder's father, an engineer, had talked about it a few times. How anyone dared to live on what had once been water was beyond Ryder, but that was a different matter.

He narrowed his eyes. King and Barrow had spent two nights at the Jumeira Beach Hotel, then another two...but one night between the two remained unaccounted for. Where had they been that night? He combed through their bank accounts and credit card records. Good god, this company used fifteen different cards and five business checking accounts in the US alone. Besides those, they had a slew of other accounts in different countries. As if they wanted to make it as difficult as possible to track their activities.

It took him an hour, but then he'd found it. One credit card had a charge from Mezyad Border Post, and when he searched for that name, the result made his heart skip a beat. They'd paid 320 dollars for two tourist visas for Oman, which would allow them to stay there for a maximum of thirty days. They must've crossed into Oman right after.

If Branson's deduction based on Hamza Bashir's clothing was correct and he was from the UAE, he wouldn't need a visa to travel to Oman. They would've had to meet somewhere, though someplace where two white Americans could stay for a night and rendezvous with an Arab man without too much suspicion. Where was for Corey and Branson to find out, while Ryder would need to trace the payment for that hotel, so he put it on his list. If they had made some agreement at that contact, money would've likely changed hands in the weeks after.

Hmm, another trip in December 2014, this time to Qatar and for just Basil King. Had he met with Bashir there? Ryder checked all payments, his frown increasing as he put all transactions side by side. Plane ticket, hotel in Qatar for one night, a withdrawal of fifteen thousand dollars in total from their various bank accounts, and then nothing for three days. No payments, nothing. Radio silence. The payments started again three days later with a charge for a different hotel in Qatar for one night and the day after, a flight to Iraq, where King spent four days before flying home through Bahrain.

Ryder leaned back in his chair, taking a sip from his coffee. Oh, yuck. He winced at how cold it was. He put the cup back down and pushed it away from him, his eyes never leaving his screen. So for three days, Basil King had gone offline, not spending a dime on his cards. The large withdrawal suggested he'd paid cash, but that was highly unlikely for a reputable business like a hotel or an airline. No, one paid cash if one wanted to fly under the radar. So where had he gone? Where could he have traveled from Qatar with that amount of money?

Ryder made some notes to discuss with Branson and added the dates to his own list of things to check for. He rubbed his hands. God, he loved his job. Untangling puzzles like this was such a challenge. His eyes fell on the donut that was still on his desk. Oops. He'd better eat that before Branson would see it and get on his case again. The man seemed to take some perverse pleasure in confronting Ryder with his flaws.

Wait, what time was it? He checked his watch. Huh? How could it be past noon already? And hadn't Branson said he'd stop by at nine? Had something come up? He could've at least let Ryder know. He'd have to meet Branson in his office, then. With a sigh, he stuffed half the donut into his mouth and grabbed his laptop. Please let the man keep it short. Ryder had more to do.

2

"I thought we were meeting at nine?"

Branson looked up from his screen, where he'd been studying the latest report from their agents on the Arabic Peninsula. They were tracing every possible lead on Hamza Bashir, and while it was slow going, they were making progress. "We were."

Ryder frowned as he pushed his thick-rimmed glasses back up his nose. His hair was sticking up in every direction, a sign that he'd been playing with it habitually. He did that when he was mulling something over, Branson had noticed. It was adorably cute and contributed to Ryder's high geek factor, which Branson found surprisingly attractive. Ryder's regular outfit of dark blue slacks with either a light blue, a white, or a blue-white-striped dress shirt shouldn't even be remotely sexy, but Branson thought it endearing.

"But it's past noon now. I don't understand."

"I stopped by at nine, but you were working and didn't seem inclined to allow interruptions."

Ryder at work was a sight to behold. *I get sucked into whatever I do.* That was what he'd told Branson when he had started working with him. Understatement of the decade. He had hyperfocus, the ability to sink into his job so completely that everything around him disappeared. Branson had stood there for minutes without Ryder ever noticing him, clacking away on his keyboard, hunched over while occasionally remembering to drink his cold coffee. How Branson knew his coffee was cold? Because Ryder winced every time he took a sip yet never got up to get himself a fresh cup.

"Oh." Ryder's frown intensified. "You stopped by? In my office?"

Branson grinned. "Stood right in front of your desk for a minute or two, then decided that I could wait, since whatever you were doing had your full attention."

A faint blush stained Ryder's cheeks. "Sorry? Corey sent me the first financial data from Kingmakers, and I found some interesting things."

"It's all good. We can talk now. Why don't we grab some lunch and eat while we talk?" He noticed a smudge of chocolate in the corner of Ryder's mouth. "Or did you only just eat your donut?"

Ryder looked sheepishly. "It was yummy. But I could eat lunch."

"Awesome, let's go."

He'd been working with Ryder for a month now, and he'd discovered a lot about the man in that time. Like the fact that he often forgot to eat, getting too immersed in his work. Branson had made it a habit to combine work meetings with meals so he could at least make sure Ryder ate. He wasn't that hungry for lunch himself yet, but he'd save some for later.

They talked little as they joined the line in the cafeteria, then each ordered their food. Ryder was a man of habits, usually choosing a club turkey sandwich with oven-baked chips and a small house salad with Italian dressing on the side, accompanied by a carton of milk. Branson picked whatever he was in the mood for, and the lasagna looked especially appetizing today. He grabbed a to-go box to take half of it back and put it in the tiny fridge he had in his office.

Ryder walked to a table in the back—as always—opting to face the wall and sit with his back toward the room. Funny how he always chose the exact opposite of what Branson would do. He always, always sat with his back against the wall so he could see what was happening. Ryder's position would make him hella nervous.

For the first few minutes, they ate in silence, Branson watching with amusement as Ryder wolfed down his sandwich. He might often forget to eat, but when he did, he could stow away a crap ton of food for someone as slender as him. He wasn't skinny, his body naturally slim and sleek.

"I guess I was hungrier than I realized," he mumbled with his mouth full when he caught Branson's eyes.

Branson smiled. "Knock yourself out, dude. It beats throwing half of it out. I hate wasting food."

Ryder cocked his head. "Did you grow up poor?"

"Why would you think that?"

"Many people who are or were poor have issues with throwing out food."

Ryder didn't have much of a filter between his brain and his mouth, which was unusual for an introvert like him. He often said things others might consider rude or too direct, though it never bothered Branson. With Ryder, he always knew where he stood, and he could appreciate that. "No, I didn't grow up poor, but my mom was pretty strict about wasting food. We had an example to set."

"An example?"

Branson nodded. "My father is a US ambassador. I was born in the US, but I spent my whole life in different countries."

Ryder's eyes lit up. "That's why you speak Arabic so well."

"Yeah, we lived in Jordan and Morocco for a few years."

"What other languages do you speak?"

"French. We stayed in Paris for six years, and I went to a French school there. My parents often chose native private schools, not American ones, so I'd be exposed to the local culture and language. My Spanish is decent, and I speak enough German to get by."

Ryder wiped his hands off on a napkin, then cleaned his mouth. A small glob of mayo stained his cheek, and Branson suppressed a smile. He'd point that out before they were done if Ryder didn't catch it himself.

"I tried to learn French, but I'm not good with languages," Ryder said. "As is often the case with people who excel in math and numbers."

Branson gave a one-shoulder shrug. "I'd say your brilliance with numbers more than makes up for your supposed lack of language skills."

Ryder pulled his salad toward him. "I suppose so. I thought it would be cool to speak French, though."

"Why French? Wouldn't Spanish make more sense, as it is the second language here in the US?"

"I like how French sounds. It's so...romantic. Everything sounds so melodious and gentle in French."

Branson chuckled. "Have you ever watched one of those videos where they compare the sounds of several languages?"

Ryder shook his head, his mouth full.

"They'll say a word in English and then repeat it in Spanish, French, Portuguese or something, and then in German. Everything sounds harsh in German. I mean, it's also the way they pronounce it, but to foreigners, German sounds angry."

"Say something in German."

"Hmm, let me think. Oh, right, this was a cool example. A helicopter. In French, it's *hélicoptère*. In Spanish, it's *helicóptero*. In German, it's *Hubschrauber*."

He made the *r* a rolling, harsh one and extented the long *au* sound in the second part of the word, and Ryder giggled. "Do another one."

"Butterfly is another famous example. It's *mariposa* in Spanish, *papillon* in French...and *Schmetterling* in German."

Ryder laughed again. "I see what they mean about it sounding angry. That's funny. What's a butterfly in Arabic?"

"*Farasha*, so another melodious sound."

"I admire you can speak all those languages. Here I am with my poor English, and I struggle with grammar even in that one."

"I'd think grammar would be the easy part for you. It's about rules and systems, and that should appeal to you, since you're such a systematic person."

Something flashed over Ryder's face. Anger? Hurt? Branson wasn't sure, but he'd struck a nerve somehow.

"Let's talk about work," Ryder said, cold and aloof.

What had happened? Something Branson had said had hit a sour note with Ryder, and he wanted to know what. Hmm, he'd have to analyze it later, try to find out where he'd gotten it wrong. "Sure. Tell me about what you discovered in the financial data," Branson said after making sure no one was in hearing distance. Everyone who worked here would have clearance, but one could never be careful enough.

Switching into work mode was like flipping a switch with Ryder. His entire body language changed from his posture to his expression and tone. "I've identified two time periods when one or both of the owners of Kingmakers were on the Arabic Peninsula and went dark for a specific time."

Branson's heart skipped a beat. "Tell me more."

"In September 2014, they both stayed in Dubai but spent one night in Oman. Then in December 2014, Basil King disappeared from Qatar for three days after withdrawing a sizeable amount of cash. I've sent you the dates."

One thing he loved about Ryder was his way of delivering information. No beating around the bush, no long-winded story, just the facts. "Oman? Do you know where they crossed the border?"

"Yes. They paid for a visa at the Mezyad Border Post. I looked it up, and it's close to Al Ain."

Branson pictured the map. Al Ain was pretty far to the south of Dubai and not the most logical choice if they'd been heading for the coastline of Oman, where touristic destinations like Muscat were located. To Sohar, maybe, since it was the most northern bigger city on the coast, but even then, they could've picked a more northern border crossing. No, from Al Ain, there was only one major tourist destination: Nizwa.

Nizwa was a beautiful and characterful old city with a stunning fort that had been built in the seventeenth century to defend the city's position on a major trade route. It sat surrounded by palm plantations that produced the dates the region was known for and, even to this day, held a large souk, an open-air market where they sold all kinds of animals—dead and alive—fruits, vegetables, handicrafts, and more. A few years before, Branson had spent a morning there, fascinated by all the sounds and smells of that male-dominated environment.

But was it a place that the owners of Kingmakers would seek out for purely tourist purposes? Hell no. If they'd driven to Nizwa, they'd done so for a meeting. A smart choice, since Oman was a safe destination for tourists, and while it wasn't overrun by them, it had enough foreigners visit that two Americans wouldn't really stand out. And if Hamza Bashir was indeed an Emirati, he wouldn't need a visa for Oman and would be able to travel there without getting flagged.

"That's really interesting." Branson added that information to the puzzle in his head. He put half of the lasagna in the box he'd grabbed, meanwhile mulling over what Ryder had said. "How much cash did he take in Qatar?"

"Fifteen thousand dollars."

"Local currency?"

"No, US dollars."

"Meaning he had to pay something in cash. Transportation, maybe. I'm assuming Bashir wanted all meetings to happen outside the UAE to avoid drawing attention to himself. Oman is a logical choice, but would they have met there again? That could be too conspicuous, especially since King would need a new visa at the border, which would've been registered. No, he would've wanted to fly under the radar, so where would Bashir have King go from Qatar?"

"Saudi Arabia?" Ryder asked.

"That side of the country is pure desert. Not a single paved road. It would be madness for King to travel there, aside from the risk of getting caught. You said three days, right?"

Ryder nodded.

Branson closed the box, then tapped on it with his

fingers. "He could've left Qatar by boat, but where would he go? The Persian Gulf and the Gulf of Oman are both heavily patrolled because of all the oil platforms. No, he wouldn't get far by boat, not unless he was meeting on the water, but even then. Too many eyes. It would have to be a private plane, but to where?" He snapped his fingers. "Yemen. If Bashir wanted to establish a base in Yemen, he would've had King fly there on a private flight. Great work, Ry. That gives me more things to look into."

Ryder had finished his lunch as well, and Branson got up, eager to start exploring this new information.

Ryder pushed his chair back with so much force it almost toppled over. "My name is Ryder, not Ry."

Branson bit back a smile as they walked over to the area where they'd throw out their trash and return the trays, plates, and utensils. "I know, but you don't mind when I call you Ry, do you?"

"I do mind, as I've repeatedly told you...and I know you're not obtuse, so why is that so hard for you to remember?" Ryder grumbled.

This time, Branson did laugh. God, he loved pushing Ryder's buttons. One thing was for certain. Life had gotten a lot more exciting since Ryder had joined his team. Despite being intrigued by him, he'd never ask him on a date, even though Branson strongly suspected Ryder was gay. His gaydar went off loudly every time he saw him.

But it didn't matter because he didn't do coworkers, and besides, Ryder didn't give off even the slightest vibe he was interested. Maybe he had a boyfriend? Branson would have to find out. Purely to satisfy his curiosity, of course.

3

Ryder groaned as the high-pitched wheezing sound of the vacuum cleaner woke him from a pleasant dream where he'd been abducted by a sheikh for his harem. Mmm, all these naked, gorgeous guys kneeling at his feet, worshiping him and preparing him for the sheikh's massive cock...until his mom had started running the vacuum cleaner. What a mood killer.

He checked the clock. Of course. Nine o'clock on a Saturday morning meant vacuuming. It had for as long as he could remember, and as annoyed as he was from having to wake up, he couldn't even be upset with her. It wasn't like he hadn't known this would happen. Every week, like clockwork. Just like they had dinner at six on the dot, ate fish on Friday—some leftover tradition from his mom's Catholic upbringing, his father had once told him, though what fish had to do with being Catholic, Ryder wasn't sure—and Monday was laundry day.

That was life in the Treese household, and since it had been his own choice to move back in with his parents when Paul had kicked him out six weeks before, he could hardly complain. He'd grown up in a quiet residential neighborhood of Frederick, Maryland, in the house his parents still lived in. On a good day without traffic—also known as Utopia or when pigs flew and hell froze over—it would take him an hour to drive to work, but in reality, an hour and a half was more common and over two hours not even exceptional.

He needed to find something closer to work, but wow, the houses around McLean, where the CIA headquarters were located, were crazy expensive. Even two-bedroom apartments sold for, like, four hundred thousand dollars, and well, Ryder didn't have that in his bank account nor the fifteen percent for the down payment. Oh, he'd have if he hadn't been such a stupid, gullible idiot who'd fallen for the oldest trick in the book.

He hadn't told his parents. They knew Ryder and Paul had broken up, but not the why...and he would never tell them. He could barely think about it without feeling a sense of shame so deep it made his heart clench. No way in hell was he confessing to his parents how stupid he had been to believe Paul had truly loved him. As if.

With a sigh, he rolled out of bed. His mom would vacuum the entire house, making noise for the next half hour, so trying to sleep was futile. He took a quick shower, then headed downstairs to the kitchen, where his father was reading *The Washington Post* at the table. "Morning," Ryder said, patiently waiting for his father to acknowledge him. He'd never had to question whom he had inherited his hyperfocus from.

"Oh, good morning."

His father put the newspaper down, and Ryder frowned as he grabbed cornflakes and milk. His father always read the whole newspaper on Saturday mornings. Even as a kid,

Ryder had known better than to disturb him. For him to voluntarily put his newspaper down was a worrisome break in pattern. Ryder took a seat across from his dad, then dumped his cornflakes in his bowl and poured milk over them.

"Your mom and I were talking yesterday," his father said just as Ryder had taken his first bite. Uh-oh. "You know we love you, and we completely understand you needed a place to stay after you and Paul broke up, but..."

Crap. Ryder's heart sunk. They were telling him to leave.

"Days before you moved back in, your mom and I had decided to sell the house and downsize."

They were moving? He hadn't expected that. "Sell? I thought you guys loved this house."

"We do, but we're not getting younger, son. Your mom's hip and knee are bothering her more and more, and the stairs are becoming an issue. It's only a matter of time before she can't climb stairs anymore. You know how much work the garden is, and while we've always loved it, we're ready for something with less maintenance."

Ryder swallowed. "Where are you guys going?"

"We've bought a much smaller house with a lovely little garden in a senior living community, where maintenance, the upkeep of the communal lawns, and snow removal are included in the monthly fee. It's adjacent to the golf course, and several of our friends have settled there as well."

He couldn't blame them. His mom had retired from her job as a high school math teacher two years before, at the same time his father had stopped working. He'd worked as an engineer for NIST, a technical research facility that was part of the Department of Commerce, his whole life. This next step was a logical one, and how could Ryder begrudge them a peaceful retirement? They'd worked hard all their lives.

"That sounds amazing, Dad. It would do Mom good to have less house to clean."

His father's shoulders lost their tension at Ryder's approval, a stark reminder that the man took Ryder's opinion seriously. He always had. Ryder had been blessed with amazing, supportive parents who had always loved and accepted him. He had been his parents' miracle after trying to conceive for years without luck. At thirty-four, his mom had finally gotten pregnant with Ryder, and after that, she'd never succeeded again. He was it, their one and only son, and he'd never had to doubt their love for him.

"It would. She needs to slow down, but you know it won't happen here."

No, it wouldn't. His mom would never be able to change her routine in this house, not when her habits were so deeply ingrained. "I understand. When are you guys moving?"

"We're putting the house up for sale this week so we can sell it before we'd have to start spring cleanup in the garden. The real estate agent says she expects it to sell fast. I'm sorry, son. I know the timing is inconvenient for you."

Ryder took a deep breath and pushed down the panic that bubbled up. "I'm happy for you guys. You deserve this. Don't worry about me, Dad. I wasn't planning on being under your feet for that much longer in the first place anyway. I need to find something closer to work because the commute is killing me."

Relief bloomed on his father's face. "Yes, I would've loved to sell you this house for a good price, but it's way too big for you...and you'd still have that long drive to work."

Thank god for those two excellent reasons. That spared

Ryder the embarrassment of having to admit that regardless of how good a deal he'd get on this house, he still wouldn't be able to buy it, since he had no savings left.

His father went back to his newspaper, and Ryder ate his cereal, his head spinning. How much time would he have? If it sold fast, it would still have to close, so at least six weeks... but maybe not much more than that. How the hell would he find somewhere else to live in such a short time? And with so little money. The good news was that he didn't have debts. If he kept saving his money—which he'd been planning on anyway—he'd have enough for a first month's rent and security deposit by then. Buying was out of the question, but maybe he could find a rental? Or search for a roommate, possibly move in with someone who already had a great place close to Langley?

He mentally groaned at the idea. He'd always hated sharing a house with someone else, even back in college. They left their stuff everywhere, ate his food, made a dirty mess of the kitchen, constantly interrupted his routine... Roommates were a fucking nightmare.

Even living with Paul had been a challenge due to their differences in preferences. Ryder was a neat freak. Paul was...not, and that was just one example. The idea that at thirty-three, he was sentenced to suffering the frustration of someone else's bad habits was...discouraging. Enraging all over again, but who could he be pissed at other than himself? Paul, but that didn't get him anywhere.

Just as he'd rinsed his bowl and was headed back to his room to brush his teeth, his phone dinged with an incoming text. Dorian, his best friend.

DORIAN: Heard you were back in town. Wanna hang out?

. . .

A WAVE of guilt rolled through him. He'd let Dorian know about the breakup about two weeks after Paul had kicked him out, but he hadn't reached out to him since, too ashamed. How could he face his best friend and tell him what an idiot he'd been? Dorian had never liked Paul, and in the end, he'd been right. Not that he'd ever rub it in. He wasn't like that. But still. The shame was real, but now that Dorian had contacted him, Ryder's desire to reconnect with his friend won from his embarrassment.

Ryder: Temporarily until I find a different place, yeah. And yeah, I'd love that.
Dorian: Got anything going on right now? If you don't mind a godawful mess and a cranky two-year-old who desperately needs a nap, I'd be happy to hang out at my place.
Ryder: On my way.

RYDER AND DORIAN had become friends in high school, naturally drawn to each other as the two gay geeks. Dorian had become a research engineer, working at the same place Ryder's dad had worked at, NIST. For as long as Ryder had known Dorian, he'd wanted to be a dad, and when at thirty, he still hadn't found his forever guy, he'd decided to become a single dad. A friend of his had offered to be his surrogate and to donate her eggs, and within a year, he'd become a father to Amelia, who was the cutest girl Ryder had ever seen.

Dorian lived on the other side of town in a relatively new

neighborhood with smaller single-family homes in a classic suburbia setup. The yards were much smaller than where Ryder's parents lived, and the houses stood closer together, but the neighborhood had a cozy family feeling. Ryder parked his Tesla on the driveway behind Dorian's Subaru, which sported a *Baby on Board* sticker.

Before he'd even reached the front door, Dorian had opened it, smiling broadly, Amelia on his arm. "Come on in!"

Ryder gave him a careful hug. "So good to see you." He turned to Amelia, who had hidden her face against Dorian's shirt. "Hey, sweetheart."

"Give her a few minutes. She's super tired."

Ryder followed Dorian into his house. Wow, he hadn't been joking about the mess. Toys littered the hallway and living room, dishes were piled up in the kitchen, and on the dining table was Dorian's laptop amid stacks of papers. If this had been Ryder's place, he'd never have invited someone over, too ashamed of the state it was in. But Dorian had always been easier, especially since he'd become a dad.

Dorian winced. "I know. It's bad. Amelia caught strep at day care last week, and then I got it too, so it's been a week. But I really wanted to see you, and if I have to wait until it's clean and tidy here, it's never gonna happen."

Ryder felt guilty all over again that he'd never reached out to him, but he pushed that feeling down. He was here now, and that mattered more. He studied his best friend for a moment. Dorian's pale skin showed the dark rings under his slightly bloodshot eyes. "You look like you need a nap yourself."

Dorian chuckled. "Dude, ever since I had her, I've learned to function on very little sleep. I'm fine. Can I get you some coffee?"

"Yes, please."

"On second thought, can you make it yourself while I try to put her down for a nap? I'll take a cup as well."

"Sure."

Ryder loved Dorian made him feel so at home. Not like a guest but like a true friend. Thankfully, that hadn't changed, even though they hadn't spoken as much as they used to the last year or so. He walked into the open kitchen, taking a deep breath at the full countertops. He might as well help out a bit while he was waiting for the coffeemaker to be done. He filled it with water and grabbed a filter and coffee, then turned it on.

Everything in the dishwasher was clean, and by opening random cupboards, he had it all in its proper place in no time. He quickly reloaded the dishwasher and turned it back on. There, that was done. A quick wipe over the countertops and stove took care of the last bit of dirt, and the kitchen looked a hell of a lot better.

Dorian hadn't returned to the living room yet, so Ryder decided to wait with pouring the coffee. He didn't want it to get cold if Amelia needed a few minutes to fall asleep. In the meantime, he could make himself useful. He picked up Amelia's toys and sorted them in the stacked bins in her play corner. He found a Swiffer in the mudroom and used it to quickly clean the floors. He wouldn't touch Dorian's papers, but he did wipe down the coffee table.

Hmm, he didn't hear anything. Amelia must've fallen asleep, but why hadn't Dorian come back yet? He'd give him another five minutes, fluffing up the couch cushions and watering the plants. When Dorian still hadn't returned, Ryder tiptoed up the stairs. Amelia's door was open, and he carefully peeked around the corner. Dorian was on Amelia's bed, holding his daughter...and they were both asleep. Aw, poor guy. Despite what he had claimed, he must've been exhausted.

Should he leave? Nah. Naps didn't last that long, and Ryder would rather spend some time with Dorian than be at his parents' all day and be reminded of impending doom. He settled on the couch with his coffee and a copy of *Surely You're Joking, Mr. Feynman!*. He'd read it in college, but he didn't mind a reread, and it would offer a welcome distraction from his housing problem.

4

From the moment Coulson and his team had learned Annabeth Markinson had a second phone, they'd assumed it concerned a cheap, simple burner phone. Asher and Diane Russell had both referred to it as such, and Coulson had had no reason to believe otherwise. Until they'd retrieved it from Diane's safe at her bank and had discovered it wasn't a simple one. On the contrary.

The BlackBerry DTEK50 was considered one of the most secure phones in the world and near impossible to hack when it was locked, which it was, of course. And it wasn't even expensive, especially compared to the latest models iPhones. About a fifth of the price, in fact, and yet that little device had caused major headaches when the FBI experts had tried to hack it.

In the end, they'd succeeded, but Coulson had been beyond frustrated with how long it had taken. They'd counted on Mrs. Markinson using an obvious password, but no matter what they'd tried with words, phrases, or numbers they could think of that might have meaning to her, it hadn't worked. In the end, they'd had to use a brute force attack—what that entailed Coulson didn't want to know—and had managed to crack it.

"Let's hear it." He gestured at Sophia, the team leader of the agents responsible for hacking the phone, to begin.

Sophia clicked on her laptop, and on the screen, a list of calls popped up. "The phone was first used in April 2019, over a year before the assassination of President Markinson. It received both incoming calls and made outgoing calls to four different numbers, all with DC area codes and none of them in use anymore. None of those numbers were registered. On average, she had contact with these people once every two weeks, but we've found a few dates when multiple calls were made in close succession, including in the weeks before her death. We've confirmed that the information we picked up from the cell tower near her house was indeed from this phone. On at least two occasions, whoever she was calling was on the same cell tower, meaning they were in close range of the house."

"How long did the calls last?" Seth asked.

"It differs. Some were under two minutes, others as long as fifteen minutes, and the longest one was almost half an hour. That one was made from the White House, by the way, three months before the assassination."

She clicked to the next screen, which showed a new list of numbers but now grouped by geographical location. "Based on the assumption these calls were between Mrs. Markinson and either Basil King or Kurt Barrow, we checked cell towers around Kingmakers' office and both men's private residences to see if we could identify these calls. The cell tower closest to Kingmakers has processed over twenty of the calls on our list, confirming our suspicion she was in contact with someone who works there."

"That's great work," Coulson said, knowing damn well that cross-referencing cell tower records with a list was a tedious task. "This will help us build our case against Kingmakers."

"Thank you, but I haven't even gotten to the best part."

Coulson held up his hands. "My apologies. Please continue."

Sophia smiled as if to show she hadn't been upset by Coulson's interruption, then took a deep breath. "The phone contains no emails, no text messages, and only one app, which I'll get to in a second. But we did find a browser history, proving that even on a secure phone, you have to use a private browser to protect your history."

She put a fresh picture on the screen, which showed the search history on the phone. Coulson scanned it. *Is being gay in the Marines safe? How to get honorable discharge from Marines. Hamza Bashir. Pride Bombing. Al Saalihin evidence.* Mrs. Markinson had done a whole number of searches, every single one showing that she'd been looking out for her grandson and had tried to find out more about Hamza Bashir and the Pride Bombing. Coulson checked the dates on those last searches. July 2020, right after the assassination. Before that, she'd shown no interest in anything to do with the Pride Bombing.

"The timing suggests she didn't know Al Saalihin would claim the assassination," Seth said, coming to the same conclusion Coulson had.

"I agree," Coulson said. "That must've come as quite a shock to her."

"This is where we get to the good part." Sophia was practically bouncing in her chair. "We don't have to guess how she felt…because she recorded it. The only app installed on that phone was a simple one that records phone calls, which, by the way, is legal in DC but not in Maryland, which requires consent from both parties."

Coulson sat up straighter. "She recorded a call?"

"Yes, sir, she did. This call took place two days after the assassination. Let me play it for you."

Coulson closed his eyes when Mrs. Markinson's voice came through the speakers. "What on earth happened? That was not what I agreed to. You promised me no one else would get hurt. And please tell me this is not the same group who carried out the Pride Bombing."

"What does it matter? You wanted him gone. He's gone." The voice was deep, male, and sounded annoyed.

"Of course it matters. How could you associate me with that horrific group that took so many innocent lives?"

"That's a funny line you draw there, ma'am. You have no qualms about having your husband assassinated, but now that other lives were lost and it's a terrorist group who carried out the order, you have a problem with it?"

"Three Secret Service agents were killed. Three honorable men who dedicated their lives to serving their country and their president. That's unacceptable. You guaranteed me there'd be no other casualties. What happened to shooting him?"

She sounded more assertive than Coulson would have thought possible from the warm, kind lady he'd met. Not that her tone was anything even remotely close to how she'd spoken to him and Seth. Her intonation was crisp and precise, her voice frigid.

"We couldn't figure out a way to get a sniper rifle into any event where we could take him out. Security was still too tight for that." Impatience simmered in his voice, his words coming out as if he was forcing them between clenched teeth.

"You broke your promise to me. I don't take that lightly. You knew very well that if I had known agents would get killed or that you would use these terrorists with their hatred against America, I'd never have agreed to this. All I wanted was for Shafer to be president and get my husband out of the picture. I didn't agree to any of this, and I won't accept it."

Silence followed. Was that the end of the recording? But then that male voice came back. "Ma'am, that sounded awfully close to a threat. Please reconsider that course of action. Much more powerful people than you have tried to take me down and have failed. Remember, your life is just as expendable as your husband's was."

Click.

Holy shit. One phone call had cleared up so many of their questions.

"She didn't know." Seth sounded relieved, almost happy. "She didn't know it would be the same group who was responsible for the Pride Bombing."

"Not unless this phone call is fake, which I doubt," Coulson said.

"We're still working on a more thorough analysis, but so far, nothing indicates this recording was altered or fabricated," Sophia said.

"Was that Basil King?" Gary, one of Coulson's most trusted agents on his team, asked.

Sophia nodded. "We think so, but we're still running everything through our voice recognition software."

"Was that the only recording?" Coulson asked.

"No, she made one more... Let me play it for you. This one was recorded the day after you and Special Agent Rodecker visited her."

They'd gone over to ask her if she'd been the source for

Henley Platt's article. The same day they'd caught someone observing them...or maybe Mrs. Markinson.

The recording started playing.

"What in the name of God are you doing?"

Mrs. Markinson was furious, spitting out every word.

"A pleasant afternoon to you, ma'am. To what do I owe the pleasure of this call, and what have I done now to incur your wrath?"

His mocking tone sent shivers down Coulson's spine.

"A second bomber, one who was supposed to take out Shafer. That's what you have done."

"Who told you that?" All amusement had disappeared from his voice.

"Is it true?"

"I don't owe you any explanation."

"You lied to me. You told me you'd use a sharpshooter to take out my husband, and instead, you used a bomber. And now I find out you've gone after the vice president as well. Why? I never wanted this."

"That's the problem when you make a deal with the devil, ma'am. It's hard to complain about my dirty hands when you have just as much blood on yours."

"You're a despicable man. I wish I had never made a deal with you."

"Tread carefully, Mrs. Markinson, or you may find you've outlived your usefulness to us." His voice had taken on a sharp edge, the threat crystal clear.

"Do you honestly think I fear death? At my age and after everything I've been through?"

"Hmm, maybe not your death, but I'm sure we can find someone you do care about. After all, an accident could easily happen to a young Marine like Noel..."

Her gasp echoed through the room, and then the only

sound left was her ragged breathing. "You would go after my grandson?" she finally whispered in a broken voice. "An innocent boy who has nothing to do with this?"

The man laughed. "You still don't get it, do you? This was never about you or your weak husband. You were just a pawn, someone we could use to get what we wanted. And trust me, we will get it. If that means arranging for a gay Marine to die young, I'm perfectly okay with that."

"I won't say anything to anyone," Mrs. Markinson said, barely audible. "You have my word."

"Good. I'm glad I made myself clear."

The call ended, and Coulson had goose bumps. The asshole had threatened her with her grandson. Was there nothing these people wouldn't do, no lows they wouldn't sink to?

Seth cleared his throat. "That confirms she had no idea of their bigger plans. All she wanted was for the president to die, which in itself is bad enough, I know."

"I understand what you're saying," Coulson said. "This doesn't exonerate her, but it does answer questions as to what she knew exactly."

"I wonder why they never considered the possibility of her recording these calls," Gary said.

"She wasn't tech-savvy at all," Seth said. "She must've asked one of her grandkids how to put that app on the phone, or maybe she Googled it. She was smart, but not with technical things."

"They must've reckoned they'd ensured her compliance after threatening her grandson. They knew what she would do for him," Sophia said softly. "As a mother, I understand that part. If someone threatened my child, I'd react the same way."

"This is fantastic work, Sophia. Please convey my thanks to your team."

Coulson had never expected to get this much from her phone. Thank fuck Diane had kept it and not thrown it out, which she could've easily done. With this, they had a few more pieces of the puzzle...and it was almost complete. Kingmakers was going down, and Coulson wanted to be the one to slap the handcuffs on Basil King, read him his rights, and then throw the fucker in jail. For the rest of his life.

5

Branson loved his job, but one downside of working for the CIA was that hanging out with friends and family was complicated. Talking about one's job was such a normal thing for most people, yet most CIA employees weren't allowed to reveal much about what they did. His parents knew where he worked, but not what his area of expertise was.

As an ambassador, his father even had clearance for some details. He didn't have the need to know, however, and after everything that had happened with Mrs. Markinson and now Mrs. Shafer, Branson's team leader had made it crystal clear that they couldn't talk with anyone about anything related to their investigation into Hamza Bashir and Al Saalihin. Branson had never shared much about his job in the first place, but he was even more careful now.

That sense of social isolation was one reason why he liked the company's socials the agency organized every once in a blue moon. In the summer, they'd always have a family day where spouses and kids could come and hang out, the sight of colorful inflatable bouncing castles a welcome change of scenery on the otherwise austere CIA grounds.

In the wintertime, they'd have a few socials on a Friday afternoon in the atrium, where coworkers could chat in a more relaxed setting while enjoying soft drinks and snacks. Nothing fancy, but still, Branson never missed one, eager to talk to people without having to watch his every word.

That day, Director Heeder attended as well, his six-foot-five frame easy to spot among the sea of people. Initially, Branson hadn't known what to make of him, a career man from within the intelligence community who had worked for the Military Intelligence Corps and the NSA before making the switch to the CIA. Heeder was an introvert, a quiet man who listened more than he spoke, and Branson had wondered if his personality would be strong enough to counter the considerable pressure someone in his position would be under.

But within weeks, the man had proven himself when he'd taken a stand and had refused to fire an analyst who had come under attack for a wrong report. That had instantly gotten him respect from the workforce, as they all knew they could easily be in that position at some point, and knowing they had the director's backing was a big plus.

Branson's eye fell on Ryder, who was standing to the side, clutching a glass with what looked like Coke. The discomfort was rolling off him in waves, and Branson had no trouble figuring out that a social setting like this was way outside Ryder's comfort zone.

Damn, he looked so stinking cute. Today he was wearing his blue-and-white-striped dress shirt, which was Branson's favorite because it highlighted his slender figure. He had a bit of stubble, not uncommon, though Branson suspected it was more because Ryder had been too rushed to shave than deliberate. His hair was neatly styled, and he'd apparently gotten a haircut the day before, which brought out the slight auburn undertones even more.

Branson had never been attracted to men who were as slim—and dare he say fragile?—as Ryder, since he liked to fuck hard and rough. Most of the guys built like that couldn't take it. But Ryder made him reconsider. Maybe it would be worth holding back for? Not with Ryder himself, obviously, but maybe with someone like him?

For now, he'd settle for helping him feel a tad less uncomfortable. He made his way over, stopping a few times when people talked to him. By the time he'd reached him, Ryder was still in the same spot, sipping his Coke.

"Want me to introduce you to some folks?" he offered.

"I'm good, thank you."

Always so polite. Someone had instilled manners in him, which Branson could appreciate. Call him old-fashioned, but he felt people underrated the importance of being polite and knowing how to behave in every circumstance so as not to draw negative attention to themselves or, even better, make a good impression. One never knew how paths might cross again and how a random person one had been rude to would turn out to be someone important. A crucial lesson his father had taught Branson.

"That's Laura Tresor, team leader for the Al Qaeda team. She's a former paratrooper, and she and I went skydiving once." Branson pointed out the laughing redhead standing right in front of them, talking to Director Heeder.

"Skydiving? Are you into that?"

"No, but she was, and I was curious what the fuss was about."

"Did you like it?"

"I didn't hate it, but I won't do it again in all likelihood. It gave me a thrill for sure, but it was too risky for me."

"My father always said he couldn't fathom why people would voluntarily jump out of a perfectly good airplane."

Branson smiled. That sounded like something Ryder would say himself, so maybe he took after his dad? "What does your father do for work?"

"He's retired, but he's a mechanical engineer. He worked at NIST his whole life."

"Ah, so you grew up around here."

"Frederick, Maryland. My parents still live there."

For a second, it seemed like he wanted to add something, but then he closed his mouth again. Maybe Branson had imagined it? He let it go. "See that short guy there?" He subtly pointed to his left. "That's Steve Koniewski. He worked undercover in more countries than you can count after 9/11. Speaks ten languages fluently and can kill you with his bare hands without blinking an eye."

"That's quite the résumé."

"His biggest hobby is fly-fishing. He's from Montana originally, and it's something he's done since he was little. A year or two ago, he took me out to Big Gunpowder Falls River, just north of Baltimore, to go fly-fishing for trout, and man, that was cool to see. He gets into this zone where he's one with his rod, his line. I sucked at it, but I loved watching him."

"I admire people who have the patience for fishing."

Branson studied Ryder for a moment. "I had you pegged as someone with a lot of patience."

"Oh, I have plenty, but not when my brain has nothing to latch on to. I gotta keep my mind busy with something, and then I have all the patience in the world."

"Hmm, that makes sense."

"I'm also not an outdoors person, and that's putting it mildly. Bugs love me, mosquitoes especially, and my natural clumsiness doesn't jell with adventurous activities. I once broke my arm while stepping off a sidewalk, just saying."

Branson snorted. "How the hell did you manage that?"

Ryder shrugged. "Didn't watch where I was going, so I stumbled when the step was bigger than I'd anticipated, then tripped over my own feet and, of course, tried to catch myself with my left hand. My wrist didn't appreciate that."

Branson tried hard not to laugh too much, but he could picture the whole scene so easily it was a struggle. "How old were you?"

"Thirteen. In my defense, I had just picked up a new book from the library, so I was a bit preoccupied."

"You were reading while walking."

Ryder made a face. "Duh. I'd discovered Umberto Eco's books and had managed to get a copy of *Foucault's Pendulum*. I literally started reading as I walked out the door."

"You read that at thirteen?"

"I was precocious."

Yeah, no kidding. Branson had tried reading *The Name of the Rose* once, Eco's most famous book, but he'd given up after a few chapters. Way too philosophical for him—and he'd been in his twenties at the time. "Good on ya. Do you still read a lot?"

Ryder nodded. "Mostly nonfiction, but yes. I have a sizable collection of books by now. And puzzles."

"Puzzles? Like jigsaw puzzles?"

"No, though I like those as well. No, I mean the brain teaser puzzles, the physical ones where you have to get a key out of an iron cage or finagle until you can free the rope or something."

"Oh my god, those things drive me bonkers. I may or

may not have thrown one against the wall in a fit of rage when I couldn't solve it."

Ryder laughed. "I own close to a hundred of them by now. They're my favorite pastime."

"And you solved them all?"

Ryder looked at him as if he'd just asked the stupidest question. "Of course."

"Considering I couldn't even crack the one I tried, it's not quite so obvious, but okay. Again, good on ya."

A slight frown marred Ryder's forehead. "What does that mean, good on ya?"

"Oh, it's something I picked up from spending a few months in Australia for an internship. It's their version of 'well done' or 'good for you.' The guy I worked with said it at least a few times per day, and I loved it, so ever since, I've been saying it."

"How many countries have you visited?"

Branson blew out a breath. "God, I don't even know. A lot. Pretty much all of Western Europe plus a few countries in Eastern Europe. The Middle East, parts of South America, Australia and New Zealand...Africa, especially Northern Africa, but I've also been to South Africa and Uganda. Asia not as much, but I did visit Japan, Singapore, and Thailand. Oh, and Vietnam and Cambodia. My father attended a memorial ceremony for the Vietnam War, and I got to go with him."

Ryder's mouth had dropped open a little. "Damn. That's...a lot."

"It really helps if your father is an ambassador who also loves to travel."

"Yeah, true. My parents aren't travelers. My dad has been to some places because of conferences for work, but my mom doesn't like to travel, so I haven't seen more than

Canada, Mexico, and a glimpse of the Bahamas, the Dominican Republic, and Puerto Rico on a Caribbean cruise with my ex."

Judging by his tone and the tension that had crept into his face, Ryder didn't hold particularly pleasant memories of that trip, so Branson didn't ask more. "Maybe you'll get to travel more in the future. What's a country you'd love to visit?"

"Italy," Ryder answered. "I'd love to see Rome. Greece too. Spain, especially the Sagrada Familia in Barcelona. And Madrid, to visit the Museo Reina Sofia and see *Guernica* in person."

Branson hadn't expected Ryder to like art. *Guernica*, Picasso's famous surrealist depiction of the bombing of the Basque town of Guernica in 1937, wasn't easy, accessible art either, like a Van Gogh or a Monet. Appreciating a complicated piece like *Guernica* meant studying it, allowing all the elements to sink into you and, in this case, to convey the horrors of that bombing.

"I've seen it in person," he said softly. "I couldn't look away. It's every bit as magnificent as you imagine it to be."

Ryder let out a wistful sigh. "One day, I hope." He cleared his throat. "What about you? Any places you would like to visit?"

Branson didn't have to think. "Peru. I had a friend who wanted to see Machu Picchu, and he never got the chance. I'd like to do it for him if that makes sense."

"He died?" Ryder's voice was soft.

"Yeah. Motorcycle accident. A truck changed lanes and never saw him. He didn't stand a chance."

"How old was he?"

Branson swallowed. He hadn't thought of Lucien in years, and yet when Ryder had asked that question, the tall, lean boy with the messy curls had immediately popped into his head. "Nineteen. He was French. We met at school in Paris."

They'd met and fallen in love in that wild, overwhelming way only teenagers could. The kisses had been frantic and had quickly led to equally passionate sex. Lucien had been uninhibited and unashamed of his sexuality in classic French nonchalance, simply not caring what others thought. He'd once given Branson the blow job of his life... in their school's chapel. They had fucked like rabbits and had loved with abandon, and with one accident, it had all been over.

"You loved him," Ryder said with a hint of surprise.

"I did. It probably wouldn't have lasted, since we were so young, but we never had the chance to find out. But I have beautiful memories of him, and one day, I'll visit Machu Picchu and think of him."

They were quiet for a bit, but the silence felt comfortable to Branson. Then Ryder said, "Maybe one day, you can also visit a place for yourself rather than for someone else."

Branson had no idea how to respond to that.

6

Ryder didn't know why, but Seth and Coulson intimidated him. Nice as they both were, they radiated a self-confidence he could only dream of and that he was envious of. They seemed to have it all: the career, the relationship, and both were insanely sexy. Hell, Ryder had been tongue-tied the first time he'd met them, especially with Seth. No man should be that good looking. Totally unfair to others. If they hadn't been so genuinely kind and professional, it might've been easy to dislike them or even resent them, but seeing as they were, that was impossible.

Disliking Branson was much easier. He certainly qualified as hot too, as Ryder's dick had made clear more than once, stirring when Branson was close. But compared to Seth and Coulson, Branson was annoying as fuck, which helped Ryder dissuade himself from getting too attracted.

"I wanted to update you all in person," Corey said as they settled into a conference room in the FBI building. "I've discovered some things that Coulson felt should be held close to our chests for now because this could have wide repercussions."

Coulson nodded. "The floor is yours."

Ryder leaned forward, and to his right, Branson mirrored his move. What had Corey uncovered?

The forensic accountant took a deep breath as he linked his laptop to the screen on the wall. A spreadsheet popped up, and Ryder scanned it, his breath catching. Oh god. This was big indeed.

"Based on the information Henley Platt got from Bill Clampton, I did a thorough analysis of the finances of Governor Winkelmann's presidential campaign when he ran against Markinson. As Clampton suspected, something fishy was going on. Not only were the donations significantly higher than in any campaign in history..."

He clicked, and the screen showed a graph, visualizing a comparison between Winkelmann's campaign and previous high-budget campaigns. Winkelmann had raised a whopping 823 million dollars—well over 200 million dollars more than any other campaign and almost twice as much as Markinson's 470 million.

Branson whistled between his teeth. "That's a big difference."

"It is...and yet he still lost," Corey said.

"Ouch..." Branson grimaced.

"But take a look at this." Corey showed a new graph. "This shows the percentage of types of donations, categorized as under 50 dollars, between 50 and 200 dollars, 200 to 1000, and above."

Ryder had already interpreted the numbers and had to resist the urge to rub his hands. This was fucking gold. Over 400 million had been raised in donations under 200 dollars, making it almost fifty percent, which was insane compared to Markinson's much more standard twenty percent. And of those 400 million, almost half had been raised in donations of under 50 dollars.

"400 million in small donations?" Seth asked. "With roughly 330 million people in the US, that means everyone over eighteen would've donated twice."

Corey nodded. "Yes, which we all know isn't likely. Now the problem with those donations under 50 dollars is that they can be reported to the Federal Election Committee, the FEC, without identifying the donors, providing they were done at campaign events. And that's what Winkelmann's campaign claimed, that they had raised this money at events. They supplied a list of events, and the keen observer will notice multiple events on the same day."

"That can't be uncommon," Branson commented. "If they're being organized by state or local organizers, they can coincide with events in other states."

"Yes, but if an event held in Bangor, Maine, is reported on the same day and time as an event in Miami, Florida, and both claim that Governor Winkelmann attended, there's an issue. That's a flight of at least a few hours, so no way could he have attended both on the same evening. And that's just one example of inconsistency. My team found many such issues, but also events that were reported but never took place, expenses for hotel rooms and town halls that were claimed but never spent, and more. The deeper we dug, the more irregularities we uncovered."

"That money had to come from somewhere else if it wasn't from actual donors, so the obvious question was who would have the motive to hide a massive donation to a political campaign," Coulson said.

Kingmakers. Ryder was certain of it.

"In the six months before the elections, Kingmakers sold

several properties at a loss, or so they claimed," Corey said. "In reality, they got much more for these sales than they reported to the IRS. They also sold vehicles, guns, and other assets, took out loans, downsized, and let people go, and they cashed in on various IOUs. Both Basil King and Kurt Barrow took a substantial pay cut, as did several of their management-rank employees. I don't have the complete picture yet, but so far, it adds up to almost 200 million dollars."

200 million? That was a significant sum...but not even close to the 400 million they were looking for. "If normal small donations would have been around 80 million dollars and Kingmakers donated 200 million, where's the other 120 million to get to 400 total?" Ryder asked.

"That's the big question now," Coulson said. "We're almost certain that the fraud Kingmakers committed in their tax returns was to cover up massive donations to the Winkelmann campaign, but it's not the whole amount. Someone else donated as well, and we need to find out who."

"You're forgetting something," Branson said. "Someone also paid Hamza Bashir because regardless of who he is, he didn't execute two attacks for free. Where did that money come from?"

Silence filled the room.

"Damn." Coulson leaned forward in his chair. "You're right. What's the price tag for a presidential assassination?"

"I have no clue, but if it was done purely for the money, I don't think it would've been less than ten million dollars. Times two, though I suspect the Pride Bombing had an even higher cost," Branson said.

Ryder did the math. If Kingmakers had paid 20 million to Hamza Bashir, they were 140 million short for the presidential donations, not 120. Granted, 20 million might not seem like a lot when talking about such high numbers, but it was an amount large enough to make it hard to hide. So how had they done it?

"Where do we search for this money?" Seth said.

Ryder closed his eyes, letting the numbers run through his head. Few individuals were capable of coughing up large amounts like that, so it would have to be an organization or a company. A PAC or a super PAC? Those were checked by the Federal Election Committee, though, and with that much money, someone would have double-checked and investigated. No, it had to be a company. Or money from outside the US, like a rich extremist who backed Al Saalihin. Someone who knew Hamza Bashir, perhaps?

But if that were the case, how would they have gotten that much money into the country? Smaller sums were much easier, especially if one kept it well under the limit of ten thousand dollars—the rather arbitrary number where it had to be reported by banks and financial institutes—but transferring 140 million dollars in transactions that small? That would mean roughly 14,000 transactions. No way would that have gone unnoticed, not unless they'd been spread out over at least a hundred different accounts, which seemed unlikely.

No, part of that money had to have come from within the US. Which domestic company had the funds and the motive to contribute that much to a presidential campaign? They would've had to have had much to lose if Markinson won, which he did anyway. And most likely, they had a shared interest with Kingmakers.

Something tickled the back of his brain. He'd read an article a few years ago that had talked about some companies suffering big losses after Markinson had won the elections. Where had he seen it? He pinched his eyes shut, closing himself off from everything and everyone else. Kingmakers hadn't been mentioned in that article, or he would've recognized the name when he'd first heard it. What other companies would have gotten into trouble when Markinson became president? Had he made any drastic economic changes? Plans that would affect certain types of companies...like Kingmakers?

Lightning hit. Oh, god. That was it. It had to be.

When he opened his eyes, everyone was looking at him. "Did I talk out loud?" he asked, confused for a second.

"You were mumbling, but we could all see your brain at work." Branson sounded more intrigued than anything else.

"Give me one minute," Ryder said, then turned to Corey. "Can I borrow your laptop?"

Within seconds, he typed in the website address for the Wall Street Journal archive. He knew exactly where to go, and he didn't even care he was still linked to the big screen. He picked the month, January 2017, then scanned the list of articles that popped up. *There.*

He pulled it up. *Military Contractors Report Staggering Losses.* "In January 2017, the Wall Street Journal reported that four military contractors that supply the US military reported big losses compared to previous years," he said, unable to contain the excitement in his voice. "It stood out because their losses were not in line with the rest of the market."

He opened a second window, then did a quick search on the four companies named in the article. "KADS, Technitron, Powers Aeronautics, and the Sytronics Group all reported losses that deviated sharply from the rest of the market...and all get over eighty percent of their revenue from their defense contracts."

Coulson's eyes narrowed. "What are you thinking?"

"I'm thinking it's interesting that four companies who had most to lose from a new president who would scale back military spending reported a loss before said president was elected. Their losses cannot have been from Markinson's new policies because he wasn't elected yet until November of that year and not in office until months later. And the rest of the defense industry reported nothing even remotely similar. We need the financial records of these four companies because if my hunch is correct, their losses were reported to cover for illegal campaign contributions to Governor Winkelmann's campaign."

Coulson reeled back, his mouth dropping open. "Holy shit, that's totally plausible. Do we subpoena these records? Or do we want to go for an indirect route and do an IRS audit again?"

Ryder hesitated. "From a financial point of view, a subpoena would be better because we could look at previous years, but I don't know how it would play out for the investigation if they know something is going on."

"They would know anyway," Seth said. "I can't imagine that if they were indeed in cahoots with Kingmakers, they wouldn't inform them if they got audited by the IRS, at which point Kingmakers would know what was up as well."

"Good point," Coulson said. "Can you two find out anything without a subpoena? Because this alone isn't enough evidence to get their financial records. We need the proverbial smoking gun."

Ryder and Corey looked at each other. "We'll get on that," Corey said. "I'm sure that between the two of us, we can find the evidence we require to convince a judge."

"If we go that route, may I suggest subpoenaing Kingmakers' records as well?" Ryder said. "If they hear about the others, they might try to destroy evidence. We'd still get them, but it would cost us a lot more time and effort."

"I agree," Coulson said. "And I think it's time we go full frontal in our attack. Let's get as much evidence as possible so we can build an irrefutable case for a judge to get a subpoena. I want one for Kingmakers, for those four companies, for the personal records of both Basil King and Kurt Barrow, and for the presidential campaign of Governor Winkelmann. We'll dig as deep as needed until we've uncovered it all. Let them know we're onto them. They might start making mistakes when faced with prosecution..."

7

Calix drummed his fingers on the armrest of the couch in the Oval Office.

"Chill, would you?" Del asked him, not for the first time. "You're acting as if you're facing the firing squad."

Calix sighed. "Sorry. In my defense, it feels that way."

He wasn't easily intimidated, but John Doty, the minister of defense and a retired lieutenant general in the Army, scared the crap out of him. The man had a coldness over him Calix had found unsettling from the moment he'd met him. Having a cool head might be a good trait to have in combat, but the degree to which Doty possessed one made for icy relationships and frigid conversations.

And now they had to give him some highly unexpected and probably unwelcome news. Calix had promised Del he'd be there for this particular conversation, and he'd never break his word, but he would've paid good money to skip this one. Doty was not someone he wanted to have as an enemy, and yet he was convinced that was exactly what was about to happen.

Del dragged a hand through his hair. "I know. I'm not

looking forward to this meeting either, but the alternative is even worse. I can't have him in the position he's in when we're not sure of his loyalty, especially when the first round of subpoenas is about to hit. I've been told a grand jury has been convened."

"You're being too kind. We're damn sure where his loyalty is...and it's not with you. Not with the constitution either. If what Marcus Pizer told Henley was true..."

"He has no reason to lie," Del said softly. "That's what I keep coming back to. Why would Victor's deputy lie? He has to be telling the truth, and let's face it, what he said explains a lot, like why Markinson kept Doty on as secretary...and why he upped his Secret Service protection."

"I know. I'm right there with you, but..."

A subtle knock on the door and then Issa stuck his head around the corner. "Do you need anything before your next appointment, Mr. President? A water, a coffee, a Coke you'll hide from everyone to make them believe you're sticking to your healthy habits?"

Calix hid his grin behind his hand. Issa was exactly as he'd presented himself in the interview: an absolute firecracker who didn't take shit from anyone, including Del.

Del looked guilty. "I'll have a water, please. And can you charge my Kindle, please, so I can read a bit later?"

"It's already on the charger, Mr. President."

Issa sailed into the room, gesturing at Del to get up. Without a word of protest, Del obeyed. Issa took a step forward, put Del's collar up, then straightened his tie, pulling it tight before folding the collar back in place. "There. Better." He nodded with a satisfied smile, then stepped back. "Water coming right up. For you, Calix?"

Calix pointed at his glass of water. "I'm good, thank you."

"My pleasure."

Calix waited until Issa had left the Oval again. "How is he working out?"

Del looked pained. "He's very organized."

"You're saying that like it's a bad thing."

"Cal, he color-coded my socks and underwear. The man went through my entire wardrobe and color-coded it. It's... mildly disturbing."

Calix snorted. "He's nothing if not efficient."

He stopped talking when Issa returned and placed a cold bottle of water and a glass on the table to the right of Del. He put a small bowl with some cashew nuts next to it.

"To prevent you from snacking on the fun-size candy bars in the bottom drawer of your desk, Mr. President."

Del merely sighed. "Thank you, Issa."

"My pleasure."

"See what I have to put up with?" Del complained when Issa had left again, but his words held no fire.

"You mean someone who makes sure you drink enough water and eat healthy snacks? Yes. Absolute hardship. You have my sympathy."

Del rolled his eyes, but before he could say anything, the door opened. "Secretary Doty is here, Mr. President," Max said.

Calix looked at Del. "Showtime."

They both rose from their seats. Del straightened his shoulders, then placed a quick hand on Calix's right shoulder. "Thank you." Del's eyes softened. "For being by my side."

Calix smiled at him. "I serve at the pleasure of the president."

Del took a deep breath, then nodded at Max. "Send him in."

Doty marched in as if he owned the place, but maybe

that was the self-confidence rooted in years of being in charge of large numbers of troops. "Good afternoon, Mr. President. Calix."

They both got a nod that at the surface seemed affable but made Calix's skin crawl with the underlying condescension.

"Thanks for coming, John."

Calix turned his head away so Doty wouldn't see the laughter in his eyes. That right there was why Del was president and Calix wasn't. Having grown up with an overbearing father, Del had become immune to power games. He played right along up until the point where he'd had enough or it no longer served his purpose, and then he put his foot down. Calling Doty *John* rather than Mr. Secretary or General was far from subtle, but judging by the tightness on Doty's face as he sat down, the warning shot had the intended effect. Del had made it clear he wasn't in the mood to be disrespected.

"What can I do for you, Mr. President? As you can imagine, I had a busy day planned until I was summoned."

And with that, the tone was set. Not that Calix had ever expected this to be a friendly, casual conversation, but the lines were drawn in the sand.

"I'm going to have to ask you to resign, John." Doty took a sharp intake of breath, but Del gave him no opportunity to protest before he'd done his whole spiel. They'd prepared this little speech together, and Calix knew Del would finish it before he allowed Doty to speak. "You've served your country far beyond what could be expected after your distinguished career in the military. I've come to understand why President Markinson kept you on, even though he may have disagreed with your views, but the Department of Defense needs some fresh blood. You've certainly earned your retirement, so it's time to get serious about making that trip to Normandy you talked about recently."

Calix held his breath. They'd come up with this exact wording so Del couldn't ever be accused of lying, but would Doty pick up on the underlying meaning?

Doty's face sported barely concealed anger. "I'm unpleasantly surprised by this, Mr. President. You've given me no indication you took issue with the way I've been fulfilling my position."

"That's because I have no issues with it. It's simply time for a change. I'm not a proponent of having people in the same job for too long. It breeds complacency."

Technically, Del was right. Even though he and Calix both suspected Doty of mixed loyalties, he hadn't done a bad job. At least not in public. The behind-the-scenes stuff was what worried them, but, of course, they couldn't bring that up.

"I assume you have an equally qualified replacement in mind?"

Del looked at Calix, his cue to take over. "We haven't formally asked anyone yet, as we didn't think that appropriate until we'd spoken to you, Mr. Secretary."

"I'm sure you have someone picked already."

"We have, but we don't feel it's the right timing to release names as we haven't approached this person yet," Calix said smoothly.

Doty turned to Del. "You need a strong man in this position. Someone from the ranks of the military who understands how to run the armed forces. After the assassination and the renewed threat we're facing from Al Qaeda and its offshoots, we need to send an undeniable signal that the US military is still the best and the most powerful in the world."

"My vision on the threat level from Al Qaeda differs

somewhat from yours, John, maybe because I have access to more information than you."

Oh, Dell was playing dirty now, and Calix loved it. They'd kept Doty in the loop on the aspects concerning Hamza Bashir and Al Saalihin, but not the domestic component—for obvious reasons.

"I still don't understand why I'm not fully read into the investigation. It's a hindrance in doing my job if I don't have all the information."

"That's a moot discussion at this point, as is your opinion on Al Qaeda. Rest assured that we'll find the best person for the job."

"You're not going to go with a military man?"

His tone grated on Calix's nerves, but he swallowed his anger back. Del had to handle this, and he would.

"We may not even go with a man, John." Del's voice was mild but with an iron edge to it. Did Doty pick up on it as well?

"You can't put a woman in this position. She'll never get the respect from the chiefs of staff and the military in general. Letting women serve is one thing, but they lack the experience at this level of leadership."

"And they always will unless we allow them the same courtesy as we do to men, and that is to give them a chance to prove themselves."

The steam was practically coming out of the man's ears, but he had the smarts to hold back. Maybe he realized that this wasn't an argument he'd ever win. "I'll stay on until you've announced my replacement."

"That won't be necessary. I'd like you to resign now," Del said.

"You can't leave the Department of Defense without a leader."

"It won't be. Deputy Secretary Karyn Barette will lead in the meantime."

"She's not suitable to lead the whole department. She's served for only four years, and that was eons ago."

"She left the Army with an honorable discharge because of injuries sustained in battle. I'd say that's a damn good reason to cut a military career short. Besides, I've only served four years, and I'm the commander in chief, so I'm confident we got this."

"With all due respect, Mr. President, but you need someone with more military experience."

"I don't, actually. The secretary of defense has always been intended as a civilian position. When President Markinson wanted to appoint you, he needed a waiver from Congress, since you'd only retired two years prior. I think it's time to bring civilian leadership back in this position."

"Mr. President, I must once again object to—"

"John, we're done talking about this. I'm giving you the chance to resign and walk away with your head held high. You have until five p.m. today. If you don't, I'll fire you, leaving you with a stain on what is otherwise an honorable career of serving your country."

Del rose to his feet, sending a clear signal this conversation was over. Doty got up as well, his face red. "You will regret this."

"That sounded an awful lot like a threat to me. Are you threatening me, General...like you threatened President Markinson?"

Del's eyes were spewing fire now, nothing left of his previous concern about what Doty could do in retribution. Apparently, he'd decided to fuck caution and confront him. Del was usually so mild-mannered, rarely losing his temper, that outbursts like this always made an impression on Calix.

"I never threatened Markinson."

The first crack in Doty's confidence was obvious, a slight tremor in his voice and a nerve that ticked right beside his left eye.

"We both know you did...and why."

The tic grew stronger. "I don't know what you're talking about."

"If that's the truth, then you have nothing to worry about. If not, you should be afraid. I'm not President Markinson. I don't run from a fight, and I sure as fuck don't hide, not even after losing my wife. And I swear I will move heaven and earth and leave no stone unturned to find each and every person responsible for her death and the senseless murders of all the others who perished...and when I do, there won't be a place to hide for them. That mighty US Army you bragged about? I'll send it to the ends of the earth if I have to, to capture them all, and I will bring them to justice. And that's not a threat, General. That's a promise."

That had gone well.

8

They had a name. Holy shit, they had a name.

Branson blinked, unable to believe his eyes. But no, he'd been right. The facts were irrefutable. A week ago, they'd made the breakthrough discovery on Winkelmann's presidential campaign, and now he had a name. Justice would be served. It had taken them much longer than it should have, but by god, they would nail these bastards for the lives they had taken.

He wanted to tell someone. He wanted to tell...

Why was Ryder's the first name that popped into his head? Why not Weston, his team leader, or even Seth or Coulson? It made little sense. It had to be because they worked so well together. Ryder was just as stubborn in resisting Branson's teasing as Branson was in calling him Ry. He didn't know why, but he liked to press his buttons. A flustered Ryder was even cuter than a normal one.

"Do you have a copy for me from—"

Branson spun his chair around at the sound of Ryder's voice. If he was here, no way was Branson not sharing his news with him. "I have his name."

Ryder frowned for a moment, but then his face lit up. "You found him? Hamza Bashir?"

"Yes. Look..." Ryder peered over Branson's shoulder as he turned back to his screen. "It has got to be him. He was in Qatar when Muhammed Bhat had his meeting in the mall. He was in Oman in September 2014 when Basil King and Kurt Barrow were there. And he was in Yemen in December 2014 when King traveled there."

He pulled up the picture he had found. "His picture matches the man we saw on the security footage from the mall in Qatar. His name is Yazid El Sewedy, and he's a citizen of the UAE, born in Dubai. He's thirty-one, he studied at Oxford, he's single...and he's rich."

Behind him, Ryder gasped. "It's him. It lines up."

"Yes, it does. Beyond a shadow of a doubt, it's him. We have our man."

He pushed his chair back and got up, joy flooding his system. He had him. After six years, they had the real name of Hamza Bashir. His face split open in a grin so wide it almost hurt. He'd done it. Not by himself, of course. It had been a massive team effort from people from all agencies within the intelligence community...but he'd been able to piece the final bit together.

On impulse, he hugged Ryder, then lifted him off the floor for a second. Ryder laughed, not giving any indication he didn't want the embrace. Why wouldn't he? It was just a friendly hug between coworkers, a celebration of a major triumph. A hug that, admittedly, felt surprisingly good, but that had to be his high from the discovery. Branson held on a moment longer, then released him.

"Congratulations, Branson. That's fantastic work," Ryder said, beaming.

Branson raised his hands in the air. "Victory is mine! I drink from the keg of glory."

Ryder giggled, a sound that always settled deep inside Branson, maybe because it was such a rare occurrence. Ryder was usually so serious. "It's a good day when you're quoting the West Wing."

"It's the best day ever. We should celebrate."

"*You* should celebrate. My work is only just beginning. You found a name. Now I have to tie him to Kingmakers financially."

Branson waved his words away. "Details. You're brilliant at what you do."

"Thank you."

He put his arm around Ryder. Yup, he really liked touching him. Still riding that high, probably. "Now let's celebrate. I'll treat you to the best lunch we can get in the cafeteria."

Ryder laughed again, and Branson loved the sound. "Don't go crazy now."

"I can afford this. I think. And after lunch, I'll set up a meeting with Coulson so we can update him."

He should remove his arm, though Ryder didn't seem to mind. In fact, he was leaning into Branson's touch a little, and Branson filed that fact away to ponder later. For now, he'd settle for a fun lunch.

His phone rang, and while he was tempted to let it go so they could leave, he had to at least check to see who it was.

Mom.

His heart skipped a beat. She never called him at work. Ever. And he'd talked to his parents two days before, since they were on a brief vacation in the US. He let go of Ryder and picked up. "Mom? Everything okay?"

"Branson, sweetie, I need you to be strong now, okay?"

Icy fear replaced the joy he'd felt only seconds before. "What's wrong, Mom? Did something happen to Brenda?"

"No, it's your father. He hasn't been feeling well lately and had some complaints, so we had him checked out while we were stateside on a quick visit. I don't know how to say this, but he's... He has cancer."

Ohgodohgodohgod. He reached out, and Ryder grabbed his hand, stepping so close to him Branson could lean against him. "What kind of cancer?"

"Colon cancer. It's... It's bad, sweetie. I'm not gonna lie. He's determined to beat it, but he's in for the fight of his life."

"Mom..." His voice broke.

"He needs you to be strong. I need you."

"I'll be there. Does Brenda know?"

"I'm calling her next."

His twin sister, an Air Force pilot, was stationed overseas in Incirlik, in Turkey. He checked his watch. It would be early evening there, so still plenty of time to call. "Where's Dad now?"

"Georgetown University Hospital. They're running more tests today, and they want to schedule surgery as soon as possible to remove part of his colon."

Ryder nudged him, and when Branson looked, he held up his phone with a word scribbled in a notes app. *Metastasis?* Oh, good question. "Mom, has it spread? Is it metastatic?"

"That's what we'll find out after today, but the surgeon said it won't change the initial treatment plan. It might mean he'll have to undergo more radiation and chemo, but we don't know that yet."

"Okay. What can I do? What do you need?"

"I'd love for you to come to the hospital if you can, but I understand if you can't get away."

"I'll be there."

"Branson, you have an important job. Make sure it's okay to leave."

"I'll be there, Mom. They'll understand."

"Okay. I love you, sweetie. We'll get through this."

"Love you too, Mom. See you soon."

He hung up, dazed. Cancer. His father, the picture of health even at sixty-three, had cancer. How was that possible? The man drank infrequently, ate super healthy, ran five miles every other day, and was still in phenomenal shape. How could this happen?

"I gotta go," he said to Ryder, who was still holding his hand.

"I heard. Georgetown University, right?"

Branson nodded.

"I'll drive."

"You don't... I can drive myself."

Ryder's eyes were endlessly kind. "You just heard some devastating news. You shouldn't be driving now."

He had a point. "I need to tell Weston I'll be gone for the rest of the day."

"I'll let him know when I tell him I'm out for a bit."

Branson packed his bag, only vaguely registering Ryder making a quick call, then hurrying out to get his own briefcase before coming back for Branson. He felt like he was sleepwalking when they made their way out into the parking lot. This couldn't be real. It had to be a bad dream, the worst nightmare he'd ever had. Except it was real, wasn't it?

He didn't say a word as Ryder drove him to the hospital, his Tesla barely making a sound as he weaved in and out of lanes, driving as smoothly as a cab driver. Branson cleared his throat. "Do you know where it is?"

"Yeah. My erm... My ex works there, and I often picked him up from work."

His ex? That confirmed Branson's sense that Ryder was gay and answered his question about whether he was single. "What does he do?"

"He's an attending surgeon, hoping to specialize in cardiothoracic procedures."

His tone was clipped, his face tight. Oh, there was a story there, but Branson let it go. Now wasn't the time. "You can drop me off at the entrance," he said.

"Okay."

Ryder navigated to the main entrance, then found a spot where Branson could get out.

"Thank you for driving me. I'm—"

"You're welcome. Go."

Branson sent him a look of gratitude, then got out of the car and hurried inside. With help from a kind receptionist, he found the waiting room where his mom sat by herself, leafing through a Vanity Fair. "Mom."

She looked up and rushed to him, then enveloped him in a tight hug. "Hey, sweetie. Thank you for coming."

He held on to her for a moment, giving in to his need for her touch. She'd always been a hugger, someone whose love language was touch, and Branson was the same. His father and Brenda were different, both focusing more on words, but Branson had always felt that one hug could affect him much more than an entire speech. And so he clung to her, allowing her subtle perfume to surround him, her soft arms to hold him.

"Did you manage to reach Brenda?" he asked when he could let go, his eyes moist.

"Yes. We agreed we'd wait on the results of today's tests, but she'll talk to her CO so he knows what's up."

"She should be granted emergency family leave under these circumstances," Branson said. "She's not in a war zone."

His mom nodded. "She didn't expect it would be an issue, but we wanted to wait until we had a clear picture of what the situation was."

They sat down on a pair of burgundy red, uncomfortably hard chairs. "How's Dad dealing with it?" Branson asked.

His mom smiled at him. "What do you think? Your dad's a fighter. He always has been. To him, this is just another battle he has to win."

Branson should have known. His father, a former Marine, had never backed down from a challenge. He always faced adversities head on, choosing to deal with reality rather than delude himself. In college, Branson had learned about the stages of grief and of coping with severe setbacks, and one of them was denial. Even then, he'd realized his father always skipped that phase. He accepted the truth...then went on to badger it, mold it, shape it purely by the power of his will until he'd made it palatable.

"Mrs. Grove?" A doctor stepped into the waiting room, her face professional but kind. "I'm Dr. Porterfield, the attending oncologist."

"Yes. I'm Lisa Grove, and this is my son, Branson."

Dr. Porterfield took a seat across from them. "I have some first results of your husband's MRI, and he gave permission for me to share these with you."

She had bad news. To others, her expression might've been neutral, but Branson picked up on the subtle signs of sadness and stress. She seemed young enough to still be bothered by having to deliver bad news. Branson mentally braced himself.

His mom took a deep breath. "Okay."

"Unfortunately, it's more widespread than we thought, which means we're now at a stage III colon cancer. It's spread to lymph nodes nearby, but his lungs and liver are clear, so that's the good news."

Branson swallowed. It had metastasized. Goddammit.

"Are you still operating?" his mom asked.

"Yes. Our first step is to perform a partial colectomy, so we'll remove part of his colon, which in itself is a complicated surgery that has serious risks. Tumors are unpredictable, so we won't know how much we can take until we can see it on the table. Depending on what we face, we may have to do a total colectomy. Regardless, your husband will have to use a bag for the foreseeable future to collect his stool, either a colostomy or an ileostomy bag, depending on where we can place it."

His father would hate that. He'd always been so proud of his body, of his health.

But Branson's mom waved her hand dismissively. "That's a small price to pay if it means he'll survive."

"We can do the colectomy the day after tomorrow, so we want to keep him to prep his bowels. He'll have to stay for at least four days after, depending on how well he recovers."

"And after that?" Branson wanted to know. "Can you say anything about his prognosis?"

He was afraid to ask because the answer could crush him, but he still needed to understand what they were dealing with.

Dr. Porterfield shot him an apologetic look. "The most likely next step is chemotherapy, but we'll have to take it one day at a time. I wish I could give you a comprehensive treatment plan, but we won't know until we've seen the tumor. And even then, colon cancer is a type of cancer that's unpredictable, so our approach will always have to be flexible so we can adapt if necessary. That's also why, in this stage, I'm not comfortable yet talking about a prognosis or statistics."

"Thank you," his mom said, sounding tired. "When can I see him?"

"We're doing some last tests, but he should be back in his room in half an hour. I'll have a nurse come get you when he's done."

With that, Dr. Porterfield walked off, and Branson took his mom's hand. "We'll get through this."

She leaned her head on his shoulder. "We will. Your dad is the strongest man I know. If anyone can beat this, it's him."

They sat quietly until a nurse came to tell them they could go up to his dad's room. Branson had to fight back his emotions at the sight of his father in that hospital bed. He looked too frail, too old all of a sudden. His hug was still strong, though. "Thank you for being there for your mom." He squeezed Branson's shoulder. "She's gonna need you."

"I'm here," he promised.

"Don't neglect your work," his father warned him, as always clear in his priorities. Branson's parents knew what he did, though obviously not the details. "The world needs people like you to keep us safe."

"I'm only an analyst, Dad."

"No, you're not. If people had listened to analysts in 2001, 9/11 would never have happened. Don't ever forget the power you have."

His father, always the man to offer inspiration. "I know, Dad."

"Make time for your friends as well," his mom said. "Especially in hard times, you need friends."

His friends. Now there was a sobering reality. What friends? He had coworkers, guys he hooked up with, acquaintances, but that was it. Somewhere along the way, he'd forgotten how to make friends...or how to be one, maybe. But he had a fulfilling career and a wonderful family, so it would have to be enough.

After meeting Seth, he'd hoped that maybe he'd found someone he wanted to get to know better, someone kind and loyal, strong and honorable. But alas, Seth's heart belonged to Coulson, and honestly, after meeting Coulson and seeing the two of them together, Branson couldn't deny what a perfect pair they were.

Maybe he should resurrect his profile on that hookup app. He'd called himself *SpookyBigDick* in a lame attempt at an inside joke combined with his best-selling feature. After what had happened with Seth, he'd deactivated it, but he could sure use a good, hard fuck right now, something to take his mind off the thought of his father fighting for his life. He might not have friends, but he'd never had trouble finding a hookup.

Sex, the ultimate distraction. It would have to be enough.

9

Seth closed the door of the boring, sparse FBI meeting room behind him. "Grab a seat," he told his fellow agent, Jules Gallagher. Damn, the guy looked like he'd been on a two-week drinking binge with bloodshot eyes and a pale face. Seth had worked maybe one or two shifts with him, but they'd never been on the same detail as Jules had been assigned to President Markinson's team and had quit after the assassination, even though he hadn't been on duty that night. And now he'd called Seth out of the blue, asking to meet with him.

Jules lowered himself into one of the uncomfortable chairs. Seth wondered if they'd been deliberately picked to be crappy to pressure people into getting to the point. He should ask Coulson sometime.

"Thanks for meeting with me," Jules said.

"Of course."

Jules rubbed his temples, and Seth waited patiently. The man clearly had something he needed to say. "I wasn't on shift when the president was assassinated," Jules finally said, his voice raw.

"I know."

"But I saw the footage and…" He let out a sigh. "My wife asked me to quit. She'd always known about the hypothetical risks, but that event made it clear the dangers were real."

"It's hard on spouses." Seth figured a listening ear would be the best strategy, since he had no idea where Jules was going with this.

"I was relieved to get a job with the local sheriff's department as a deputy. A demotion, but one that came with the perk of seeing my kids, having a more predictable schedule, and, considering the rural county we live in, little danger."

"I can imagine. The Secret Service life is high pressure and can be rough to combine with having a family."

"When I received Director James's repeated requests for anyone who had information concerning the assassination to come forward, I ignored them. I figured it was in the past, and what was done was done. Besides, we all knew that even though, technically, we were at fault, the reality was that we had to do an impossible job under untenable conditions. This one had been coming for a long time."

"Hmm." Seth would keep it noncommittal at this point.

Jules met Seth's eyes. "And since I wasn't on shift, I didn't think I had much to contribute. Especially since I happened to be off the three days prior to the assassination due to a nasty stomach bug that forced me to stay in close proximity to the bathroom."

Seth winced. "Oy. Those are the worst."

"Bad chicken, man. Don't recommend it." He took a breath. "But a week ago, I finally read the director's requests in more detail, and I realized I did know something. She listed specific issues you were trying to get answers to, and one of them was how the bomber got his hands on a Secret Service pin."

Seth leaned forward. "What do you know?"

"It was mine. I lost one and didn't report it."

Bingo. Another piece of the puzzle. Seth forced himself to stay calm. "How did you lose it?"

"Mind you, I didn't notice losing it, but in hindsight, I connected the dots. That guy who called into the radio broadcast with claims about Mrs. Markinson and Mrs. Shafer?"

"Gavin Wedmore?"

Jules nodded. "I collided with him four days before the assassination. I was walking patrol in the West Wing, and he bumped into me, spilling coffee and some kind of salad all over me. He apologized profusely and helped me clean myself up. Because I was on shift, I had to rush down to change into another shirt and suit, and when I did, I noticed the pin missing. I figured it had come off while cleaning myself up, but when I went to look for it, I couldn't find it. I wanted to report it, but things got hectic, and then I got sick, and…"

"And then the president was killed, and it didn't seem important anymore."

"It didn't, not until I read Director James's email. I'm so sorry, Seth."

Seth nodded. "I know. We have tapes of him wearing the pin, but the thing is that we can't know for sure it was your pin, since it was obliterated in the blast. I think your explanation is likely, though, and it eliminates a major concern."

"You were afraid they had an inside man in the Secret Service." He grimaced. "Other than Diane, I mean."

The news about Diane's arrest had made the rounds, first inside the Secret Service and then in the press, though the charges had been kept secret so far, citing national security—not a stretch. "Yes, so you can imagine my relief to know that it was procured through different means. I wish we could've asked Wedmore for details, but alas... I'll check the security tapes to see if we caught the accident on camera, just for full closure, but this seems most likely. Thank you for coming forward, Jules."

"I feel so stupid..." Jules said with a sigh. "I should've known better, should've figured out the connection much sooner."

As much as Seth wanted to agree with him and kick his ass for not speaking up sooner, in all fairness, Jules couldn't have known. Yes, he should have read the emails sooner, but that incident couldn't have made him suspicious on its own. "We weren't trained to look for the enemy in our midst," he said gently. "You weren't expecting a White House staffer to have such sinister intent. You couldn't have known."

"Thank you for saying that. I'm not sure I'll ever be able to forgive myself, though."

"I get that, but remember this. After what happened to President Markinson, we were on high alert...and they still managed to get to Mrs. Shafer."

"Yeah... The whole thing is one big fuckup and an embarrassing tragedy for the Service."

"It is. No one feels that more deeply than me...aside from Director James, perhaps."

"I don't envy your position. I will say that."

"Thank you. It's not easy, I'll admit. But thanks for coming forward, Jules. I appreciate it."

Jules nodded. "Will this have repercussions for me?"

"I can't tell you. That's not my call. I'll report this back to Director James, and what happens after that is on her."

He doubted the director would pursue legal actions

against Jules, but he didn't say it. They had bigger fish to fry than someone who had made a stupid but not deliberate mistake.

As soon as Jules had left, Seth walked into the office he shared with Coulson. More than a few people had commented that they could never survive being with their partner twenty-four seven, but Seth loved it. He and Coulson both had found a good distinction between personal and professional, and only in rare cases did they cross that line.

"What did he have for you?" Coulson asked as soon as Seth sat down. He'd known about the appointment.

"A lead on how Ghulat Babur got his Secret Service pin." He caught Coulson up on what Jules had shared. "I'm glad he came forward. It's a minor detail, but it'll make us feel better we don't have another traitor in our midst."

"For sure. I have some news to share myself. Gary stopped by when you were in with your fellow agent. We have an ID on the boat that was used to let the divers into the water and Mrs. Markinson's boathouse. You'll never guess who owns it..."

Seth raised an eyebrow. "Don't keep me in suspense. Judging by your face, it's a good one."

"Rex King, father of Basil and Regina King..."

Seth's heart skipped a beat. "Holy shit. That's insane. How the hell did he ever give permission for that? Or did he?"

"That part, we don't know about, but it's obvious they didn't think they'd ever get caught. The boat was launched several miles downstream, and it never got close enough to Mrs. Markinson's property to be spotted. Those divers must've swum a good distance. But get this. The boat was transported on a trailer, one that was borrowed from a marina and put back afterward, but the truck that pulled it wasn't borrowed or stolen. It belonged to one Dwayne Gable, a former Army diver, whose current employer is..."

"Kingmakers."

"Bingo."

"How did they ever think they'd get away with this? Did they really think we'd stop digging before we found the truth?"

Coulson looked pensive. "I've asked myself that as well, and even Sheehan brought it up the other day. Here's the thing, though. In my experience, being a criminal always comes with a certain amount of stupidity and arrogance, and it's one or both of those that will get them caught."

"True, though you'd have to be arrogant to the extreme to think you'd get away with a presidential assassination."

"It makes me wonder what they've done over the years that no one ever noticed, other than that one case of their unit raping and killing civilians in Iraq. We see this all the time in our investigations. Criminals become bolder over time if they don't get caught for smaller stuff. They develop a sense of being untouchable...and it always leads to their downfall."

"How many big cases did the FBI never solve?" Seth asked.

"I haven't counted them, but if we're talking about famous cases, it's not more than a handful. The biggest and most notorious one is the aircraft hijacking by D.B. Cooper in 1971. The guy hijacked an airplane, then jumped out of it midair with the ransom money, never to be seen again. It's no longer an active case, but I know plenty of agents who studied the evidence, hoping to notice what everyone else had missed. Oh, and let's not forget the disappearance of Jimmy Hoffa. That one bugs us still as well."

Seth smiled at Coulson's use of the word *us*, as if he personally felt responsible, even though both crimes had taken place decades before he'd joined the FBI. Hell, before he'd even been born. He understood it, though, just like he still cringed at the failure of the Secret Service to protect JFK.

"But to get back to Kingmakers, I suspect that if we dig deep into their actions, we'll find more crimes they committed. Smaller ones, escalating over time," Coulson said. "Time will tell. One thing is certain. They won't evade justice this time. The grand jury has been convened, and Legal told me they're expecting the first round of subpoenas to go out this week. The proof is stacking up against them, and it's irrefutable."

Tears burned behind Seth's eyes. Why was he crying? Coulson shot him an intense look, then got up and closed the door. "Come here, baby." Before he'd even finished, Seth had jumped up and stepped into his embrace.

Those strong arms wrapped around him, and he clung to him, literally and mentally leaning on Coulson. Why was he so emotional?

"It's okay. This has been one hell of a year for you, baby," Coulson said softly. "It's so much more personal for you than it is for me or anyone else from my team. And I love you for it, for your sense of honor and duty and the pride you have in what you do."

Seth was exhausted. The fisting had helped, but it was becoming clear he'd drained his reserves, depleted them. "I wanna see this through till the end."

"And you will. We're almost there, baby. Hang in just a little longer, and then we'll go away together. Find a remote cabin in the woods or something and just sleep and read and watch TV...and fuck. Lots and lots of fucking."

Seth smiled through the tears that were still clouding his vision. "I'd love that. I miss you."

"I miss you too." Coulson was quiet for a moment, then dropped his voice to a whisper. "Want me to fist you again?"

"Would you?"

"It would be my privilege. I loved sharing that with you…and this time, we can do it without Asher."

"Thank you. I need it badly."

"Tonight, baby. You, me, your ass, and my hand. It's a date."

The warmth that spread through Seth at that promise proved once again that love could be communicated in many different ways other than through saying "I love you."

10

What a weird day it had been. Ryder had gone back to Langley after he'd dropped off Branson, but he'd kept thinking about him for the rest of the day. He'd even texted him to ask how he was doing and had gotten an immediate reply that things weren't looking good but that he was trying to stay positive.

Poor guy. Ryder knew little about his background other than the bit Branson had shared with him, but it seemed he was close with his parents, so this news had to hit him hard. He'd have to keep checking in on him, and Ryder had set a daily reminder for himself on his phone. Without systems like that, he wouldn't even remember to get gas on time or file his tax returns, distracted as he tended to be.

Luckily, he had the perfect way to distract himself from worrying about Branson too much. Dorian had asked if he wanted to come hang out. For real.

Ryder knocked softly, not wanting to wake Amelia up in case she was already in bed.

"Attempt two," Dorian joked as he opened the door for

Ryder. "Let's see if I can stay awake this time. Amelia is already asleep, so that should help."

Ryder grinned. "Hey, I had a lovely time sitting on your couch and reading...for three hours."

Dorian rolled his eyes. "I still can't believe we slept that long."

Ryder laughed as he followed him into the living room, which looked considerably neater than last time. "Tea?" Dorian asked. He knew Ryder didn't drink caffeine after six.

"Yes, please. Large mug."

It didn't take long for Dorian to make himself a cup of coffee and prepare an herbal tea for Ryder, which he put down in front of him on the coffee table. "I'm glad we get the chance to hang out," Dorian said as he sat down. "I feel bad about Saturday. By the time we woke up, we only had half an hour left before we had to go to my parents."

"Don't worry about it. It was clear you needed it, and I was happy to be somewhere else for a bit."

Dorian winced. "Things not good with your parents?"

"They're great, as always, but it's not easy being back there after so long."

"I bet. So if I may address the enormous elephant in the room, what happened with Paul?"

Ryder sighed. "You never liked him, did you?"

Dorian hesitated.

"It's okay. You can be honest."

"No, I didn't, sorry. I never quite understood what you saw in him other than that he was hot."

"He was... He was everything I wasn't. Popular, social, sexy... It drew me in."

"Ry, I've said this before, but you're super sexy, just in a different way. He's more obvious, too obvious even, like a ridiculously attractive movie star. You're... You're like that gorgeous hidden spot you can only discover after a strenuous hike, but once you do, it's so worth it because of the view."

Ryder blinked. "Damn, that was poetic for a fellow geek."

Dorian laughed. "I surprised myself there, I'll admit."

Ryder's laugh faded, and he let out a sigh. "I couldn't believe someone like him would want me. I know you've told me repeatedly that I think too little of myself, but it's how I felt. He liked me, wanted to hang out with me...and the sex was good. At least, I thought so."

He frowned. Had it been good? He'd always told himself so, but now that he thought about it, Paul had rarely given him what he wanted. Or needed. Or maybe Ryder had never been open and honest enough about what he craved?

"Good or great?"

Ryder shrugged. "Decent with the occasional good? You know I can be demanding in bed, and I've had far, far worse, trust me."

"That's setting the bar damn low. You can expect more from your partner. Sexual compatibility is important, considering how much you like sex...and you're not *that* demanding."

"Maybe, but I always thought there were reasons, extenuating circumstances. He made such crazy hours as a resident that I understood he was often tired. Too tired for the kind of sex I prefer."

"Makes sense...but I doubt that was the reason you split up."

"No, he broke up with me as soon as he became an attending."

Dorian's eyes widened. "*What?*"

"Turns out he wanted me for my income and money.

Otherwise, he wouldn't have been able to afford a place so close to Georgetown. But once he made attending, he could pay for it on his own."

"You're fucking kidding me…"

The anger in Dorian's voice was comforting to Ryder's wounded soul. "I wish I were. And I wish that was all…"

"There's more?"

Ryder took a deep breath. "He fucked every pretty boy he could get his hands on, all while spending my money and making me believe we had a future together. He bought furniture, had the apartment we rented all painted and spruced up, he got a new car…and I paid for it because we were together, and I thought we'd marry one day, and I made twice as much as him. And then he broke up with me, kicked me out, and I ended up back with my parents with an empty bank account."

"What a fucking dick." Dorian's eyes were blazing. "In fact, that's how I'll refer to him from now on. Dr. Dick."

Despite everything, that made Ryder smile, but then the memories flooded him, and his happiness seeped away. He'd been so fucking stupid. The shame of it burned inside him.

"How the hell did he get away with it?" Dorian asked.

"His name was the primary on the lease, not mine. I discovered he'd changed that two years ago without my knowledge. The money, I was aware of, but I didn't mind him spending it. You know I don't give two shits about material things, and if it made him happy to buy an expensive couch… We weren't in debt. I made sure of that, so I figured once he became an attending, we'd start saving."

"But you should have at least gotten half of the things he bought, like his car, the furniture…everything else."

"He hurt me so deeply that I didn't care anymore. As if I

wanted that couch he bought that wasn't to my taste in the first place. It would only remind me of him. No, thanks. I took my own stuff, like my books and my collection of puzzles, and of course my car, and I walked away with my head held high."

"I'm so sorry...and he cheated on you as well?"

Oh, that had hurt as much as the money had. "I was such an idiot. I never even suspected him because whenever we were out, he was always so attentive and sweet to me. Everyone kept telling me how lucky I was to have such a smart, successful, and sexy boyfriend."

Dorian huffed, clearly disagreeing with that statement. "How did you find out?"

"One of his coworkers told me. We'd met at some hospital party he took me to, and she and I had connected over a shared love for those brainteaser puzzles. She loved them as much as I do, and we had a fun conversation. When she caught him fucking some nurse a few weeks later, she thought I should know. I confronted him, and...he told me the truth."

"What truth?"

Ryder looked at the floor, studying the pattern in the hardwood. This part hurt the most, and he'd barely admitted it to himself. Dorian would understand, though, and he would be kind. "He said I was way too bossy and demanding in the bedroom, utterly boring outside of it, and that I'd never done something spontaneous in my life. He told me that my whole life was one big predictable combination of systems and structures and that he'd suffocate if he had to be with me for the rest of his life..."

Dorian was up in a flash and took a seat next to Ryder on the couch, then pulled him against him. "He was out to hurt you where it would hit you the hardest. What a despicable thing to say."

Tears burned in Ryder's eyes as he leaned into Dorian's embrace. "Is he wrong?"

"What do you mean?"

"Yes, it hurts, but is he wrong? I do live for routines and structure, both in my job and my personal life…"

"So do I, and even more now that I have Amelia. Hell, my whole existence is one big routine. Does that make me boring?"

"No, but… You became a dad. You made that decision, and you went after what you wanted."

"So did you. You chose to be a forensic accountant, and you did whatever you had to to get there."

"But…" Ryder sat up, then half turned so he faced Dorian. "He said even my job was boring."

"Is it?"

"What do you mean?"

"I know you can't tell me much about what you do, but is it uninteresting?"

Ryder thought of the intense joy he'd felt that morning when Branson had told him they finally had Hamza Bashir's real name. The events afterward had eclipsed his emotions, but what a rush that had been. And Ryder might've only played a small part, but his financial digging had helped them find Bashir…and it would allow them to ultimately nail Kingmakers; of that, he had no doubt.

"No, absolutely not. It's like a challenging puzzle to me, one of those giant ones with ten thousand pieces, and you don't know where to start. So you find the corner pieces first and then search for patterns, colors, anything that stands out. But no matter how long it takes, I finish it, and my reward is to see the entire picture and take in all the intricate details...and then I start on the next one. Except in this case, the puzzle matters because my part is connected to a much bigger part, and if I do my job right, it helps prevent a lot of bad things from happening. I love it."

"So he was wrong about that. Your job isn't boring."

Funny, now that Dorian said it so calmly, Ryder could easily see what he meant. Paul had been wrong about that. "To him, maybe, but not to me."

"So the problem was with Dr. Dick. Big surprise there."

"I suppose so."

"I say this with all my love, Ry, but Paul was a douche. A second-rate jerkwad who used you and cheated on you. Why would you take a single word out of that lying bastard's mouth seriously?"

Ryder giggled at Dorian's description. "Why don't you tell me how you really feel?"

"Oh, I have more choice words for that mothereffing son of a bitch, trust me. Just getting started here."

Ryder's laugh rang out. "Thank you. Strangely enough, that does make me feel better."

"All joking aside, you can't take Dr. Dick's opinion seriously. He lied to you this whole time, so what makes you think his parting words contained even a shred of truth?"

Huh. Ryder hadn't looked at it like that. "They hurt me real deep," he said softly.

"Which was his intention, I'm sure, but he told you those things, knowing they'd hit you hard. He's lived with you for five years. He knew exactly what to say."

Ryder swallowed. "He really is an asshole, isn't he? How could I have been such an idiot? I'm supposed to be this super smart guy."

"You are, just not with relationships...and let's face it, neither am I, or I wouldn't be a single dad. But he's the one who's wrong here, Ry, not you. Even if you had been the biggest moron on the planet, that still wouldn't have made it okay for him to cheat on you and use you. That's all on him."

Ryder gave in to his need for physical comfort, and he snuggled up to Dorian, who smiled as he draped his arms around him and held him close. Funny how despite both of them being gay, they'd never so much as kissed. The attraction had never been there, not even a little bit. Dorian was like his brother and best friend, all wrapped into one.

"I'm sorry I allowed Paul's dislike of you to come between us," he whispered. "I should've ignored his opinion."

Dorian caressed his hair. "I understand…and believe me, if you hadn't reconnected with me when you did, I would've come find you. Nothing can come between us, Ry, and especially not Dr. Dick."

How had he ever gotten so lucky with a friend like Dorian? "Thank you. I'm still sorry."

"I know. You're forgiven. I love you."

"I love you too." He blew out a long breath. "I don't think I ever want to be with someone again," he said hoarsely. "I'm way too scared I'll get hurt again."

"Give it time. You'll feel differently in a few months."

"Maybe. I kinda want to keep it casual from now on, though. Really get to know someone before I take the next step. You know, like hook up."

"I used to do that before I had Amelia. Now sex is a distant memory… Pretty sure I'll need hours of prep if I ever have sex again. I haven't so much as had a good-sized dildo up there in months."

Ryder chuckled. "Your poor asshole, all lonely down there."

"You have no idea. Single fatherhood isn't for the faint of heart, let me tell you. But I wouldn't miss it for the world."

"I'm happy to babysit if you ever want a night off. I mean, I have zero experience with kids, but I doubt I could kill her in a few hours, right?"

Dorian snorted. "That's reassuring. Great sales pitch, bro."

They were quiet for a while, Ryder's heart finding peace as he pondered Dorian's words. "My parents are selling the house," he finally said. "They're moving into a senior living complex. I have about a month to find a new place."

"Oh, crap. Good for them, of course, but that's the worst timing ever."

"I don't have the money for a down payment to buy something, and I can't cover a security deposit yet. If they had waited, like, three months, I would've been fine. But they don't know the details of what happened with Paul, and I'll never tell them."

"The commute would be even worse than from your parents' house, but if you can't find anything else, you and your vast collection of books and puzzles are welcome here."

Warmth filled Ryder's chest. "Thank you. It would add another fifteen minutes to my drive, but it's great to have something, so thank you."

"And I may take you up on your offer of babysitting. I could use a good dicking."

Hmm, there was an idea. A good dicking. Ryder's ass contracted at the thought but in an eager way. It had been seven weeks since Paul had broken up with him, eleven or twelve since they'd had sex, which, in hindsight, should have clued him in something was wrong. Ryder could do with a hard fuck himself to help him get his mind off everything.

Maybe it was time to score himself some dick. Find an app he could safely use, considering his job, and arrange a hookup. Mmm, yes, the more he thought about it, the more it appealed to him. He would fuck Paul and all the insecurity he'd caused out of his system. There. Problem solved.

11

He couldn't concentrate. Branson pushed his chair back from his desk and rubbed his temples. A faint headache brewed behind his eyes, the result of a night of restless sleep where nightmares in which his father was dying kept waking him up, gasping for air. Twenty-four hours before, things had been fine...and then everything had shifted.

The surgery had been scheduled for four days later—the delay caused by the doctors wanting to run more tests first—and Branson had told his team leader, Weston, he'd be taking that day off. Weston had been supportive, though Branson knew that the timing couldn't have been worse. Now that they knew who Hamza Bashir was—which Branson had only told Weston once he'd come back from the hospital and could think somewhat straight again—his absence was a big hindrance in making progress in the investigation. It couldn't be helped.

To his credit, Weston hadn't shown even a hint of frustration. They had a meeting with Coulson and Seth scheduled for the next day, and the Director of National Intelligence had already briefed the president. Weston had reached out to their British counterparts for help, as well as a few handpicked foreign intelligence agencies who had excellent contacts in the region. Hopefully, they'd be able to make progress together. Al Saalihin's attacks had been against the US, but other countries were all too aware of the risks of this new terrorist cell growing. Of course, the CIA hadn't shared the suspected link with Kingmakers yet. That couldn't leak before they had cold hard evidence.

"Hey," a soft voice spoke behind him, and Branson spun around. It didn't happen often people were able to surprise him, least of all Ryder, who couldn't ever be accused of being stealthy.

"Hi."

Ryder jammed his hands into his pockets, but the *How are you holding up?* Branson had expected never came. "Are you hungry?" Ryder asked instead.

Branson frowned. "What?"

"It's lunchtime. Are you hungry?"

"It is?" Shit, he hadn't even noticed it was past noon already. "Not really, to be honest."

"You owe me a lunch."

"What do you mean?"

"Yesterday, we were supposed to go out for lunch to celebrate your big breakthrough, and it never happened, so I'm collecting my debt."

Branson's heart softened. Ryder's phrasing might be slightly awkward, but the deeper intention was sweet. He was reaching out to Branson, attempting to distract him. "True. Let's go."

Ryder's face lit up, and Branson's belly grew warm. He loved Ryder's smile.

In the cafeteria, Ryder got his usual sandwich while Branson opted for the chicken burger with fries and coleslaw. Not healthy, but he couldn't care less. Now that he'd smelled the food, his stomach had changed its mind about craving sustenance.

"Thank you again for driving me yesterday," he said once they'd settled at their table in the back. Ryder always picked the same one.

"No problem."

Branson cocked his head. "I keep waiting for you to ask the expected questions. About my dad, I mean."

Ryder shrugged. "I figured if you wanted to talk about it, you'd bring it up yourself. I didn't want you to feel obligated to share personal things with me. After all, we're coworkers, not friends."

For some reason, that stung. "We could be."

"Friends?"

Branson nodded.

Ryder blinked a few times as he studied Branson, then turned his attention back to his plate. "Why would you want to be friends with me? I'd think someone like you had plenty of friends."

Ouch. Ryder had intended it as a compliment, no doubt, but the realization that he didn't have friends left Branson aching inside again. How had that happened? He'd always been someone who loved having people around him. He was a social butterfly, and he found it easy to connect with all kinds of people. So why hadn't he managed to cultivate deep friendships over the years?

"I actually don't have that many friends," he said, surprising himself by admitting the truth to Ryder.

Ryder's hand stopped halfway to his mouth, and he slowly put his sandwich down. "You don't?"

"No. I realized that yesterday, which was a little unsettling, I'll admit."

Ryder opened his mouth, then closed it again.

"What did you want to say?" Branson asked.

"Nothing. No, that's not true. I did think of something, but then I decided that was rude to ask, so I didn't. A rare case of my filter functioning properly."

Branson chuckled at the self-deprecating remark. "I don't mind you being direct."

"No? That makes you an exception. Most people don't appreciate it."

Branson shrugged. "I like knowing where I stand. You don't hide your feelings, and that saves me a lot of guesswork."

Ryder rolled his eyes. "I couldn't hide it if I tried. I'm, like, the worst actor on the planet. We had to perform this shortened Macbeth play in my junior year of high school, and my English teacher thought it would be a good idea to give me a speaking part. I warned him I would fuck it up, and lo and behold, I fucked it up. I can't act. Memorizing the lines, no problem, but delivering them with even a modicum of emotions, nope."

Branson laughed, and for a few moments, his chest felt loose and free of the tightness that had invaded him after hearing the news about his dad. "I'm sure it can't be that bad."

"I beg to differ, but you don't have to take my word for it. It's all been recorded for posterity… My parents digitalized all their old tapes from their video camera, so you can now watch seventeen-year-old me in all my puberty glory. Hypothetically, if I were ever to give you access to said tape."

Branson laughed even louder. He'd never known Ryder

could be this funny, but his dry humor cracked him up. Where had that been hiding the whole time? "What do I have to do to, to persuade you to let me see that?"

Ryder cocked his head. "I'll consider it."

"Okay, I'll help you remember, no worries. But in the meantime, what did you want to ask and then decided not to?"

Ryder averted his eyes, playing with the last bits of his sandwich. "I was curious how someone like you couldn't have friends."

"Someone like me?"

"Yeah, you're... You're so easygoing, so social. You talk to everyone, and everyone likes you. Plus, you're..." He gestured at Branson as if that said it all, and Branson quirked an eyebrow.

"I'm what?"

Ryder stubbornly kept his gaze downward. "Attractive. You're attractive. As you damn well know, I suspect."

"Thank you."

Finally, Ryder looked up. "*Thank you?*"

"That's the appropriate reaction when someone compliments you, isn't it?"

Ryder blinked. "I meant it more like... It was a statement of a fact."

"Mmm, doesn't make it less of a compliment. Maybe even more, since you clearly didn't say it to butter me up."

Ryder seemed horrified at that suggestion. "Why on earth would I want to do that? And that's providing I'd even know how to do it in the first place."

"I don't know, but it's a hypothetical case, so let's get back to what we were talking about. Me and my lack of friends."

"You don't have to answer that question."

"I know. I'm not even sure I can. Like I said, I only realized it yesterday, and I haven't figured out the cause."

Ryder bit his lip. "At the risk of offending you, but how can you not realize you don't have friends?"

How indeed? Branson wished he knew. Had he been so out of touch with himself? "The truth is that I don't have a clue. I should, obviously, but... I don't think I ever missed having friends. Between my work and my social life, I kept myself plenty busy."

"Your social life? Isn't that the same as hanging out with friends?"

"That depends on your definition of a friend. I consider someone a friend when I wouldn't hesitate to call them for help if I needed it, and the truth is that right now, I can't think of anyone I'd feel comfortable enough reaching out to. I have a boatload of acquaintances who would be there in a second if I announced something fun and exciting or promised them a good time, but they won't show up for this. That, and an app full of hookups."

He wasn't even sure why he'd added that last line, but Ryder almost choked on his chips. "H-hookups?"

Branson raised an eyebrow. "You're familiar with the concept of a hookup app like Grindr and similar ones, I assume?"

"Of course... Though I haven't had... Up until recently, I was in a committed relationship, or at least, I thought I was, so I haven't used one in years."

He'd *thought* he was? That sounded like his ex had cheated on him, and anger bubbled up inside Branson. He loved fucking and enjoyed sex, but he wanted nothing to do with cheaters. He didn't always know if someone who wanted to hook up with him was involved with someone else, but he'd become an expert at picking up signs, and if he suspected even a sliver, he was out. Loyalty was crucial to him. No judgment for those for whom monogamy wasn't important, but he couldn't do it.

"Well, I used them a lot until…" He thought of Seth and the crazy idea that had taken hold of him that he could've seen himself in a relationship with him. Not anymore, obviously. The man was besotted with Coulson, but even then, they might not be as good a fit as Branson had thought. Nevertheless, it had changed something in him, although it had taken him a while to realize. For the first time in his life, he wanted more. He was done with the anonymous sex, no matter how good it was.

"Until what?"

He sighed. "Until something happened that made me think I should maybe aim higher than mere sex. Like a relationship."

"Trust me, relationships are overrated. If I could do it all over again, I would…" Ryder let out a long sigh, and his shoulders stooped. "I don't know what I would do, but I wouldn't spend so many years with a guy who wasn't on the same page with honesty and monogamy."

That confirmed the cheating, but Branson couldn't resist asking the obvious question anyway. "He cheated on you?"

After a short hesitation, Ryder nodded. "Repeatedly, I found out later. In fact, he went behind my back for the entire time we were together."

"What a dick."

Ryder's eyes widened. "That's what Dorian, my best friend, keeps calling him. Dr. Dick."

"Apt."

"It is. In hindsight, I feel so stupid."

"Why?"

Ryder frowned. "I'd think that's obvious. We were together for five years. How did I never notice it? And not only the cheating but a lot of other red flags as well."

Oh, the *pain* in that statement... Branson felt it deep in his soul, even though Ryder had spoken in a flat voice with only a hint of the emotions he had to feel. "I refuse to accept that if you don't see someone else's bad behavior, that makes you stupid. It's not stupid to trust someone you're with, especially not for such a long time. I'm not an expert on relationships, but I'd argue it's the norm to trust your partner. So the fault is not with you, Ry. It's with Dr. Dick."

"But if I..." Ryder sighed. "That's wishful thinking, isn't it?"

"What, that if you had done things differently, he wouldn't have cheated on you? Yes. The blame lies with him, not with anything you did. Cheating is always a choice, and he made that choice time and again. How can you blame yourself for that?"

"Oh, quite easily," Ryder said with a touch of humor. "I have no trouble at all putting all the blame with myself... even though rationally, I know you're right. It's unsettling, as I'm not someone who's guided by my emotions."

"This must've hurt you deeply."

Ryder's eyes clouded with sadness that hinted at even more behind his story. "It did. But we were talking about you and your lack of friends."

Branson suppressed a smile at that blunt segue. "Technically, we were talking about me wanting to be friends with you."

Ryder pushed his glasses back up. "Right."

"So what do you say?"

"Even though I now understand you don't have friends, I'm still baffled why you would pick me to build a friendship with. Aside from the fact that neither of us is straight and we both work for the CIA, we don't seem to have much in common."

Not straight. Branson loved the inclusive way Ryder had formulated that, even after he knew Branson had at least once been with another man. "I'm gay, to slap the correct label on me."

"Okay."

Ryder said nothing else, and it stung.

"Am I so awful that you don't even want to get to know me better?" Branson couldn't keep the hurt from his voice. Sure, he hadn't expected him and Ryder to be BFFs instantly, but Ryder didn't even seem the least bit interested in the possibility of a friendship.

"I offended you," Ryder said slowly.

Branson swallowed. He hated how emotional this whole conversation made him. "Not offended, but it's painful to realize you don't even want to try to be friends."

"I don't have sufficient data to make that decision."

"We've been working together for six weeks now."

"Yeah, so? That doesn't mean I *know* you."

"I'm confused. We've shared plenty of lunches and talked about other things than work."

"No, you ask me questions, and I talk about myself, but you don't."

"What do you mean?"

"You always focus on others and distract attention from yourself."

What was he talking about? That made no sense at all. "I'm still not sure I know what you mean."

"You went fly-fishing and skydiving because someone else loved it, not you. You want to visit Peru because someone you were in love with wanted to go there. But what about you? What do you want or love or hate? I could fit what I know about you on a Post-it, and I wouldn't even have to write small."

Panic bubbled in his stomach. That wasn't true...was it? It couldn't be. That would imply he'd always been... No, Ryder had to be wrong.

Ryder cocked his head. "Want me to summarize what I know about you?"

He stopped talking after that and watched Branson expectantly, awaiting his reaction. Oh, he hadn't meant it as a rhetorical question, then. "Yes?"

"I'm checking because I don't want to hurt your feelings."

How much worse could it get? "I'll take my chances."

Ryder took a deep breath. "I know you lived in various countries and speak several languages and that you're fantastic at your job. Your father is a US ambassador, you're gay and once were in love with a French boy, and you're a social butterfly who excels at adapting to others. I also know that despite my repeated protests, you keep calling me Ry and that you seem to derive some perverse pleasure out of teasing me. You rarely talk about yourself, and that appears to be a deliberate choice. Now please tell me, what in all that should give me the idea that we'd have something in common other than working here and being gay? What in all that tells me you'd be a good friend to me, someone who respects me and the boundaries I set?"

For once in his life, Branson didn't know what to say, struck mute by Ryder's honest and factual analysis. Ryder hadn't been out to hurt him, to hit him where Branson would feel it. He'd given the facts as he'd observed them, unfiltered and straight. And that it made Branson sound like a selfish, shallow person? Well, that wasn't his fault. Nope, that was all Branson, and once that truth sank its claws into him, a deep sadness filled him. He didn't like what he saw in the mirror at all.

12

The day after his conversation with Branson about becoming friends, Ryder still wasn't sure if he'd done the right thing. He felt like he'd kicked a man who had already been down and that he'd only added to Branson's stress and low emotional well-being. What else could he have done when Branson had asked him directly, however? Lie? He couldn't do that. He sucked at it, but he also had a hard time with it emotionally. The few times he'd told a lie, the guilt had been overwhelming.

But as he noticed Branson's pale face and the bags under his eyes as he settled in his chair for a meeting with Coulson and Seth, another kind of guilt washed over him. Should he have handled it differently? Branson looked like he hadn't slept since they'd last talked, and all traces of his usual sparkly personality had disappeared. If Ryder had caused that, he was deeply sorry, and he would tell Branson that in no uncertain terms. After the meeting.

"We're excited to finally have some great news to share after a long period of plodding and plugging," Weston said, and the room grew quiet. "In my experience, it's often like this. For months and months or even for years, we only seem to make minuscule steps forward, and then all of a sudden, we hit one big breakthrough after the other. Over the last weeks, we had some fantastic new developments, but this one beats all. Branson, will you do the honors?"

Branson sat up straight, and a little energy returned to his posture. "We've positively identified Hamza Bashir."

Coulson and Seth gasped at the same time. "Seriously?" Coulson's face broke open in a wide smile. "You've ID'd him?"

Branson nodded, then turned on the screen to show a picture. "Meet Yazid El Sewedy, a thirty-one-year-old natural citizen of the United Arab Emirates, born and raised in Dubai."

"Holy shit," Coulson said, studying the picture. "How certain are you? No offense. Is this an undisputed fact, or are we working within a margin of error?"

"One hundred percent certain. We have confirmation from several agencies who have used their resources to dig into his background, for example, from the British. It turns out El Sewedy studied at Oxford for a while, under his real name, of course. He speaks British English fluently, almost without an accent."

"That explains the faint British accent in the videos," Seth said.

Branson nodded. "And everything else we already discovered pans out as well, including the Yemeni angle. He speaks both San'ani Arabic, also known as Peninsular Arabic, and Gulf Arabic. That's because his mother, Halimah Thabet, was from Yemen. She died when he was fifteen, but before then, he'd often visited her family in Yemen, so he knows his way around there."

Ryder knew all this already, but he was amazed again at

how all the details they had picked up on had been correct. Now that they had a name and an identity, every puzzle piece fit.

"Both Yazid and his father, Sameh El Sewedy, are wealthy businessmen," Branson picked up, "and the rest of his family is affluent as well. Yazid travels extensively on multiple passports and under different names, mostly in the Middle East but on occasion also to North Africa. They've been involved in some shady business deals, for example, in arms and military supplies, and seem to have few morals. They're Muslim but more out of habit and tradition than out of personal interest. We've found no evidence that Yazid El Sewedy is radicalized. Everything so far indicates he's a hired gun, someone whose only goal is to make money."

"Thirty-one?" Seth raised his eyebrows. "That meant he was only twenty-four when he started preparing for the Pride Bombing. That's damn young."

"He's smart," Branson said. "Very smart. He returned from England the year before. The British are still investigating the time he spent there, but their first reports show he was popular with his fellow students. Amicable, smart, a hard worker. He excelled academically, and his professors had nothing but praise for him. No evidence of radicalization during that time either. He frequented a local mosque, but that one is known to be liberal and well integrated into the British culture."

"If I may ask, what's the evidence that makes you so sure this is Hamza Bashir?" Seth asked.

"We have cross-checked dates of his travel with the periods we know Basil King and Kurt Barrow were in Oman or Qatar. They overlap. His picture matches the video we have from the Qatari mall, where he met with Muhammed Bhat. But most importantly, he spent a few months in

Yemen around the time the first reports popped up about a new terrorist cell developing there…and he traveled to the Kashmir region several times. There's no logical explanation for that from a business perspective. It's not an affluent region and not an area he or his father has business dealings with. He went there to recruit…and he succeeded."

Seth and Coulson looked at each other, sharing a look that made Ryder's belly all warm. "That's amazing work, Branson," Coulson said.

Branson held up his hands. "Team effort, not my own accomplishment. This wouldn't have been possible without close cooperation between a lot of intelligence agencies, foreign ones as well. Because we agreed to share information, we managed to assemble all the puzzle pieces in one place, and that's what led me to find him."

"Fair enough, but I know how hard you personally worked on this as well," Coulson said.

"So what's the next step?" Seth wanted to know.

"Digging into his background until we know everything about him," Branson said. "We're especially interested in how Kingmakers established contact with him. How did they know each other? One of our working theories is that they might've done business before, since El Sewedy was involved in military supplies, including arms."

Weston nodded. "He's priority number one for the entire US intelligence community. Based on this new information, the NSA will reevaluate the historical data they already have to see if they can find out more now that they know what and whom to look for. They'll also make sure we have eyes and ears on him as much as possible. On our end, the CIA will increase our assets in the UAE and try to get closer to him."

"But our biggest challenge is to tie El Sewedy to Kingmakers financially," Branson smoothly took over again. "We need proof that money changed hands from Kingmakers to El Sewedy. And that's where Ryder and Corey come in."

Ryder cleared his throat. "I'm working on getting El Sewedy's financial records, which is a challenge, as you can imagine. We're making progress with the authorities in the UAE with help from the British, who have a better in with them than we do. Meanwhile, Corey is pouring over the information we have from Kingmakers to see if they had previous deals with El Sewedy, but we need more access. What's the status on the subpoenas?"

"The grand jury has determined there's probable cause to go after Kingmakers, and it's ready to issue the first round of subpoenas," Coulson reported. "I wanted to wait for this meeting to see if we could add anything more to the request, but I think we'll keep this part under wraps for now. We'll file as soon as this meeting is over."

"Unless there's a reason not to." Seth looked around the room. "Will this guy go to ground if we subpoena Kingmakers? Will they contact him?"

Ryder hadn't even thought of that, but Seth raised a valid point. What if El Sewedy disappeared after all the trouble they'd had to identify and locate him?

Weston scratched his chin. "Let me run that by Director Heeder. He may have to take that up with the president."

From what Ryder understood, Seth and Coulson had direct access to the president, but of course the chain of command had to be respected.

Coulson nodded. "I'll inform Legal to hold off until we have confirmation we wouldn't be risking the investigation into El Sewedy."

The meeting ended soon after that, and Ryder was still

gathering his things when Seth walked up to Branson. "You okay?" he asked him softly. "You look like crap."

Branson didn't respond immediately, and much to Ryder's surprise, Seth put a hand on his shoulder, even though Coulson was watching them from the doorway. "I'm here if you need me," Seth said, dropping his voice even lower. If Ryder hadn't been standing right next to them, he wouldn't have been able to hear it.

Wait, did they know each other from outside of work? Ryder sucked at interpreting body language, but Seth seemed overly personal with Branson for someone he'd only had professional contact with. No, something else had happened between them.

"I know. I'm dealing with some personal issues. My dad..." Branson shook his head. "I can't talk about it, but thank you."

"I respect that, but if you need a listening ear, I'm here."

Branson's smile was watery. "I wouldn't think you even had the time."

"I make time for what's important."

Branson took a deep breath, and his face lost a bit of tension. "Thank you. That means a lot to me. I didn't think you'd ever wanted to talk to me again after..." He gestured at Coulson, who was still waiting by the door.

Ryder had been correct, then. They had a history.

"He understands. Hang in there, okay?"

Seth squeezed Branson's shoulder, then walked off, Branson's eyes following him until he'd reached Coulson and the two of them walked out. Only then did Branson tear his eyes away, startling when he noticed Ryder. "I didn't know you were still here."

"I suspected as much."

Branson stared at him, letting out a sigh. "You never do what I expect you to. It's unnerving."

"What should I have done, according to you?"

"Everyone else would've asked me about what you just witnessed. I'm sure you have questions."

"I do, but I know that you don't like to talk about yourself, so I won't ask and put pressure on you to share things you may not want to."

Branson rubbed his temples. "I keep thinking back on what you said to me yesterday."

He wouldn't get a more perfect segue. "I apologize if I hurt you. That was never my intention."

"I know."

"Did I hurt you?" He needed to know for reasons he didn't even fully grasp himself. The idea of Branson being in pain over something Ryder had said grated.

Branson hesitated. "No. You pointed out some truths that were painful to face, but none of that is on you. In fact, I owe you an apology."

"You do?" What on earth could Branson have to apologize for?

"Yes." Branson met his eyes straight on. "You were right that I kept calling you Ry even after you repeatedly asked me not to. I thought it was funny, but it wasn't. It was disrespecting your boundaries."

"Yes." Relief filled Ryder. If nothing else, Branson had understood that. "Thank you for acknowledging that."

"I really am sorry, and you were correct to point it out. Few people would have. I'm... It wasn't easy to hear everything you said, but you weren't wrong."

"My timing was awful. I should've waited until you felt better."

"I flat out asked you. You double-checked, and I told you

I wanted you to say it, so you bear no blame. Granted, I wasn't expecting that, but still."

"Okay."

"I'm... Seth and I have a history," Branson said. "He and I hooked up a few times before he met Coulson, but we didn't know each other's name or occupation."

Ryder winced. "That must've been awkward when you ran into each other and found out."

"God, yes. We both pretended we'd never seen each other, though Seth later told Coulson the truth, of course. But I'd hoped..." He sighed again, his shoulders drooping. "Never mind."

He'd hoped what? Not that Seth would've kept it hidden from Coulson. That didn't make sense. Then what? Oh, wait. Maybe he'd meant he'd hoped Seth would've wanted to continue their relationship, even after they'd found out who they were. But then Seth and Coulson had gotten together, and well, that had been it. Ryder felt bad for Branson.

"I'm sorry," he said.

"Sorry for what?" Branson's tone held an edge.

"Sorry you got hurt."

"Oh. Yeah...I did. Thank you."

Ryder stayed silent, watching Branson as one emotion after the other flashed over his face.

"You were right about something else," Branson finally said. "And I can't believe I never realized it. I don't like to talk about myself, and I don't know why. I love chatting with people, and until you mentioned it, I'd never recognized how unbalanced those conversations have always been with me listening and asking questions, maybe talking about things the other person was interested in. But I rarely opened up about my life, and I don't know why."

"You'll figure it out. And maybe now is not the best time for a lot of introspection."

"Maybe. Anyway, thank you. I hope you'll continue to tell me the truth."

Ryder chuckled despite everything. "Little chance of anything else with me."

"I look forward to it." Branson looked at him in a way he never had before, and it made Ryder's belly tickle.

"Me too." God, that was stupid. He rolled his eyes at himself. One day, he'd be as socially smooth as Branson... but not today. Whatever. At least he hadn't fucked up with Branson, and that mattered much more, though why, he wasn't sure.

13

"Amzi, thanks for stopping by." Calix gestured at the sitting area in his office. "How are things?"

He figured they'd do a bit of professional talk before he'd break the big news to him. News that he had no idea how Amzi would react to.

"Good. The talks we've had so far with Islamic scholars and imams have been well received, both by them and by the broader community." Amzi sat down. "In fact, multiple leaders have contacted me to express their interest in talking to us."

"What kind of leaders?"

"Youth workers, cultural workers, community activists... It's a broad spectrum, but they all have in common that they want to share their ideas on helping Islamic youth integrate better into American society."

"That's great news." Calix winced. "I'm not sure how many more appointments I can add to my schedule, though."

"I suspected as much, so I wanted to suggest we set up a task force. Create a bigger group of people to have these dialogues and gather ideas, then come up with a plan to present to the president."

As much as Calix liked this idea, he needed to tell Amzi the news first. "Before we get into the details of that, let me catch you up on an important development first. One that will impact not only your plans but the Muslim community as a whole."

"Oh?" Amzi's eyes widened for a moment, but then they clouded with fear. "Please don't tell me it's bad news."

"Bad? No. Unexpected, I would say." Calix took a deep breath. "I'll share a few more details in a moment, but the bottom line is that Al Saalihin didn't initiate the Pride Bombing or the assassination. Someone else hired them. A domestic group."

Amzi paled, his jaw dropping open. "Did you say domestic? Islamic fundamentalist domestic?"

"No. Right-wing nationalist terrorist."

Amzi opened and closed his mouth like a fish on land and stared at Calix as if he'd grown wings. "*Americans* were behind this?"

Calix slowly nodded. "Yes, born and raised white Americans. This was domestic terrorism, coordinated from the US but executed by a group pretending to be Muslim fundamentalist but is, in reality, a terrorist group for hire. Hamza Bashir is a ruthless mercenary who used genuine Muslim young men and deceived them into believing he was fighting for their cause, an Islamic state in Kashmir."

Amzi leaned back in his chair, hiding his face in his hands. "Excuse me," he stammered. "I need... I need a moment."

"Take your time," Calix said kindly. "I can't even imagine all the emotions you must be feeling."

When Amzi finally looked up, his eyes were misty. "I

don't know what to say. I'm profoundly relieved this wasn't the work of a true Islamic terrorist group, but the truth is... just as troublesome, if not more. Since when do we have terrorist groups for hire? Where is Hamza Bashir even from?"

"I'm sorry, but I can't share much more with you at this time, but I can tell you he's doing it purely for the money."

"Can you tell me anything about the domestic terrorists?"

"No, sorry, but religion plays no role here...and from what we have discovered, neither did the LGBT+ factor."

Amzi raised his eyebrows. "They didn't choose the Pride Parade on purpose?"

"We think they chose it because it's a big event with the potential for a high casualty count...and because they figured it would be a target that would sell the message of this being an Islamic terrorist attack."

Amzi ran his hands through his hair, his posture slumping. "I don't even know what to say to that."

"We're all right there with you, though for you, it would be even harder, as you're Muslim yourself."

"I'm going to need some time to process this."

"Keep in mind this is classified information. I only told you because with your project in the Muslim community, you needed to know. The president and I would love to hear your thoughts on how you expect the community will react when this becomes public. Not immediately." Calix held up his hand when Amzi opened his mouth to react. "Take your time. I understand this is a shock."

"Good. Because right now, I have no clue. No clue at all. Hell, I don't even know what I'm feeling myself. Relief, sure, but also...disappointment? Anger that they used the concept of an Islamic terrorist group, thus fueling Islamophobia and hate against Muslims throughout the world and that the only reason they did that was money."

Calix sighed. "Wait until you find out what the motive of the domestic group was... It's all so awful and horrific, and it has definitely impacted my trust in people."

They sat for a while in silence, emotions still flashing over Amzi's face. "How long until this news will break?" he finally asked.

"We don't know for certain, but a few weeks at the most. The investigation is making significant progress now."

"Okay." Amzi rubbed his temples. "Let me get back to you on my thoughts on how the Muslim community will react, okay?"

"Sure. In the meantime, let's talk about your idea for a task force. I like it, and I think the president will too. Once this is over, building better relationships with the Islamic community will have to become a priority. The incidents against Muslims have decreased, thank god, but a lot of work remains to be done."

"You're right, the numbers are going down, but minor incidents occur every day, spread across the country. When *60 Minutes* did a piece on Syrian refugees a month ago, we saw an uptick in aggression aimed at Muslims. So it's still brewing, and one little spark can create a new combustion, but for now, the situation is steady."

Calix scribbled down Amzi's comment on the effects of that broadcast. That was the kind of stuff Del was always interested in. "Any other updates?"

"The good news is that I'm getting signals from within the community that they want a solution for men like Abdullah Shahin, that fundamentalist imam in New Jersey. His fan base is mostly outside the US. Domestically, his support is limited to his fellow hard-liners and, sadly, young people. The latter is worrisome and not just to us. Multiple leaders have told me they're open to any ideas to fight this risk for radicalization."

"Talk to me about Shahin. What is he teaching?"

"He's extreme in his views, way beyond conservative. Take women, for example. Islam teaches women should be respected, but he regards them as babymakers who should have no voice at all. His view is basically that a wife is her husband's property and he can do to her as he wishes. He disses other religions, like Christianity and Judaism, which he openly and fervently hates. He supports fatwas and has expressed his wish that certain penal codes would be reinstated. Think stonings and amputations, along those lines. When the Arab Spring hit in 2011, he was in favor of a harsh crushing of the protests. Much more problematic is that he publicly denies Muslims were behind 9/11, and instead blames the Jews, but privately, he expresses his support for ISIS, urging young men to join this terrorist organization. So far, six Americans who traveled to Syria to join ISIS have been traced back to his influence."

Calix whistled between his teeth. "That's quite the résumé."

"And that's only the tip of the iceberg. The FBI has an entire file on him, which I only know the highlights of. I think it may be time to pursue legal options against him before he spreads even more hate. It would also send a powerful signal to the community, both his supporters and those who want to see his influence curtailed."

Calix made another note. "Why don't you reach out to the FBI and the AG's office and take their temperature on where they stand on this? Then I can take it to the president."

"Will do."

"Anything else?"

Amzi shifted in his seat. "One more thing. I've been asked to represent the White House at an interfaith symposium on LGBT+ issues in religion."

"I know. I suggested they approach you."

"Calix..." Amzi pinched the bridge of his nose. "I can't do it."

Calix frowned. "Why not?"

Amzi worked for the queerest White House in history. Certainly, he couldn't have an issue with this topic.

"I'm... I'm not ready for this yet, not for a public event like this."

Calix's fusion grew. "What do you mean? I've heard you speak in public with great confidence...and for a much larger audience than this will be."

"I know, but it wasn't about a similar topic. This is... It hits too close to home for me." He took a deep breath, and then it hit. Calix knew where this was going, and he held up a hand.

"You don't owe me anything more."

"It's okay. I'm gay, Calix. I've known for a while now, but I'm not out. I can't be. Even more liberal interpretations of Islam still preach against homosexuality. Their opinion is that people who identify as homosexual should live a life in celibacy and submit to conversion therapy. The idea of losing my family, the support of my Muslim friends... It's too much, too high a price."

Calix leaned forward and put a hand on his arm. "Thank you for trusting me with this. I understand."

"It would be impossible for me to stand there and speak with the required and expected objectiveness and distance about that topic. I wrestle with this so much that it would feel disingenuous to keep up a front and pretend it's a theoretical debate for me."

"I get that, and it speaks to your character. And, Amzi, if you ever need a listening ear, I'm here. Off the record, outside our work relationship. Just from one gay man to another, someone supportive you can talk to and who will listen."

"Thank you. I appreciate that a lot."

Calix pulled his hand back and sent him a warm smile. "My pleasure. And I'll find someone else for that conference, no worries."

After Amzi had left, Calix sat by himself. He always tried not to speculate about people's sexual identity, but with Amzi, he'd never even picked up on the slightest hint that the man wasn't straight. What a struggle and a burden it had to be to suppress his true identity and present himself as straight. For Calix, who had been out since he'd been a teenager, it was impossible to imagine. Hopefully, one day, things would change for Amzi so he could be himself as well and live free. Wasn't that one of the major goals of their administration anyway? One day.

14

Milan had been tasked with assisting the FBI agents who were once again pouring over the footage of the site of the Pride Bombing as well as all traffic cams and video recordings the FBI had painstakingly cataloged back in 2015. They were hoping to find more clues now that they better knew what to look for. Coulson had suggested that Milan, as a native New Yorker and an NYPD detective, might be able to offer valuable insights, and Milan had agreed.

Besides, it offered a welcome distraction from the whole shitstorm his relationship with Asher and Denali had caused. The serious press had long since stopped caring, having moved on to the next scandal, but the tabloids loved it. They'd had to resort to staying in the White House rather than in Asher's apartment, and the White House staff had proven to be incredibly loyal. They hadn't leaked the relationship in the first place. That had been one of Asher's neighbors who had recognized Milan and had tipped the press off. Asshat.

Del had fired him as an advisor to the president, but

when Milan had called his NYPD captain, the man had made it crystal clear he didn't give two shits about Milan's sex life...or love life. "Legal and consensual, that's where I draw the line. Other than that, I don't even want to know what kinky shit you're up to, Bradbury," he'd said, and Milan had never loved the blunt, grumpy guy more.

Even better, NYPD had loaned him out to the FBI as a special consultant—something he knew Coulson had made happen. The man had valued Milan's contribution, and Milan had to admit it felt good to be appreciated. And so he sat down with the team that focused on the bombing, led by Supervisory Special Agent Ashley Foerster, who possessed a sharp mind that had impressed Milan from the moment he'd met her.

The upside of Manhattan being an island was that there were only so many ways someone could get something big in like, say, a bomb. And still they had no hard evidence of how the bombs used in the Pride Bombing had been transported into the city. All they knew was that one of the three bombers had rented a storage space close to the site of the bombing—under a fake name, but one that had been easy to discover—but the camera covering the hallway where his storage unit was located had been tampered with, so the owners hadn't been able to hand over any CCTV footage. Same for the cameras around the storage facility, which had all suggested a highly skilled bomber.

"Detective Bradbury, how would you approach this?" she asked him.

The use of his title was much more formal than Milan would have preferred, but he knew enough about the FBI culture by now to know that trying to change that was futile. "What do we know about the bomb maker?"

"The ATF has traced the blasting caps and other

elements used in the bombs back to Jon Brooks, so we're certain he either made the bomb or supervised someone making it. He was flagged a few years ago for missing materials, but the case was never picked up because he didn't trigger any suspicion otherwise," Ashley said.

"Before the Pride Bombing?"

Ashley nodded, a frown creasing her forehead. "Six weeks before. But no priors, no warning signs, nothing."

"Shit. That's gonna look bad when it leaks...and you know it will."

"It's 9/11 all over again. But it's so easy to see it in hindsight. The man owns a construction company, no record, and he's an American. How does that trigger suspicion?"

"Terrorists don't look like they used to, that's for sure." Milan took a deep breath, shoving his anger down. "Okay, so Brooks made the bombs, which means they had to be brought in from Oklahoma. Who do we think transported them to New York?"

"Based on the profile we have now, we're assuming they kept the number of people in the know limited. That would mean that the bombers, the bomb maker, or someone from Kingmakers transported the bombs into the city," Ashley said.

Milan shook his head. "Not the bombers. They're brown, which draws more suspicion than a white driver. Regardless of how you feel about it, racial profiling is still very much a thing with the NYPD. Kingmakers would've known that, so they would've picked a white driver."

Ashley wrote that down on the gigantic whiteboard she used for their brainstorm session. "So either the bomb maker or someone from Kingmakers."

"Kingmakers is located in DC," Brandi, one of the agents on the team, said. "If one of the Kingmakers men drove, that meant they either had to pick it up in Oklahoma or meet Brooks somewhere. DC isn't on the way unless Brooks made a massive detour."

Ashley added it to the list.

"Considering the weight and size, we're looking for a van, a pickup truck, or even a dump truck or something similar," Xander, another agent, said.

"Driving a dump truck on Manhattan is difficult," Milan pointed out. "Especially if you're not familiar with the area."

"Sure, but Jon Brooks would be used to them, considering he owns a construction company," Xander replied.

"Yeah, but would he drive one all the way from Oklahoma? Those things can't be comfortable for such a long distance."

Another note on the whiteboard.

"Let's leave the identity of the driver for now. The question is, would he have used one of the high traffic routes, like the Lincoln Tunnel, or a more obscure route to get to the storage facility?" Ashley looked around the table. "Both have arguments pro and con."

"Were any of them familiar in New York?" Brandi asked. "Do we have any evidence of them ever spending time in the city?"

"Oh, great question. As far as I know, not, but let me double-check," Ashley said. "But what are you thinking?"

"Look, traffic on Manhattan is a nightmare, even for those of us who live there and are used to it. Everyone knows this. Hell, every tourist guide about the city mentions this. If you're not familiar with it, it's ten times worse. So if the driver didn't know the area well, my guess is he took the easiest route."

Brandi was from New York. Brooklyn, judging by her

accent, and while she made a good point, something about it niggled Milan, but he couldn't put his finger on it.

Ashley pulled up a map and plotted a course from Oklahoma City to the Stonewall Inn. "In that case, he would've come in through the Holland Tunnel."

Milan clicked his tongue. "That's debatable. First of all, if he drove anything else but a van or a normal pickup truck, he wouldn't have been able to use it. That tunnel has strict limitations on size and weight. Depending on whether he was transporting all bombs at the same time or just one, he'd have been over the weight limit as well. But more importantly, you can't transport explosives or any hazardous materials through the tunnel."

Xander frowned. "Do they check that?"

"They do random checks, especially when they see a vehicle that's overweight. I don't think he'd take that risk. Everything we've seen so far confirms that Kingmakers plans things into detail. My guess is the driver took either the Lincoln Tunnel or a bridge."

Brandi narrowed her eyes, and Milan could practically see her brain spinning. "If he'd kept on driving on the 95..."

"He would've taken the George Washington Bridge," Milan said.

"Then south on the Harlem River Drive and the FDR Drive."

"Houston would've been the easiest, then north on Sixth Avenue."

Ashley highlighted the route Milan and Brandi had suggested on a detailed map of Manhattan. "OK, let's start here. Pull all footage from traffic cams from this route and mark any vans and trucks. Don't rely on previous analysis. Fresh eyes, people."

Milan leaned back, staring at the map while the others

got up. The route they'd come up with made sense, and yet something didn't sit right with him. If Brooks or one of the Kingmakers guys had transported the bombs, where would he have dropped those off? At the storage facility? But how did you carry something that big into a building and not draw attention, especially when it included three young brown men? Someone would've remembered, and no one had. The FBI had asked everyone, and no one had noticed anything around the storage facility.

"Wait," he said. The others, who were already at the door, turned around.

"What's up?" Ashley asked.

"What if we've been wrong about the storage facility?"

Ashley cocked her head. "I'm listening."

"The storage facility showed no traces of explosives when forensics processed it, correct?"

Everyone walked back again and retook their seats.

"Yes, but more than a week had passed since the bombing, which explains the lack of physical evidence," Xander said.

"The fake name that was used was too easy to find. What if the whole thing was a decoy? What if they wanted us to focus there, knowing we'd run into a dead end, and they stored the bomb somewhere else?" The more Milan thought about it, the more he was convinced he was right.

The room grew quiet. "If Brooks transported the bomb close to the storage facility, we're talking about a rough-looking, middle-aged, white male...who met up with three young, brown students," Brandi said slowly. "That would stand out on Manhattan. In the other boroughs, not so much, but in the area around Stonewall? It would. And even if it had been one of the Kingmakers guys, like Basil King, Kurt Barrows, or Steve Duron, we're still talking about three people, including two brown men, carrying something big and heavy from a van into a building."

Milan nodded. "Exactly. Someone would've noticed, and if they didn't call the cops at that time, they would've at least come forward after the bombing. The faces of the three bombers were plastered all over the news. No one confirmed seeing them here with the bombs. Canvassing the area, yes, but never with the bombs. So how did those get there?"

They all looked at each other.

"Let's assume for a moment the bombs weren't stored at that storage facility. That means they somehow had to be brought to the area. How and by whom?" Ashley asked. Milan loved that she kept trying to see the entire picture rather than focus on one minor aspect at the risk of missing connections.

"Go through the placement of the bombs again," Milan said.

Ashley gestured at Brandi, who connected her laptop to the projector and pulled up a map. "The first bomb was hidden in a trash can close to the Stonewall Inn. We have partial camera footage of someone matching the physical description of one of the three bombers placing it. It was the smallest of the three bombs, carried in a suitcase."

Milan nodded. "What about the other two?"

"Both were hidden on a float. The second bomb was on the float from the Rainbow Pride Foundation, a nonprofit that helps homeless LGBT+ kids in New York. And the third bomb, the biggest, was on Club 69's float. Both floats were held at the same location on Washington Street, along with two more floats."

She marked the locations on the map with a red circle. The floats had been built only a couple of blocks away from the Stonewall Inn. Close enough to walk—but not with a bomb that size.

"How did they get into that building?"

"We still don't know. There was no sign of forced entry. The building was locked and had no security cameras. In the week before the parade, people constantly walked in and out, from what we've gathered. We questioned every single person who worked on those floats or even at that location, and none of them saw any of the three bombers inside. We showed their pictures everywhere."

Milan leaned back, mentally organizing the information. "How long would they have needed to place the bombs?"

"At least fifteen minutes. They would've had to cover them up well enough so no one would discover them."

"Show me the footage from the parade."

For an hour, they watched and rewatched, then went back to the map and puzzled, still not getting anywhere, though everyone kept coming up with ideas and suggestions that Ashley wrote down. Milan looked at the images of Seth chasing the suspect. "I know he still died, but if Seth hadn't chased him, the blast would've taken him out," Brandi said.

Milan froze. "Wait. Was he expecting to die?"

"I don't know for sure, but we don't think so. Why?" Ashley asked.

"If he placed the bomb himself, he would've known how powerful the thing was. He would've been a hell of a lot farther away from it when it went off. Instead, he was standing there, waiting for it to go boom."

"He had to be close to detonate it. They had remote detonators."

"But he ran away. When did he set it off?"

Brandi rewound, then paused the frame. "Here. See? He

has the remote in his hand, and he's looking over his shoulder as he's pressing it. That was Seth's signal to warn everyone."

"It doesn't make sense, not if he expected to walk away from the blast. He only set it off there because Seth chased him. Otherwise, he would've been on that sidewalk when he pressed the button, and it would've killed him. Unless he didn't know its power and wasn't even sure what he was setting off."

Brandi frowned. "How's that possible? He placed it on the float."

"Did he? Or do we assume he did?"

"We have surveillance footage of him the week before, canvassing the area, both around Washington Street and along the route of the Pride Parade. Same for the other two. They hired a storage facility. We have them on camera when the bombs go off, and we know they set them off," Ashley said.

"The one element that's missing, at least for bombs two and three, is how they got them into the building and onto the floats. Think about it. Three Indian-looking students. Or maybe two. Around a building where floats are being built for a Pride parade. They would've stood out like a sore thumb. The queer community is hella diverse, but we don't have many Indian-looking members..."

"What are you saying?"

"What if they didn't place the bombs? They set them off and took the fall, but what if they never placed them on the floats because they would've drawn too much attention? What if they had no idea what they were doing, how much damage they would inflict?"

Brandi swallowed. "But if they didn't place them, who did?"

Things clicked into place for Milan. "We're talking about three guys from an impoverished area in India with no confirmed prior knowledge of explosives or any terrorist training. Would Kingmakers really have trusted them to set up the bombs, knowing they might make a mistake? Or that the very color of their skin would arouse suspicion? No, they used one of their own. They placed the bombs themselves."

"Shit." Ashley slapped her fist on the table. "I think you're right. And of course when we did the interviews, we only knew about the three bombers. We had no idea of Kingmakers' involvement, so we never thought to ask about anyone else. In general terms, yes, but these guys are good. I'm sure they found a way to infiltrate that building without arousing anyone's suspicion."

"Start over, ask questions all over again," Milan said. "Only now show pictures of Barrow, King, Duron, and even Wesley Quirk. My money is on one of them."

Ashley nodded, furiously scribbling on the whiteboard.

"If they placed the bombs themselves, where did they store them?" Xander brought up their previous dilemma again.

"After 9/11, people on Manhattan are suspicious." Milan steepled his fingers. "I think it would be impossible to carry something that big into a storage unit and not have someone ask questions." An idea struck. "How long did they work on the floats?"

"Two weeks," Ashley said.

"If I had to do it, I'd volunteer for one of the crews. Show up every day, be nice, and work hard so no one would ever suspect me. I'd be white, present myself as queer, and make sure I'd fit in. Bring in the bomb the day before when everyone is used to you being there and won't ask questions."

"Yes." Ashley tapped the marker against her chin. "That's the smart way. But they still would've had to store it somewhere. And I doubt they did it in that storage facility."

"No, nowhere close. Too many questions and risks. South Bronx," Milan said. "That's where I would do it. People know better than to ask questions there. And for the right money, you don't need a storage facility. You use an empty building and pay off whoever controls it. It's one of the few areas left that still could be called a ghetto. A simple Google search for the worst neighborhoods in New York would've turned that up."

"And if they were smart, they smuggled the bomb in long before the parade, so we'd look for it in the wrong time period," Brandi brought up.

"What are our chances of finding surveillance footage from that area from six years ago?" Xander asked.

"About zero," Milan said. "Cameras don't survive for long in the South Bronx. But...if you send the right agents to ask around, showing pictures of all the suspects, asking if they recognize any of them, and offer certain *benefits*, you may hit gold."

Ashley, who he knew was from rural Pennsylvania, looked at him questioningly. "How?"

"Tell them flat out it's about the Pride Bombing, pay them cold hard cash, and send local agents or cops, plainclothes people who speak the language. These guys are wary of outsiders, but one of their own who can appeal to the common ground of being pissed as fuck someone set off bombs in their city again may get lucky."

"Let me run this by Coulson, but it's worth a shot," Ashley said.

"If you need volunteers for this, let me know," Milan said. "I know a couple of guys who've done undercover work in criminal organizations, and this would be right up their alley."

"Let me check that with Coulson as well, but I may take you up on that. I'm sure you've discovered by now, but the FBI can be bureaucratic...and slow."

"Slow? A sloth would get a speeding ticket here." Milan winked at her.

That earned him some chuckles.

Ashley straightened her shoulders. "In the meantime, let's review all traffic cam footage again, now going back two months. Flag any vans, trucks, any vehicles large enough to transport the materials. And we'll start with the George Washington Bridge because even in the South Bronx scenario, that would still be our best bet."

15

The waiting room in Georgetown University Hospital smelled so clean it stung Branson's nose. He'd turned the volume down of the TV that was anchored to the wall, not in the least interested in watching *Good Morning America*. The water cooler gently bubbled every few minutes, but otherwise, the room was quiet with him as the only occupant, waiting for his sister to arrive. She'd texted him she was on her way—and knowing Brenda, she'd make it in record time. Need for Speed was like her personal credo.

He paced the room, too restless to sit down in one of the thin-padded beige seats. Hell, the entire room was beige from the walls to the floor and the chairs. He hated beige, in his opinion the most horrendous color on the planet. since it lacked any personality. Bland, boring, beige. There was a reason those words alliterated.

Quick steps in the hallway *click-clacked* toward him, and seconds later, Brenda rushed into the room. Dressed in jeans, boots, and a bomber jacket, she looked every inch the tough Air Force pilot. She stepped straight into his open arms.

"The circumstances are awful, but I'm so happy to see you," he said, hugging her tightly.

Brenda held on to him for an uncharacteristically long time. "Likewise, but I'm grateful we get to hang out for a bit," she said as she finally let go, her voice thick with emotions.

"When did you come in?"

She looked tired, her eyes small and her face pale. No wonder after her travel from Turkey.

"Yesterday evening late through Germany. Spent the night in a motel, too exhausted to drive anywhere."

"I would've picked you up if you'd asked me."

She put her head on his shoulder, leaning into him. "I know, but I was on a military flight to Andrews, and that's such a shitty drive for you. Plus, I wasn't even sure what time I'd be arriving."

"How long can you stay?"

"I have initial approval for forty-eight hours, excluding travel time, but if something goes wrong during the surgery…"

She didn't finish her sentence, but she didn't have to. If their dad didn't make it through the surgery, she'd get bereavement leave. Branson couldn't even allow himself to entertain that option. His dad had to make it.

"Mom is with Dad," he told Brenda. "She can stay with him until they bring him to the OR, which should be"—he checked his watch—"right about now."

"We're in for a long day. Did you bring something to do?"

He grinned at her. "Of course I did."

Her eyes widened. "Oh no, you didn't…"

"Hell, yes, I did."

He grabbed his backpack and pulled out Stratego, the board game his sister loved to play, beaming as he held it up.

"God, I love you," Brenda said. "You're the best brother I could've ever wished for."

"You're welcome. Wanna play?"

They set up on the small, somewhat rickety table in the corner, sitting down on wobbly folding chairs that would kill their backs and asses in an hour, but whatever. Branson had just made his first move when his mom walked in.

"How was Dad?" he asked.

His mom dragged a more comfortable-looking chair over, then sat down with a sigh. "He was in good spirits, excited to get this step over with."

"Did the doctors say anything?" Brenda asked.

"Nothing new. His chances of making it through the surgery are good, but there are always risks."

"You know how Dad feels about risks," Brenda said.

Branson nodded. "There can be no life without risk..."

"...and when our center is strong, everything else is secondary, even the risks," Brenda finished the quote from Elie Wiesel that had always hung in their dad's study.

They both extended a hand to their mom, and she took them, smiling. "Our center is still strong," she said, her voice clear. She squeezed their hands, then let go, straightening her back. "Now, who's winning?"

"We just got started, but obviously, I'll beat him," Brenda said with a wink at Branson.

They resumed playing while his mom dove into one of her romance novels, and it seemed his sister had been right, as she quickly gained the upper hand. Not that Branson minded. He'd never taken losing board games personally. In fact, he'd never been as competitive as Brenda and his dad were. He'd mostly played board games because they loved them.

His hand halted as the realization sunk in. Was this another example of what Ryder had said? How often had Branson not even considered an alternative he preferred just because he wanted to please the other person? Brenda loved board games and especially strategic games like this one, so he'd brought Stratego. He hadn't even debated picking something for himself.

"Bran?" Brenda asked. "You okay?"

He mentally shook himself. "Yeah. No. I don't know."

She frowned. "What do you mean? What's going on?"

"Nothing. It's something someone said to me the other day, and it keeps playing through my head."

"What did they say?"

His mom had looked up from her book and was now studying him. He shouldn't have brought this up. She had enough to worry about. "It doesn't matter. It's not important."

Brenda clicked her tongue. "Yeah, that won't fly. Cough it up, Bran."

Funny, before, he might've done the same thing, might've reacted the same way if the roles had been reversed. But Ryder's simple remark about not respecting his boundaries had opened his eyes to how others might experience his persistence. "Not to sound like a stubborn two-year-old, but if I don't want to talk about it, please don't try to make me."

Brenda narrowed her eyes. "Why would you say that?"

"Because I told you it didn't matter, and you put pressure on me to talk about it anyway."

She blinked. "That's something new. I'm assuming this has to do with whatever this person said to you?"

Yeah, his sister was smart. Plus, she knew him better than anyone else. Although they were unmistakably related in their appearance, they were different in character, but they'd always been close. Probably because they'd had to start over so many times in their lives. New country, new culture, new school, new language...new friends. They'd always leaned on each other.

"Do you think I'm hard to get to know?" he said after a long pause.

She leaned back in her chair, studying him. "You're super easy to get along with, but I'm not sure about getting to know you... Maybe that's not as simple as people would expect."

"Why not? I've always made friends easily."

"Real friends? Or casual acquaintances?"

Dammit, how was it possible she'd immediately zeroed in on the problem? Had she known all along? "How many true friends do you have?" he shot back, then winced at his sharp tone. "Sorry, I didn't mean it like that."

"Bran, what happened? I've never seen you like this..."

Genuine worry colored her voice, and that convinced him to confide in her. "You know what I realized when Dad fell ill? That I don't have close friends... I have acquaintances galore, but no real friends, the kind I can count on in times like this."

Understanding lit up on her face. "I know how that feels."

"Aren't you super close with Lucia and Melinda?"

She shrugged. "I like hanging out with them, but they're not the type of friends I'd call to hide a body, you know?"

He knew exactly what she meant. "How did this happen to us?"

Brenda glanced at their mom, who looked guilty. "Mom and I talked about this a few months ago, about the effect moving around has had on me. I loved living in different countries, and it never felt like a negative thing to me, but I can't deny it's affected me."

Branson's mom nodded. "After that talk with Brenda, I did some research, and it showed that it's a similar struggle to what Army brats experience. Moving so often can cause bonding issues and an inability to develop long-term friendships."

Damn. Now that he thought about it, it made total sense, but how had he never realized this? But even then, not having real friends was only part of the problem. "Someone told me I don't talk about myself, that I always focus on the other person. He said that even though we'd worked together for a while and had spent time together, he still knew little about me. And he was right."

His mom cleared her throat. "One of the coping strategies I came across was extreme adaptability."

"What's that?" Branson tried to picture it but wasn't sure if he understood correctly.

"It means that you become so flexible that you respond and adapt to others to get accepted, to the point where you forgo developing your own identity."

Wow. That was... Damn, that hit awfully close to home. Was that what he'd been doing? A wave of emotions rolled over him, then another one, and his throat became tight.

"Bran?"

He held up his hand to his twin. "Give me a moment."

Extreme adaptability. He'd erased himself in order to fit

in. And he *had* fit in, always finding new friends. But those friendships hadn't been real because he'd never been himself. He'd presented the Branson he'd thought would fit best, not his true self. In other words, he'd been a fake. All his life, he'd been phony...and no one had ever called him out on it until Ryder. How was it possible that he had seen what no one else had? And that for someone who, by his own admission, wasn't that socially gifted. *Yeah, right.*

He took a deep breath, then faced his mom and sister again. "Can we drop this for now? It's not the best timing. I'm sure we can agree."

"Absolutely. Let's continue with me beating your ass," Brenda said, clearly attempting to lighten the heavy mood.

Hard as he tried, Branson couldn't let go of what he'd learned. Memories kept popping into his head, occasions where he'd denied himself and had presented what he'd thought was the best version of him, where he'd adapted and changed. Moments where he'd pushed down his feelings, his opinions, where he'd convinced even himself he was interested in something when he hadn't been. Skydiving and fly-fishing were just two examples of an endless row that also contained playing board games with his twin. How depressing that even with the person who knew him best, he still hadn't been able to be himself.

They grabbed some food from the hospital cafeteria, dry sandwiches that tasted like wallpaper glue. Branson swallowed them down, years of eating strange food having trained him for moments like this. He could eat anything if he had liquids to wash it down with, in this case, a Sprite.

Just after lunch, his phone beeped with an incoming text.

. . .

Ryder: How are you?

Branson smiled. He would bet his year salary that Ryder had set an alarm. He'd texted him at the exact same time over the last three days, and Branson found it adorably sweet.

Branson: Hanging in there. It'll be a few more hours before we hear more.
Ryder: Okay. Just wanted to check in.
Branson: I appreciate it.
Ryder: Do you want me to text you later to ask for an update?

Branson stared at the words for a while. What was Ryder offering here? Merely attention or was he making an effort for the careful start of a friendship? Branson wasn't sure, but he didn't want his pity attention. That was even worse than Ryder's initial reluctance to become friends.

Branson: Only if you want to. No pressure.
Ryder: I guess my feedback on consent stuck, huh?

Classic Ryder, no filter and calling it as he saw it.

Branson: Yeah. You were right. About more than just that.

Ryder: Yeah? You can tell me if you want to.
Branson: I think I do, but not today if that's okay.
Ryder: Absolutely. I'll text you at 5 to check in.

W͏ITH A SMILE, Branson closed his phone. He was looking forward to Ryder's text.

16

Seth yawned, stretching his arms above his head. "God, I slept like the dead."

Coulson smiled at him as he finished the Windsor knot in his tie. "I'm glad to hear that, baby."

Seth's stomach went soft at the tender look in his man's eyes. "Thank you for taking care of me."

Coulson had taken him apart the night before, fucking him relentlessly until Seth had been a whimpering, boneless mass, too exhausted and spent to even lift a finger.

"Always."

Seth finished filling the two travel mugs with coffee, then turned off the coffee maker and emptied it. "We're good to go."

"You have my peanut butter and banana sandwiches?"

Seth quirked an eyebrow. "Would I ever forgot those, boo?"

"Good point. Let's get out of here, then."

Usually, they were out the door much earlier, but for once, they had slept a little later, both needing to fuel up on sleep—and sex—if they wanted to continue the grueling hours they were putting in. Coulson had informed his boss the night before, and even Sheehan had told him to come in as late as he wished, proof that he knew how hard they were working.

As soon as Seth drove off, Coulson's phone rang, and after a quick look at the screen, Coulson picked up, connecting it to the car's speaker. "Special Agent Padman."

"Hey, Coulson, Iris here. I have a call you should take."

Iris was one of the newer agents on Coulson's team. A former lawyer, she was methodical in her approach, building cases no one could argue with.

"Who is it?"

"His name is Warren Stack, and he says he's received an email that was intended for someone else... Coulson, I think it was supposed to be sent to Donnie Smith."

Donnie Smith? The security guard from the Baltimore Convention Center had been dead for almost ten months now. Why the hell would someone still email him?

"Patch him through," Coulson said. "Good morning, this is Special Agent Padman," he said as soon as a click indicated she'd connected the call.

"Good morning, agent Padman. My name is Warren Stack. I contacted the FBI because I received a rather disturbing email. Actually, the email was sent to my son, Damon, and the content itself wasn't concerning, but the website it linked to was."

Seth smiled. The man was clearly trying to be accurate, but the slight tremor in his voice betrayed his nerves.

"What kind of email was it?" Coulson asked, his tone warm and calming.

"You know those emails you get when you forgot your password for a website and they send you a link to reset it? My thirteen-year-old son is, quite frankly, not always the smartest when it comes to internet safety, so I monitor his email. He received one of those reset password messages, except I didn't recognize the website, so I figured Damon must've gotten into something he shouldn't have. I clicked the link, and that's where it got weird."

"Where did the link lead to?"

"At first, it showed a normal website for a store or maybe a service called DITS, Durrick IT Services."

Seth's heart skipped a beat. Durrick? Naomi Beckingham's current boyfriend was Ralph Durrick. Not common enough of a last name for this to be a coincidence.

"But then it automatically logged me in, and I ended up on some kind of backend of the website, like a second site hidden behind the first one, only this one was called Proud Patriotic Nationalists. It had some information, but it mostly was a forum where people were exchanging messages with each other as well as private messages."

"What kind of messages?" Coulson sat ramrod straight now, at full attention.

"Agent Padman, I think they're about the assassination of President Markinson. There's talk of money, details about the Baltimore Convention Center and the guards' schedule, and of what this person whose account I got into had to do."

Oh my god. What the hell had happened here? "Mr. Stack, this is Special Agent Seth Rodecker with the Secret Service, listening in on this call. Could you tell me what email address this reset password email was sent to?"

"Yes. My son has a special account he only uses for his online games and things. It's dsfanboys@gmail.com."

Holy crap. Someone had tried to get into Donnie Smith's account and had mistyped his email address by one letter: it had a *z* at the end of boyz rather than an *s*.

"Mr. Stack, do you know how to make screenshots?"

Coulson asked, urgency coloring his voice. "And if you don't, do you have a cell phone you can use to take pictures?"

"I can do screenshots. What do you want me to screenshot?"

"Everything. Once they discover someone else has gained entry, they'll shut this site down, so we need everything you can get. Please start doing this right now."

"On it."

Coulson blew out a slow breath. "Okay, while you do that, I'm going to connect you with one of our IT specialists who will ask for remote access to take over your computer so they can see what you see. If we're fast enough, they may be able to download the entire website. Please do not log out of that site."

In the background, Seth could hear the faint clicks of an app for screenshots.

"Got it. I'm already screen shooting. Want me to do the private messages to whoever they were intended for too?"

"Yes, please. Thank you so much, Mr. Stack."

Coulson pointed at Seth's phone, and Seth nodded he could use it. In the office, placing someone on a brief hold was easy, but on their cell phones, it could get tricky, and it was all too easy to accidentally end the call.

"I'm going to make a brief call, Mr. Stack. I'll mute myself, so you won't be able to hear me, but we can still hear you. If anything happens, just let us know."

"Okay. I've got ten screenshots already."

Thank fuck they'd gotten lucky with someone who was savvy enough to follow directions. Seth knew plenty of people who wouldn't have known how to take a screenshot on a desktop computer if their life depended on it.

Coulson got through to someone from IT and gave quick instructions for her to call Mr. Stack in a minute. "Mr. Stack?

Special Agent Amy Niles will call you as soon as we hang up. If for some reason, you don't get her call, please call the FBI again and ask for me by name."

"Okay, will do."

"And, Mr. Stack? Thank you. In time, I'll be able to tell you how crucially important this information is you've given us, but thank you."

"My pleasure, Agent Padman. Just doing my patriotic duty as an American citizen."

Within twenty seconds after ending the call, Coulson received a text message. "Connected with Mr. Stack," he read out loud. "That's from Amy. She's on the phone with him."

"Holy shit," Seth said, his head still reeling. "If that website is what I think it is, we just hit the jackpot."

"Proud Patriotic Nationalists?" Coulson said. "They might as well have called themselves the KKK. Sure as fuck sounds the same to me."

"Do you think Naomi's boyfriend runs that?"

"Wouldn't surprise me. With her support, most likely, considering her history of being a right-wing extremist."

"He's an IT specialist," Seth said. "He'd have the skills to build something like this."

They were all but sure it had been Naomi's boyfriend who had hacked into the Secret Service's server, using the entrance Christopher Hales had unwittingly provided by clicking on the link Naomi had sent him to her "résumé." According to what they'd discovered about him, he had experience with hacking, having been warned by the FBI back when he'd still been in high school for illegal online activities. If he were behind this, he'd upped his game.

When they arrived in the office, Amy had already uploaded the first screenshots into their system, and Seth pulled them up. His heart caught in his throat as he went through them, Coulson sitting next to him and reading along with him.

"Twenty thousand dollars," Seth whispered. "That's what they paid Donnie Smith to let the bomber and the bomb in. For twenty thousand dollars, he had the president killed."

"It's so little." Coulson put his hand on Seth's lower back in silent support. "You can't even buy a new car for that. I know it shouldn't make a difference, but the fact that they bought him for so cheap is… It somehow makes it worse. If they'd paid him millions, at least I could've understood what he got out of it. But twenty thousand dollars? That's nothing. Peanuts."

"I doubt Hamza Bashir was a similar bargain, but we'll find out."

Amy called twenty minutes later. "The site kicked me out, and it's shut down now, but I was able to download a lot. I have all private messages to Donnie Smith and some from the forum. I wasn't able to get any other private messages, since they were behind another firewall that I couldn't get through that fast. But I've already sent a request to Legal to contact their web host and prevent them from deleting their backup. Hopefully, that will get us the rest."

"That's amazing work, Amy. Thanks for jumping on this."

"We got lucky with Mr. Stack. He wasn't merely cooperative, but he knew enough about computers to quickly give me access so I could take over his computer within two minutes."

Together, they poured over the screenshots. Mr. Stack had been right. The private messages had been about the assassination, and they contained all the details Donnie had provided. He'd given them the guards' schedule, a detailed map from the convention center with cameras and security elements marked, all the information he'd picked up about the Secret Service protection, and more. And he'd received instructions on what time to be at the back door to let Ghulat Babur in, including a line that whoever would be escorting him would be dressed like a cop.

It was all there, the whole plan, all the details. The proverbial smoking gun in all its glory. They'd figured most of it out, but to see it all spelled out was still shocking. Donnie had had second thoughts at some point, but whoever had sent him these messages had reaffirmed his decision to be a true patriot, to liberate his country from the socialist, left-wing rule of a corrupt president, to bring honor back to the White House, and more similar statements that made Seth's stomach turn sour.

Everyone on the forum—and they were still figuring out how many people were members or at least had access—used nicknames. Donnie Smith's nickname had been Benjamin Tallmadge, after the man who had organized the famous Culper Ring, a network of spies during the Revolutionary War that had helped George Washington obtain critical knowledge about the British. Seth doubted Donnie Smith had picked that name himself, since from all the info they'd found out about him, he didn't strike him as a history buff. Maybe he'd been given that nickname in another effort to butter him up, make him feel important.

Then the information Amy had downloaded came in, and with every word Seth read, his anger grew. "They boasted after the Pride Bombing about using Muslims to divert the attention so they could strike again," he said bitterly to Coulson.

"They" being Kingmakers, they determined from

reading through everything. Even though Ralph Durrick owned and administrated the site, he didn't seem to be the one in charge. Whether it was Basil King himself or one of his men, they hadn't figured out yet, but someone from Kingmakers ran the show...calling himself George Washington. Subtle, they were not.

Ralph Durrick had labeled himself Paul Revere, and they suspected that Virginia Hall was the nickname for Naomi Beckingham, since it was the only female name they'd found so far. A quick Google search had shown that Virginia Hall had been a famous American spy in the Second World War.

"Yeah," Coulson said with a sigh. "Proud Patriotic Nationalists, but by all means, let's use a group that represents everything we stand for and let them take the fall. How do these people live with themselves?"

"What's this?" Seth pointed at an exchange on the forum. It was dated only weeks before. "Who the hell is this Eisenhower?"

Paul Revere: Sissy has no idea of Eisenhower's plans. He's so stupid.

Virginia Hall: @GeorgeWashington When will Eisenhower make his move?

George Washington: We gotta lie low for a while. Too much heat from the feds. But fear not, he'll step up when the time is right, and he'll be the man we need.

"No clue," Coulson said.

Seth studied the snippet again. "Sissy... That could refer to President Shafer. It's still a derogatory term for any cis man not considered masculine enough. Him being bisexual would qualify."

"Hmm, could very well be. But how does Eisenhower fit in? So far, we've had a theme of spies and revolutionaries. He doesn't fit. He was a…"

They looked at each other.

"…a general who became president," Seth finished his sentence.

Holy shit. General John Doty, former Secretary of Defense. Could it be?

17

"What kind of picture should I use on that app?" Ryder sat curled up on Dorian's couch, frowning as he studied the profile he'd been filling out. No more talking about hooking up. He was gonna do it. He needed sex, and he was done waiting.

It had been another crazy busy time at work, with Branson catching up after missing the day before for his father's surgery, and then the news of the website Coulson had been tipped about had come in, and they'd spent hours going through every line of that, looking for clues. Ryder had been happy having concrete information to search for, but he was just getting started, so no results yet. Hence the need for some distraction…and relaxation.

Dorian shot a quick glance at Amelia, who was building impressive constructions with her Duplo blocks. From the looks of it, she'd inherited her father's technical skills. "Is it to date or to…" He dropped his voice. "Hook up?"

Right. Amelia might only be two, but she was a smart cookie. "The latter."

"Then show your bestselling feature."

Ryder quirked an eyebrow. "Not sure how you want me to take a picture of my sparkling personality."

Dorian snorted. "Your ass, dimwit."

"My ass?"

"Yeah. It's rather spectacular in case you hadn't noticed, and since you're a full-on bottom boy, you might as well advertise it."

"Bottom!" Amelia repeated happily, beaming at her dad as if she was proud she'd managed to say it.

Dorian groaned. "We're totally ruining my daughter's innocence." Then he smiled at the little girl. "Yes, sweetheart, bottom. Good job saying such a difficult word."

"Daddy!" Amelia giggled, then went back to her colorful bricks.

"If you didn't want her to know that term, why did you repeat it?" Ryder asked.

"Tip from my mom. She said that kids pick up on forbidden words and will repeat those at the most unfortunate moments, but if you act as if the word is normal, they're much more likely to forget it."

"I wonder how she found that out."

Dorian grinned. "Apparently, my sister once yelled 'goddammit' at the top of her lungs at some work event my parents attended. My father had dropped something heavy on his foot a few days earlier and had let that heartfelt exclamation out, and when she'd asked what that meant, he'd tried to distract her. Clearly, that approach hadn't worked."

"Oops."

"Yeah, oops indeed. So I'm trying a different strategy…"

"But back to my question. You think I should take a picture of my ass…ets?"

"Yes. From the right angle, no top will be able to refuse that blatant invitation."

Funny, Ryder had never thought of himself as sexy, but the way Dorian made it sound, he'd been wrong. "I never knew you were so invested in my...assets."

Dorian shrugged. "You're like a brother to me, but I'm not blind. Besides, I'm as much a needy bottom as you are, so it's not like I don't know what you should work with."

"Bottom!" Amelia exclaimed again, seeking her dad's approval.

Ryder laughed. "Good luck explaining that at day care."

"At least it's a relatively innocent expression. Imagine if she'd drop the word c-o-c-k there."

Ah, spelling, the old adult strategy of keeping things from their kids, at least until they could read and write well enough to spell quickly. "True. Anyway, what's the best angle for that pic?"

"I keep forgetting you haven't done this in years."

"Neither have you. Can I just point that out?"

"Two years in my case. Almost six for you. If we're keeping score."

"Semantics."

"Look, she's gonna go down for her nap in a few minutes, so if you can wait until she's asleep, I'll help you."

True to his word, Dorian put Amelia in bed ten minutes later, and the kid was out like a light. Dorian rubbed his hands as he walked back into the living room. "Okay, horny boy. Strip and show me those assets."

"What, you're not even gonna take me out on a date first? Why, sir, you are moving awfully fast..." Ryder pretended to fan himself, batting his eyelashes, and Dorian chuckled.

"You're having way too much fun with this."

They kept laughing and joking as they found a spot in Dorian's bedroom with a suitable background. Ryder stripped without thinking about it twice. Weirdness didn't exist between him and Dorian. They'd been through too much together for that.

"Push your ass back," Dorian instructed. "Now put one hand on the wall and look over your shoulder."

"Are you including my face?"

"No, but that twist in your spine makes your ass pop."

Okay, then. Ryder dutifully followed instructions while Dorian took one pic after another on his phone. "You should start a career in porn," Ryder joked when Dorian was satisfied. "You're good at this."

He got dressed again, then checked out the pics Dorian had taken. Damn, he hadn't been kidding. Framed like that, Ryder's ass did look spectacular.

"Thank you," he said.

"Don't mention it. What are friends for if not for taking dick pics or, in this case, ass pics?"

Someone should put that on one of those inspirational quote things on Instagram: "True friendship is taking a picture of your best friend's ass so he can score some quality dick."

They settled back on the couch, where Ryder added the three best pics to his profile, took a deep breath, and made it live. There, done. With any luck, he'd get laid tonight. And with even more luck, he'd get fucked into the mattress.

"What did you put into your profile?" Dorian asked.

"Hungry bottom looking for an aggressive top."

Dorian's eyes widened. "Wow, not exactly subtle, is it?"

"It's a hookup app. Subtlety is not the point."

"Mmm, true. I keep forgetting that when it comes to sex, you're not shy and introverted."

Dorian wasn't the only one who made that mistake, and he'd known Ryder for many years. People often assumed that because he was introverted and a geek, he'd be like that in bed as well...but he wasn't. Ever since he'd discovered sex —and he'd been a late bloomer at nineteen—he'd decided to go after what he wanted. Why settle for bad sex when he could get better? Except, it seemed, with Paul. Why had he accepted mediocre sex with him? It still baffled him.

His phone dinged. "Oh, I recognize that sound. Someone took the bait." Dorian grinned.

Before Ryder could open the app, his phone dinged again and then once more. Look at that; he still had it. Good to know. He checked the responses. The first one was an immediate no. "Stern Daddy Looking for a Boy to Spoil" the profile's headline read. Nope. No offense, but Ryder wasn't into Daddy kink. Or much older guys. To each his own, but not his thing.

The second one was a maybe. Thirty-seven years old, and if that truly was the guy's body, he was in excellent shape.

"Let me see." Dorian curled his fingers in a "gimme" gesture, and Ryder scooted over closer to him so they could look together. "Mmm, he's hot."

"If that is really his pic, then yes."

Dorian winced. "Good point. What about that one?"

Ryder opened the profile he pointed at. Dorian whistled. "Damn, boy, that is one fiiiiine piece of equipment."

He wasn't wrong. The pic showed off one hell of a cock, close up in every veiny detail, with a thick drop of precum dripping from the slit. How long was that thing? At least eight inches if Ryder had to take a guess. "That's a work of art." He swiped to the next picture, which showed a little more of the guy's body with tight abs and a nice cum gutter.

A guy like that had to have his pick of bottoms to fuck, and yet he'd responded to Ryder. Maybe Dorian had been right. Maybe it was time to delete everything Paul had told him from his system and start over. A hard fuck would help with that, and especially a hard fuck by a dick that size. Sign. Him. Up.

I'm in, he messaged back. *When and where?*

"What did you put in as location anyway?" Dorian asked. "Around here?"

"Fuck, no. Way too much chance of running into someone I know from school or some shit. Nope, I did DC and suburbs. Plenty of horny fish in the sea there."

A ding alerted him to an incoming message. *Are you available tonight?*

Yes.

Madrassa Motel, room 61. 8 p.m.?

I'll be there.

See? He liked this. No complicated rituals, no endless required socializing, no need for negotiations. Dick and ass, top and bottom, easy as that. He turned off his phone.

"I'm out of here. I have a booty call I gotta answer."

Dorian hugged him. "Have fun. Be safe."

Ryder nodded. "I'll turn on my location for you."

"Good."

He spent the next two hours preparing, showering and cleaning himself, then doing some grooming and manscaping. He hadn't bothered since he'd broken up with Paul, but he needed to feel pretty and wanted tonight, and so he waxed himself until his balls and ass were as smooth as velvet. Perfect.

Choosing what to wear had always been a challenge, since he didn't give two fucks about clothes and brands, but Paul had badgered him enough over the years to look presentable that Ryder owned a few outfits that looked great on him. He picked a pair of tight jeans and a black button-down shirt made of some slightly shiny material. He refused to wear uncomfortable shoes, so his Converse would have to do, geeky or not. Dress shoes gave him blisters.

He gave himself a last check in the mirror, nodding at what he saw. That was as sexy as he would ever be, and Paul might be an asshole, but he hadn't been lying when he said those jeans made Ryder's ass pop. They totally did.

He snuck out before his mom could ask him what he was up to—another major drawback of moving back in with his parents—then drove to DC. The Madrassa motel was on the northwest side of downtown, which made it a quick drive for him, and the parking lot had plenty of space. Easy-peasy.

He waited in his car until a few minutes before eight, then walked in and took the elevator up to the sixth floor. For a motel that rented rooms by the hour, it looked pretty decent and clean. He took a deep breath, then knocked on the door of room 61. He'd prepared a casual greeting for when this guy would open the door, but when it happened, his mouth dropped open.

"What the fuck are you doing here?" he asked Branson, who stood there looking equally mystified, wearing only a pair of tight underwear, showing off every perfect muscle on his body.

Wait. Branson had been expecting company, or he wouldn't have opened the door. And dressed like that, he'd been expecting a hookup.

Oh, no. It couldn't be...

Ryder's eyes dropped to Branson's crotch, where a sizable dick lay half-hard under the thin cotton of his underwear.

Shit, shit, shit. Out of all the dicks in the world, he'd picked Branson's.

18

For the second time in a few days, Branson was speechless, his brain spinning as he tried to comprehend what was happening. What was Ryder doing here when Branson had been expecting...?

Oh.

Oh.

Ryder had... That had been Ryder's ass. That drool-worthy, absolutely perfect butt had been Ryder's. He cleared his throat. "Same thing as you, I suspect."

Confusion marred Ryder's face. "What?"

"You asked what I was doing here. The same thing as you. Hook up."

"So it was you, that... That dick pic."

Branson fought to keep his face straight. "Yes. I didn't use a dick double if that's what you wanted to know."

Ryder groaned. "Can we move this conversation inside your room? I'm not comfortable discussing this in the hallway."

Branson stepped aside and let him in, then closed the door behind him.

"And maybe put on some clothes?" Ryder waved at Branson's body.

Right. His poor dick had deflated, which Branson couldn't blame it for because talk about a cold shower. Though he had to admit Ryder looked hot AF in those tight jeans. He snuck a few glances as he got dressed, and yup, that picture had definitely been Ryder's own ass. Yummy.

"How the fuck did this happen?" Ryder asked.

Branson didn't like the hint of suspicion in Ryder's voice. "It's not like I had anything to do with it."

Ryder studied him for a few beats, then nodded. "Okay. Pure coincidence, then?"

Branson sighed. "Yeah, combined with the fact that most guys use Grindr now, but I suppose you don't have that app for the same reason as me."

"Can't have that location service turned on."

"Exactly. Plus, the encryption of Grindr is too weak, leaving it vulnerable to being hacked."

The downside of working for the CIA or for any intelligence agency was that they had to be extremely careful not to expose themselves to potential scandal and especially blackmail. Being gay was fine, but evidence of hookups? Dick pics? Anything that could be used for blackmail? Not so much.

"So what do we do now?" Ryder said, looking dejected with stooped shoulders, shuffling his feet.

Warmth spread through Branson at his vulnerable expression. "I'm sorry. Neither of us is at fault, but I truly am sorry…"

Ryder slowly nodded. "Me too. I'd been looking forward to…" He gestured at the bed.

"Same. After this week, I thought it might provide some necessary relief for me. Even though the surgery went well,

I'm still stressed about my dad." He hesitated, then decided he might as well be honest. "I know it sounds stupid, but fucking is a great way for me to get rid of stress."

Ryder only blinked. "Not weird at all."

"No?"

"Why would it be? Sex can be many things for people, so why wouldn't stress relief be a valid experience?"

"Was that what you were looking for?" he dared to ask.

Ryder's eyes widened for a moment, but then he caught himself. "Not primarily, though I do appreciate a good...dicking."

Branson grinned. They were speaking the same language now, and how about that? It was like talking to a different person. Instead of introverted, geeky Ryder, he was this sexy guy, radiating a special kind of confidence. "Likewise, though I prefer to do said dicking."

"That's why I picked your profile."

Branson tilted his head. "You into big dicks?"

"Yes. That and a hard fucking. I'm not a fan of the slow, tender stuff. I want to still feel it two days later."

Branson swallowed. "You're being awfully forthcoming all of a sudden."

Ryder sighed. "I know. I shouldn't be. It's just...bad timing, I suppose. I spent two hours preparing for this, and now...I'm disappointed."

He'd prepared for two hours? Doing what? "Care to share details?"

Ryder's mouth pulled up in one corner. "That depends on whether we can agree to apply the Vegas rule."

Vegas? Hell, yes. "Yes. I solemnly vow this is Vegas."

"In that case, I waxed. Everywhere."

Branson groaned, easily picturing how that would look...and even better, how beautiful his cock would look, sliding between those peachy, smooth ass cheeks. "Not sure I should've asked."

Ryder sobered. "What are we doing? We can't…"

"We shouldn't."

"But…"

Their eyes locked, the air between them crackling.

"Vegas."

Ryder took his glasses off and threw them carelessly onto a chair. "Fuck, yes. Vegas."

Branson wasn't even sure who moved, but Ryder was in his arms, and their mouths met in a frantic kiss. Tongues came out, dueling, pushing, probing, and Ryder gave as good as he got. Branson needed to taste him, sink into him deeper, explore every inch of his mouth and his body. He walked them backward until he had him backed against the wall, moaning when Ryder's minty flavor filled his mouth. Slick, smooth, sexy. On fire.

Their kiss didn't slow down, not even a little bit, and when Branson nipped at Ryder's bottom lip, he was rewarded with a low moan of pleasure. He kissed the bruised spot, then did it again. Ryder took over, invading Branson's mouth with an aggression that was the hottest thing ever. Shy, geeky Ryder was a fucking beast in bed, and Branson loved every second of it.

They were almost the same height, with Ryder being a hell of a lot more slender, and Branson used his weight to pin Ryder's hands above his head, rubbing himself against him while Ryder still devoured his mouth. He hadn't been kidding when he said he liked to fuck hard. God, Branson was so on board with that. His last good fuck had been with Seth, and if he thought about that now, he felt guilty because the man so clearly belonged to Coulson.

Ryder tore his mouth away, his eyes dark with want. "You can't ever use this against me. Ever."

It stung that Ryder found it necessary to say this, but Branson couldn't blame him. "I won't."

"Not in teasing, not in a joke, not when you're pissed at me. Not ever. Vegas."

"I promise. For real."

"Good. Then for the love of everything holy, fuck me."

Clothes went flying as they both undressed in a hurry, and Branson's cock was back in action. No wonder. Even the sight of Ryder stepping out of his underwear, that luscious ass on full display, was enough to make him swallow. How had he never noticed that in the office? Right, Ryder's baggy dress pants. He'd been hiding his assets, which had been smart because if Branson had known what he sported underneath his clothes, he might not have been able to resist him.

Ryder plunked down onto the bed on his knees, bent over, and spread his legs. "You waiting for an engraved invitation?"

Branson laughed. "I really like you like this."

He took his time to appreciate the view, studying every line and curve of that perfect ass.

"Yeah? Well, you'd better hurry up, or I'm gonna have to get aggressive."

Thank fuck they were on the same page. Branson wanted Ryder with a fierceness he barely recognized in himself. No subtleness, no foreplay necessary. Just sex. He'd prepared well, and so the condom was already on the butt-ugly nightstand, as was the lube. He rolled it on, squirted some lube, and coated himself.

"Do you need…?" He pointed at Ryder's ass. Usually, with pre-arranged hookups like this that were preplanned, the guys would prep themselves, since it saved time and awkwardness, but he didn't want to assume.

"I'm ready for you. Just go slow. You're...big."

No matter how often he heard it, it never failed to make his heart beat faster. What was it about that compliment that appealed so much to him? Rationally, it was stupid because his cock wasn't his accomplishment, something he could take credit for. And yet he loved it when men admired it.

He crawled onto the bed, then lined up behind him. Ryder hadn't been lying when he said he'd waxed. He was smooth everywhere. Smooth belly, smooth balls, the softest ass right up to his pink little hole, all perfect and edible.

He hesitated. Was Ryder truly okay with being fucked like this without any foreplay or tenderness or words? But then Ryder shamelessly wiggled his ass, and Branson had his answer. If he loved to fuck hard, why wouldn't Ryder?

He pressed against that hole, surprised when he slid in almost instantly. Someone was being a good bottom...or simply horny and eager. *Hungry bottom looking for an aggressive top*, Ryder had advertised himself, so Branson should start believing him. Taking a deep breath, he sank inside him, going slow but steady.

"Fuck, fuck, fuck..." Ryder panted, tensing every now and then before relaxing again.

"You good?"

"Goddammit, that thing is big..."

Branson grinned. "I'll make you feel every inch."

"You'd better keep that promise. Don't go easy on me."

"I won't."

He took his time opening Ryder up, all too aware that with a dick his size, bottoms needed time to adjust. As always, he felt when he could move for real. Ryder let out a sigh, and his body relaxed around Branson's cock.

He thrust in an inch to test the waters, and Ryder let out the most beautiful moan. Yup, they were good to go.

The room smelled of sex already, the mix of sweat and body odors and precum making him even hornier. His next push had more power behind it, and Ryder's breath left his lungs with a whoosh. Mmm, yes. He wanted harder and faster and more. Claim that ass, that hole, sink inside him again and again. Breed him, fill him up...then do it all over again.

A daze came over Branson as he snapped his hips and drove into him, his balls slapping against Ryder's ass.

"Jesus fuck!" Ryder groaned. "Harder."

Branson obliged, putting even more force behind his movements, and was rewarded with a pornstar-worthy moan. Oh yes, that was what he craved to hear. He wanted to make Ryder moan, make him whimper, make him scream. He wished to be the best fuck Ryder had ever had, though why that mattered so much, he had no clue. Not something he'd waste energy on right now. Not when he had more important things to do, like sink inside that tight hole again and again and again.

A myriad of sounds filled the room. Jagged breaths, moans, and grunts. Wet squelches as his body collided with Ryder's when he pushed back in. Erotic music in a sexy symphony that the two of them were composing on the fly. Ryder moved back against him, eager and hungry, signaling he could take whatever Branson dished out.

He pulled out and grabbed Ryder's wrist, then forced him onto his back and pushed his legs up. He slammed back into him. "Again," Ryder shouted. "God, do that again."

Branson's angle had to be spot on because every time he

rammed into him, ecstasy exploded on Ryder's face, his eyes going glassy as he fisted the sheets with both hands. His smooth balls were tight, tucked up against his body. "Oh, fuck…" he moaned. "Ohgogohfuckohgoddammit, fuck me harder. Make me come. I'm so fucking close."

He never made a move to touch himself, and Branson didn't reach for his cock either, figuring that Ryder wanted to come hands-free. Hell to the fucking yes. He sped up, snapping his hips in a brutal rhythm, fighting to stay coordinated and keep the angle right.

Ryder clenched his eyes shut, his body pulling taut as he threw his head back, his back perfectly arched. Branson gave one more thrust as hard as he could, and Ryder's cock erupted, shooting thick, milky ropes all over his own stomach that dripped down the sides, turning his body into a canvas of cum.

Holy shit, it was the hottest thing Branson had ever seen. He slowed down as he fucked Ryder through his orgasm, his channel clenching and spasming around his cock, which brought Branson dangerously close to the edge.

When Ryder finally stopped shaking and opened his eyes, Branson pulled out of him and ripped off the condom. He stroked himself fast and rough, only needing a few tugs to come. He grunted between clenched teeth as his cock pushed out its load, adding it to Ryder's on his stomach.

The second spurt forced out, and Branson shuddered, his belly flaring red hot inside him at the sight of their mixed cum. He'd marked him. What a primitive need and yet he couldn't deny how *right* it felt. The third squirt was thin, and he crashed down as soon as it was out, and rolled onto his back next to Ryder. Holy shit, that had felt like a marathon.

Their ragged breaths calmed down, and the sweat on

Branson's body evaporated, even more when the AC turned on, blasting them with cold air.

"That was spectacular," Ryder said, sounding raw.

"Yeah."

"Do you think we could..."

Branson turned his head toward him. "That we could what?"

"If you want, we could..."

Branson's heart skipped a beat. Hell, yes. "You wanna go again?"

Ryder faced him. "I really do. If we make a mistake, we might as well make it twice, right?"

"Couldn't agree more. Wanna shower and go for round two?"

"What time do we need to leave? How long did you rent the room for?"

He grinned. "We got all night."

19

He should never have agreed to a shower. Ryder was already regretting it as he rolled off the bed. Showering together was way more intimate than sex, strange as it might sound. It meant looking at Branson, *seeing* him, and that seemed the worst idea ever. Not that Branson was bad to look at. Hell no. The guy was insanely hot, even more so naked when every one of his perfect muscles was on full display, rippling like they did now as Branson walked into the bathroom.

Stupid, stupid, stupid. But if Ryder backed out now, he'd be an asshole. Or it would appear as if he regretted this, which he was sure he should and would the day after, but right now, he didn't. Branson had perfectly scratched his itch for a hard fuck, and if he could repeat that once more, all the better. So maybe Ryder should initiate sex in the shower. He could suck Branson until he was hard again, then entice him to fuck Ryder again. Shower problem solved.

Decision made, he took a deep breath and headed in.

Steam was already filling the bathroom, and Branson stepped under the hot water as Ryder joined him. "I thought you'd changed your mind." Branson studied him.

"Nope, just needed a moment."

After a long look, Branson tilted his head back and let the water run down his hair and face. He rubbed his wet face, then moved aside. "Your turn."

Ryder fought to keep his features neutral as he inched closer to him, positioning himself under the showerhead. Branson grabbed one of those little hotel-sized bottles and squeezed some liquid out, then washed his hair. Okay, this was good. Ryder could do this casual stuff. He wet his hair as well, then took the shampoo from Branson and soaped his head. And if he made an effort to avoid meeting Branson's eyes, well, that was to prevent it from getting awkward.

He peeked at him from between his lashes, averting his eyes when Branson was watching him, a soft smile playing on his lips as if he knew what Ryder was doing. Maybe he did, but as long as he didn't bring it up, Ryder had plausible deniability, or so he kept telling himself.

The shower gel might come in a small bottle, but the scent was penetrating. The bathroom reeked like it had just been cleaned with the Mr. Clean lemon spray Ryder always used. Not exactly sexy. Branson crumpled his nose. "Jesus, I smell like Lysol."

Ryder snorted, finally daring to look at Branson. "I know, right?"

"I understand they have to use something that's suitable for all genders, but who the fuck wants to smell like a lemon grove?" Then he smiled. "We'll just have to replace it with the aroma of sex..."

Ryder swallowed. "I think that would be preferable, yes."

Branson's smile was slow and sexy, making Ryder's belly flutter. Uh-oh. Nope, he wasn't going there. Sexy was all fine and well, but he'd been there before, and that had brought him nothing but heartbreak and money issues. He might've been an idiot with Paul, but he wasn't stupid enough to make the same mistake twice.

"Yeah? You're up for round two?"

Should he make a lame joke about being *up* all right, considering his cock was perking up? Nah, too easy. And too tacky. "Yeah."

Branson turned off the water, then licked his fingers, taking his time to wet them thoroughly, all the while pinning Ryder down with his eyes. His hungry gaze shot hot sparks straight to Ryder's dick. Branson brought his hand to Ryder's ass, his move casual, as if he'd done it a thousand times before, as if he had every right to touch him like that. And then his wet finger pressed against Ryder's still slick hole, and Ryder opened up, letting him in.

"Fuck," he moaned, widening his stance.

Branson sank his finger inside Ryder, and as if that wasn't good enough, curled it until it rested right against his sweet spot. His touch was tender as he rubbed it, every gentle circle sending fireworks through Ryder's body. One finger became two, but still his movements were slow and deliberate.

Ryder hissed, alternatively pushing his ass back for more and trying to move away. It felt too good, too close, too intimate. The thrills that raced through him made him rise on his toes, his body taut with the effort of processing it all. The fire in Branson's eyes became too much, and he dropped his head against Branson's shoulder so he wouldn't have to look at him. As a response, Branson yanked him closer, pumping his two fingers in and out of him.

How could that feel so good after already being fucked? He'd expected it would be pleasant, nice, but not this crazy good. Not the goose bumps-inducing, cock-hardening, take-my-breath-away level of pleasure that was coursing through his body. If Branson kept that up, Ryder would come on the spot.

Every breath became a shallow one, him desperately sucking in air as Branson made his body rise higher and higher. Himalayas high. Mount Everest high. The pressure built in his balls, his cock. His whole body was tingling and humming, buzzing with electricity and sparks. Despite the steam still present in the bathroom, he shivered. Too many sensations.

"If you don't stop, I'll blow," he said between gritted teeth. "And I can't guarantee I'll have enough energy left after that to let you fuck me again."

Branson's hand stilled. "Your choice."

Dammit, the man had been paying attention, and how sexy was that? "Considering this is a one-time thing, I'd rather you fuck me again."

Branson pulled his fingers out, and Ryder leaned against him for a moment longer to catch his breath. His body retreated from that cliff, grumbling and reluctantly. When he was sure he could walk again, he let go of Branson. Would it get awkward now? Transitions in sex could be so impossible to navigate.

But Branson didn't seem to have that problem. He snagged two towels from the towel rack and handed one to Ryder. He dried off fast and rough while Branson did the same, and then they both walked back into the room. Before Ryder could even feel awkward, Branson grabbed his wrist and yanked it, making Ryder tumble against him. His squeal of surprise was caught by Branson's lips, and he moaned.

They ended back up on the bed, still kissing, and this time, Ryder took the opportunity to run his hands down Branson's body. Fuck, his strength was such a turn-on, those powerful muscles, big arms, wide chest. The freaking six-pack that tapered down into a pair of perfect cum gutters. He wanted to worship those abs, kiss every inch. Lick them and claim them.

Branson flipped Ryder onto his back, then sank his weight on top of him. He rolled his hips, dragging his hard cock over Ryder's body. He whimpered with impatience. How long was Branson gonna make him wait? Ryder wanted that thick cock inside him again, like, yesterday. His hole twitched with need, and his cock was leaking like crazy onto his stomach, making it all wet and sticky.

Maybe if he spread his legs, Branson would get the hint. He rolled his hips, bowing into him, meeting him with a move of his own that had Branson moan. "Jesus, you're so perfect..." he grunted. "So fucking perfect. Your ass, your body, that tight little hole of yours that sucks my cock right in. Perfection."

The stronger Branson's hold on him, the more he put his weight on Ryder to pin him down, the hotter Ryder's blood ran. He was hard, so fucking hard. *Aching* with need. Branson pushed him into the mattress, holding him in place with one hand while rubbing against him, smearing his precum all over him. What should've felt dirty and a bit demeaning instead was hot as fuck. And the effortless way Branson did it all, not even panting or sounding winded, made it all the more arousing. Maybe because Ryder felt safe, trusting Branson to stop if he protested. Despite Branson being a solid wall of muscle, unmovable even when Ryder tried, he wouldn't hurt him.

"Condom," Branson mumbled against his lips. "I need a condom."

"Yeah." Ryder felt light-headed as Branson rolled off him for a moment, then returned all sheathed up and slick.

He pulled up his legs, sighing with pleasure as Branson's cock found his entrance and slid in. He loved that burn from the first fuck, but this effortless entry, the slower second round where they'd both last much longer, was equally pleasurable, if not more. And Branson took his time, kissing him until his lips were throbbing and swollen, until the fire in this belly had roared so high it threatened to engulf him.

He felt every inch as Branson surged back into him again, then retreated until only the tip was inside him. Precise, controlled, every thrust measured for maximum effect. His ass was burning, tingling with the slow buildup. Their first round had been frantic and fast, but this one dragged him higher step by step, stroke by stroke, kiss by kiss as Branson didn't let go of his mouth.

They shouldn't kiss this much. Kissing was intimate. Kissing was for lovers, not hookups. Yet Ryder couldn't make himself pull away, turn his head, evade the firm lips that kept seeking his, the slick tongue that kept dueling with his own, Branson's feel and taste and smell. He invaded every cell of Ryder's body, and Ryder was helpless to stop it. It felt too good.

He'd missed this for so long. Branson's focus was on Ryder as if nothing else existed, and the outside world faded away. No distractions, no sighs or frustration at being interrupted, no quick fuck just so Ryder would be satisfied. Branson might not love him, like Paul had claimed—and look how that had turned out—but he loved fucking him, and that was enough. Ryder didn't need love anymore. An eight-inch cock and a man who knew how to use it were enough. At least for the foreseeable future.

The constant friction in his ass and on his cock, which was trapped between their bodies, built his desire, his need little by little until it burned hot and bright inside him. Thrills meandered down his spine, then back up again, as if his body couldn't decide which way to go. His balls ached, churned, flush against his body. His cock...oh, it *throbbed*, caught where he couldn't touch it, but he wouldn't have, even if he could. This was so much better, this fight to come, this pressure rising and brewing everywhere.

Until he couldn't take it anymore, the need to come too big, too demanding. "Please..." he begged against Branson's lips. "Please, Branson..."

If Branson had asked him to explain, he wouldn't have been able to, but he didn't. Instead, Branson pushed himself up on his elbows, and Ryder wrapped his legs around him, holding on to him as Branson sped up. His thrusts went from smooth and sleek to rough and hard until he was jackhammering his ass.

Ryder's brain shorted out, frizzling and sputtering as his whole body went haywire. His vision went white, then black as he screamed, and a millisecond later, his trapped cock released its second load. It hurt, but god, it hurt so good. His breath caught in his lungs, his body spasming and shaking until it finally released all the tension. He vaguely registered Branson coming as well, but it took a long time before he came back to earth.

When he did, Branson had rolled off him and was asleep, the condom tied down and discarded. He studied him, Branson's sexiness not even dimmed in the slightest by his closed eyes. Damn, that had been the best fuck Ryder had had in a long, long time. Maybe even the best fuck ever.

Too bad it had been with the one guy who was off-limits for him for too many reasons to count.

No, this had to stay a one-time thing, a Vegas experience neither of them would ever mention again, but it would have to be enough. Anything more was impossible.

20

Now that everyone had had a chance to read through the content of the Proud Patriotic Nationalists website, Coulson had set up a meeting with some of his FBI agents and Branson and Ryder. As always, Coulson had come to the CIA building, making it easy for Branson, who hated wasting time on a drive downtown.

Branson sat knee to knee with Ryder—in itself a kind of torture since that unexpected encounter they'd shared Friday evening. Being so close to him, Ryder's scent enveloping him, triggered too many memories. When he'd woken up, Ryder had been gone, and neither of them had brought it up when they'd seen each other again that morning.

Vegas, Branson kept telling himself. He'd promised not to talk about it, so he wouldn't. The first hour had been awkward as fuck, but funnily enough, after that, it had become easier. Almost normal again. He'd been surprised, then grateful that they'd both managed to keep things separate. But sitting this close to Ryder? Not a smart idea.

"What do you make of these statements, especially the ones by George Washington?" Coulson asked Branson.

"Remember what we said about the proclamations Al Saalihin made, how over the top they felt? This is along the same lines. So cheesy and extreme it's like a bad movie script."

"But do they believe it? Or is it lip service?"

"I think the person they sent those messages to believed it. Donnie Smith did, and if I had to take a guess, so do Naomi Beckingham and Ralph Durrick. They're the true believers. Maybe Wesley Quirk and Jon Brooks as well. They fit the profile. But Kingmakers? Hell no. They have their own agenda, and while it happens to align with these right-wing nuts, they're only spouting this to appeal to that base, to those people."

"I wonder if they all know about each other," Seth said. "Do they know Hamza Bashir is a hired gun? Do they realize Kingmakers has a different end goal than they do?"

"Mmm, good question. We can identify three distinct groups. We have Hamza Bashir, aka Yazid El Sewedy, and possible accomplices on his end, who do it for the money. The second group comprises the true believers like Naomi and her boyfriend, who think they're helping their white nationalist cause. And then there's Kingmakers, who seems to have their own monetary gain as main interest, combined with the political goal of having a pro-war president who would hire their firm. For now, I'm assuming that the military contractors we suspect of election donation fraud are on their side with similar interests, but who knows? They may have their own agenda as well."

"I'm still not sure how Mrs. Markinson fits in," Seth said. Branson knew the question of how she'd gotten involved with a plot this dark and sinister kept plaguing the Secret

Service agent. Seth had expressed multiple times that he couldn't reconcile the warm, loving grandmother he'd known with a cold plan to take out her husband.

"I've thought about that too," Branson said. "And I have a comprehensive theory about the whole chain of events, though I can't prove it. Yet."

Seth raised his eyebrows. "Hit me with it."

"Here's what I think happened. Markinson became the Democratic nominee for president, and when he polled much better than Governor Winkelmann, the Republican candidate, Kingmakers got scared. They figured that if Markinson won, he'd not only scale back the US presence in the Middle East but also limit the use of military operators like Kingmakers. He wanted to rely on US troops only, which would have put them out of business. So they approached some other military contractors and together poured money into Winkelmann's campaign."

"But he still lost," Coulson said. "So they required a plan B."

"Right. So they came up with the idea for the Pride Bombing. They needed a new 9/11, an attack by Muslim extremists that would make Markinson reconsider his war strategy and maintain a much stronger presence in the Middle East to fight Al Qaeda. So they approached Hamza Bashir or he them. That part I'm not sure about. And initially, their plan worked because after the Pride Bombing, everyone assumed Al Qaeda was back, just under a different name. At least, the public did."

"It didn't have the effect on Markinson's policy they had hoped for, though," Seth said.

"No. He did limit our overseas commitments, but while he didn't stop working with Kingmakers and others altogether, he did minimize their influence, and they took a financial hit. So they wanted another president, one who would be much stronger against the supposed terrorist attacks. To do that, they needed to get rid of both Markinson and his VP."

Seth nodded. "Following you so far."

"By now, Diane had convinced Mrs. Markinson to approach Henley Platt with classified information on how weak the Secret Service was, thus giving Kingmakers valuable intel on how to get to the president. They had set that in motion already, I assume, but they needed more help. Either they figured out Mrs. Markinson had been the leak for Platt's article, or they got lucky, but I suspect Basil King knew about his sister's affair with the president and used it to his advantage. In fact, it wouldn't surprise me if the affair wasn't a coincident at all, but a carefully planned attack on Markinson."

At first, Regina King had only been a name to Branson, someone the president had cheated with on his wife, but then he'd realized that as Basil King's sister, she might've shared characteristics with her older brother. That had made him see the affair in a different light.

"You think he sent her? His own sister? Maybe to blackmail Markinson?" Seth's eyes widened.

"We said it before," Coulson said. "If Annabeth Markinson had gone public with the affair, the president would've lost the reelection. The idea that Basil King convinced his sister to go after Markinson intending to discredit him is valid. Except it didn't work."

"No. In fact, Mrs. Markinson used it to get her way and get Shafer on the ticket as VP. And I think that would've been the end of it for her had the president not made the mistake of bullying his grandson. That was Markinson's big fuckup, coming at Noel Markinson, Mrs. Markinson's favorite grandson. That set her off, thus priming her for whatever Basil King said to her at that party. Maybe he knew about it, maybe he used the affair to get her riled up, but he played her like a fiddle, using her anger against her husband to get her cooperation to assassinate the president."

"And it was supposed to be only him, and with a sniper, so no one else would get hurt." Seth was clearly putting the puzzle pieces together in his brain. "She didn't know about any of it, not about Hamza Bashir being involved or that they would go after Shafer. She thought they'd take out her husband, and that would be the end of it."

"That's my theory based on what we know," Branson said. "She showed genuine remorse about the Pride Bombing, and that recorded phone call made it clear that she wasn't a part of that."

"I concur. She didn't know the same people would be involved, or she would never have agreed," Coulson said.

"And the phone calls show her anger that Shafer was targeted and that they were watching you guys, possibly coming after you." Branson waved his finger between Seth and Coulson. "That's when she became a liability, and they took her out."

"But since their attack on Shafer failed, they tried again with having him poisoned by Gavin Wedmore." Coulson looked at Seth. "Maybe you can update them on what you found out there?"

"Yes, we've discovered some new things. I told you we had confirmation that it was Wedmore who obtained a Secret Service pin. My theory is that initially that was all they recruited him for, but then when their plan to kill Shafer didn't pan out, they needed him again."

"You think he was approached?" Branson asked. "He wasn't part of this network already? I know he didn't show up on that website anywhere. At least, not that we know of..."

"No, he wasn't. I've spoken to various White House staffers who, in hindsight, recognized they were approached as well. I showed them pictures of everyone we've identified so far, and they positively ID'd Naomi Beckingham, Ralph Durrick, and Steve Duron. A few staffers also mentioned another man, but we don't know who he is yet. They chatted them up in social situations, like at a bar, a restaurant, a party, and even in church. They were asked about their lives, their hobbies, their jobs, and in some cases, the questions became uncomfortable. Two of them reported the conversations to a Secret Service agent because they felt too obvious to be coincidental, and it turns out they were right."

Branson sighed. "They were looking for an in."

Next to him, Ryder frowned. "An in?"

Branson loved that Ryder was never afraid to ask questions, never feared it would make him look stupid. "They needed background information so they'd know where to search for skeletons, for things they could blackmail people with, anything they could use against them. That's probably how they found out about Gavin Wedmore's gambling issues."

Seth nodded. "Wedmore was approached in a similar fashion, most likely, and gave them enough info to find out he had a gambling problem. We discovered he took out a twenty-thousand-dollar loan with a loan shark, and when he wasn't able to pay that off, Kingmakers must've made him a deal. The loan shark told us that Wedmore's loan was suddenly paid off...by Steve Duron. Not that he'd known his name, but after Coulson's agents leaned hard on him, he picked Duron's picture out of a large lineup."

"Jesus," Branson mumbled. "One moment you're in over your head with a gambling debt, and the next, you've murdered the First Lady..."

"We're convinced by now that he didn't intend to kill anyone. Our theory is that he was pressured to take out the president, based on the fact that he usually ate a banana and the First Lady didn't. But Wedmore didn't put in enough to kill him. If the president had eaten that banana, he would've been violently ill, but it wouldn't have taken him out. The First Lady, however..."

His voice broke, and Branson's heart went out to him. Seth still wasn't over losing not one but two First Ladies, and Branson wasn't sure which death had hit him harder. He smiled when Coulson put a quick hand on his boyfriend's thigh. Under the table, of course, and maybe others hadn't even noticed, but Branson loved seeing his care and concern. He'd never have pegged tough alpha male Coulson as a man capable of such tenderness, but now that he'd gotten to know him, he knew better. Underneath that professional, hard-ass exterior hid a kind, gentle man. Funny, for the first time, it didn't hurt anymore to think of Seth and Coulson together. They belonged, and Branson didn't. Not with Seth anyway.

"With her pre-existing condition and her much smaller mass, the poison was enough to take her out," Coulson finished. "And while it doesn't excuse what Wedmore did, that was never his intention. He most likely didn't see a way out and figured that if he tried, they maybe wouldn't get upset with him. Except he ended up killing the wrong person, which must've pissed off Kingmakers."

Silence descended. "So there we have it, their grand plan," Branson finally said. "It's the stuff of movies...except in this case, it's real."

"We have almost all the puzzle pieces. Now all we need is proof." Coulson slapped his hand on the table. "Let's get back to work so we can nail these bastards."

21

With the help of Donnie Smith's mother—who was deeply ashamed of her son's involvement in the assassination and had been more than willing to assist law enforcement—Ryder had gotten full access to the man's financials. At first glance, there had been nothing out of the ordinary. No major debts, no sudden weird changes in income or debt, no wild splurges. A second more thorough review hadn't revealed anything either.

Ryder had asked Corey to come over to his office so they could combine their brainpower and because Ryder had to be careful working on domestic connections, which Donnie Smith was. Sure, with the Al Saalihin/Hamza Bashir angle, he could defend himself focusing on this, but why make it difficult? And so Ryder and Corey had booted up their computers, sitting side by side, and went over everything together.

Thanks to the information found on that Proud Patriotic Nationalists website, they now knew what to look for. Donnie and whoever he'd been messaging with had been so stupid as to share a few specifics—enough to give them an idea of where to search. They'd opened a bank account for him where they'd deposited the money in. That way, they'd told him, the IRS couldn't trace the money, which made no sense at all to Ryder.

"How does opening a domestic account keep the money hidden from the IRS?" he asked Corey, whose short, blond hair looked like he'd plugged his fingers into an electrical socket. The geek factor was high with him, and Ryder had felt a kindred spirit connection from the moment they met.

"It doesn't. So why would they claim that?"

Ryder looked at the exchange from the website again. "They're saying it's not in his name. So did they make him an authorized user?"

Corey double-checked the information on his screen. "It doesn't show up on his credit report, which it would have if it had been linked to his social security number."

"They could've given him access without putting his name on the account. With online banking, that's easy to do."

"True. And with only twenty thousand dollars, setting up something complicated doesn't make sense. It's not like you'd open an offshore bank account for that amount."

"But if he ever cashed that money, what did he do with it? It doesn't show up anywhere on his own accounts."

Corey slapped his forehead. "Of course he didn't. They killed him before he could access the money. He never had the chance."

"What if that had been their plan from the get-go and they never intended for him to have the money?"

"In one of his messages, he mentions he'll check as soon as they've wired it, so they must've given him real log-in credentials."

"And why wouldn't they if they knew he'd never be able

to use them and get to the money? They knew he was going to be dead before then. Which means…"

They looked at each other. "They probably gave him info to an account that's still active," Corey said, almost squealing with excitement.

"And it's gotta be a domestic account. No way would they have given him access to a secret, offshore account. Donnie Smith might not have been the brightest bulb, but they wouldn't have trusted him with that much information."

"Agreed," Corey said. "And there would've been exactly twenty thousand in there because why give him extra money? So let's see what we can find in Kingmakers' accounts."

They went over every line of the financial information they'd obtained from Kingmakers, reasoning that the money would have to have been deposited somewhere in the weeks around the assassination. With the number of financial accounts Kingmakers used—undoubtedly a deliberate strategy to make it harder to follow the money—it wasn't a quick task, but they kept looking.

"Here, what's this?" Ryder pointed at a transfer of seven thousand dollars. "That's a strangely round number."

"Hmm, it's going out from one of their main accounts to…a dormant bank account with Capital One, which is an online bank. I wonder if we can find more round numbers… Here's another seven thousand."

Ryder thought the same thing. People might not realize it, but transferring round numbers indicated a manual transaction. Automatic payments of, for example, credit cards or bills seldom consisted of perfect numbers. "Which leaves us with six left. All well below the ten thousand where the bank would report to the IRS."

It took another ten minutes, but then they found the last transfer from yet another account but into that same dormant account, and lo and behold, the balance right after the assassination was...exactly twenty thousand dollars.

"They moved the money again after his death." Ryder tapped on the date. "See? July 11, they transferred almost all of it, leaving only five hundred. Donnie Smith was murdered on July 10."

"Holy shit, they barely waited until the body was cold." Corey cocked his head. "Actually, Quirk dumped his body in the water, so I'm pretty sure it was cold. Although it's the Caribbean, so it would depend on the water temperature, I suppose. Anyway, moot point, and I'm getting off track. Where were we?"

Ryder snorted, happy he wasn't the only one who would get caught in weird thought tangents like that. "I wonder where they transferred the money to." He refocused on the bank statements.

"I assume back to the accounts it came from."

Ryder checked the last payment. "No, it was sent to an account at...Evolve and Trust bank."

"So was the second payment..." Corey clicked away on his keyboard. "And the first. What account is that?"

"It's not a known Kingmakers account, not according to the information we have. The name on the account is listed as John Smith. That's gotta be a fake name."

Corey rolled his eyes. "Yeah, no shit. Someone was shit out of creative inspiration. Let's see if we can find more payments to this account."

They did. Every two weeks for the last six-and-a-half years, money had been sent to this account from various Kingmaker accounts. Small amounts, some larger amounts, but never over eight thousand dollars, and the last payment had been only weeks before. "One million exact," Corey said. "That can't be a coincidence."

"It's too low for El Sewedy. Unless he's much cheaper than the going rate, but I doubt it."

"True, but I can't imagine them sending a higher amount than to one account. That would raise red flags at some point, even if spread out over lower payments."

"Maybe El Sewedy is using multiple accounts to collect the money," Ryder said. "Wait, Evolve and Trust? That's a bank that's used by Wise, the international money service."

"That would allow El Sewedy to have a US bank account that Kingmakers could send money to without it being seen as a foreign transaction."

"It would, and since he's not a US citizen, the IRS wouldn't care...and I doubt the UAE does. That's an easy way to get money to him. But that means he'd have to have multiple accounts there to still spread the risk, all under fake names. How would we find those?"

Corey inhaled sharply as if to say something, but Ryder held up his hand. "Gimme a moment. I'm thinking out loud here. We'll never find John Smith, not with a name that generic, and if he used similar names for the other accounts, we won't be able to trace those either. But that money left the account at some point, presumably to a bank account El Sewedy owns, maybe with the Central Bank of the United Arab Emirates or in some foreign country with strong bank privacy, like Switzerland or Brunei, which wouldn't be that much of a stretch for him."

"So if we subpoena the records for this Evolve and Trust account, we should be able to trace the money right to El Sewedy." Corey was beaming, bouncing with energy.

Ryder thought the steps out in his head again, but he couldn't see any fault in his reasoning. "Yes. Even if he transferred it from there to yet another bank before depositing it in his final account, we should still be able to trace it. The Central Bank of the United Arab Emirates has promised to hand over information if we give them specific account numbers, but they refuse to say which accounts are associated with El Sewedy. This is how we could get there."

"I'll need to run this through Legal, but I'll get on that right away," Corey said, already packing up his stuff.

Ryder stretched as he yawned, then got up from his seat. "Thanks for coming over. I feel like we made progress."

"We did." Corey looked around, probably checking if he had everything, then leaned into Ryder. Before Ryder knew what was happening, Corey had kissed him on his cheek and was out the door with a happy "Bye now," leaving him standing in utter befuddlement. What the hell had just passed?

"I see you two are getting along well."

Ryder spun around. Branson was leaning against the doorpost. "What?"

"You and Corey."

Wait, why did Branson sound so sharp? That wasn't like him, Mr. happy-go-lucky. Maybe the stress about his dad was getting to him. "I suppose so, but why?"

Branson crossed his arms. "Because he kissed you? Or is that so normal you don't even realize it?" Something flashed over his face. "You know what? Never mind. None of my business."

He was right, of course, since what Ryder did with Corey was none of Branson's business. And yet Ryder felt a deep urge to explain and maybe even defend himself. "I don't know why he did that. He's never done it before. But I'll talk to him about it because...I didn't like it."

Branson stood straighter. "You didn't?"

"No. I mean, maybe I'm making it into much of a bigger deal than I should, but..."

Understanding lit up in Branson's eyes. "He kissed you without your consent."

"He did. And I know I'm weird about that, but it matters to me. We live in this culture where somehow people have made it okay to kiss people without seeking permission, strangers even. The other day, I saw a video about moments of respect in sports, and this tennis player accidentally hit the umpire who sits by the net? Not sure what that's called. But anyway, he hit that lady and then walked over and kissed her on the cheek. Everyone was cheering that on as a lovely gesture, and all I could think of was that she never consented to that. It's not okay to do something so intimate without asking first."

Branson had walked into the room during Ryder's mini tirade, his brown eyes warm and understanding. "I'd never have looked at it like that before, but you made me think about consent in a whole new way. In case I never thanked you for that, thank you. It was something I needed to hear."

Ryder studied him. Branson's attitude had changed, though Ryder had trouble putting his finger on how exactly. "You're different," he said, hoping it wouldn't come across as offensive.

Branson didn't seem to take it the wrong way. He just looked at Ryder, his gaze gentle. "In what manner?"

"I don't know. It's not so much calmer as...less flashy? Like you've toned something down?"

Branson nodded, a smile showing on his lips. "I'm trying to be more myself. One thing I realized was that I was often playing a role, being the person I thought people wanted me to be."

"That sounds exhausting."

"It is. And somewhere along the way, I became so good at it that I lost sight of who I am. I focused on what I thought I should be for so long that I forgot who I really am."

"I like you much better as you. You're far less tiring."

Oops, that had come out much harsher than he'd intended, but Branson's smile widened. "Thank you."

"I thought I might've been too direct again."

"Nope, not at all. I appreciate your honesty, your directness. I know you'll tell me the truth, and right now, I need that."

"Oh, well, in that case, you're welcome. Anytime."

They stared at each other, and Ryder's eyes dropped to Branson's mouth. He had such a nice smile…and perfect lips…and he was an amazing kisser. God, Ryder wanted to kiss him again, wanted to be pinned down with that strong body on top of his again. He wanted to feel every inch of that fat cock inside him, stretching him, wrecking him…

"Ryder…"

Branson's voice was hoarse.

"Yeah?"

"You need to stop looking at me like that."

Ryder swallowed, dragging his eyes away. "Like what?"

"Like you're imagining me inside you again."

How had he known? Then Ryder noticed his own body, his increased heart rate, his fast breaths, the warmth in his cheek…and his hard cock. Shit. "I'm… I'll try."

"Try harder. You're sexy enough as it is without seeing how much you want me back."

"We can't." That hadn't even sounded remotely like he meant it.

"No, we can't. Which is why I'm gonna walk away and pretend this never happened."

Ryder watched him walk out, his body protesting fiercely. How could one night of fantastic sex have made him addicted to Branson Grove?

22

Branson had always thought he was disciplined in the things that mattered. He'd definitely considered himself as a man who had self-control, but that iron resolve was crumbling when working side by side with Ryder every day. He wanted him. God, he wanted him. His whole body reacted to Ryder every time he stepped into the room. Like a homing beacon that recognized it was close to what it craved, what it needed.

It made no sense. Yes, he and Ryder were highly compatible, sexually speaking. He'd finally found someone who'd topped his experiences with Seth—no easy feat. But phenomenal sex alone shouldn't be enough for him to think about Ryder this much. Although…hadn't he done the same with Seth? Granted, his mild infatuation with Seth hadn't developed until they'd hooked up a few times, but still. He'd wanted more with him, and that hadn't turned out well. Maybe he was imagining things again, seeing an attraction that was more than physical where there was none.

Regardless, he had to stop thinking about Ryder. They were at a crucial phase in the investigation, and they both needed their heads in the game. So when Ryder walked in with his laptop under his arm, Branson shoved down the happiness that bubbled up inside him and plastered a more neutral expression on his face. "Hey."

"Hey."

They stared at each other. Wow, award-winning conversation they had going there. "How have you been?"

Ryder's eyes twinkled. "Since two hours ago when we last spoke, you mean?"

Branson rolled his eyes, though more at himself. "I'm trying here. I deserve points for that."

"Totally. Bonus points awarded."

"Thank you. Glad you agree this isn't easy to navigate. Anyway, what can I do for you?"

"You asked me to stop by when I was done with the Kingmakers spreadsheet."

"Right. Sorry. I need to switch gears for a moment." Yes, because he'd been thinking about how spectacular Ryder's ass was, but he'd better not mention that.

"No worries. So what's up?" Ryder dropped in the seat next to Branson's desk.

"Coulson has a theory, and he's asked me to look into it on our end. Remember Laurence Paskewich? He was a guard at the federal prison where the three bombers died."

"Right, the guy who quit shortly after and who had worked for Kingmakers before."

"He popped back up on Kingmakers' payroll a couple of months after the bombing, working some off jobs in between. He's still working for them."

"Okay," Ryder said slowly. "What about him?"

"Coulson's reasoning is that the core group of people who know everything has to be small. Basil King, Kurt Barrow, Steve Duron...and he thinks Paskewich is part of that inner circle. He's former Army, and he's worked for Kingmakers since, except for his brief stint as a prison guard. They have evidence that suggests he was the guy Seth and Coulson ran into when they visited Mrs. Markinson, the man who had been watching her, and he may have been one of the men who approached White House staffers."

"Oh, wow. So he's not afraid to get his hands dirty."

"Now Coulson has asked us for possible proof of any activities the guy might've carried out outside the US."

"Such as?"

"Such as the murder of Muhammed Bhat in Islamabad, which has never been solved. Our agent there has built a good rapport with the Pakistani cops, and they agree his death was staged to look like a suicide. Another agent managed to get close enough to Bhat's parents to ask some questions, and they gave him the address of the safe house in Islamabad Bhat had been told to go to. They also described the American who checked in on them a few days after Bhat had left for Islamabad, the one who gave them money again. He fits Paskewich's description."

"So you want me to look for a money trail that leads to him?"

Branson nodded. "The idea is that Kingmakers paid him extra for that murder. I mean, not exactly the kind of thing a normal salary covers, right?"

"One would hope not." Ryder bumped Branson's shoulder, and he got the hint and scooted as far to the right as he could, making room for Ryder at his desk. Ryder flipped open his laptop, hit a few keys, then cracked his knuckles. "Okay, let's see what we can find. When do we suspect that murder took place?"

"November 24 or 25, we think. We were informed on the

twenty-seventh, but Bhat had been dead for a while then."

"Hmm, okay."

Ryder's hands flew over his keyboard, and the mother of all Excel sheets popped up. Good god, that monster was a thing of beauty, all color-coded and organized. Ryder's mind was a scary entity.

"Was it a last-minute flight?" Ryder asked Branson.

"I don't think so. Bhat had been back in Kashmir and walking around since early July, so it doesn't look like they were in an awful hurry to get to him. He disappeared early September, but if his parents told the truth, he went to a safe house provided by Kingmakers, so they knew where he was. It would've been a straightforward job for Paskewich, since Bhat would have been expecting him."

"Was there a specific reason for them to kill him? I mean, like something that triggered them?"

"Not that we can think of. It looks like they were tying up loose ends."

"Okay. That gives me an idea of the date and price range I need to search in. I'm assuming he made a stop in Qatar to meet up with El Sewedy?"

Oh my god. Branson had never even thought of that, but he should have. It made total sense for anyone from Kingmakers to connect with El Sewedy when they were in the area, so to speak. "That seems logical, but I never even looked into that. That's something for me to check."

And so they worked side by side, their shoulders brushing whenever one of them moved, Ryder's subtle smell invading Branson's senses. Only it didn't arouse him this time, but it did somehow comforted him, like a reminder of the friendship and companionship they shared. He glanced sideways every now and then, but Ryder was lost to the world, murmuring something to himself occasionally before bursting out in another staccato attack on his keyboard, pulling up more spreadsheets, different files, comparing them, followed by more mumbling.

After about an hour, Branson grabbed two bottles of cold water, happy when Ryder guzzled his down almost instantly. He'd discovered Ryder preferred salty snacks in the afternoon, and so he'd stocked up on little bags of pretzels. They were perfect, since they hardly resulted in crumbs and didn't leave your fingers all greasy. And indeed, Ryder wolfed those down, his eyes never even leaving his screen.

Two hours later, he looked up, then blinked and rubbed his eyes. "Welcome back," Branson said with a wink.

"Thanks. Also for the water and the pretzels that I only now realize you must've provided, since I still haven't mastered teleportation."

Branson chuckled. "You're welcome. What did you find?"

"Proof that Paskewich was in Qatar and Islamabad. Assuming he intended to travel to Pakistan legally, he'd need not only a plane ticket but a visa as well. I'd noticed before that Kingmakers uses a visa service for that called Visas Express, so I searched for any payment to them in that time frame between the bombing and late November. A few popped up, and it was an easy cross-check. They applied for a business visa for Paskewich on August 15, and it was granted September 3."

"A business visa?"

"Yes. According to the documents they supplied, he was invited by the Pakistani government as a consultant on anti-terrorism."

Branson let that sink in. "You're telling me that the Pakistani government invited a man who shared responsibility for two domestic attacks on US soil and possibly a couple of murders to teach them about anti-terrorism? A man who most likely used that same trip to kill a terrorist... on behalf of another terrorist?"

Ryder pushed his glasses back up his nose. "The irony is rather thick."

"I'll say."

"Anyway, he booked his flight on September 3, so immediately after hearing his visa had been granted, and he flew to Islamabad on November 23...from Doha, where he spent twenty hours. He left Dulles on the twenty-first, arrived in Doha on the twenty-second because of the time difference, and then spent twenty hours there before catching his next flight to Islamabad. His return flight was December 1, again through Doha, but now with only two hours between the flights. Both tickets were paid for by Kingmakers, as was the visa. On December 2, which was a Sunday, three cash withdrawals of five thousand dollars each from three known Kingmakers' accounts were made at an ATM in Georgetown, two blocks away from where Basil King lives."

Branson whistled between his teeth. "You're thinking that's the cash bonus."

"Paskewich returns and asks for the money. Wouldn't you? He did his job, so he wants to get paid. So Basil King walks over to the nearest ATM and withdraws. But the max is five thousand per ATM per card, so he has to use three different accounts. I checked, and all three were funded only days before, so he knew this withdrawal was coming."

"Wow. That's great work."

"There's more."

"There is?"

Ryder nodded. "I figured that if Paskewich had done more assignments like that for them, he would've been paid cash as well, so I tracked all large cash withdrawals. None of them match the crucial data we have. So I went through his personnel records and the W2 forms Kingmakers provided him with over the last years. They showed bonuses that were paid out, so I traced those. It turns out he got a fifteen-thousand-dollar bonus in December 2015, with the first paycheck he received after working for Kingmakers again after the Pride Bombing."

Branson immediately made the connection. "That had to be for the supposed suicide of the three bombers."

"That's what I suspect. The timing seems suspicious. But he received another bonus in that same year, another fifteen thousand dollars...with the last paycheck of June, right around the Pride Bombing. And that while Kingmakers had sold a lot and had downsized, laying people off."

"Shit." Branson's head was spinning. "So he was involved directly with that."

"The only other employee who earned a bonus that year was Steve Duron, who was paid twenty-five thousand...also in June."

"Those two are their executioners, their henchmen, so to speak."

"There's one more payment to Paskewich...a Christmas bonus of ten thousand dollars, but it wasn't paid out until January."

Branson let that sink in, but then he snapped his fingers. "Mrs. Markinson. He was one of the divers."

"I can't confirm that, but again, the timing is suspicious to say the least."

"Let me check on something real quick." Branson turned back to his computer and pulled up the file on Laurence Paskewich. He speed-read through their information until he found what he'd been looking for. "Paskewich was trained as an Army diver and specialized in underwater demolition and salvage and reconnaissance."

"Army diver? Why does that sound familiar?"

Branson slapped his forehead. "We found another connection. Remember Coulson said they'd traced back where the boat had entered the water and had found the truck that pulled it? The owner of the truck was a guy named Dwayne Gable...and he was a former Army diver as well. How much do you want to bet he and Paskewich knew each other?"

"Another piece of the puzzle." Ryder pumped his fist.

Branson leaned back in his chair again. "It amazes me they didn't even try to keep those bonuses secret...except for that payment to Paskewich. Why did they pay one out in cash?"

"I suspect because another fifteen thousand would've put Paskewich in another tax bracket and would've ended up costing him more than it was worth. That's probably also why they didn't pay him his Christmas bonus until January. We're dealing with tax-savvy criminals here. And they had no reason to be secretive about those bonuses. Both Paskewich and Gable were and are on their payroll, so the timing and amount of those bonuses wouldn't have raised any flags in any normal audit. Not if the auditors didn't know the significance of those dates."

"Jesus, just when you think you've seen it all."

Ryder stretched, yawning, and Branson smiled as he watched him. Ryder could be so uninhibited in his expressions and reactions. He'd sure as fuck been in bed. Even the thought of how Ryder had responded to his every touch made Branson swallow and look away.

He cleared his throat. "It's past seven. Why don't we grab a quick bite to eat before you drive home? I don't want you to crash because you're too hungry to drive."

23

Ryder wasn't even sure how it had happened. One moment, Branson had mentioned dinner, and the next, they were sitting at a cozy table in a pizza restaurant in McLean, where the delicious smells made Ryder drool. Going home would've been smarter for too many reasons to count, but most of all because it was becoming harder and harder to look at Branson and not remember. Remember how exquisite he had felt inside Ryder, how perfect that fat dick had stretched him, what a great kisser he had been...and how desperately he wanted a repeat.

"What's good here?" he asked, forcing himself to change the subject.

"Honestly, all their pizzas are amazing, but their variation on a Caprese is my favorite. It has fresh tomatoes, real mozzarella made from the milk of a water buffalo, sun-dried tomatoes, arugula, and parmesan cheese, and it's to die for."

"Sold." Ryder put the menu down.

"That was easy." Branson laughed.

"You were very persuasive."

That, and Branson had licked his lips when he'd described the pizza, and of course, Ryder's mind had gone straight to the gutter again. Jeez, when had he become such a sex-obsessed person? He would've thought that the hookup with Branson would've lasted him a while, but nope, it had only made him crave more.

When the server came, they both ordered the Caprese, and Ryder treated himself to a Coke. He never drank caffeine after six p.m., as he feared it would keep him up at night, but he was too tired to function now.

"I'm exhausted," he said with a sigh, taking his glasses off and rubbing his eyes, then putting them back on. Maybe he should consider contacts. They'd be much easier, but he was afraid he'd forget to take them out.

The way Branson shifted until their legs touched under the table sent sparks through his body. "You've worked crazy hours the last few days."

"So have you, and you also have your father to worry about." As soon as he said it, he winced. Had that been too direct? Insensitive? Should he ask a follow-up question, show that he was empathetic? He never knew what to do in situations like this.

But Branson didn't seem to take offense. "True. It's not been easy, though my father is doing well under the circumstances. He's home from the hospital and recovering well. But he has a long road ahead of him."

"Do they have a treatment plan now?" Since Branson had never shown he didn't want to talk about it, Ryder figured this was safe to ask.

"The next step is chemotherapy, probably for six months, but they'll monitor how he responds."

"Are you worried?"

Branson was quiet for a long time. "I've never been so scared in my life."

Ryder pressed his leg against Branson's for a moment, not saying anything. What could he offer but empty platitudes? Nothing. Words wouldn't suffice. "How's your mom?" he finally asked.

"Stronger than I had ever thought possible. She always taught us that you don't know how strong you are until you have no choice, but I never realized how true that was until now. She's a rock, and my dad is the same. But they've always been like that, no matter what happened. They set the bar high for me for a relationship, you know?"

Right. Branson wanted a relationship, and Ryder had better remember that and be crystal clear in his signals. He didn't want Branson to think he'd be interested in anything more. Not that they had discussed the possibility of a repeat, but just in case. "With stories about unsupportive parents being so common for gay kids, we both got lucky with ours," he said.

"We did. I never feared coming out to them. They'd always been so open and accepting that I knew they'd be okay with it."

"Same. I remember that when I was maybe ten, my father took me to the Museum of Natural Science. He gave this whole talk on how biology wasn't as binary and as straight as people wanted it to be and how sex and gender were different things. Way ahead of his time, but he'd always been a man of science, someone who followed the facts."

"Do you think he maybe suspected you were gay already?"

Ryder nodded. "I never asked him, but I'm sure my parents had picked up on it by then. There was never much doubt with me. Not that I was flamboyant or anything, but just...I wasn't interested in most things other boys were."

"I know what you mean. It's that vibe a lot of gay men have, that combination of sensitivity and vulnerability."

Their food came, and Branson hadn't been lying. That pizza was orgasmic, and Ryder tried to savor it, but he was too hungry to go slow. "Man, that's so good."

Branson chuckled. "I'm always amazed at how much you eat. You're so slender, but you devour quantities like you're starving."

Ryder shrugged. "I have to compensate for often forgetting to eat, especially lunch."

"I noticed that."

"But I also love good food, simple as that."

Paul had often commented on Ryder's eating habits, especially in public. Something about it being bad manners to clear your plate because it made it seem like you hadn't had enough. That had always sounded silly to Ryder, but like with many other things, he'd trusted Paul to know better. In hindsight, that had been a monumentally stupid habit.

"Are you in a hurry to go home?" Branson asked.

Ryder sighed. "Not really."

"No one there to wait for you, huh?"

Branson knew Ryder had broken up with his boyfriend, so the conclusion he lived alone was a logical one. He could easily let him assume that, and yet somehow it didn't feel right. "Actually, I moved back in with my parents. Temporarily."

"Oh man, that sucks. Your ex kept your previous house, then?"

"Apartment, and yes. It turns out he'd removed my name from the contract."

Branson gasped. "You're kidding me."

"I wish."

"So he'd planned to break up."

"Yes."

"So why aren't you getting your own place?"

Yeah, he should've seen that one coming. The thing was, Branson wasn't asking because he suspected something. Ryder was certain of it. The way he'd asked was too casual for that. It was a normal question from someone who was curious. So once again, Ryder had to choose to either evade, lie…or tell the truth.

"He cleaned me out," he said quietly. "I was an idiot who believed him when he promised me he wanted a future with me, and so I used my savings to furnish our apartment, to buy him a car, to pay for everything…and when he broke up, I walked away with an empty bank account. I can't afford a down payment for at least a year, and renting on such short notice is impossible if you want something decent."

Branson frowned and slapped his hand on the table. His visceral reaction felt good. "What an unbelievable bastard. He not only cheated on you but deliberately spent your money, knowing he would break up with you?"

"Dr. Dick, right?"

"Dr. motherfucking son of a bitch is more like it." The genuine anger in Branson's tone was balm for Ryder's wounded soul.

"I concur."

"So now what? You're going to stay with your parents for an entire year? That sounds like hell, no offense."

Ryder sighed. "My parents are amazing and very supportive, but yes. It's hell." He hesitated. He'd already shared so much he might as well come clean. "Even if I wanted to, I couldn't stay that long. They're selling their house and moving to a senior living community."

"Oh, shit. Can you buy their house?"

"Aside from not having the money, they live in Frederick. It's too far a commute for me. I need something much closer to Langley."

"The housing market around here is insane."

"You live close, don't you?"

"Yeah. I own an apartment in McLean, about a fifteen-minute drive. A little less without traffic. But I know I'm lucky. I'd never have been able to afford it if my parents hadn't helped me out. The median house price in McLean is, like, eight hundred thousand. Apartments are cheaper but still horribly overpriced. My parents loaned me the money for a large down payment so my monthly payment would be doable."

"My parents do well enough, but they're not in that range." He yawned. "I'm sorry, but I'll have to leave now. I have at least an hour's drive ahead of me."

He groaned as his exhaustion hit him. He'd offer good money if he didn't have to drive home now. Or since he didn't have any, maybe a blow job would work? He laughed at his own lame attempt at humor.

"Come home with me."

Ryder jerked up his head and gaped at Branson. "What?"

"Come home with me. To sleep. So you don't have to drive."

"I...I can't." The answer came automatically.

"Why not?"

Ryder's brain went blank. He had to have a reason, right? But what was it? Something about being coworkers... But if all they did was sleep, why would that be a problem? If any other coworker had offered, would he have refused as well? No. He would've jumped at the opportunity, though he didn't like the disruption in his routine. That was a small price to pay for saving two hours of driving...

"I promise I won't put any pressure on you to do anything more than sleep."

Branson sounded hurt. Did he think that Ryder's hesitation was because he didn't trust Branson? "I know. You've proven that to me."

Relief bloomed on Branson's face. "Okay, glad to hear that. I wasn't sure if that played a role, if you thought I wouldn't honor my promise of keeping my hands off you."

"It doesn't, I assure you."

"Then why did you hesitate?"

He stared at him, thoughts tumbling through his head, none of them helpful. Finally, he took a deep breath. "Let me text my parents that I won't be home tonight."

He felt the joy on Branson's face deep into his soul, though why it hit him so hard, he didn't understand.

24

"Come on in." Branson was feeling strangely nervous as he led Ryder into his apartment. At least it was clean, since the cleaning lady had done her job the day before. Paying for a service to stop by weekly to clean had been the best investment ever. "Alexa, turn on the living room."

God bless technology.

"Nice place," Ryder said. "Roomier than I had expected."

"It's a two-bedroom. When I bought it, I had hoped that… Well, I'd hoped I'd find a partner at some point, hence the extra bedroom so we'd have the space for, I don't know, a guest bedroom or a study or maybe a family."

Branson took Ryder's jacket and hung it on the coat rack, along with his own.

"You'd want a family?"

"I've always wanted kids. It hasn't happened so far, but it's not too late." He kicked off his shoes. "Can I get you something to drink?"

When he met Ryder's eyes, he found him studying Branson. "You're much more open about yourself."

He sighed. "Yes. After you told me that, I had a conversation with my mom and my sister, and it turns out you were right. I never realized it, in my defense. They erm... My sister had some more truths to share with me."

"I never meant to make you face things you weren't ready for."

"I know. You didn't. I needed to hear it, confronting as it was. But ever since, I've been conscious about answering your questions rather than deflecting them. It's strange and a little scary, but you make it easy."

"I do?" Ryder looked surprised.

"Yes. At first sight, you seem like a nerd, a total geek, and I know that for me, a lot of preconceived notions came into play. I didn't expect you'd be good at social interactions, for example."

"I'm not."

Branson smiled at him. "You're much better than you think. I reckoned your analytical skills would be limited to numbers, but they're not. You're a highly systematic thinker in general, detecting patterns and changes in them."

"I have a hard time correctly interpreting emotions. Back in high school, they thought I was on the spectrum."

"I'm not a psychologist, so I won't argue with that diagnosis, but I haven't seen much evidence of it."

"My responses often offend people."

"Yeah, but I think that's because you're very direct, and that's what they take issue with, not the fact that what you're saying isn't true. And maybe they feel you don't show empathy. You do, but you're highly respectful of boundaries, and people may interpret that the wrong way, as if you're not interested. They expect certain reactions, like questions, and you don't ask them."

Ryder seemed shocked. "Really?"

Branson nodded.

"I wanted to have a family too with my ex, but he never felt it was the right timing. In hindsight, I'm grateful, and now I don't know if I ever want that again. The kids, maybe, but not a relationship," Ryder said, and Branson needed a moment to realize he was referring to their earlier topic. "My best friend, Dorian, has a two-year-old daughter, and she's amazing. When he was thirty and still single, he found a surrogate who was willing to donate her egg cells and carry his baby, and it worked out wonderfully for him."

"You smile when you talk about him," Branson said.

"I do? We've been friends since high school. The two geeky gay kids, natural friends."

"Never dated?"

A look of horror passed over Ryder's face. "God, no. He's like a brother to me. Sort of." He giggled, the sound settling low in Branson's belly. "Although he did take that picture of my ass for the app."

Branson swallowed. "He did? That was a work of art... but then again, so is your ass."

"As is your cock..."

The tension between them was heavy, thick, and Branson had to make an effort to turn himself away. "If we want to keep this platonic, we need to change the subject. I already need a cold shower as it is." He took a deep breath and straightened his shoulders. "I'll show you where the guest room is."

Ryder was quiet as Branson pointed out the bathroom they'd have to share, as well as the guest bedroom. "Let me grab you a towel. I'm sure I have a new toothbrush somewhere. I don't have guests often, but I buy them in bulk."

"You don't bring hookups here?"

"Never. No exceptions."

"I guess I should feel honored, then."

Branson picked up on Ryder's effort to keep it light, but he still wanted to set the record straight. "You're not a hookup. You're a coworker and...maybe a friend?"

"Maybe?"

Ryder said it in a teasing tone, and Branson played along. "Considering the jury is still out on whether you wanted to become friends with me, I thought I'd be careful in how I worded it."

"You know, I think I'll take you up on that invitation after all."

The joy that exploded inside Branson at those words was completely irrational and disproportional, but he couldn't help it. "Yeah?"

Ryder put his hand against Branson's cheek, and he froze. Ryder had never touched him spontaneously before, and he was afraid to even breathe. "You've proven yourself to me. You don't have to worry about me not trusting you anymore...Bran."

Branson snorted at that last addition. "Unlike you, I don't have a problem with you calling me that."

"No?" Much to Branson's disappointment, Ryder dropped his hand. "I'll have to find something else to call you, then, if my goal was to annoy you...but it's not, I assure you."

"Not to bring back the whole topic, but why do you hate it so much, being called Ry?"

"It's Dorian's name for me, and he deserves that honor. He's earned it."

"Fair enough. I won't use it again."

"You haven't, not since our talk."

"Are you sure? Because I might've used it out of habit."

"Oh, I'm sure. Trust me, I would've called you out on it otherwise."

Branson grinned. "Yeah, you would've. I like that, you know, that you're not afraid to confront me. Not everyone has the guts."

"Why? It's not like you're so scary..."

"I think it's more of a mental thing, but whatever. Anyway, do you want to borrow some underwear from me? Clean underwear, I mean."

Ryder was silent for a moment, then burst out in laughter. "What, like I'd want to borrow your dirty underwear?"

Branson laughed sheepishly. "I dunno, maybe you wanted to use them to jerk off to? You know, help remind you of the greatest fuck of your life?"

Ryder's laugh stilled. "I don't need your underwear for that, believe me. My memories of that night are vivid enough without them."

And here they were again, staring at each other, standing way too close, while the room seemed charged with electricity. "So far, that whole concept of staying away from you isn't going great," Branson said hoarsely.

"No, it's not." Ryder sighed. "Though we did manage well enough at work."

"True, but we're in a professional environment there, everything reminding us of the importance of our jobs. Here, we're..."

"We're two guys who shared something special."

"You thought it was special?"

"Yes. I thought it was spectacular while we were at it, but I analyzed afterward, and it's safe to say it was the best sex I ever had."

Branson didn't know what to say. Sure, that was a wonderful compliment, but what a sad truth for Ryder, who had been in a relationship for years. "It's none of my business, and feel free to tell me to fuck off, but were things not good with your ex?"

Ryder looked at the floor, jamming his hands into his pockets. "He thought I was too demanding."

"Demanding?"

"Yes. Because I was too vocal in expressing my sexual wishes. Paul favored a more traditional bottom, I suppose. One that was content to let the top do whatever he wanted."

Branson hadn't thought it possible to hate someone he'd never even met and had no idea what he looked like, but here he was. What an unbelievable asshat. "You know that's BS, right?"

Ryder nodded. "I do now, but it took me a while. I think it was because he wanted to be able to focus on his own pleasure without having to worry about me getting what I wanted from it. In his opinion, an orgasm was an orgasm, and he did the bare minimum to make me come, which really isn't that hard. But orgasms definitely come in levels or maybe categories, and whatever system you use to classify them, the ones he gave me rank low."

"Like jerking off because you have to, because it's been too long or you have something important coming up where you can't allow your dick to distract you, so you rub one out, but you're tired and not invested in it, so you come, but it's all meh, and minutes later, you can barely remember you had an orgasm."

Ryder blinked, then burst out laughing. "Yes, exactly like that! I've never heard someone describe it like that, but that's perfect."

How Branson loved the sound and the sight of Ryder's laugh. He did it in the same way he did everything else: with full devotion, all in. The visceral way Branson reacted made him take a step back.

Ryder's smile faded. "Did I do something wrong?"

Branson's heart broke for him. "No. Not unless you count being so goddamn adorable that I needed to create some physical distance, or I would kiss the shit out of you."

Ryder swallowed. "Oh."

"And I don't want that."

"You don't want to kiss me? Now I'm confused."

"Oh, make no mistake. I want to not only kiss you but do a hell of a lot more."

"L-like what?" Ryder whispered.

Branson couldn't stop now if he'd wanted to. The words just tumbled out. "Like spend a few hours worshiping your ass with my hands, my tongue, my cock...especially my cock. I love edging, and I bet I could prevent you from coming for a long, long time to the point where you'd beg me. But I also want to suck you off, taste you, swallow down your load. I'm a dirty man, *chéri*, in case you missed it."

Ryder's mouth had dropped open, and he needed a few seconds to compose himself again. "Ch-chéri?"

"It means someone you treasure, who you cherish, in French. I figured if I can't call you Ry, I'd come up with a term of endearment of my own."

"Oh. Okay. That's... That was quite descriptive. I'm not sure if... I think I'd be on board with that, actually."

Branson's heart skipped a beat. "Yeah?"

Did Ryder even notice he'd drifted closer to Branson? They were only inches apart now, close enough for Ryder's smell to embrace Branson, hardening his cock even more.

"Mmm."

Branson inhaled deeply, then balled his fists and took a step back. "As much as I'd love to rip off your clothes and bend you over the couch right now...I won't. I made a promise I wouldn't touch you, and I need to keep it. If not for you, then for myself. I would love, love, love to take you to bed again...but you'll have to come to me. It needs to be your choice, made in a moment of rational thinking, not another impulsive decision guided by our dicks. We both deserve more."

He took a deep breath, then slowly released it as he retreated even farther, feeling prouder of himself than he had in a long, long time. "Sleep well, chéri."

25

Home. To anyone else, the constant blare of cars honking, of snippets of conversation caught as people rushed past, their ears glued to their phones, of traffic and music and street vendors shouting, would've been enough to make them go crazy, but to Milan, it was home. New York. His heart beat faster just from the smell, that unhealthy mix of car fumes, garbage, wisps of body odor and scents, and even the signature smell of Abercrombie & Fitch as he strode by their store. He had come to appreciate DC, but this craziness was home…and it always would be.

"Hey, Bradbury," O'Donnell, one of the other detectives, greeted Milan as he sauntered into his precinct. "What brings your ugly mug back to us lowly servants? Don't you have two boyfriends to fuck?"

His faint hope that his fellow boys in blue wouldn't have learned about his love life evaporated. Oh well. "They'll survive without me for a day. Had to check in on you assholes and see if you already managed to burn down the place without me."

He eyed his desk, once a hot mess of papers but now neat as a pin and occupied by a guy who couldn't be a day over twenty-five. "Who the fuck are you?"

The kid jumped to his feet. "Detective Collins, sir."

Detective? Was he fucking serious? Milan looked for confirmation at the others. "He's our newest addition," Sanchez, a former partner of Milan's, said.

"For real?" Milan turned to Collins. "Do you even shave yet?"

Much to his surprise, Collins didn't blush, merely raised his chin, determination settling in a pair of gorgeous gray eyes. "My lack of facial hair bears no significance on my ability to do my job, sir."

Damn. The boy had a backbone. "Okay, point taken. Mind telling me how old you are?"

"Thirty-two, sir."

Thirty-two? Dude looked ten years younger. "You good at your job?"

Collins didn't so much as blink. "At being a detective? Not yet, sir. I only started three weeks ago. But I will be."

Milan had to admire his confidence. To succeed in the NYPD, one needed that. Confidence and grit because it was one hell of a job. "Good. Glad to hear it. Welcome to the team, kid."

Oh, he could see the struggle on Collins's face, the debate with himself whether he should call Milan out on calling him a kid. But he wisely decided to keep his mouth shut, which earned him more bonus points in Milan's book. Knowing when to take a stand and when to shut up was a crucial skill for a cop and even more for a detective.

He chatted for a bit with his fellow cops, Collins observing without chiming in, then asked, "Anyone know where Reyes is?"

"Interrogating a suspect," Sanchez said, checking his watch. "He should be out in minutes."

"Okay."

"What do you need Reyes for? We heard you were working with the feds now," Alexa Christiansen, a kick-ass female detective Milan respected the hell out of, asked.

"I am."

She cocked her head. "That didn't answer my question."

"That's right. Can't talk about it, but I need someone who can blend in."

A chorus of affirmative sounds rose around him. They all knew that Reyes was as close to a human chameleon as someone could get. Born in Puerto Rico, he was fluent in Spanish but with a mixed heritage, which meant he could pass for black, brown, and anything in between. The guy had a knack for languages, flawlessly switching from accentless American English to Bronx, Brooklyn, and Milan had even heard him speak Cockney once.

Minutes later, Reyes walked in, and after a warm bro hug, Milan pulled him aside so they could talk in private. "You in for a visit to the South Bronx? I cleared it with the captain."

"Sure. Who we looking for?"

Milan met his inquisitive gaze. "This is classified."

Reyes's eyes lit up. "My neighbors were wondering what was up when some feds showed up yesterday, asking questions about me."

"This is about the Pride Bombing."

Reyes's expression hardened. "I'm in."

Milan had known he would be. Reyes had lost a cousin in the bombing, a young woman who'd been watching the parade with her girlfriend. He gave him a quick briefing, and after they'd both gotten changed into a more casual outfit, they left.

Their first stop was the 40th precinct, where cops did their best to police the most southern tip of the Bronx. The keyword being *tried* because while New York crime rates had plummeted in recent years, this precinct didn't share that decline. The combination of poverty, housing projects where people were packed too closely together, lots of homeless shelters, methadone clinics, and a variety of gangs and drug dealers made for fertile ground for crime, including murders, drugs trade, and plenty of violence aimed at cops. The New York Times once had done a whole series of murders in the 4-0, as they had called it, describing the backgrounds of each murder in detail. With its fair share of undocumented immigrants and people fearing retribution from gangs, the neighborhood didn't even report half of the bad shit that happened.

Still, things were improving, albeit at a slower rate than they should have. Not that all change was always good. Milan was frustrated by the ongoing gentrification in the city, seeing once vibrant neighborhoods being slowly but surely bought by project developers and transformed into luxury housing, pushing out the original residents. It was only a matter of time before the same would happen to the South Bronx.

"What can I do for you?" Feliz Matos, captain of the 40th, asked Milan and Reyes after leading them into his office. He was curt but cordial, and Milan didn't sense an unwillingness to help, more the tiredness of someone who was flat out overwhelmed.

"2016, the months before the Pride Bombing," Milan said. "You were a detective here."

Matos sighed. "Not exactly the good ole days."

"Can you remember any talk of strangers coming into the 'hood, asking questions about storing things here?"

"What kind of things?"

"The kind that go *boom*."

Matos's eyes widened. "You're talking about the bombs."

"I'm talking about storage for big things, the size of a barrel, maybe. A small container."

Matos got the hint and didn't ask for more details. "Ground floor then, easy to carry it in."

Milan nodded.

"In a residential building?"

"We don't know."

"I don't recall anything off the top of my hat, but...I can tell you who to ask. For the right price, he'll talk. Nothing happens around here that he doesn't know about."

Armed with a name and a location of where they might find this guy, Milan and Reyes left. They found Big Julian where they'd been told he'd be, behind the counter of a neighborhood mini store, and the moniker *Big* was no joke either. The guy was six feet six, if not more, and built like he could crush you with one hand. Without breaking a sweat.

Milan had agreed to let Reyes do the talking, and after making sure the store was empty, Reyes leaned in. "We wanna ask you some questions. We'll make it worth your while."

Big Julian looked them up and down. "Cops?"

"Yeah, but the good kind."

Big Julian snorted. "Never met a good cop."

"Today's your lucky day, then." Reyes's tone was light yet radiating strength. His accent was spot-on Bronx and not forced, like someone trying too hard, but effortlessly, like Chazz Palminteri in *A Bronx Tale*.

"What we be talkin' about?"

This was where they had to take a risk, and Milan had okayed it. No one would talk otherwise. "Bombs," Reyes said softly.

Big Julian leaned forward, his eyes razor-sharp now. "What kind of bombs?"

"The kind that blew up in Greenwich six years ago."

"Shit," Big Julian said. "Still fucking pissed that those Osamas keep thinkin' they can come over here and blow shit up."

"I feel ya."

"So why you talkin' to me? I had nothin' to do with that."

"We think you might know something."

Milan pulled the photos out of his pocket and laid them on the counter.

"Six years ago, weeks before the bombing. Remember seeing any of these guys around here? Hearing about a white dude looking for storage?" Reyes asked.

Big Julian paled. "Goddammit. Ricky!"

A young teen appeared. "Yeah, Big J?"

"Stand outside the door and don't let anyone in. If someone asks, tell them to come back in thirty."

"Yeah."

Big Julian waited until the teen had left. "This guy." He tapped the picture of Laurence Paskewich. "I know him."

Holy shit. "How?" Milan asked.

"I ain't talkin' until I have protection."

Reyes looked at Milan, who nodded. He wasn't authorized to offer this, but he doubted any charges would stick against Big Julian anyway. The man hadn't known about the bombs before, so it wasn't like he'd willfully aided and abetted.

"Full immunity," Reyes said. "But only for anything related to this."

"You break your word, you'll pay," Big Julian said, and it sounded more like a statement of fact than a threat. Milan had to admire his balls for threatening two cops.

"Understood. Talk," Reyes said.

"He showed up in the 'hood," Big Julian said. "Musta been March or April. Stayed for a coupla weeks, then disappeared."

"Where?"

"Apartment on Alexander. Guy who lived there was sent to Rikers, so his mom sublet it."

"How'd you hear about it?"

"One of my boys alerted me. We don't like white guys movin' in like that. You never know what trouble they bring."

"What trouble would that be?"

"Cops, feds, gangs, drug dealers...anything."

Milan could see why any of those options would pose a problem for Big Julian.

"What else?" Reyes asked.

"Something weird was goin' on. He said he had no car and took the red line downtown at 149th every mornin', but one of my guys saw him load a van that didn't look like no rental."

"What kind of van?"

Big Julian slowly shook his head. "Fuck, I never even thought of it." He seemed lost in thoughts for a moment. "Black van that looked reinforced, not a scratch on it. Had New York tags, but old ones, dinged up. We figured the van or the plates or even both were stolen."

"Where did they see him?"

"Port Morris, next to the recycling."

"Any idea what he was loading?"

Big Julian shook his head. "Somethin' big was all they

said. Covered up. But so heavy they carried it into the van with two men, this dude and another white guy. He disappeared the day after. Never gave him another thought until now."

"You remember a lot of details," Milan said.

Big Julian shrugged. "I remember everythin', keep track of everythin'. That's why I'm still alive...and not in prison."

"Would you remember a name, by any chance?"

"I gotta make a call. Come back in fifteen. Ricky will give you a note at the door. You need anythin' else, call the number on the note. Don't come back here."

"What do we owe you?" Milan asked.

Big Julian didn't hesitate even for a second. "Nothin'. This one's on the house. We don't fuck around with bombs here, and any motherfucker who does is fair game."

When they returned fifteen minutes later, Ricky gave them a folded piece of paper, and Milan didn't read it until they were back in their car, which was a beat-up civilian car Reyes used often. To his credit, Reyes never even asked what was on the paper, and Milan wouldn't have told him anyway. The less Reyes knew, the better, and in this case, it had held only a phone number and one name.

Ryan Wallace.

26

Coulson was reading through the latest 302 forms when his phone rang. Who the hell called this early in the day? It was seven thirty. He and Seth had come in at daybreak, as they'd done often lately, attempting to stay on top of things.

With a sigh, he picked up, his eyes still glued to the report he was holding.

"Coulson, I have an urgent phone call for you," Rebecca, one of their phone operators, said.

Coulson frowned, tearing his eyes away and focusing on the call. "Who is it?"

"A young guy named Elya Abramson. He says he's a police officer with the Baltimore PD."

Officer Babyface. "Put him through."

"Okay."

As soon as the line connected, Coulson heard panting. "Officer Abramson?"

"Yeah. Yes, I mean. I'm... I don't know what to do."

He sounded flat out panicked. "Take a deep breath for me. First things first. Are you in a safe place right now?"

Coulson snapped his fingers at Seth, who just walked in, then put his phone on speaker. Seth sat down on the edge of Coulson's desk, listening intently.

The young cop sucked in a breath. Good. He could still follow instructions. "I'm in the bathroom of a McDonald's."

Not the safest place to talk, but at least he was around other people. "Okay. Is your life in danger right now? Do I need to send backup?"

A half-choked sob. "I don't want to panic, but... Maybe? I don't know."

"Tell me why you think you might be in danger."

"Remember my friend Emery?" His voice had dropped to a whisper.

Emery... The name rang a bell, but Coulson had encountered too many names to place it.

"IT guy," Seth mouthed.

Right. "Yes, your friend in IT. What about him?"

Another sob. "He's in the hospital. In the ICU. Someone hit him yesterday as he was driving home on his motorbike. A hit and run."

Shit. Coulson didn't like the sound of that at all. "Will he make it?"

"The doctors aren't sure yet. I talked to his sister, and she said that the cops have no clue who hit him. No leads, even."

"You suspect foul play?"

Abramson was quiet for a few beats. "The cop who took the car from the impound lot? Wesley Quirk? He stormed out of Emery's office yesterday morning, looking mighty pissed. I wanted to ask Emery, but I feared they were watching him or monitoring his phone. I figured I'd stop by his house after work...but he never made it home."

"Do they know about you?"

"They have to realize we're close. Emery and I hang out

all the time at work... And Quirk knows I work in the impound lot."

Yeah, he was right to be cautious. "I can imagine you're worried. Where exactly are you?"

"I'm at the McDonald's around the corner from the precinct. My shift started at seven, but I'm too scared to go in. If they came after Emery..."

In any other situation, Coulson would've sent a uniform, but how could he when the kid's own brothers in blue were after him? Coulson wasn't sure who to trust, and that meant not relying on any outsiders. "Stay where you are and text me your location. I'll come get you."

"Thank you. I'm scared. I know I shouldn't be, but..."

"You were right to call me." Coulson packed up as he continued the conversation, and Seth did the same. "Are you wearing your uniform?"

"Yes, sir."

"Your gun?"

"Yes, sir."

"Stay in that bathroom, okay? We'll get to you as fast as we can. I'll stay on the phone with you."

He'd let Seth drive. He was the better driver out of the two of them anyway, having done all kinds of special driving training with the Secret Service. They raced down to the garage, then jumped into the car. Coulson slapped the blue light on top as Seth already backed out, then rubber-burned it out of there.

"We're on our way, okay? Sorry, what was your first name again?"

"Elya. Elyakim, officially, but my friends call me Elya."

"Okay, Elya. Stay calm for me."

"I know I shouldn't be scared as a cop."

"Fear is a normal reaction, even for a cop...and especially when it's one of your own that's after you."

He kept chatting with him as Seth bulldozed his way through the morning congestion, honking and driving whole stretches on the shoulder where possible. Rush hour was the worst possible timing to drive to Baltimore, but they had no choice. The young cop calmed down a bit, sharing everything he knew about the hit and run. Coulson made a mental note to have one of his agents look into it. The chances of it being a coincidence were slim, especially with what Elya had said about Quirk coming out of his friend's office.

"We're a couple of blocks away," he said when they'd finally made it to the area. "Why don't you come outside to the parking lot? Stay on the phone and put it on speaker. I'll mute it on my end unless you ask me a direct question, okay? That way, no one will see or hear you're on a call."

"O-okay."

A door creaked—probably the bathroom stall. Abramson's shoes shuffled on the floor as he walked out of the bathroom. In the background, people were talking, ordering food, and calling out order numbers. Then the environment changed as he stepped outside, traffic coming in. Honking cars, squealing brakes.

"What the fuck do you think you're doing? Why aren't you on shift?"

The voice was stuffed with venom, spitting out each word. Oh, shit. The kid had run into trouble.

"I w-wasn't feeling well, sir. I had to throw up and could barely make it to the bathroom here on my way to the precinct," Elya said. Great, the kid could think on his feet.

"Bullshit. Not that it matters. You're coming with me. You're gonna tell me exactly what your faggot little traitor friend shared with you about what he saw on that footage. We don't like snitches here."

Coulson's stomach sank. It had to be Quirk or at least one of his friends.

"I don't know w-what you're talking about, sir. Officer Quirk."

They had their confirmation. Smart kid.

"Oh, I think we both know that's a fucking lie." Quirk sounded like he was standing close, his voice low and threatening. "Give me your gun."

"Why? I don't understand. What are you doing?"

"Stop talking, or you'll meet an unfortunate fate, just like your friend."

Holy shit. The guy had no idea Abramson was on a call.

"No. I'm not going anywhere."

Much to Coulson's surprise, Abramson sounded resolute, like he meant it. Maybe he was emboldened, knowing his rescuers were close? This wasn't how Coulson had intended things to go down, but they'd have to adapt and deal with it. His priority was to keep Elya safe.

He looked at Seth, who nodded, weaving in and out of traffic, then driving straight over a sidewalk to get to the McDonald's. When he saw the yellow M pop up, Coulson removed the blue light off the roof of the car. No need to announce their arrival.

A smack and then, "Ow!"

He'd hit the kid, no doubt about it. That took some serious guts, considering they were in public.

"Hey, asshole, why you hittin' him?" a female voice called out. "He's a cop, you dumb fuck."

If she called Abramson a cop, Quirk must not be wearing his uniform, or she would've worded it differently.

"Stay the fuck out of it," Quirk snapped. "I'm an undercover detective, and he's impersonating a police officer."

Smart move, casting doubt about who the bad guy was in this scenario. Seth whipped the car into the parking lot, and Coulson's eyes scanned until he found them. Quirk stood behind Abramson, holding him in a rear choke hold. Quirk was a head taller and a good forty, fifty pounds heavier. No way would the rookie be able to retract himself from those arms. Shit. This wasn't going to end well.

"You sure? 'Cause he don't look like he's old enough to even shave. I can't see him hurting no one," the same woman said, and Coulson spotted her standing at a safe distance. She was Black, early forties, and she had her hands on her hips in the telltale fashion of someone who had seen her fair share of things and didn't take shit from anyone anymore.

"Back. Off." Quirk held up his gun, or maybe it was the one he'd taken from Abramson. The situation was escalating by the second.

Seth parked as close as he could. No matter the urgency of the situation, Coulson still took the time to put on his vest and FBI jacket, and Seth did the same. They couldn't afford mistakes here. He slid his phone into his pocket—making sure not to end the call with Abramson—then touched Seth's hand for a second. "Stay safe," he whispered, and Seth nodded.

He didn't need to tell Seth to follow his lead. He would.

They slipped out of the car and stayed low, leaving the doors ajar. A man who got out of his vehicle saw them and gasped. Coulson put his finger on his lips, then pointed at Quirk and the rookie. The man immediately went back into his car, thank fuck.

"Look, all I'm sayin' is that—"

Quirk pointed his gun straight at her. "Shut. Up."

She took a few steps back. "You ain't no cop, not with you waiving that gun. Imma call 911."

Damn, she had guts. And Coulson had no idea if she'd noticed him and Seth or not, but she sure was creating the perfect distraction. They crawled into position behind a car, as close as they could make it.

"Bitch, do I need to fucking shoot you to get you to shut your trap?"

Coulson took a deep breath, then rose in one fluid move, his Glock trained at Quirk. "FBI. Put down your gun."

Quirk jerked, then pivoted, still holding Abramson, and pointed his gun at Coulson. "I'm a detective with the Baltimore PD."

"I don't care if you're the queen of England. Put. Down. Your. Gun."

Quirk hesitated. "Show me your ID!" he called out.

"This is not some game of who has the longest, asshole. Put your gun down, and I'll be happy to show my ID."

Quirk's posture changed, and Coulson reacted before he'd even consciously processed the danger. He dove to the ground.

Pop! Pop!

He hit the asphalt with a smack that took his breath away for a second. That asshole was fucking firing at him!

Pop!

A scream. The *thud* of something heavy falling to the ground. A clatter. More screams.

But that hadn't been Quirk. This shot had come from right behind him... He raised his head a fraction. Seth stood, his SIG Sauer in his hand after he'd just fired straight over Coulson's head. "Don't fucking move," he said, his tone so commanding that even Coulson had the urge to obey.

He stepped past Coulson, who scrambled to his feet.

Seth strode forward, his gun still trained at Quirk, who was now on the ground, clutching his hand while his standard-issued Glock 9mm lay next to him. Seth kicked it away. He'd hit Quirk's hand? That was some excellent marksmanship.

He followed Seth, who loomed over Quirk, his gun still aimed at him. Coulson's heart rate slowed down again. Jesus, that had been way too close. Where was Abramson? Coulson looked around. There. The rookie cop was hiding behind a car several feet away. Good. The scene wasn't secured yet.

"You fucking *shot* me," Quirk spat out. "I'm a cop."

"And I'm a federal agent who told you to put down your gun, so bite me," Coulson snapped back. An idea popped into his head. Quirk didn't know who they were and why they were here. They could use that to their advantage.

"That was a lucky coincidence that we happened to be driving by," he told Seth, who didn't miss a beat.

"Yeah, good timing we saw this asshole hold a cop hostage."

Quirk groaned again, clutching his hand, which, Coulson had to admit, was bleeding profusely. Still, first things first. "You're under arrest for assault with a deadly weapon on a federal officer."

Seth kept his SIG trained at Quirk as Coulson kneeled next to him, turned him onto his stomach, and handcuffed him. He patted him down, discovering another gun in his ankle holster as well as a knife. He also found a wallet, which was perfect. It would help their facade that they didn't know who he was.

"You're Wesley Quirk?"

"Yes. I'm a detective with the Baltimore PD. I'm telling you, you've got this all wrong."

He sounded a lot less cocky than before, so the seriousness of the situation was probably sinking in with him. "Hmm, so you shooting at me was a figment of my imagination?"

Technically, he didn't have to read him his rights, since he hadn't declared his intention to interrogate him, but as with everything else in this case, he preferred to risk nothing, not even the slightest chance of anything the man said being inadmissible. With Quirk already trying to twist the facts, he might end up incriminating himself, and when he did, Coulson wanted to be able to use it. And so he went by the book.

"You have the right to remain silent. Anything you say can and will be used against you in a court of law. You have the right to an attorney. If you cannot afford an attorney, one will be provided for you. Do you understand the rights I have just read to you?"

"The fuck is wrong with you? I'm a cop. Why are you arresting me? I was doing an undercover operation."

Boy, was he glad he'd read him his rights because the man was digging a hole for himself that would only get deeper, and Coulson wanted to use every word he said against him. "Do you understand the rights I have just read to you?"

"Of course I do. I'm a fucking cop."

Perfect. Hook, line, and sinker.

"Let me request an ambulance and grab the Medkit," Coulson told Seth. A small crowd had gathered around them, and he didn't like it. Situations like this could change in a flash, and in this case, he couldn't be assured of the support of cops. He needed backup. He dug out his phone, ended the call with Abramson, then stepped away far enough so no one could overhear him and called it in, requesting immediate backup from the closest FBI agents as well as the Maryland State Police. In hushed tones, he instructed the operator not to inform the Baltimore PD, though how long they would stay out of it, he wasn't sure.

Once that was done, he put a quick pressure bandage around Quirk's hand, which showed a through-and-through shot. It was still bleeding, but his main artery wasn't hit, so he'd live. Whether he'd ever be able to use that hand again was another question, but not one Coulson wasted any energy on. He caught Abramson's eye again and signaled for him to stay hidden. Coulson didn't want his face even associated with them. Let Quirk think the rookie had fled. Abramson nodded, then snuck back into the McDonald's, probably heading for the restrooms again. Perfect.

While they waited for the proverbial cavalry to arrive, Coulson had everyone back up, then asked for witnesses. He wrote down their contact information so the FBI could reach out to them later for statements. The chances of needing them were low, but he wanted Quirk to assume this was a routine thing.

When backup arrived—an ambulance, two state police cars, and two cars with four FBI agents each—so did the Baltimore PD, and the air grew tense with impending conflict. Coulson mentally braced himself.

"What the hell is going on here? I hear you're arresting one of my men." A man in police uniform stalked toward Coulson, a scowl on his face. Coulson rested his hand on his gun. He recognized the Baltimore PD police commissioner from pictures he'd seen of him.

"Keep your distance, sir. This is an active crime scene."

Oh, the man didn't appreciate that. "Crime scene? What crime are we talking about?"

"Detective Quirk is under arrest for assault with a deadly weapon on a federal officer."

The police commissioner paled. "What? What happened?"

Coulson raised an eyebrow. "You expect me to discuss details in public? I don't think so."

"Detective Quirk has rights."

"He sure does, and I've read them to him. You should be well familiar with them. Feel free to contact the FBI, but at this point, we are not releasing information."

Fuck that asshole. Luckily, his fellow agents swarmed the scene with assistance from the state police, cordoning off the area and keeping everyone, which included several police officers—presumably from Quirk's precinct—at bay. Coulson took one of his agents aside. "Quirk thinks we were here by accident," he said softly. "Don't reveal we know who he is."

She nodded. "I'll make sure of it, sir."

"Don't let him out of your sight. Not even for a second. If he has to pee, someone goes with him. If he's in a holding cell, someone will watch him at all times, and I mean all times. Understood?"

"Yes, sir."

He waited until everyone had left, then headed into the McDonald's. "Elya?" he called out softly in the restroom, even though he saw no feet under any of the stalls. "It's Coulson."

Feet appeared, and then the stall opened. The young cop looked shaken but steady. "Is it over?"

Coulson nodded. "He's under arrest. How are you holding up?"

"I thought he was gonna kill me."

Coulson put a hand on his shoulder. "We wouldn't have let that happen."

"I was terrified."

"I know, and that's understandable."

"What happens now? Am I safe now that he's gone?"

Coulson squeezed his shoulder. "Unfortunately not. I can't tell you more, but he's a part of a large network. I'll have someone take you to a safe place to stay for a while, okay?"

Abramson nodded. "Sir?"

"Yeah?"

"I recorded the whole call from the moment you picked up."

Halle-fucking-lujah. "That's excellent thinking, Elya. Well done. Make sure to turn your phone in to the FBI agent who's driving you to a safe location, okay?"

"I will."

Coulson waited until another agent had picked the rookie up, bringing a change of clothes and a baseball cap so he could change out of his uniform and no one would recognize him. Only then did he make his way back to his car, where Seth stood waiting for him.

Coulson looked around. Everyone had dispersed, no one watching them. He pulled Seth in his arms, hugging him tightly. "Thank you."

"That was close, boo," Seth said, his voice choked. "Let's try not to do that again."

"I'm down with that."

He held on to him until their heartbeats had slowed down and were calm and steady again. Only then did he let go, but not after a firm kiss.

As Seth drove back to the office, Coulson didn't let go of his thigh, giving in to the deep need to touch him, to know for a fact they were both still alive.

Then it sunk in. They had Quirk in custody. This would disrupt their plans. Now what?

27

Branson had never been in the same place with so many powerful people. Coulson had called an emergency meeting, and they had crammed themselves into a way-too-small conference room in the CIA building, but nothing else had been available on such short notice.

Everyone had shown up, including the directors of the FBI and the CIA, the attorney general, FBI Special Agent in Charge Sheehan, and the national security advisor. Plus, of course, the usual suspects like Coulson and Seth. Branson was once again knee to knee with Ryder, asking himself why the fuck he'd subjected himself to this torture. Even Ryder's smell turned him on, his cock half hard in anticipation. Traitor.

"Due to unforeseen circumstances, we have Wesley Quirk in custody," Coulson started the meeting, and boy, that had everyone's attention. He explained how Officer Abramson had contacted him and what had happened afterward. Branson's heart sped up as the story unfolded, and he forgot all about Ryder. Damn, that had been a close call for both Abramson and Coulson.

"You shot him in his hand?" Suzy Girardi, the attorney general, asked Seth.

"Yes."

"Why his hand?"

"Because if I'd hit him anywhere else, he might've squeezed the trigger in a reflex, and with that many people around, including Officer Abramson, someone might've gotten hurt."

FBI Director Huebner whistled between his teeth. "That's excellent marksmanship, son."

Seth shrugged. "I'm Secret Service. I don't miss."

Branson loved the man's quiet confidence. He wasn't bragging. He'd stated a fact, and in Branson's eyes, that made it even more impressive. In his experience, people who excelled in something rarely bragged.

"The problem is that this may impact our investigation," Coulson said. "We postponed the first round of subpoenas to prioritize building our case against El Sewedy, but this could jeopardize our timeline. For now, Quirk is in federal custody for assault with a deadly weapon on a federal officer. We got lucky he took a shot at me. Otherwise it would've been hard to charge him with a federal crime."

"The Baltimore PD police commissioner contacted us," Sheehan said. "He wasn't happy, but when we informed him Quirk fired his gun at an FBI agent, he backed down. I didn't get the impression he knows about Quirk's involvement in the assassination, though he's well aware the man is not squeaky clean in other areas."

Coulson nodded. "The problem is that the security cameras around the McDonald's caught the whole incident, which shows Officer Abramson. We're not releasing it for now, but once we do, his precinct will know he's involved."

"They'll know something is up anyway," Gary said. "Abramson didn't show up for his shift yesterday, and he's in a safe location now. He called in sick, but at some point, his chief will figure out it's connected."

"What about his friend, the IT guy?" Seth asked. "How is he doing?"

"Emery Licari is still in the ICU, listed as stable but critical. We have plainclothes state police guarding him in case someone wants to finish the job. Traffic cams caught the accident, and it was a direct attempt to take him out. If he hadn't been wearing a leather jacket and leather pants as well as a high-quality helmet, he'd be dead," Coulson said.

"Did Quirk do it?" Branson asked.

Coulson shook his head. "No. He was on shift, and his alibi checks out."

"State police are investigating, with our quiet assistance. As harsh as it sounds, finding out who was behind that is secondary to our investigation, so we haven't provided a list of names of people who could be behind it to the state police," Huebner said.

"What's the impact on the investigation?" Heeder asked. "Give me the worst-case scenario."

"Worst case is that everyone we're investigating finds out we're onto them now that Quirk is in federal custody, and they all go to ground...and destroy evidence," Ella Yung, the national security sdvisor, said. "It would make everything a hell of a lot harder and time consuming."

"Has Quirk used his right to speak to an attorney?" Branson asked.

"He contacted his union, the Baltimore City Fraternal Order of Police, and talked to one of their lawyers," Gary said. "That's good news because that means he still thinks this is unrelated to the assassination. Otherwise he would've reached out to a whole different type of lawyer."

"In my estimate, we have twenty-four to forty-eight hours before the shit hits the fan," Suzy Girardi said. "If we keep the current charge of assault with a deadly weapon of a federal officer, there'll be an arraignment. The magistrate judge will release him pending trial on his own recognizance, since he's a police officer with no priors, and the charge carries a sentence of under ten years of prison. Once he's out, he can contact whoever he wants."

"And if we add domestic terrorism charges?" Branson asked.

"That's a whole different ball game. He wouldn't be released, and the judge would most likely agree to strict confinement and no contact with anyone but his lawyer."

"Are we ready to charge him?" Heeder asked. "Do we have enough evidence against him?"

Suzy Girardi gestured at Sheehan. "I think so, but I'd like to hear what the FBI thinks."

Sheehan smiled weakly. "Coulson is our expert here."

The man might technically be in charge, but he had so little input, Branson wondered why he even bothered showing up for these meetings.

"Yes." Coulson's answer was fast and firm. "We've had enough against him for a while, at least for the murder on Donnie Smith and for his role in the assassination. We've been surveilling him for months now, monitoring his calls and activities outside of work. That's the only reason he could get to Abramson. He was on duty and walked over from the precinct. For obvious reasons, we can't shadow him on the job, though we do monitor him there as much as we can."

"And everyone else?" Heeder asked.

"We have sufficient evidence to link Naomi Beckingham and her boyfriend, Ralph Durrick, to the hacking of Christopher Hales's laptop. Our cybercrime division has traced the hack back to Durrick, who's an infamous hacker, so we have that all wrapped up. The ATF is confident Jon Brooks was the bomb maker for both the Pride Bombing and the assassination and has physical evidence for his arrest, linking the components to materials he bought, like the blasting caps. All we were waiting for was more proof on the role of Kingmakers and their connection to Hamza Bashir." Coulson looked at Branson. "How are things on your end? Any fresh developments?

Branson loved that Coulson asked him and not Weston, who was also present. "We've dug up a lot more on Hamza Bashir, or Yazid El Sewedy, I should say. The Emirate authorities are cooperative after the British put pressure on them, and we have confirmed most of the details of his two meetings with Basil King, including the mysterious trip to Qatar where King disappeared for a few days. We have evidence he paid for a private plane to take him into Yemen, where El Sewedy had set up base by then."

"What about the financial link between him and Kingmakers?" Coulson asked Ryder, who cleared his throat.

"If you'll allow me to share some other developments first, I'll get to that in a second," he said, and Coulson smiled, as did Branson himself. Ryder was so adorable when he was all serious and nerdy.

Ryder took a deep breath. "Based on the assumption that someone else had paid for the Pride bombers to come to the US, Corey and I traced the tuition payments to the colleges they attended. They all came from a US bank account set up through Wise, which is a go-between financial service that allows non-US residents to set up a bank account in the US. That's where we ran into a problem. That tuition was paid months before the first established contact between Kingmakers and El Sewedy. These three guys arrived in the US in July 2014. The first contact with Kingmakers wasn't until September of that year."

Silence descended in the room as the implications sank in. "You're saying El Sewedy set these three guys up as sleepers in the US before he ever talked to Kingmakers?" Heeder then asked.

"Yes." Ryder didn't even hesitate for a second.

"We think that El Sewedy planned to do some kind of terrorist attack on US soil for the highest bidder," Branson said. "He set everything up way ahead of time, before he'd even talked to potential clients, so it would all fly under the radar. And it did. The intelligence community didn't pick up chatter on a new terrorist cell until February 2015, and the Pride Bombing happened in June of that year. El Sewedy set everything in motion, but he waited with establishing the terrorist cell until he had a client and knew what it had to look like. It all fits with our theory that he's doing it purely for the money."

"Jesus," Huebner muttered. "Just when you think you've seen it all, we now have to worry about people committing these atrocities for money? I don't know why, but that makes it ten times worse."

Branson had thought the same thing when it had hit him. On some level, he could understand people who committed crimes out of a deep religious conviction. They were wrong, no doubt about it, but he could follow their reasoning. But killing for money? That meant having no soul at all, no compassion. No humanity.

"We subpoenaed Wise for the records, and the money

was transferred into that account from another Wise account, one that Kingmakers paid a million dollars into over the course of the last six years. So for the first time, we've established a financial trace between Kingmakers and El Sewedy," Ryder said.

"That's fantastic work, guys," Coulson said, and Ryder's beaming smile made Branson's belly flutter. Fuck, he was so stinking cute.

"Thank you, sir. We're still working with the Central Bank of the United Arab Emirates to get access to El Sewedy's account, but I'm positive we'll find what we need in time."

Ryder sounded confident, as always when he talked about numbers, and it never failed to amaze Branson how sexy that was.

"Does that mean we have enough on the financial links?" Coulson asked.

Ryder looked at Corey, who gestured Ryder should answer. "For an arrest, yes, but a conviction in court would require more. To get that, we'd need full access to all Kingmakers' financials, straight from the source, so to speak, not from third parties. I assume they have multiple hidden accounts we don't know about yet."

"The same is true for the companies we suspect of involvement in the fraud regarding Governor Winkelmann's presidential campaign. I need access to their full financial information," Corey said.

Coulson nodded. "I figured as much. The bottom line is that we have two choices. We can either let Quirk walk on charges of assaulting a federal officer and risk him alerting everyone in his network, thus compromising and complicating our investigation. Or we can make our move now and execute search warrants and indictments across the board for everyone on our list...except El Sewedy."

"He'll know we're on to him," Calix said.

"Yes. He'll disappear," Branson said. "And it may take us a while to find him again."

"I have a third solution," Ryder said, and the room fell quiet. "It's what I would call the Al Capone approach."

Al Capone? What did he have to do with anything? Oh, wait. In the end, they'd convicted him for tax fraud, not for the crime empire he'd built. Shit, of course. Tax evasion.

"You propose going after Kingmakers for tax fraud?" Huebner said. "Color me intrigued."

Ryder nodded. "For tax fraud and the illegal elections contributions to Governor Winkelmann's campaign. The IRS already flagged Kingmakers' returns and set up an audit, so we have that precedent. There are plenty of factual anomalies in their returns, enough to build a case for tax evasion and fraud. We could go after the other four companies for illegal campaign contributions, and it wouldn't surprise me if they committed fraud to cover those up."

"You're saying use those charges as an excuse to subpoena everything, then later indict them for domestic terrorism," Heeder said.

"Yes, sir. It would give us some extra time."

The room grew quiet again. "All we'd have to do is classify the McDonald's footage so the Baltimore PD or the media can't get their hands on that," Coulson said.

"And find a reasonable excuse for Abramson to quit his job," Branson added.

"But Quirk knew Emery had that video of him stealing the car from the impound lot," Seth brought up. "How will you make that go away?"

"We don't. Quirk doesn't know we already connected the dots. He fears he might get busted for stealing a car based on that video, not for anything else," Coulson said. "And I doubt he'll be shocked when Abramson leaves, not after the way he threatened him. In fact, he probably figures that solved his problem. The IT guy is in the hospital, and Abramson is gone. He'll never expect them to contact the FBI because stealing a car isn't a federal offense, not even if it involves a cop."

"Do we have any evidence they're planning another attack?" Ella Yung asked. "Because if they are, we can't delay arresting them."

"Not even a hint. We've been monitoring communication between all suspects as much as we can, and we've seen nothing that suggests they're gearing up for another attack. They're lying low."

"Putting the pressure on them with Quirk's arrest, followed by indicting them for tax fraud may, cause them to make mistakes. Even the most hardened criminals have a tough time keeping their heads cool when they suspect the feds are on their trail," Huebner said.

The man made a good point. "They might contact each other to compare notes," Branson said.

"If they do, it would play right into our hands." Coulson rubbed his hands in a way that made Branson smile. "And the tax fraud indictment will prevent them from destroying financial evidence."

"This is our course of action, then?" Huebner looked around the room. "Any objections? No? Okay, then everyone has their marching orders. Let's get them, people."

As everyone left the room, Director Heeder walked over to Ryder. "That was excellent work, Ryder."

Ryder beamed, his entire face lighting up. "Thank you, sir."

"From you as well, Branson," the director said. "How's your father doing?"

Branson was taken aback. How did Heeder know about his dad? But Heeder smiled, putting a hand on his shoulder. "I met your father several times throughout my career, especially when he was stationed in Jordan. He's a good man, and I was sorry to hear about his diagnosis."

"Thank you, sir. I'll let him know you asked about him. He'll appreciate that. He's hanging in there. The surgery took a lot, and his recovery isn't as quick as we'd hoped, but I'm confident he'll fight his way through this."

Heeder squeezed his shoulder, then let go. "He's a fighter, that's for certain. Tell him to kick this disease's ass, would you?"

He walked off, leaving Branson and Ryder behind. "That was really nice of him," Ryder said.

Branson smiled at him. "His compliment to you or what he said about my dad?"

"Both...but I'd lie if I said I didn't value him affirming me."

"It was well deserved, chéri. That was a brilliant suggestion."

"Thank you." He shuffled his feet, then looked up at Branson again. "I like it when you call me that."

"What, chéri?"

"Yes."

"Good. I'll keep calling you that, then."

"Yes, please. I mean, that would be okay. Good. Fun even. Anyway, I'm rambling. Wanna grab lunch together?"

Warmth filled Branson's heart. Ryder had initiated hanging out together—and this time not because of something that had happened with Branson. "I'd love to."

28

Without looking, Ryder reached for his coffee while triple-checking the numbers in front of him. Was he certain he'd included everything? He had to submit this to Legal in—he checked his watch—twenty-two minutes. No pressure.

He took a sip, then frowned in surprise. Huh? He was damn sure his coffee had been cold mere minutes ago. No wonder, since he'd been glued to his screen for at least a few hours. So how was it possible the liquid was now warm again?

He looked up. Branson was standing in his office, leaning against the wall with a big smile on his face. "I put it there minutes ago. I was wondering how long it would take you to notice."

Ryder sighed, then took another sip of his coffee. "And what's the verdict?"

"Six minutes and thirteen seconds."

"You've been standing there for six minutes and thirteen seconds?"

"Yup."

Ryder shrugged. "I take after my dad, who also has hyper concentration. It once took him twenty minutes to realize my mom was standing in the room, waiting for him to notice her."

Branson whistled. "She must've been upset."

"Not really. I think by then, she was more curious than anything else. But it did become a kind of legendary moment."

Branson chuckled. "I can imagine."

"Anyway, thanks for the fresh coffee. Much appreciated. Anything I can do for you?"

"Just wanted to check in and make sure you were good for the deadline with Legal."

Ryder nodded, turning back to his screen. "I was running a last review, but I think I've got it."

After the decision to go after Kingmakers and the four defense contractors for tax fraud and illegal campaign contributions, things had moved fast. The FBI and the US Attorney's Office had worked around the clock to switch gears and prepare the grand jury for a different case. That session would take place on Monday, and everyone had received detailed instructions on what information to submit so the picture would be complete and irrefutable. Ryder and Corey had been charged with detailing all the financial evidence they had so far.

None of this was new. They'd been building their evidence from the get-go, always anticipating the moment when they'd have to convince a judge. But the focus had shifted for now, plus the process had been accelerated, so they'd had to recheck everything. This case was too important to fuck up even the smallest detail.

"Give me five more minutes," he told Branson, already running down the last lines of his Excel sheet.

"Sure."

Ryder read through the numbers one more time. He couldn't explain how it worked in his brain, but he'd once described it to his father as a built-in computer that automatically checked numbers. They ran through his head like they were projected on his mental screen, and if something was off, the screen froze. But nothing popped up this time, and when he had assured himself of that, he hit Send on the document and let out a long sigh.

When he turned around, Branson sat on the floor, leaning with his back against the wall as he flipped through his phone. As soon as Ryder turned his chair, he looked up. "Done?"

"Yeah. Thanks for waiting." He cocked his head. "Why were you waiting for me, actually? If you only wanted to ensure I would make the deadline, my answer would've been enough, no?"

Branson smiled. "Sure, but I was done anyway, so I figured I might as well kill time here."

"Not ready to go home?" A quick check on the clock showed it was almost nine p.m.

"Not really. I'm so pumped up I wouldn't even know what to do with myself. Knowing what's going to happen on Monday, that years of work are going to culminate in the first legal actions, even if they're only the precursor to the real event, I could never fall asleep."

Ryder finished his coffee, then lowered himself on the floor next to Branson. "Have you ever seen that movie Gladiator, with Russell Crowe playing Maximus?" Ryder asked.

Branson nodded.

"It reminds me of that opening scene, where the Roman army lines up for the final battle. They're trained, battle-hardened, and ready. Maximus inspects the troops, and once he's satisfied, he tells them, 'On my signal, unleash hell.' That's what it feels like, like we've done everything we could to prepare...and now we're waiting for the signal to unleash hell."

"I like that comparison. There's this anticipation now as if we're expecting war to break out."

They sat shoulder to shoulder. "When this is all over, I'm going to take a leave of absence," Branson said.

Ryder looked at him sideways. "To do what?"

"To find myself. I've had a few long hard looks in the mirror, and I didn't like what I saw. I need some time to decompress and discover who I am."

"I feel like I should say sorry again, though I don't know what I'd be apologizing for."

Branson bumped his shoulder. "No need at all. It's the best thing that could've ever happened to me."

"Why?"

"If you hadn't said anything, I would've kept on pretending and putting on a mask for years to come, probably never developing true friendships...or a relationship."

Branson had dropped that word several times now. "That's something you long for, isn't it?"

"A relationship? Yes."

"Why?"

Branson was quiet for a long time. "Because I'm tired of being alone. I thought it was enough, the hookups and casual sex, but it's not. I want to be together instead of by myself, if that makes sense. Be part of something bigger. A team. I want someone to share my life with, the highs and the lows. To laugh and cry together, to love and fight, to travel and make a home. "

Ryder didn't understand why, but his eyes grew moist as

Branson's soft words sank deep into him. "You make it sound so poetic. So perfect."

Branson moved, lifting his arm, then dropping it again. "Can I...?" He gestured.

Ryder nodded.

Branson draped his arm around Ryder and pulled him against his body. "I know it was far from perfect for you."

"Yeah."

"But spending the rest of your life alone would be punishing yourself for what your ex did, don't you think? You'd allow him to dictate your life, even years later."

Ryder had never looked at it like that. "How can I trust again after that? What if I get hurt again?"

"What if you don't? What if your fears would rob you of a wonderful relationship? Of finding your soul mate?"

A soul mate. Did he even believe in that? Ryder had always approached the concept of love from a practical point of view. If everyone only had one soul mate, many people would be unhappy if they missed meeting theirs. Or maybe he—and everyone else—had multiple soul mates? Or was a soul mate another label for the man he'd have his happily ever after with? If he even trusted he'd ever achieve that.

Branson had made a good point. If Ryder closed himself off for a new relationship, he'd also miss out on the wonderful things that came with having a partner. Morning sex. The intimacy of showering together. Cooking together. The joy that flowed from being in tune with someone else. Rare as those experiences had been toward the end with Paul, he remembered them from the beginning...and those memories were good.

But how would he find someone? What would he look for? His thoughts automatically went to Branson and their epic sexual encounter. What was it that Dorian had said? Sexual compatibility was important, considering how much sex meant to Ryder. And he couldn't deny he and Branson fit perfectly, sexually speaking. But that was all. The idea that they fit well in other areas was preposterous.

He leaned away from Branson for a moment, seeking his eyes. "You've given me food for thought."

Branson's smile was sweet. "Good. I want to see you happy, chéri."

For a moment, they gazed at each other, and Ryder's belly tickled at the openness of Branson's face. Such a stark contrast to the mask he'd always sported before. He relished it when Branson smiled at him like that, though deep down, he knew he shouldn't. Because thinking about Branson's smile made Ryder remember how he'd studied him after they had fucked, and that only caused him to want things he had no business wanting…

"I should go," he said, turning his head away. He checked his watch, then sighed. It would take him another full hour to get back to his parents. He was tired just thinking about it.

"You're welcome to use my guest room. It's the weekend anyway, so you could even sleep in tomorrow."

Sleep in. Fuck, that sounded good. The idea of not waking up at nine thirty from a vacuum cleaner was tempting. But was it smart to stay at Branson's again?

After Branson's little speech three nights before, Ryder had lain in bed awake for a long time, debating with himself whether he should go to Branson's room or not. In the end, he hadn't, and even the next morning, he hadn't been sure if it had been the right call. Until they'd both gotten up and things had been wonderfully easy and casual between them, and Ryder had used that as proof that he'd been smart not to have taken Branson up on his offer.

But would he be able to turn him down again? Did he even want to, especially after the direction his thoughts had taken earlier?

"Thank you for offering," he finally said, his head such a conflicting mess that he didn't know what to do. *When in doubt, don't do it.* That was what his father had always taught him. *Don't make the jump unless you know you can stick the landing on the other side.* This particular jump had the potential to end in a disaster of cataclysmic proportions, so why would he even consider it? He shouldn't.

"You're going home?"

The disappointment in Branson's voice was barely hidden, making Ryder doubt himself all over again. No, his father's advice was solid. He should heed it. "I have to."

"Okay."

Branson let go of him, and they both scrambled to their feet. Ryder felt awkward, guilty that he'd rejected him, but Branson's smile was friendly. "Safe drive home. I'll see you Monday."

"See you Monday. Have a good weekend."

He stood there for a long time after Branson had walked out, then packed his stuff and took the elevator down. If he was doing the right thing, why did it feel like a mistake? Once he was in his car, he started the engine but didn't drive off the parking lot yet. Instead, he called Dorian. He'd kept him in the loop on everything that had passed between him and Branson, including every sexy detail about their night together. Dorian would know what to do.

"Hey, Ry," his best friend said, sounding tired. Oops, he'd called him after nine thirty. Dorian was usually in bed by then.

"Sorry, did I wake you?"

"No, I was reading in bed... What's up?"

"I'm in the parking lot at work."

"Okay...and?"

"Branson asked me to spend the night."

"In his bed or his apartment?"

"His apartment... But he never retracted the other invitation, so I suppose that's still on the table as well."

"But he didn't bring it up."

"No, but he said last time it had to be my choice and that he wouldn't put pressure on me."

Dorian hmm'ed in understanding. "Just to be clear, you want him to fuck you again, correct?"

Ryder moaned. "You have no idea how much."

"Are there any legal reasons you shouldn't?"

"No. He's not my boss, we're not reporting to each other in any way, and I can't think of any rule that prohibits a consensual relationship between coworkers."

"So..."

"So what?"

"So why aren't you naked, in his bed, with that monster cock halfway inside you by now?"

Ryder almost choked on his own breath. "Dude..."

"I'm serious, Ry. After years of bad sex, you've found a guy who can make you kiss the stars. He's nice, he's your age, he's single, he's got a dick to die for, and he's a great fuck. Why are you holding out? This was what you wanted, wasn't it? Find great sex?"

"Yeah, but... This has complications written all over it. What if..."

He wanted to say *what if we break up*, but they couldn't split up if they weren't boyfriends. And arguments weren't that likely either if all they craved was sex. Besides, they'd both shown already that they could separate work and private. So what, exactly, were these complications he feared? Now that he wanted to list them, he couldn't name even one.

Yes, Branson had made him think with his questions about Ryder closing himself off from future relationships, but that wasn't on the table right now. Maybe he had a point, but Ryder could take the time to think that through and decide on a course of action. It bore no relevance for the far more pressing question of whether he should sleep with Branson again or not.

"What if you're being a nitwit who's overthinking it and imagining complications where there are none?" Dorian asked softly, then yawned.

"Go to sleep. Thank you for listening to me be an idiot."

"You're welcome. So where will you be twenty minutes from now? In your car by yourself, driving back to your parents? Or...?"

Ryder grinned. "Hopefully, as you so succinctly put it, naked, in his bed, with that monster cock halfway inside me..."

"Good. Enjoy for both of us. Love ya."

"Love ya too. Sleep well."

His heart was ten times lighter as he drove off the lot and set course for Branson's apartment. He walked in after one of his neighbors, thus skipping the phase of buzzing the intercom downstairs. After he knocked, the door swung open. Branson wore only a pair of tight boxer briefs that outlined a massive hard-on. He looked stunned to see Ryder.

"I want to spend the night...in your bed," Ryder blurted out before he could start questioning himself again.

Branson stepped aside and let him in, then closed the door behind him. "You're sure about this?"

"Yes. Very su—"

Branson's mouth was on his before Ryder had even finished the last word, his lips eager and hot and demanding.

29

Branson had always loved kissing. Such an underappreciated act of intimacy. Take the way Ryder was kissing him back, making sexy sounds as he stroked his tongue along Branson's and pressed his body against him, his hands roaming his naked chest. So. Fucking. hot.

He teased the outline of Ryder's lips with the tip of his tongue, chuckling when Ryder got impatient, and sucked him back into his mouth with a growl. The heat flared up hot and heavy, settling in Branson's belly, in his cock and balls. He swirled his tongue around Ryder's, groaning when Ryder bit his bottom lip with a sharp sting. Damn, the man could kiss.

Branson didn't even need to ask him to shed his clothes. Ryder took his hands off Branson, unbuttoned his pants, yanked them down, and kicked them off. He broke off the kiss and whipped his shirt off, sending a button flying. Hell yes. Branson loved Ryder's honest eagerness. None of it was fake or played up. Ryder wanted him for real, and the thought set Branson's body on fire.

The second Ryder's shirt was off, Branson curled his hand around Ryder's neck and pulled him close again, covering his mouth with his own. Ryder's lips were warm, moist, and so soft, but his kiss was anything but. He kissed with the same passion as he did everything else, with all his energy sinking his whole being into it.

"Bedroom." Branson tugged Ryder with him. He'd changed the sheets that morning in a hopeful mood that maybe Ryder would come home with him. Thank fuck for being prepared.

"Underwear," Ryder mumbled against his lips as they stumbled into Branson's bedroom, constantly kissing and touching.

Branson unceremoniously dragged down his underwear, then watched in awe as Ryder did the same and crawled onto the bed on his side, his hand under his head as he shot Branson an impatient look. The unadulterated lust in Ryder's eyes was only surpassed by the cock-hardening sight of his ass. His naked, luscious ass, which was at an angle that showed off every perfect inch of skin, every glorious line of his curves. Oh, how Branson wanted to get his hands on that ass again. Cup it, squeeze it, then sink his fingers into him, followed by his cock.

"Fuck, you're so beautiful," he said with an appreciative sigh. "I could study you for hours."

"That sounds nice, but I'd much rather you touch me."

Branson chuckled. "My remark was hypothetical. No worries."

"Good, because my need to feel you inside me isn't. That's very real, and it's getting more urgent by the minute."

Branson smiled as he grabbed supplies from the nightstand, then climbed onto the bed next to him. Ryder had turned, his ass toward Branson. He brushed his fingers down the smooth, hairless trail leading to Ryder's pretty hole. Mere months ago, Branson would've sworn someone like Seth had been his type if anyone had asked him. Tough, strong, super masculine, and hairy. But now? He much preferred Ryder's smooth body, the silky feel of his skin, the velvety texture of his taint, his most intimate places. Those balls, so tight already but so satiny. He longed to kiss them, lick them, take them into his mouth, and gently suck.

For a moment, a foreign emotion coursed through Branson. A mushy tenderness he wasn't familiar with. A desire to...cherish. He pushed it down. That wasn't what Ryder was here for, and it wasn't what Branson wanted either. He wanted to let loose, to unleash his own kind of hell on Ryder —the kind that would usher in heaven right on its heels.

"Let's get this party started," he said, and if it sounded as forced as it felt to him, Ryder didn't comment on it.

Branson opened him up with his fingers, efficient and fast. He'd love to take his time someday, play with Ryder's hole—damn, he should do anal beads with him; he bet Ryder would love those—but not tonight. He had other plans...and so did Ryder.

Just as quickly, he rolled on a condom and lubed up. With a cock his size, more lube was better. He fisted himself a few times, shuddering when his cock thickened even more in his hands. "On your stomach, chéri."

Ryder obeyed without protest, putting a pillow under his belly to create the proper angle. Perfect. Branson crawled in place and braced his arms on either side of him, his cock sliding to where it wanted to be, right between Ryder's ass cheeks. He thrust a few times between his legs, loving the slick feel, the way Ryder shuddered. A pleased whimper drifted in the air, Ryder clearly enjoying himself. He rocked his hips, blatantly pushing his ass back even more. The invitation couldn't have been clearer if it had come engraved and hand-delivered.

"I need your cock," he said, proving Branson's point. "Fuck me. Fuck me *hard*."

He'd promised him edging, but right now, Branson wasn't even sure if he'd be able to. The urge to do as Ryder had begged was overwhelming. To sink inside that tight hole and claim it, loosen him up, and then fuck him as roughly as he could. Go to town on that ass until Ryder was a wreck.

But he'd shortchange both of them if he gave in to that urge. If he kept himself in check, followed his original plan, the payoff would be so worth it. He wanted Ryder needy and pleading, to make him beg for real. He wanted him sobbing for his release, out-of-his-mind crazy with the need to come.

Branson took a deep breath, then slowly let it out. "We're on my timetable now, so buckle up, buttercup."

"Oh, fuck," Ryder grunted. "You're going to torture me, aren't you?"

"Yup, and I intend to enjoy every second."

The first touch of his cock against Ryder's hole sent an electrical current through him that made his balls tingle. He went slow, not even inch by inch, but a millimeter at a time, never pulling back but pushing gently, sinking deeper and deeper. He couldn't tear his eyes away from the sight of his dick spearing into Ryder, opening him, stretching him. Oh, Ryder's body clenched and pulsed around him, fighting to keep him out, but Branson wouldn't be deterred.

"Ohfuckohfuckohfuck," Ryder panted. "Why are you so goddamn big?"

"You like my cock, chéri," Branson said smugly. He'd be lying if he said he didn't enjoy watching Ryder struggle to accept him. It had to be some kind of caveman instinct, but to see Ryder's slender form take him in, that pretty hole stretching obscenely wide, was such a fucking turn-on.

"I do...in theory."

Branson laughed. "You will in a few minutes. I promise."

He took his time, holding still when he sensed it became too much, then picking right back up the moment Ryder relaxed. Yeah, he might've needed a bit more prep, but Branson would be careful.

Ryder's knuckles were white from the force of his grip on the comforter, and he had his eyes closed, moaning and whimpering as Branson fucked his way inside him. He dragged his ass up, and Ryder got the hint as he half kneeled, pushing his bottom up as he lowered his upper body and his head. Oh yeah, perfect. That whole ass wide open for him to fuck, to take, to *wreck*.

"Please don't take this the wrong way, but you have the most fuckable ass I've ever seen. I just want to...ravish you."

"No...offense...taken. Just..."

Branson pushed forward in one long thrust, burying himself completely. Ah yes, like coming home in the most perfect place ever. Hot, snug, and with such insane pressure on his cock his whole body tingled.

"Jesus..." Ryder hissed, his hole contracting and then releasing again. "I forgot how good it feels to have that monster inside me."

"I'll make you feel even better, chéri," Branson promised.

He still went slow, taking his time to fuck Ryder wide open until every trace of resistance was gone. Then he flipped onto his back, bringing Ryder with him. "Ride me."

Ryder's eyes lit up. "Fuck. yeah."

He straddled Branson, then reached backward and held Branson's cock up as he lowered himself. "Fuckfuckfuck..."

He rose, then sank down again with another breathy

moan. Branson couldn't look away. The look on Ryder's face as he closed his eyes, threw his head back, and started fucking himself on Branson's cock hard and fast was more erotic than the hottest porn Branson had ever seen.

He held Ryder's hips, assisting him as he lifted himself, then screwed down. Every time he bottomed out, Ryder's eyes all but crossed, and the sexiest moans flew out of his mouth. His cheeks were rosy, his expression one of fierce concentration with bursts of pure bliss, and Branson couldn't look away.

Ryder rolled his hips, taking him in again, and Branson couldn't stay still anymore. He snapped his hips upward as Ryder lowered himself, meeting his thrusts. Raw, choked sounds rose from Ryder's chest, from his lips, his eyes going hazy and unfocused as he took his pleasure from Branson's cock. Ryder circled his dick, and he matched the movements of his hand with the rhythm of his hips, going faster and faster, growing more uncoordinated as he chased his release.

Branson's jaw set, his body going tense as it protested against the tight hold Branson had on his release. Not yet, not yet, not until Ryder had come. But goddammit, he'd better come fast because Branson wasn't sure how much longer he could hold out. Ryder's moves grew urgent, frantic, and Branson matched his pace, unable to restrain himself. Their bodies slammed into each other, flesh smacking into flesh with wet slaps.

Ryder let out a curse, his muscles tensing as he jerked on Branson's cock. Oh, thank fuck. Branson let go as well, and their bodies shuddered and shivered as they came at the same time. Ryder spurted his load all over Branson's chest, hitting even his neck. Branson filled the condom, a nagging voice in the back of his head insisting he should ask to go bare next time. He chalked that up to orgasm craziness.

Panting, they broke apart, and Branson tied the condom with his last bit of energy. They dropped on the bed, side by side, saying nothing until their erratic breaths had slowed down. Branson turned his head sideways, just in time to see Ryder's eyes flutter closed. He didn't move as Ryder slept, his face relaxing and his mouth making little smacking sounds. He was fucking adorable, and before Branson knew it, he'd been studying him for a good five minutes.

Should he wake him so he could go to the guest room? Nah. Why would he? Ryder had chosen to have sex. He could damn well deal with waking up in the same bed. But Branson would clean him up because dried cum on your skin was…yuck. He rolled out of bed and cleaned himself in the bathroom, then brought back a warm washcloth.

Ryder moaned as Branson cleaned him, his eyes opening for a moment, looking unfocused. "Sshh, go back to sleep, chéri," Branson whispered.

Ryder smiled, a sweet smile that made Branson's stomach flutter, and then his eyes drifted shut again. When Branson crawled back into bed next to him, he couldn't resist the urge to pull him close. Spooning Ryder, he fell asleep in seconds.

30

Ryder woke up like he always did. One moment he was asleep, and the next he was awake, his brain firing on all cylinders—which was why he realized instantly that something was off. He wasn't in his own bed. This mattress was too soft, too comfortable. Too warm, courtesy of the body that was wrapped around him from the back. Branson Grove was a snuggler. Who would've thought?

What was more surprising was that Ryder didn't mind being his little spoon. Paul hadn't been a fan of cuddling, especially in bed. Too hot, too sweaty, he'd always complained to Ryder. And if Ryder had hugged him nonetheless, if he'd even so much as taken his hand, he'd been told he was too clingy and needy. It was easy to see in hindsight that had been all about Paul. He'd probably felt guilty. Or it had been too intimate for him, considering he hadn't been in love with Ryder in the first place.

Ryder had always been a tactile person. As much as he loved a rough fuck, he could equally enjoy a cuddle on the couch while watching a movie. Or simply holding hands while walking. What had happened to that? When had he accepted that Paul never touched him anymore? When had he decided that crumbs of affection were good enough for him? He wasn't sure if it made him sad or pissed off. Maybe both.

Regardless, he was in no hurry to get out of bed, not when he loved the sensation of waking up in another man's arms. Even better, it was Saturday morning, so they had the time to sleep in. No early vacuum cleaner for him today, thank fuck. He much preferred this way of waking up, though he hadn't planned to spend the night in Branson's bed.

Naïvely, he'd thought he'd go back to the guest room after their rather spectacular fuck, but that had never happened, of course. How could he have when he'd been exhausted, fucked into complete oblivion? He'd considered their first sexual encounter a bit of a fluke, their chemistry fueled by high sexual needs on both their sides. But the second one had been even better, though how it was possible, Ryder had no clue.

Behind him, Branson stirred, his body going tense before he relaxed again. "Mmm, morning," he said, his voice deliciously low and sexy.

"Morning." Ryder wasn't sure what else to answer. Did he need to say something? Do something? What was the etiquette here? It had been ages since he'd been in this position.

"Did you sleep well?"

Small talk, okay. He could do small talk. "I did, thank you. Your bed is very comfortable."

"It is. I don't give a crap about a lot of material things, but I spent good money on the most perfect mattress."

"Worth every penny." If Branson wanted to talk about

mattresses, Ryder would oblige. "Much better than my bed at my parents'."

"Well, you're more than welcome to share my bed..."

Oh. Wow. What did he say to that? Was Branson serious? Or was it one of those flirty, supposed-to-be-sexy things that were more of an empty gesture? "I wouldn't mind a repeat at all," he said, deciding that something similar in tone was the appropriate reaction. Why was this shit so hard?

"You in a hurry to go home?"

"No, not at all."

"Good."

"Why?"

"'Cause I'm in the mood for a little protein..."

Before Ryder had even processed what that meant, Branson had let go of him, pushed him onto his back, and ducked under the covers. Oh shit, Jesus fuck, he was... Branson's hot, wet mouth suckled on Ryder's semihard cock, then took him in.

The most embarrassingly loud moan ever rose from inside him, and he mentally apologized to any neighbors who might be listening in. But fuck, the way Branson was sucking him, having him rock hard in no time... He'd dreamed of things like this, of his boyfriend being so hot for him he'd take care of him spontaneously, without Ryder having to beg or even ask. Branson wasn't his boyfriend, and he never would be, but he was sure as fuck fulfilling erotic fantasies Ryder had had for years.

Branson let go of him for a moment and mumbled something that Ryder couldn't make out. "What?"

Branson whipped the covers back. "Fuck my mouth. Don't hold back. I like it."

He *liked* it? Oh fuck, did he even understand what those words did to Ryder? Branson took him back into his mouth, and Ryder didn't even hesitate. He put his hands on Branson's head and pulled him on his cock, pushing into his throat until it gave way. A few seconds, then he retreated. "Okay?" he checked.

"Fuck, yeah." Branson's voice was raw. "Again."

Ryder didn't need to be told twice. As soon as Branson's mouth closed around his cock again, he surged in deeper, fucking his mouth, his throat until he gagged. That sound shouldn't even be remotely sexy, but it was, and so was the way Branson gazed up at Ryder with tears coming out of his eyes...looking hotter than ever.

Ryder gave him a breather, then went right back to it, and within a minute, he was on the edge. "I'm close," he warned Branson. "Can I...?"

Branson held up his thumb, and Ryder moaned as he let loose, letting go of the tight grip he'd had on his release. Branson gagged as Ryder thrust in deep one more time, then pulled back as soon as he felt his balls unload. The first spurt was in Branson's mouth, but he pulled even farther back for the second, spraying his lips and chin, even his cheeks.

"Ungh... Fuckfuckfuck, so good..."

He lay panting for a moment, his rapid breaths mixing with Branson's shallow, raspy ones. A dirty idea popped into his head, and where before, he would've suppressed that shit as soon as it came up, he now let it roam free. "Let me clean you up," he whispered to Branson.

With one shove, Branson tumbled onto his back, and Ryder climbed on top of him, licking his own cum off Branson's cheek, smacking his lips once he tasted it. He didn't even want to know why he liked this so much. He cleaned up Branson's lips, then followed the trail of cum into his mouth. One thing led to another, and before he knew it,

Branson had flipped them and was on top of him, kissing Ryder as if he'd be graded for it while rutting against him with his steel cock, smearing his precum all over Ryder's body.

The scent of sex hung heavy in the air, and Ryder breathed it in between Branson's passionate kisses. Fuck, he'd missed this. He'd missed spontaneous sex. Hell, he'd missed sex in general. Feeling wanted, feeling beautiful and desirable. Branson might've wanted to give Ryder just great sex, but he'd gifted him with something deeper and more important. Maybe Ryder could make Branson feel the same.

He slipped his hand between their bodies and curled it around Branson's cock, causing him to gasp into Ryder's mouth. "You don't have to."

"I know."

"I didn't blow you in the expectation that you'd do something for me."

"Shut up and enjoy the ride."

From the way had Branson fucked him, Ryder deduced his cock wasn't too sensitive and that he appreciated rough stimulation. So he wasn't too gentle as he squeezed the tip.

"Oh, fuck," Branson grunted.

Happy he'd been on the right track, Ryder repeated his move. Maybe if he...? He used his middle finger to drag his nail over Branson's wet cockhead. A sharp hiss flew from Branson's lips, and for a moment, his body froze. Then he blew out a long breath and relaxed again.

"Good?" Ryder checked.

"Fuck, yes. Perfect."

He pushed against Branson's shoulders, and the man got the hint and turned onto his back. "Widen your legs," Ryder told him.

He'd always been a visual person. As important as touch

was to him, he loved watching during sex. And even though he'd had sex with Branson twice now and had even taken a shower with him, he hadn't taken the time yet to study him. He settled between his spread legs, sighing with admiration at the man's massive cock, which lay on his stomach, wet and occasionally twitching.

"I can't claim to have looked at hundreds of dicks, but I've seen my fair share, including in porn, and yours is by far the most perfect one." He stroked it with his index finger, reveling in the satiny softness of the skin.

"Yeah?" Branson's voice croaked. "What do you like about it?"

"The size, but that's obvious. I guess I'm a bit of a size whore, and with you, that itch is completely scratched. I've never been as full as when you're inside me."

He rubbed his finger over the slit of that gorgeous cock, then gently lifted, creating a thick string of precum upward.

"Fuck, you're killing me here, chéri..."

Funny how much he'd come to love that nickname for him. Someone who was treasured, cherished. He shouldn't attach meaning to it, and yet every time Branson said it, Ryder's belly fluttered.

"But it's also your shape, that perfect angle, not crooked even in the least. I don't have an artistic bone in my body, but if I did, I would immortalize it in art... In pictures, like Michael Stokes does. Or draw it. Make a dirty manga out of it. Or a sculpture."

While talking, he kept stroking him, and he couldn't tear his eyes away from the sight of that cock in his hand. How weird that he was waxing poetic about a dick. Maybe he'd been more sex-starved than he'd even realized. That had to explain all those funny, tender feelings inside him. Not something he wanted to spend time on right now. Not when he had said dick in his hand and Branson was moaning so beautifully with every move Ryder made.

He'd forgotten how much pleasure it could bring to take care of someone else. Not forced, not out of obligation or habit. But like this, when it had been his own choice, born out of a genuine desire to make Branson feel good, feel wanted, it was deeply satisfying.

He scooted closer and went to work, taking his time to fist him, tease his slit with his thumb, scratch him some more, then circle his base as he jerked him off hard. As soon as Branson started fucking into his hand, he stopped, grinning at the loud moan of protest.

"Fuuuuuck..." Branson groaned. "Dammit, do you want me to beg you?"

Ryder just grinned harder. Hmm, would Branson like anal play? He'd said he was a strict top, but that didn't mean he couldn't appreciate his hole played with. Many people underestimated how much ecstasy a single finger in your ass could bring if the person knew what he was doing.

He drew a careful trail with his thumb from Branson's balls backward, giving him every opportunity to protest. Branson met his eyes. "One finger," he said. "Anything more is not comfortable for me."

Ryder nodded. "Okay. Just say stop if you need to."

Some people felt conversations like that took them out of the mood, but Ryder thought that was bullshit. Consent was sexy, and knowing what Branson was comfortable with and what wouldn't bring him pleasure only made things easier. He grabbed some lube—the bottle was still on the nightstand from the night before—coated his right middle finger, and squirted some into his left hand as well, then went back to work.

Now that his hand was slick, he could squeeze Branson's cock even tighter, and judging by the sound Branson made, he appreciated it. Good. Let's see if he could find his prostate and bring some ecstasy to his ass. He'd never been ambidextrous, but he could handle a cock and a hole at the same time, even after years of not practicing that particular skill. Paul's loss for sure. Not that Ryder would spend a second longer thinking about Dr. Dick. Not when he had this sexy-as-fuck man right in front of him.

Branson definitely had experience with anal play because after a gentle pressure, he let Ryder's finger in. Ryder went slow, sliding in and out until he was certain Branson had relaxed. Only then did he twist his finger, curling it as he sank deep inside him, searching for that spot. Sometimes, it was easy to find because the texture was slightly different, but that wasn't always the case.

"Little deeper," Branson said huskily. "Right...there...oh, yes, fuuuuck."

Within seconds, Ryder had him thrashing on the bed as he rubbed that sweet spot inside him while fisting his cock tightly. He'd been teasing Branson for a while now, and he wasn't surprised when Branson's body stiffened in the telltale signs that his orgasm was about to hit. Ryder kept going, squealing with excitement when Branson let out a low moan that seemed to come from his toes, then jerked as his cock spurted out his load.

"Fuckfuckfuckfuck...don't stop. Please don't stop...fuck me through this...keep going. Keep going..."

Ryder didn't even catch all Branson was babbling, but he understood the gist of it. He wasn't to stop. That was easy enough. He slowed the intensity down but kept going until Branson let out the longest grunt and shook with a heavy tremor. Ryder had never excelled at reading body language, but that one, he knew. That was the signal for being boneless after an amazing orgasm when even the slightest touch would hurt.

He let go, pulled his finger out of Branson's ass, and wiped it on the sheets. Branson would have to wash those anyway, considering they'd both sprayed their loads partially on them. He dropped on his back, wincing when he hit a wet spot. Oh well, a shower would fix that.

"Holy shit, that was epic," Branson said after a while, his panting breaths returning to a more normal rhythm.

"I agree."

Branson angled his head toward him, and Ryder did the same. "Yeah? You liked…pleasuring me?"

"Mmm. I was just thinking that it's satisfying to see someone experience ecstasy. Plus, you're nice to look at. Especially naked."

Maybe he should stop talking now, though the smile that spread over Branson's face didn't look like he'd minded Ryder's remarks. "I enjoy looking at you as well."

"Thank you. Glad it's mutual."

That was awkward, right? But again, Branson didn't seem to mind. "Did you have anything planned for today?" he asked.

"Not really. Laundry at some point, but it's not urgent. Maybe hang out with my friend, Dorian. Why?"

"It's almost eleven. I thought we could maybe do brunch together?"

Everything inside Ryder was screaming that brunch didn't sound like casual sex at all but like much more, but when he opened his mouth, all that came out was "Sounds good 'cause I'm starving."

31

Branson blamed the morning sex. That spectacular orgasm Ryder had given him had melted his brain, and that was what had caused his mouth to blurt out the invitation for brunch. It didn't explain why Ryder had accepted, though, but maybe he'd experienced the sexual tension between them in a different way? In many aspects, Ryder was hard to read, which seemed so contradictory, since he was so honest and direct. He just didn't react the same way most people did, and his brain operated on a whole different frequency.

Branson pondered it as he took a shower after stripping the bed and throwing the sheets into the washing machine, which he'd turn on after he was done showering. His hot water system didn't like the shower and the washing machine running at the same time. It slowed the water pressure down to a trickle. He'd had to wait anyway, since he'd graciously allowed Ryder to use the bathroom first. The downside of having only one bathroom.

But now that Ryder had agreed, what should they do? Make brunch themselves? He had some stuff in the fridge, like eggs and bacon, but he was short on almost everything else. He had little coffee left, no juice, no fresh fruit. In other words, it was Saturday, the day he always did grocery shopping. No, they'd have to go out. Otherwise it would be too meager an offering.

They could go to Pete's Place, a deli he loved that was run by two gay men. They made the most delicious sandwiches, and they were across from the supermarket, so he could get groceries right after. That could be the perfect excuse to sell it to Ryder, right?

It turned out Ryder didn't need any selling. As soon as Branson dropped the words *delicious food*, Ryder was on board. He even volunteered to ride with Branson so he wouldn't get lost. They chatted easily in the car, and that continued as they found a table in the bistro.

"Hey, Branson, good to see you again," Pete, one of the owners, said as he came to take their order.

"This is my friend Ryder, who's eager to try your egg salad sandwich." Branson pointed at Ryder.

"Oh, excellent choice. With or without bacon?"

Ryder looked almost offended. "With, obviously."

"I like you already." Pete grinned. "And for you, Branson?"

"I'll have the tuna salad, please. With an orange-mango smoothie."

"Perfect. Anything to drink for you, Ryder?"

"Oh, right, I'll have the berry smoothie, please."

"Coming right up, guys."

"I was wondering why you always order the same for lunch at work," Branson asked when Pete was gone. "Not that there's anything wrong with it, but I was curious."

"It's to eliminate decision stress. At work, I have a lot on my mind, and I don't want to waste energy on things that don't matter. So I have certain outfits I wear, combinations of shirts, slacks, and socks that go well together. That prevents me from having stress about what to put on in the morning. And I eat the same thing for lunch for similar reasons. It's easy, and I genuinely like it. So why not?"

"But you do appreciate trying new things? 'Cause they have a club turkey sandwich on the menu here, but you picked something else."

"Yeah, 'cause it's the weekend. I don't have to use my brain capacity for much else, so now I have the free space for more decision-making, so to speak."

"I'm fascinated by how your mind works, you know that? I haven't met many people who do things so deliberately."

Ryder shrugged, but his eyes showed he was pleased with the compliment. "Both my parents are rational, deliberate people. I guess it's how they raised me."

"I'm much more of a go-with-the-flow guy, as I'm sure you've figured out by now. Maybe I should try your strategy."

Ryder cocked his head. "Is what you're doing working for you?"

Huh. Interesting question. "I suppose so."

"Then why change it? Just because something helps me doesn't mean it will work for you or anyone else. Our brains are not the same, and neither are our characters. Do what works for you."

Branson wanted to reply, but Ryder's phone dinged. He picked it up, cringing as he read it. "Gimme one sec," he said, then typed out a response to whatever had come in and put his phone down again. "My mom. I hadn't mentioned I wasn't coming home last night, and she was worried."

"Understandable."

"Yeah, but also a little...awkward. It's been a while since I had to explain about sex and hookups to my parents, you know? One would think that at my age, I was past that stage."

Pete came to bring their drinks and food, and Branson waited until he was gone again. "Have you thought about what you're going to do when the house is sold?"

Ryder had just taken the first bite of his sandwich, and his eyes grew big. "Oh, damn, this is good," he said with his mouth full, and Branson laughed. He loved how unfiltered Ryder was, so honest in his reactions.

"I know, right? Their soups are amazing as well."

"Mmm, I'll have to try one next time."

Why did the idea of coming here again with Ryder make Branson so happy?

"Anyway, to answer your question, I don't know yet. I'm on a waiting list for everything that's doable for me financially and in terms of a commute, but so far, nothing has opened up. I fear I'll end up moving in with Dorian, which will kill me because of the even longer drive to work."

Branson cleared his throat. The idea had been there in the back of his mind, simmering. Why not voice it? "You could move in with me. In the guest room, I mean. You'd have a short commute, and you wouldn't even have to pay rent. I won't pay anything more in mortgage with you living there, so why would I ask you for money? We could share the costs for food and stuff. And I'm sure we could work out some kind of schedule for the bathroom."

Fuck, he had to stop talking now before he sounded like a rambling idiot, though maybe that ship had sailed already. Ryder was fighting not to laugh. "A bathroom schedule? That one closed the deal for me."

"Shut up," Branson said, laughing as well. "I'm trying to be nice here."

Ryder grew serious. "I realize that, and I appreciate the offer more than I can say, but...I don't know if it would be smart."

Branson swallowed. "Why?"

If Ryder told him he wouldn't feel safe, Branson wasn't sure what he would do. The idea that Ryder still didn't trust him hurt far deeper than he'd ever expected.

Ryder covered Branson's hand with his own, and not for the first time, Branson was amazed by how open and free Ryder could be in sharing affection. "It's not because of a lack of trust."

"For someone who claims not to be able to read body language well, you certainly nailed that one."

"Not that hard, considering our history. But, Bran, you need to let go of that now. I didn't say you violated my trust in the broader sense. I was talking about some specific incidents. That doesn't mean I would extrapolate that into distrust of your behavior in general. Of course I feel safe with you. That's not the issue."

"Then what is?"

Ryder lifted an eyebrow as he let go of Branson's hand, which still tingled from the way-too-brief contact. "You have to ask after last night?"

Ah. Yeah, that made sense. "You're afraid we won't be able to keep our hands off each other."

"Oh, I'm not afraid we'll have sex again. I know we will. We both do. The chemistry between us is too strong to be ignored, especially if we'd be sharing an apartment. I'd end up in your bed in no time."

Branson slowly shook his head, smiling. "You're such a fascinating puzzle to me, you know that? You so rarely react the way I expect you to in situations like this."

"What did you think? That I'd deny the truth?"

"Maybe not so much deny as ignore it or pretend it wasn't that strong? You so easily acknowledged the attraction between us."

"Sexual attraction," Ryder corrected him, his tone a tad sharp. "I'm talking about chemistry, just so we're clear. Not...more."

It shouldn't sting, this adamant statement that Ryder only wanted Branson's body. They'd been on the same page from the get-go, hadn't they? Anything more had never been on the table, so why did this hurt? "I understand, and I wasn't implying more." Branson managed to keep his voice level.

"Oh, okay. I know we talked about it yesterday, but I'm not ready for anything else. I'm still recovering from my previous relationship, and for now, I just crave some fun and hot sex."

Again with that ache inside him. Had he gotten so attached to Ryder already? "That, I can deliver."

"Then we're on the same page. All I'm saying is that if I became your roommate, we'd end up having sex again."

"Mmm, yes. And that's a problem, why?"

He had to play this cool, had to pretend everything was fine. If he showed even a bit of pain, a hint of another emotion, Ryder would reject his proposal. Branson wasn't sure how he knew, but he did, and for some reason, he needed him to say yes. He wanted Ryder to become his roommate...and his bedmate. Fuck, he was starting to suspect he wanted him to become a hell of a lot more than that, but that, too, wasn't a feeling he'd allow himself.

"You don't think it would get too complicated if we're roommates and...lovers? Fuck buddies. Whatever you want to call it."

"Friends with benefits," Branson said. "Because I'd like to think we're friends first."

Ryder studied him as he chewed, and Branson's stomach got into a twist. Why was Ryder hesitating? Had Branson misjudged what had happened between them?

"We are," Ryder finally said, and Branson breathed out with relief, his throat unclenching.

"Thank you. I'm glad to hear that."

"And I like the friends-with-benefits label. Though if I decide to accept your offer, it would be more like friends who are also roommates with benefits. That does sound more complicated."

"It's only as complicated as we make it. Haven't we proven so far that we can separate sex and friendship and our personal and work relationship?"

"True. Good point."

"So you'll do it?"

Ryder laughed. "You should know better by now than to expect me to make a decision on the spot. Not about something like this."

Of course. Ryder was right. "My apologies, I stand corrected. I'll eagerly await your verdict, in that case."

"Eagerly?"

Shit. Had he sounded too eager? "Haven't had my fill of your ass yet," he said quickly, shoving down all those feely feelings.

Ryder's eyes lit up, and his mouth curled up in a sexy smile. "Gotcha. I'll let you know when I've made my choice, but that doesn't mean we can't enjoy each other in the meantime."

"How about we get some groceries, and then we can *enjoy* the rest of the day?"

Ryder's smile widened. "Sounds like a plan."

32

"I've decided to accept Branson's offer to become his roommate," Ryder said.

After another spectacular round of sex, he'd gone home, where he'd taken a shower and then had hurried over to Dorian. He was now lounging on Dorian's couch, right next to his friend, while they were enjoying a nice bottle of red wine. That was, Ryder was still sipping his first glass, since he had to drive home, while Dorian was about to finish his second. Amelia was in bed, the baby monitor on the coffee table blissfully quiet.

Dorian's eyes went wide, and he swallowed before coughing frantically. "Dude, can you wait with saying shit like that until I'm not drinking? I'll have you know that this wine is intended to be drunk, not snorted out through my nose."

Ryder grinned. "What, because it's such high quality?"

"I paid a whole ten bucks for that bottle, asshole. You'd better appreciate it."

"I do. You know how much I love hanging out with you."

Dorian let out a sigh. "If you move, you won't be here

that often anymore. It will be like when you were with Paul. I loved having you close."

He'd spent more and more time with Dorian, eager to escape his parents. They were nothing but nice, but he felt suffocated. "Same. But I promise it won't be like that. That was because Paul..."

"...didn't like me," Dorian filled in the rest.

"Yeah. And I was stupid enough to attach way too much weight to his opinion. You not liking him should've been a red flag."

Dorian put his hand on top of Ryder's. "It's okay. You'll know better next time."

"Oh, there won't be a next time."

"What? You plan on being single for the rest of your life? You'll end up like a sad fiftysomething who's still chasing tail, convinced that he's just as hot as he was thirty years before."

"Jesus, that's quite the picture you're painting there. No, not for the rest of my life. Just for now, for the foreseeable future. At least until I know I'm smart enough not to erase myself for a guy ever again."

"I understand where you're coming from, but don't close yourself off from possibilities, is all I'm saying."

Ryder frowned. Dorian's words sounded an awful lot like what Branson had said to him. "Possibilities? What do you mean?"

"Like, I don't know, maybe the sexual attraction between you and Branson could grow into something more."

"Branson? Fuck, no."

"Why? What's wrong with him?"

"Where do I start? We're coworkers, so there's that. Plus, he's annoying. At least, he used to be. I think he's changed, or maybe I've grown more accustomed to it. And he's hot and all, and the sex is great, but we have little in common other than that we both work for the CIA. Not exactly a stellar base."

"Didn't you say he was easy to talk to? That you had fun conversations with him?"

Ryder waved his hand dismissively. "Sure, but Branson can converse with anyone. He's super socially gifted."

"Ah, okay."

"We're opposites. He's an extrovert, whereas I'm an introvert. He's a people person, while I'm into numbers. He's good at languages, and I'm a math whiz."

"Gotcha. In that case, I say go for it."

Ryder frowned in confusion. "Go for what? I just told you I don't need any more from him than sex."

"I meant go for it as roommates. If you're convinced he's all wrong for you, there's no harm in moving in with him, right? If that weren't the case, you'd have to fear getting sucked into a relationship that you don't want, but since that's not the case, you're all good."

"Right." Something about Dorian's tone was *off*, but Ryder couldn't put his finger on it. His friend sounded a tad too...happy? Almost smug, but that didn't make sense. Nah, he was imagining things. "So you think it's the right choice to accept his offer?"

"Absolutely. You said his place is nice and tidy, which is important to you, and you have work schedules that are well aligned. Plus, you're both gay, so no awkwardness or issues there. If either of you decided to have sex with someone else, that wouldn't be a problem."

Have sex with someone else? Why would Ryder even want that? Not that he wanted to idolize it, but the sex with Branson had been spectacular, exactly what Ryder craved, so why would he try to find someone else?

Oh, wait. Branson might. They weren't exclusive. If Branson wanted, he could find someone else and bring him home. That was what Dorian was talking about. That wouldn't be awkward, since they were both gay, and Ryder didn't want more with Branson anyway. Then why did the idea of Branson with someone else make Ryder uncomfortable? It had to be because he was too used to thinking in relationship terms, a remnant of the insecurity Paul had caused with his cheating.

"Yes, all that. And it cuts my commute back by forty-five minutes at least, which saves me an hour and a half a day. That's a big one for me. And I think we're well suited as roommates. We eat the same kinds of food, and like you said, we both value tidiness and cleanliness."

"Sounds perfect to me."

"Glad you agree. I'm hoping to move in tomorrow afternoon. I love my folks, but my mom gave me the third degree about where I had spent the night. The sooner I get out of there, the better. Any chance you could help? I'll rent a small van for a couple of hours."

"Shouldn't be an issue, providing my parents can babysit Amelia. Let me text my mom."

While Dorian texted his mom, Ryder went over what he'd need to buy in his head. His parents had said he could bring the queen bed he had in his bedroom at their house. They wouldn't have a place for it in their much smaller home anyway, so he was all set there. The room in Branson's apartment had a closet that would be large enough for Ryder's clothes. He didn't have that many.

His books, that was the biggest issue. He'd packed them up in boxes that were still in his parents' garage, but he'd have to find another place for them. The bookcases in Branson's living room had been full, so maybe he'd have to buy another two Billy bookcases. His room should be able to accommodate that, though he also liked the idea of putting them in the living room, next to Branson's. It would complement the whole look, and the living room was spacious enough for two more. He'd have to ask him.

"My mom is happy to babysit, so I can help tomorrow. What time do you want me to be at your parents'?"

"Maybe around three? I'll make sure everything is packed so we can load it."

"Sure, no problem."

Ryder put his glass down and dropped sideways against Dorian, who put his arm around him and pulled him close. "I promise I won't ignore you like before. I'll drive up here at least once a week to hang out with you."

"Yes, please...and bring Branson sometime. I'd like to meet him."

"You want to meet Branson?" Ryder turned around and rested his head on Dorian's thigh, facing him. "Why?"

"Because you'll be spending a lot of time with him, whether in bed or otherwise, and I want to see the man who you talk about so much."

"I don't talk about him *that* much."

"More than about anyone else, let me put it that way."

A strange sadness filled Ryder. "That's because I have no friends other than you. Who else am I going to talk about? Paul?"

Dorian shuddered. "Please, let's leave Dr. Dick out of this. And I know what you mean. All I can talk about is Amelia...and you if it's to someone other than you."

"When did we turn into these sad guys whose social circle is nonexistent? For me, that was all Paul. Thanks to him, I lost contact with most of my friends over the last few years. That's something I'll never do again, I swear."

Dorian squeezed his shoulder. "Maybe you can reach out to some of them and explain. I'm sure they'll understand."

"Yeah, maybe."

"That doesn't sound like you plan to."

"Not anytime soon, no. Work is crazy at the moment. I can't tell you what I'm working on, but it's big, and it's taking up all my time."

"Is Branson working on the same project?"

"He is. We work well together. He's very intuitive, thinking out of the box, and I'm super structured and linear, so we complement each other well." His cheeks grew warm when he remembered. "Heeder, the director of the CIA, complimented me last week, telling me I'd done a great job. Proud moment."

Dorian's eyes lit up. "That's amazing, Ry! Wow, high praise from the director himself. That alone should tell you how important your job is, regardless of what Dr. Dick thought."

"Thank you. It's highly fulfilling."

They chatted for a while, but the whole time, Ryder's mind kept returning to Dorian's reaction about Branson. Why had his words felt off, as if he'd said one thing but had meant something else? Dorian wouldn't lie to him, that much Ryder knew for a fact, but what had he picked up on, then?

He had to bring it up. If he didn't, it would bug him for days. "Did you mean what you said about me moving in with Branson being a good idea?"

When Dorian didn't answer, he sat up straight.

"Why do you ask?" Dorian said eventually, looking guilty.

"There was subtext, and it's driving me crazy because I don't understand what you were trying to say."

"I'm sorry. I didn't mean to frustrate you."

"So I was right. There was subtext."

"Ry..." Dorian reached for his hand. "Sometimes I struggle if I should tell you something or if you need to figure it out for yourself. When you were talking about Branson and your decision to move in, I picked up on something, but I don't know if you're ready to hear it or not. And I realize how cryptic this sounds, but it's the best I can do."

"Was it something good? Something that would make me happy?"

Dorian smiled. "To hear? Not at the moment, I think. But if I'm right, yes."

Ryder took a deep breath. "Then I'll figure it out myself. You wouldn't keep something crucial from me, like something that would hurt me not to know."

"Never," Dorian swore.

"Thank you for giving me the space to discover whatever it is at my own pace."

"You're welcome. Now, go home and get a good night's sleep so you're all rested for moving day tomorrow. I'm counting on the two of you fucking like bunnies in the beginning, and since I'm living vicariously through you, I want every sexy detail."

Ryder laughed so hard it hurt.

33

When Branson lived in Paris, his French school had made one major field trip every year. They'd visit a few museums or something throughout the year, but they'd do one bigger event. When he was a junior in high school, Rome had been the destination. By then, Branson had traveled extensively with his parents, and though he'd never been to Rome and it seemed like a cool city to visit, that hadn't been why he'd been so thrilled he couldn't sleep.

It had been the knowledge that for a week, he'd be away from his parents, hanging out with his friends, which had included Lucien and thus the promise of lots of dirty sex. He'd been so excited he'd barely slept the week before, unable to think of anything else.

The hours before Ryder showed up to move in had felt the exact same. Heart palpitations, bursts of nerves followed by a crazy exuberance, sexy daydreams of endless rounds of sex... The entire day had been a veritable roller coaster, and the clock had never moved slower. Finally, just after five, the intercom rang. He buzzed him in downstairs, then opened his front door and blocked it with a wedge so it would stay open.

A minute or two later, the elevator doors slid open, and Ryder came out, carrying a large box.

"Why the fuck did I let myself get roped into this?" someone else muttered, and then he stepped out as well, bringing another box. That had to be Dorian. "I knew you own a gazillion fucking books. I'm such a moron."

Branson snorted. He was quite familiar with that problem. He'd long run out of acquaintances willing to help him move once they'd discovered how many boxes of books they'd have to carry.

Ryder laughed, then came up short as he spotted Branson. "Hi," he said breathlessly.

"Hi."

They stared at each other for a few seconds. Then Ryder cleared his throat. "Think you could let me pass? This box is rather heavy."

"Yes, of course. Sorry." Branson stepped aside.

"Hi, I'm Dorian. I'd be happy to properly greet you if you'll allow me to put this box down somewhere first because *someone* needs a different hobby than collecting the heaviest things on the planet."

Branson laughed. "Walk right in. You can put them in the living room. I already assembled the two new bookcases."

When Ryder had told him he was moving in and had suggested purchasing two more Billy bookcases, Branson had offered to get them so Ryder could focus on packing. While impatiently counting down until Ryder's arrival, he'd figured he might as well make himself useful and had put them together.

"You did?" Ryder called out from inside. "Oh, you did!"

Branson walked into the living room. "I figured it would make things easier if you could unpack right away."

Ryder was staring at the two bookcases with stars in his eyes. "I haven't seen my books in months. Thank you."

"No unpacking yet," Dorian said sternly. "We have a million more boxes to drag upstairs, plus your clothes, bed, mattress, and everything else."

Branson liked him already, and that was before Dorian turned to him, flashed him a blinding smile, and said, "Hi again. Like I said, I'm Dorian. You look strong enough to lift some boxes as well."

"Do, he's already doing enough by offering me hospitality," Ryder protested, but Branson laughed.

"Happy to help. Just put me to work."

It took a few trips, but finally, they had lugged everything Ryder and Dorian had managed to cram into one van upstairs. Ryder's bed turned out to be one that was simple to put together, and aside from his clothes, the rest seemed mostly books and his collection of puzzles. Branson had caught the longing looks Ryder had thrown in the direction of said boxes. He'd missed seeing them, and how adorable was that?

Dorian turned out to be an absolute riot, and Branson would never have guessed he was a single parent. "That was the last box," Dorian declared as he closed the front door behind him. "Jesus fuck, Ry, if you move again in the next two years, you're on your own. I'm dead."

Ryder raised an eyebrow. "Could that perhaps be because the only exercise you're getting is from chasing your daughter?"

Branson slapped a hand in front of his mouth. Those two were hilarious.

"That's rude, bro. Plain rude. Like you're engaging in any aerobics."

Ryder hesitated a moment, then nicked his head in Branson's direction. "Sex with him totally qualifies as aerobic exercise."

That had all of them exploding in laughter, although Ryder seemed surprised he'd dared to make that joke.

"I gotta go," Dorian said as they'd finished laughing. "I want to put Amelia in bed myself."

He hugged Ryder. "Thank you," Ryder said, his voice muffled against Dorian's shoulder.

"Despite my bitching, anytime."

Much to his surprise, Branson got a firm hug from Dorian as well. "Hurt him, and I'll be a lot less nice," he whispered in Branson's ear.

Hurt him? That suggested far more than he and Ryder being roommates. Dorian let go of him and winked, leaving Branson befuddled. What was he referring to? Not something he'd ask in front of Ryder.

A minute later, Dorian had left, leaving Ryder and Branson. "He's a riot," Branson said.

Ryder grinned. "He's the best thing that ever happened to me."

"I've got something for you." Branson pulled a set of keys out of his pocket and handed them to Ryder. "This is the key to the front door, this one is to the downstairs door, and I also have a small storage box downstairs, so I gave you a key to that as well. You could store your boxes there when you've emptied them."

"Thank you. For everything. I hope you won't regret letting me move in."

Never, Branson wanted to say, but that seemed too much.

"I'm sure I won't. Want to unpack your books? I've seen you eye them with longing."

Ryder nodded. "I'd love to."

"Can I help?"

Ryder hesitated. "I do have a certain system and order for my books."

"Duh. I expected nothing else, and by the way, so do I. Just tell me where they go."

Soon they had a good rhythm going. Ryder had been smart and had packed books he wanted to display together in the same box as much as possible, so Branson just opened the boxes and handed Ryder books.

"I'm strangely nervous about tomorrow," Ryder said a few minutes later. "Massive anticipation."

"Same. I know it'll be a while before we get to the good stuff, but still. It's a crucial first step."

"Is Coulson arresting them himself?"

Branson shook his head. "No. First of all, they're not under arrest yet. They're indicted, and subpoenas will be delivered, so the FBI will seize their computers and files. But Coulson said he doesn't want to do the arrests himself. He wants to be part of the interrogation team and start fresh with them, especially with Basil King, not establish a bad first impression by arresting him. He needs to build rapport."

"What does that entail, building rapport? I've heard of it, but I'm not sure what it means," Ryder asked.

Branson used a utility knife to open the next box, careful to lift the carton away so he wouldn't damage any books while cutting. "It's a crucially important aspect of interrogations, especially in big cases like this. The interrogator wants to find common ground with the suspect so he can build trust with him, make him feel like they are the same in some ways."

Ryder frowned. "How does that work? I mean, the suspect knows the interrogator is out to nail him, doesn't he?"

"Rationally, yes, but a good interrogator can make the suspect temporarily suspend that belief and instead convince him he wants the best for him. Research has shown that developing rapport leads to more useful intelligence than coercion or even torture. One study showed that detainees were fourteen times more likely to disclose information earlier in an interview when the interviewer used rapport-building strategies, like providing basic comforts, including food and drinks, treating the suspect with kindness and respect, and showing genuine interest."

"Really?"

Branson handed him a stack of books from the new box, and Ryder filled the second Billy bookcase. "Remember late senator John McCain? During the Vietnam war, he was taken prisoner. The Vietcong tortured him for a long time, but he never gave them anything useful. He later said that he knew from personal experience that the abuse of prisoners will produce more bad than good intelligence, that victims of torture will offer intentionally misleading information if they think their captors will believe it and will say whatever they think their torturers want to stop their suffering. They asked for the names of men in his platoon, for example, and he ended up giving his captors the name of some Green Bay Packers because he wanted to tell them something."

"But..." Ryder hesitated. "Didn't the CIA use torture as well?"

Branson's face grew tight. The question was a logical

one, but that wasn't a part of history anyone liked to talk about. "We did, and it's not something we should be proud of. After 9/11, we made some horrible errors in judgment that caused us to violate everything we stand for. In my opinion, at least."

"You don't think torture is justified when it would help save American lives?"

Branson handed him the next pile of books. "It's not quite that black and white. If we were certain that the information retrieved through torture was true, then maybe. But we don't. And it's a slippery slope, you know? How can we condemn dictatorial regimes for torturing prisoners or political enemies when we do the same? You lose the moral high ground."

The CIA had a complex history, one that didn't always give reason for pride, and yet Branson was proud to work there to help keep his country safe.

"How do you know all that? I mean, you didn't work for the CIA yet after 9/11."

Branson gestured at his own books. "Like you, I read. A lot."

"I haven't had a chance to study the contents of your bookcase. What are some of your favorite things to read?"

"History, biographies, sociology, and psychology, especially anything to do with how our brains work. Like, how we make decisions, how our subconscious and our conscious work together, but also how trauma affects our brain and our body. And if I'm in the mood to relax, I read the occasional steamy gay romance."

Ryder's head spun. "You read romances?"

"Yes. Don't diss it until you've tried them. They're an amazing escape when life gets rough."

Ryder chuckled. "Okay. Sounds intriguing. And sociology, can you give me an example?"

"I'm fascinated by the social dynamics in groups, like power differentials, the process of conformity or nonconformity and peer pressure, and racism." He held up the books he'd just pulled out of a box. "I see you're into literature, aside from reading Umberto Eco?"

Ryder grinned. "I love his books. I like stories that make me reflect and think. Many people feel literature is depressing, and I suppose it is to a certain degree, but I appreciate the depth of the stories and the beauty of the language used. I also read a lot in mathematics, physics, and philosophy. In short, pretty much everything you're not reading."

"We'd make a great team, though, covering almost all subjects together," Branson joked as he continued unpacking the last few boxes.

"True. And it's not that common anymore to find people who love to read. It's kind of a dying hobby."

"My parents are both big on reading, and my earliest memories are from my mom reading to my twin, Brenda, and me. No matter where we lived, our house was always filled with books. My dad reads a lot of the same stuff I do, whereas my mom is more into fiction and travel books, like Paul Theroux."

"Same, though my parents focus mostly on science topics, like I do. But they stressed the importance of reading to me at a young age. I could read when I was four and read well by the age of six. Both my parents are introverts, and we'd spend whole weekends reading, the three of us in the same room, devouring books. I know it sounds boring, but those are some wonderful memories."

Branson shook his head. "Not boring at all. There are days

when all I want to do is curl up on the couch with a book and read for hours. I do feel it's becoming harder for me to find the mental rest to read for longer stretches. It's like my brain is too used to processing chunks of information now, like emails, texts, social media. Even my work entails a lot of tidbits of info."

"That's an interesting theory that sounds plausible. I wouldn't consider my work being the same. Most of it consists of endless numbers, so not really condensed. It's more like finding the needle in the haystack of data."

"I'm in awe of how you can find those proverbial needles," Branson said. "I know it's a specialized form of pattern recognition, or rather, spotting the breaks in normal patterns, but it's fascinating to me."

Ryder smiled at him. "Just like how I'm impressed by how much information you can distill from a simple transcript or a picture or video."

Branson emptied the last box, then cut the tape and folded it flat, like he'd done with the others. "You know, you remarked once that we had little in common except being gay and working for the CIA...but maybe we have more similarities than you think."

34

He'd slept in his own bed the first night. Ryder hadn't been sure what to do when it was time to call it a day. He and Branson had spent the rest of the evening getting Ryder settled by assembling his bed, putting his clothes in the closet, and they'd had fun with all of Ryder's puzzles for a good hour. Branson had tried a few, but he hadn't been able to solve even one.

But then it had been bedtime, and Ryder had wondered what to do. Would Branson assume they'd have sex? Did he have to initiate something, give some kind of signal? In the end, Branson had made it easy. He'd leaned in, giving Ryder plenty of chance to protest, and then kissed his cheeks and said, "I'm thrilled you moved in, chéri. Sleep well."

And with that, he'd walked out. Ryder had taken a shower, sticky from sweating during the move, and crawled into his own bed. So they weren't in each other's way as they got up that morning. He drew a deep breath, then walked into the kitchen, where the coffee machine was already spluttering as it filled a large travel mug and where the smell of bacon hung in the air.

"Good morning," he said hesitantly.

Branson swiveled around. "Good morning. Did you sleep well?"

"I did."

"What do you eat for breakfast? We didn't discuss that yesterday."

"Oatmeal with milk, but anything else is fine."

"Oatmeal?" Branson shuddered. "Why on earth would you subject yourself to that horror every day? You genuinely love that stuff?"

"Love? No. But it's quick and easy to make, and it's healthy."

"Perhaps, but so is avocado, and that shit tastes like snot."

Ryder snorted. "I don't like it either."

"See? We can agree on that. Anyway, the discussion is moot, since I don't have oatmeal. I can make you some scrambled eggs and bacon?"

Ryder bit his lip. "You don't have to cook for me. That's not... That isn't part of the deal of me living here."

Branson put a hand on his shoulder. "It's breakfast, chéri. I'm making it for myself anyway."

"Okay. Yes, please, in that case. I love bacon."

Branson let go of him. "If you didn't, I'd have ordered your head examined. I'm suspicious of people who hate bacon."

Ryder chuckled. "What about vegetarians and vegans? You don't trust any of them?"

Branson scratched his chin. "I'll make an exception for them, but if you like meat but not bacon, there's something wrong with you."

He turned back to the counter, where he deftly cracked a

few eggs in a bowl, added some salt and pepper and a dash of milk, then whisked them.

"Why don't you grab plates?" he said to Ryder.

"I...I don't know where everything is."

"So open all the cabinets and drawers to find out. You live here now, chéri. This is your home, so treat it as such."

Right. This would take some time to get used to, wouldn't it? He found plates and silverware, as well as napkins. Branson's coffee was done, and so Ryder put a lid on his mug. He studied the machine. He was used to a Keurig, but this was a different kind. Did it even use pods?

"I'll show you how to make coffee after we're done eating," Branson said. "Why don't you pour what's in my travel mug into two mugs so we can share it?"

Bless him. This was way too much thinking before Ryder had drunk his coffee. Minutes later, they both sat at the high top in the kitchen behind a steaming plate with eggs and bacon, though Ryder was far more interested in the coffee that tickled his nose with its tempting aroma. He tentatively took a sip. The rich, robust flavor exploded on his tongue, and he moaned. "Holy crap, this is good coffee..."

Branson grinned, raising an eyebrow. "If I'd known that was all it takes to make you moan..."

Ryder laughed but quickly took another sip. This was by far the best coffee he'd ever had. They chatted during breakfast, then put everything away. Operating the coffee machine was complicated, but Ryder was certain he'd be able to do it himself next time. For now, they both had a lovely travel mug filled with delicious goodness.

"Do you want to drive together?" Branson asked.

Oh, right. Ryder hadn't even thought about that. His initial reaction was to say he'd drive himself, but why would he? They went home at the same time anyway. He might as well lower carbon emissions by ridesharing. "Sure. Your car or mine?"

Branson quirked an eyebrow. "Do I want to take the brand-new, environmentally friendly Tesla or my fuel-guzzling SUV? Sheesh, hard choice."

Ryder held up his hands. "Fine, fine."

The ride to work was quick and relaxed, and Ryder was surprised by how normal it felt. He'd expected some awkwardness, especially considering they'd slept together, but it felt natural.

The morning flew by as he caught up on emails, and before he knew it, it was time for lunch. Should he ask Branson to come with him? They'd been sharing lunch more often than not lately, so why wouldn't he? The fact that he had become his roommate shouldn't make a difference.

He stopped by Branson's office and found him chatting with Weston. "Hey, Ryder," Weston said. "What's up?"

"Nothing. I mean, I wanted to check if Branson wanted to have lunch, but I can come back later."

"No, you're fine," Weston said. "We were done anyway. Coulson called. We can expect the first boxes and files here around three. The FBI has raided Kingmakers and the four contractors, and they've taken all computers, files, and paperwork. They're still cataloging it to preserve the chain of evidence, but they're sending the first batch over as soon as possible."

"Yay." Ryder rubbed his hands. "I can't wait to see what they've been hiding."

Weston and Branson both laughed. "I love how excited you are about fraud," Branson teased.

"Not about fraud. About discovering fraud, about proving it," Ryder corrected him, but he hadn't taken offense.

"You two make a great team," Weston said. "I'm stoked you fit in so well, Ryder. You're an asset to our group."

"Thank you. Oh, I wanted to ask you. I moved over the weekend. Should I tell you the new address or send an email to HR?"

"To HR is fine. Where did you move to? You were up in Frederick, no?"

Ryder nodded. "To McLean, so a much shorter commute. I moved in with Branson."

He saw no reason to keep that a secret. HR would find out anyway when he put in the change of address.

"Oh, congrats! I didn't know things were going that fast between you two," Weston said, sounding warm.

Things were going fast? What was he talking about? Ryder shot Branson a sideways glance.

"He moved in as my roommate, Wes. Not my boyfriend," Branson said, and as soon as his words registered, Ryder's cheeks heated. Oh shit, did Weston think they were *together*? How the hell had that happened?

"Oh, I apologize," Weston said quickly. "I meant no offense."

"None taken," Branson said.

"We're not together." Ryder cursed himself for even opening his mouth. "Not that there would be anything wrong with it, seeing as how we don't report to each other, but we're not. I just wanted to make that clear. Not that I'm offended you would think so. I mean, I'm gay, and Branson is..." He let out a sigh. "I'm going to shut up now."

Weston laughed. "All good, Ryder. See you guys later." He was still laughing as he walked down the hallway.

"I'm sorry." Ryder felt miserable. "For some reason, I blurt out really stupid things when I'm nervous."

"Do you now? I hadn't noticed."

Ryder had been staring at his feet as he shuffled them across the gray carpet, but now he looked up and found Branson smiling at him, his eyes dancing with laughter. "You're mocking me."

"I'm not, chéri, I promise. You're adorable when you get all flustered..."

He swallowed. "Adorable?"

Branson stepped closer to him, and Ryder's heart skipped a beat. "You don't like being called that?"

The faint smell of Branson's cologne surrounded him, a sensual aroma that was all masculine, a fascinating mix of leather, bitter, and sweet. *Tom Ford's Fucking Fabulous*, it was called. Ryder had spotted it in the bathroom that morning and hadn't been able to resist taking a whiff.

"I...I don't know. I don't think I mind. You mean it in a positive way, don't you?" he stammered.

Branson caressed his cheek with a single finger. "Of course, chéri. I mean it in the highest of praise, the bestest of ways. Come, let's eat lunch. You look hungry."

Ryder followed Branson to the cafeteria. *The highest of praise?* At the surface, it sounded like mocking again, but his tone had been genuine. Plus, Ryder had asked him, and somehow, he knew Branson wouldn't lie to him...which meant he'd been serious. He really found Ryder adorable in a good way. What did that mean?

He was still pondering it when he reached the cafeteria, his brows furrowed, when Branson cupped his cheek and met his eyes. "Let it go, chéri. I promise it's all good."

He took a deep breath. He'd trust him. "Okay."

At three fifteen, Ryder received the first batch of files from Kingmakers, and he dove straight in. It only took him half an hour to find a foreign bank account he hadn't known about and then another hour to find two more. When

Branson walked in just after five, Ryder was bouncing in his chair with excitement. "I've got it!" he exclaimed as soon as he saw Branson. "I've found the link."

"What link?"

Ryder clasped Branson's hand, then tugged him close so he could look over Ryder's shoulder. "Look." He pointed at his screen. "That's a wire in October 2013 from a secret account Kingmakers had in Switzerland to another Swiss bank, registered to the Alhuriya Group, a company headquartered in Dubai. The owner of the Alhuriya Group is Sameh El Sewedy...Yazid El Sewedy's father. I found the first link between them."

Branson's face broke open in a wide smile. "That's fantastic! I can't believe you found this so quickly."

The joy on Branson's face hit Ryder. Not just his brain, which was happy with the compliment, but something inside him. He loved Branson's smile. It *did* something to him, deep in his belly, where feelings swirled he didn't understand.

He swallowed. "Bran?"

Branson's brown eyes grew dark. "Yes, chéri?"

"Can I kiss you?"

"You can kiss me anytime, chéri. Consider this blanket approval for any and all occasions where you feel the urge to kiss me."

"Okay."

He'd half expected Branson to take the initiative, but he didn't. He kept his head close, though, patiently waiting, it seemed. Ryder brought his mouth to Branson's, then pressed it against those soft lips. A moan escaped him at that first contact, and he deepened the kiss. And Branson let him, allowed him to set the pace, which, much to Ryder's surprise, was far slower than he usually wanted.

This kiss was endlessly tender, making him feel like he was floating.

"Chéri?" Branson whispered against his lips.

"Mmm?"

"I need you to stop kissing me now before we commit multiple counts of indecency in the office…"

It took Ryder a moment before it registered, and then he pulled back. "Good point."

"But you know what the good news is?" Branson kissed him one last time, a firm, much more claiming kiss.

"What?"

"We can continue this when we get home."

35

His existence had become simple and somewhat predictable, but Kenn loved it. Every morning, he woke up in Warrick's arms. Every day, they spent together. And every night, he fell asleep right next to his Daddy. How perfect could life be?

It couldn't last; he knew that. The press hadn't picked up on the relationship between him and Warrick, but that was because they never went out together. Not that they never left the White House. Of course they did. But never together. That was the price they had to pay right now to keep their relationship secret—and Kenn was okay with it, as was Warrick.

"You daydreaming, baby boy?" Daddy asked, and Kenn turned around from where he'd been staring out the window.

"I'm looking forward to the day we can go places together. As a couple, I mean."

Daddy pulled him close. He'd gained some weight since he'd moved into the White House—courtesy of Mrs. Morelli's cooking—and while he complained about it, Kenn secretly loved it. Well, he also not so secretly loved it, as he'd made it more than clear how much he adored Daddy's softness. Highly conducive to cuddling.

"I can't wait to have you on my arm and show you off." Daddy kissed the top of his head.

"It may be a while, though." Kenn sighed. His father's reelection campaign would kick off in a few months. Until he was reelected, Kenn didn't want his relationship to become public. He didn't want to risk his dad losing the elections because of him.

"I understand. Your dad has the opportunity to initiate policies that will have a positive effect for decades to come, and I don't want to endanger that. It doesn't change anything for me, you know that."

"I know, Daddy."

"Good. Now, let's go. Everyone's already here."

"They are?"

His father had decided to throw a dinner party for his inner circle for no particular reason, and everyone would be there. All he'd said was that he wanted to spend some time with his people and that it had been way too long since they'd all come together, which was true.

Kenn took Daddy's hand, and they walked into the dining room, which was full of excited voices and outbursts of laughter. Daddy had been right; they were the last to arrive. Even Kenn's father was already there, immediately coming over when they walked in.

"Hey, kiddo." He kissed Kenn on his cheek.

"Hi, Dad."

"Warrick."

Kenn had feared that things might get awkward between his dad and his Daddy, but neither of them had ever allowed that to happen. His father treated Warrick as he did anyone else, with the same warm affection and, in this case, a kiss on his cheek that made Warrick smile.

"Thanks for organizing this, Del," Daddy said. "It'll be fun to catch up with everyone."

He'd gotten good at calling Kenn's father by his first name, though it had taken a while.

Kenn spotted Denali, who was standing next to Milan, looking uncomfortable. His friend still had trouble switching from White House employee to Milan and Asher's boyfriend—and Kenn couldn't blame him. That was one hell of a transition to navigate. "Daddy, I'm gonna say hi to Denali," he said.

"Good idea. He looks a bit lost."

Daddy kissed him and sent him off, and Kenn's stomach tumbled like it always did when Daddy made so crystal clear in public who Kenn belonged to. He loved it.

"Hey." He pulled Denali into a firm hug. "I'm happy to see you."

"You too."

Denali clung to him a tad longer than Kenn had expected, and he frowned as he let him go. "Are you okay?"

He'd asked softly, but Milan must've still heard it. He sent a worried look at Kenn that he couldn't interpret. Was something wrong with Denali?

Denali looked at Milan, then tugged Kenn's sleeve. "Can we talk somewhere else?"

"Of course."

They snuck into the Yellow Oval Room, then walked out onto the Truman balcony. It was still light out, the temperature in the high sixties after a sunny, pleasant spring day. In mere weeks, the temperatures would become oppressively hot, especially combined with the humidity, but for a few weeks in the spring, the weather was always perfect.

"What's wrong?" Kenn asked.

Denali let out a long sigh. "We're trying to figure out our next step, and it's hard."

"Next step?"

"We can't keep living in the White House."

"Oh, that. Yeah, I know. So what have you guys talked about?"

Denali shrugged, his face sad. "Asher's work is here, and so is mine, but Milan's heart is in New York. He longs to go back to his old job as a detective. How can we find a compromise when what we want is so far apart?"

"Is Milan putting pressure on you?" Kenn knew his uncle well enough to realize the man could be a steamroller when he wanted his way.

"No. He just wants to talk about it, which is fair, but I get so frustrated and sad because someone will lose."

"Can you see yourself in New York?"

Denali nodded. "As much as I love my job here, my happiness is with my men. I'll go wherever they go. It's Asher who's dug his heels in. He's been in the doghouse with Director James since she found out about his relationship with Milan and me. He's hoping that in time, she'll forgive him and he'll be appointed to a protective detail again rather than getting all the shitty jobs like he has for the last months."

"Asher is from New York, isn't he?"

"Yeah. He started working for the Secret Service there. To him, going back to New York is a step back, like history repeating, he says...and I understand where he's coming from. But we can both see Milan isn't happy here, so what do we do?"

Kenn's heart broke at the sadness in Denali's voice, and

he slung his arm around him. "I don't know...but I doubt you expected me to have the answers."

Denali put his head on Kenn's shoulder. "No. Though it would've been nice."

They sat, silent. "We should go back," Denali said after a few minutes. "Thank you for listening to me."

"Anytime. I'm sorry you guys are facing this tough call. I wouldn't know what to do either."

Denali bumped his shoulder. "Yeah, but you have a hot Daddy who makes all the decisions for you, you lucky boy."

Kenn grinned. "I do. Ten out of ten, would highly recommend."

Denali laughed. "I bet you would." Then his face grew serious. "But I wouldn't want to trade in my men for the world. They're my anchor, Kenn, my safe place. There's no bigger joy for me than being with both of them...preferably in bed, with both of them inside me."

Kenn winced. "Yeah, that still doesn't appeal to me, but you do you. I'm so happy for you...and for Milan because he's so much happier than he was before he met you and Asher."

"Asher caught him whistling yesterday when he took Rogue out for a walk. Let's just say the teasing was merciless."

They were still giggling as they walked back into the dining room, where everyone had found a seat. Kenn slipped into the chair next to Warrick. "Is everything okay with Denali?" Daddy asked softly.

Kenn nodded, not wanting to talk about it in public.

The appetizers were being served, and they started with a lovely asparagus soup Kenn loved. Creamy and full, it hit all the right spots for him.

"I see you guys still haven't bashed each other's heads in

after working twenty-four seven," Milan said to Coulson and Seth, who looked at each other and grinned. Those two were as besotted as ever.

"Nah." Seth took Coulson's hand and pressed a kiss on it. "His head is way too pretty for that."

Everyone laughed.

"But seriously, it doesn't get too much?" Milan asked as the laughter had died down.

"For now, it doesn't, but who knows what the future will bring," Coulson said.

"When this long nightmare is behind us, will you return to full-time active protective duty?" Asher asked Seth, and Kenn sat up a little straighter.

Seth looked at Coulson again, then at Asher. "I'm not sure, but let's keep that between us, please." Silence descended. Then Seth let out a long sigh. "It's been... This whole investigation, everything that has happened, has been a lot. I'm running on empty, hanging on by a thread. I want to see it through until the end, but after that, I don't know if I'll have anything left to give."

This time, it was Coulson's turn to take his man's hand, lacing their fingers together. "Seth and I have talked about becoming parents, and we think we're ready for that when this is done. So maybe Seth will decide to stay home for a bit and spent time with our..." His voice broke, and he swallowed. "With our child. Excuse me... I'm... I never thought I'd ever become a dad, since I found out I'm sterile a few years ago. So this is a miracle to me."

"Guys, that's amazing," Kenn's father said. "Being a parent is such a privilege and joy. Are you guys adopting or...?"

"No. Remember Gaby Santos, the ATF agent who credits me with saving her life at the Pride Bombing?" Seth asked.

Murmurs of recognition rose.

"She named her daughter after me, Rody. When Coulson and I visited them a few months ago, they asked me if I would be willing to donate sperm for a second child, a brother or sister to Rody. In return, Judith, Gaby's wife, offered to be our surrogate should we want kids. Coulson and I talked it over, and regardless of whether we will take them up on the offer, we wanted to give them the gift of life, so they used my swimmers...and Judith became pregnant on the first attempt. They told us two days ago."

Kenn's eyes grew wet, though he didn't understand why. He didn't even know these people, but what Seth had done for them made him so happy.

"What a wonderful gift you've granted them, Seth," Asher said. "You've given them the most precious thing you could have. I'm sure they're elated."

Seth smiled widely. "They're over the moon, and I have to admit that the idea of fathering a child is special. They want me to be part of the child's life, and I'd love that."

"You know what makes me happy?" Calix sounded a little choked up too. "That something this amazing has come out of that horrible day, like beauty from the ashes."

Seth nodded. "Coulson and I said the same thing... Us meeting and now this, it's helped us process what happened and let go of the pain of that day."

Kenn's father raised his wine glass. "To Seth and Coulson and the little mini-Rodecker. May they become a healthy and happy baby."

They all toasted to that, Seth still beaming.

"Since it seems to be the time for announcements," Kenn's father said. "I have one as well."

The room grew quiet again, and a shiver trickled down Kenn's spine. An announcement? About what? His father hadn't spoken to him about it, and a quick look at Calix showed he was equally baffled.

"Del?" Calix asked. "What's going on?"

Kenn's father straightened his shoulders, then looked around the room. "I've decided not to seek reelection for a second term."

36

Calix blinked, unable to believe his ears. Surely he must've heard that wrong, and Del had not just announced he was done and walking away from it all. "Come again?"

"I'm not seeking a second term, Cal."

Del's voice was firm, laced with a finality that told Calix he'd made up his mind.

"I...I don't understand."

Rhett reached for his hand, and Calix took it, as much to signal to him he'd be okay as to seek comfort. Why had Del not spoken to him about such a crucially important decision?

Del looked around the room. "I know this will come as a shock to most of you...maybe even all of you. Rest assured that I've thought long and hard about this. I hope you'll be willing to listen when I explain the why behind it."

"Of course." Calix's voice joined in with others.

Del took a deep breath. "The first reason is that I'm tired. Exhausted. Ever since Sarah...I'm not sleeping well. Being president means running on pitiful amounts of sleep anyway, but for me, it's even worse because I lie awake in bed for hours, unable to fall asleep. I miss her beside me in every way. The burden of the presidency is a heavy one, and I can't bear it alone. If I were to go on, I know I'll be killing myself slowly but surely. That's not worth it."

Calix had known Del had trouble sleeping, but he hadn't realized it had gotten this bad. Guilt filled him. No one worked more closely together with Del than him. He should have seen this. He'd thought that Del had been drowning in the small stuff, which was why he'd hired Issa. And boy, had he made a difference. Del never had to worry about any of the details anymore. Issa took care of all that, lightening both their loads.

But at night, when Del went back to the residence, he was still alone...and Calix couldn't help him there. He'd figured that with Kenn and Warrick staying there, plus Milan, Asher, and Denali, Del would have enough company to not feel lonely, but he should've known better. The nights had been the worst for him as well. Not having Matthew in his bed, waking up alone...it had broken his heart again and again.

"But the second reason and the one that sealed the deal for me is the knowledge of how this is impacting all of you." Del gestured at Kenn, his eyes full of love. "I want you to be able to build your life with Warrick, kiddo. You belong together...and not under the same roof as me. You're hiding the nature of your relationship as if what you have with Warrick is something to be ashamed of. It's not. Love is beautiful, and you shouldn't have to hide how much you love your Daddy..."

"Dad..." Kenn said, sounding shocked.

Del smiled at him. "Warrick has been patient, but asking him to continue this charade for another four years…or even another eight, considering I would be allowed to run once more, since my first term wasn't a full one… I can't ask that of him. Or of you. I want you to be happy, Kenn. More than anything in the world, I want that."

Kenn was out of his chair in a flash, and Del was ready for him, hugging him as he whispered words to him no one else could hear. When they let go, Kenn's cheeks were wet with tears. "I love you, kiddo. More than life itself."

Del kissed his forehead.

"I love you too, Dad."

Kenn walked to his seat again, but instead of sitting down on his own chair, he nestled on Warrick's lap, a sign of how accepted he felt in this group.

Del breathed out a long, slow breath. "My son isn't my only concern, though he is my biggest. The last year has been hell for all of us. We've been thrown into carrying a responsibility we may not have been ready for…"

He looked at Levar, who nodded.

"Or somewhat forced to quit our jobs…"

A meaningful gaze at Henley, then at Milan.

"While others have been doing work that's been a heavy burden on them, especially mentally."

Seth and Coulson shared a look, and then Seth dropped his head on Coulson's shoulder. That simple gesture of leaning on his partner made Calix's stomach weak for a moment. He'd always seen Seth as the strongest man he knew, but he was showing how depleted he was here.

"And let's not forget the impact this has had on relationships. Rhett, I know you don't get to spend as much time with Calix as you'd want, and the same is true for Henley with Levar. Both of you have had to endure many hours of being alone because your partner was working late…again."

"I'm... I would never complain about that," Rhett said. "I understand how important Calix's work is to him."

He was speaking the truth. Not once had he objected to Calix's long hours, to him interrupting dinners and evenings at home, even sex, because this job needed him.

"I know you wouldn't, honey," Del said, and Calix's heart warmed at that sweet endearment, proof of the tender feelings Del had for Rhett. He evoked that in almost all of them, that urge to protect him. "But I see it hurts you. You need him, and that's valid and important."

Rhett looked at Calix as if to check it was okay to acknowledge that. Calix leaned in for a quick kiss. "He's right. You need me home a lot more than I'm able to manage."

"B-but I don't want you to sacrifice your career for me," Rhett protested.

"I wouldn't, sweetheart. It's not a sacrifice when nothing brings me more pleasure than to be with you."

"And that leads me to the three of you." Del turned to Milan, Asher, and Denali. "Don't think I don't know the price the three of you are paying..."

"Del," Milan said, but Del held up his hand and cut him off.

"No, let me finish. When you moved in to support Sarah, I was beyond grateful. She needed you, but frankly, so did I. Having you there to lean on, both you and Calix, has been the only reason I'm still standing. And after she died, you stayed...and I'll never be able to thank you enough for that. But I also know how much it costs you to be by my side and to hide what shouldn't have to be hidden. All three of you. When your relationship leaked, you were made to feel like your love was something to be ashamed of, something dirty and improper. It's not, and I deeply regret that you were forced to hide."

"Please tell me you didn't make your decision because of us," Milan said, worry flashing in his eyes.

"And what if I did? What if the happiness and well-being of my son and my friends are more important to me than whatever duty people assume I have toward my country? Haven't we sacrificed enough? Haven't I?" Del's voice broke near the end, and he took a deep breath, closing his eyes for a moment. "I know how much change I could realize if I were to get reelected. But I'm not so arrogant to believe I'm the only one who could. It's not even been a year for me, but I can't do this for another four years. I can't. It would kill me, physically and mentally."

Calix's heart hurt for his friend, and he gave Rhett's hand a quick squeeze, then got up. On the other side of the table, Milan did the same, and they both rushed over and hugged Del. "It's okay," Calix whispered. "You've done enough."

And then Del broke, his body shaking with violent sobs as he cried his heart out. Calix and Milan held him, meeting each other's eyes over Del's bowed head, understanding without words that this had been a long time coming and that he needed them. A breakdown like this wasn't Milan's forte, but he stood tall, holding on to Del as much as Calix did. The man had truly changed, and Calix had never been more proud of him.

"Let's give them some privacy."

That was Coulson, of course, and as always, everyone followed his lead, and the room emptied. That man was born to be in charge.

Calix had no idea how much time had passed when Del calmed down and the tears stopped flowing. Calix's shirt was soaked from where Del had rested his head, but he couldn't care less.

"How did you do it, Cal? How did you move on after Matthew?" Del's small voice as he stepped out of Calix's and Milan's embrace broke Calix's heart. His eyes were red-rimmed, and when he wiped his cheeks with an almost childlike move, Calix wanted to roll him in bubble wrap and keep him safe.

"I didn't, not for a long time. Grief comes and goes, and sometimes, it can hit you like a wave out of nowhere. It'll be like this for a while, I'm afraid."

Maybe not the best news, but he refused to lie to Del. Losing a partner was a blow that left deep wounds. Del would need time to recover from this, especially since he had so little opportunity to grieve.

"Yeah..." Del inhaled, removing the last of his tears from his eyes. "I was afraid that was the case." He turned to Milan. "Do you think I'm making the right choice?"

Calix knew why Del asked Milan first. The man had no filter. Granted, he'd developed a new sense of tact and sensitivity since he'd gotten together with Asher and Denali, but he'd always be a straight shooter. Not that Calix wasn't, but Del could count on Milan to give him the cold, hard truth.

"Yes." Milan's answer was fast and firm.

"Why?"

"Do you remember the conversation we had when Markinson approached you to be his VP?"

Del nodded. "You advised me against it."

"You never dreamed of being president, Del. That was your father's dream, your grandfather's, but never yours. You accepted that role out of a sense of duty to your country, out of the knowledge you could be a trailblazer and make a difference, especially for all of us on the rainbow. But you never sought this. Even if Sarah hadn't died, I still would've felt the same. Can you honestly say the presidency doesn't feel like it's crushing you? Like you can't breathe? You already bucked against the system when you were a senator. Now you *are* the system. How could you ever be happy here?"

Calix had forgotten about Milan's vehement opposition to Del accepting the vice presidency. He'd warned him from the start it would suffocate him, especially working under Markinson, who hadn't been known for allowing his vice president a lot of leeway.

"Cal?" Del asked.

He squared his shoulders. "Milan is right. I didn't see it back then, and I didn't want to see it now, but he's right."

"I feel like I'm letting you down," Del said softly. "You're so good at this."

"I am, but I can be just as great elsewhere. We both know that after this job, I'll have my pick of board or consultancy positions. You were right with what you said earlier. Rhett needs me, and another four years of this wouldn't be good for our relationship."

The relief that filled Del's expression was so stark a wave of guilt rolled over Calix. He should have seen this, should have picked up on this.

"Not to get all touchy-feely," Milan said, rolling his eyes at himself, "but Delani taught me this... How do you feel about the idea of leaving this behind? He says that's a great indicator whether you're on the right path or not."

Calix smiled. What an impact that boy had had on Milan. Calix would never have picked him for Milan, let alone with Asher, but those three were magical together, showing that love was beautiful and unexpected.

"All I feel is relief. Joy. Mixed in with a good dose of guilt, but that's understandable. I have a job many people dream of, and to leave that behind voluntarily..."

"Sure, but there's your answer. You deserve to be free and happy, Del. So throw all your political weight behind Joanna Riggs and help her become a trailblazer for women. She's smart, she's kind, and she's a moderate, so she'll have a broad appeal. She can win this...and you'd be free."

Wow. Milan Bradbury as the voice of reason with some free political advice thrown in for good measure. Miracles really did still happen.

37

Living with Ryder was so easy it felt like he'd been there for months. Branson had expected to experience the occasional irritation, but one week in, he hadn't. In fact, they'd found a perfect rhythm, the two of them on the same page with keeping the apartment tidy. With Ryder preferring to shower in the evening and Branson in the morning, sharing a bathroom had been a breeze too.

They'd had sex twice more, both times as spectacular as before. The first time had been a quick fuck—in the hallway, of all places—and they'd both cleaned up and had gone back to whatever documentary they'd been watching. The second occasion had been the night before, and after a double orgasm, Ryder had crashed hard in Branson's bed... where he still was this Sunday morning, snoring in the most adorable way.

Branson turned on his side, then rested his head on his arm and watched Ryder sleep. He needed a haircut, his dark hair even messier than usual. His skin was like a perfect white peach, so satiny and unblemished except for his stubble.

Funny, Branson missed seeing Ryder's eyes. He had the opposite of a poker face, his eyes betraying everything he felt. His face was so much more closed off now that he was asleep...though he was still beautiful. He was always beautiful.

Branson's heart contracted painfully. How had he grown this attached to Ryder this quickly? If he wasn't careful, he'd fall head over heels for him. Oh, who was he kidding? He was already in love with him. He had been for a while, maybe even before he'd been aware...before they'd slept together, which told him all he needed to know about the depth of his feelings. Sexual attraction played a role, but it wasn't the base. At the core, he just...loved him.

He *loved* Ryder. He loved his geekiness, his kind heart, his dry sense of humor, and how smart he was. He loved that Ryder was honest, that he'd told Branson the truth before anyone else had, and that he'd given him a second and maybe even a third chance. He loved how uninhibited he was in bed, how genuinely attracted to Branson's body...but what about the rest of Branson? Could Ryder grow to love him as well?

There had been moments when he'd been convinced the attraction on Ryder's side ran deeper than pure sex, but as open as Ryder was about most things, he kept that part of himself firmly hidden. Or maybe he didn't want to acknowledge his feelings to himself, which would make sense after the way his ex had treated him. He'd gotten hurt, so of course he would protect himself.

In the past, Branson might have forced the issue, kind of like he'd done with Seth—only to get rejected. But he wouldn't with Ryder. He'd learned from his mistakes, and besides, he was smart enough to know that attempting to force Ryder to do anything would backfire. No, he'd have to be patient and wait for Ryder to see how good they already were together...and how much more perfect they could be if they were boyfriends.

Ryder stirred, making smacking noises as he opened his eyes. He blinked twice, and then a sweet smile spread across his lips that had Branson's heart dancing in his chest and his belly fluttering with the force of his feelings. "Bonjour, chéri."

"Bonjour, monsieur," Ryder replied after a short hesitation, then turned on his side, facing Branson.

Ryder replying in French? That was new. Branson rewarded him with a big smile. "Look at you, speaking French."

Ryder's eyes lit up. "I looked it up for the next time you'd greet me in French."

"Cool. Your pronunciation was good. What did you use, Google Translate?"

"At first, yes, but then I saw an ad for an app called Duolingo? It helps you learn the basics of a language, and it's both reading and writing and speaking and listening, so I figured I'd try it. I did the first two lessons yesterday."

"I've used Duolingo myself in an attempt to learn Dutch. I'd met this guy from The Netherlands, and he was really hot, so I thought I'd impress him by learning some seductive phrases in Dutch."

"How did that work out?"

Branson grinned. "It's an impossible language to learn, and the sounds are insane, so I gave up after ten lessons. Besides, Duolingo teaches you basics like how to introduce yourself or ask where the train station is, not how to say someone has a spectacular ass or can I fuck you pretty please."

"A missed opportunity," Ryder said dryly. "I'll be sure to mention that in my review."

"Please do. Every gay man in the world will thank you."

Ryder yawned as he stretched. "I slept like a baby."

"I guess you were pretty worn out."

Ryder laughed. "Yeah, no shit. You went to town on my ass."

"Not too rough, was I?" Branson was worried for a second.

"Fuck, no. It was perfect."

"Ah, good. We're a good match…sexually."

"We are." Ryder scooted a little closer. "In fact…"

Branson lifted an eyebrow. "You up for another round?"

Ryder froze. "That not okay? Am I too demanding? Too forward?"

Branson curled his hand around Ryder's neck, preventing him from moving back. "It's more than okay, chéri. I like it when you're eager and confident, showing me you want me."

Ryder searched his eyes, then breathed out, tension leaving his body. "Okay. I'm s—"

Branson cut him off with a finger on his lips. "Don't apologize. I understand. Just know that I don't feel that way, okay? I love it when you show me what you crave. It turns me on."

He took Ryder's hand and brought it to his dick, which had peaked at the idea of morning sex. He didn't put Ryder's hand on it but let go when they were close, so the choice to touch or not was Ryder's. Ryder's eyes darkened as he circled his hand around it. "I love your dick."

He sounded hoarse, and the sigh he let out made Branson's cock throb.

"Thank you."

"Can I...?"

Branson nodded.

"Sit on the edge of the bed."

He obeyed Ryder's soft instruction, and Ryder slid out on the other side of the bed, then walked up to him. Branson's eyes narrowed. Were those...? "Did I *bruise* you?"

Ryder looked down at his hip, where four bruises showed, matching where Branson's fingers had been. "I guess so." He checked the other side, then turned it toward Branson. "They're on this side as well, though less pronounced."

"Ryder..." Branson had to swallow before he could continue. "I'm so sorry. I didn't mean to hurt you."

Ryder gazed back up at him with a puzzled expression. "Were you under the impression that I'm upset about this?"

"I don't know, but shouldn't you be?"

"Why? I loved every second of it. A few bruises won't kill me. Besides, I always bruise easily."

Branson caressed the spot on Ryder's right hip with his fingertips. "I'll be more careful next time."

Ryder put a finger under his chin and forced eye contact. "Did you not hear me? I love it when you pin me down like that and fuck me rough. That second orgasm damn near took me out, it was so intense. You did that with the way you held me, so please don't say you'll be more careful. I don't want you to be."

Ryder's face was open as always, showing every word he'd spoken was the truth. "Okay. But if that ever changes, or if I do anything you don't like or want, please tell me."

"Of course. I promise. Now, can we move on to the good part?"

Branson's mouth curled up in a smile. "What part would that be?"

"The part where it's my turn to get some morning protein in..."

Ryder sank to his knees between Branson's legs, but not in submission. Not that Branson wanted him to, but he'd never mistake Ryder's honest expression of what he wanted for submission. Ryder didn't want Branson to dominate him. He wanted his cock. His desire was raw and pure, and Branson reacted with his whole body.

He threaded his fingers through Ryder's hair even as the man leaned in and pressed his lips against Branson's throbbing cock. Branson pulled Ryder's head forward, rubbing himself against those soft lips that would feel so amazing wrapped around him. "You want this, chéri?"

"Mmm."

He wouldn't beg. And funnily enough, Branson didn't want him to. They were on equal footing in every way, and that was how it should be for them. He offered Ryder his cock, moaning when Ryder attacked it with his mouth. He lapped and licked, kissed and nibbled, then created a wet trail from the base to the tip. Branson spread his legs, his body tense with the fight against the urge to slam his cock into Ryder's mouth. He'd have to let Ryder set the pace.

Ryder nuzzled Branson's balls, inhaling deeply as if he loved the scent. His tongue kept darting out, his lips so warm and wet as they explored his nuts, licking and sucking gently. Branson gasped with pleasure, the tension inside him building up rapidly. And god, when Ryder finally sucked the tip of Branson's cock into his mouth, Branson thought he'd fucking lose it. Ryder let go with a plop, then worked his way down again, giving Branson's balls another round of loving attention before he wrapped his lips around his cock again and sucked him in.

"Oh, fuuuuck," Branson moaned. "Oh, that feels good, chéri... So fucking good."

His fingers tightened on Ryder's hair as Ryder took him in as deep as he could, fondling Branson's balls with his right hand. Jesus, he was so eager, so desperate for his cock. Branson couldn't think of a stronger aphrodisiac than that. And dammit, Ryder knew how Branson liked it by now, handling his balls with just that touch of roughness, that edge of discomfort and pain that got him so fucking hard he could pound nails.

Ryder bobbed his head, his left hand around the base of Branson's cock as he sucked him. He didn't hold back, slurping noises filling the room as he worked that wet, hot mouth until Branson shook with need. "Can I fuck your mouth?" he rasped.

"No, I need you inside me."

"Then you'd better move on to that part because I'm about to blow my wad."

Ryder grinned, then pulled off. "Moving on."

They both climbed back onto the bed, Ryder installing himself on his back with his legs pulled up and spread wide. Branson made a show of sucking on his own fingers, licking around them, wetting them thoroughly. Ryder watched him with hooded eyes, his cheeks flushed. They both knew where those fingers would end up. When Branson retracted them with a *pop*, Ryder swallowed. Branson trailed his thumb over Ryder's ass, but as soon as he'd reached his pretty little hole, he sank those two fingers right in, aided by the lube that was still present from the night before.

"Oh fuck, oh god, oh please..." Ryder babbled, tensing, then letting Branson's fingers in. Branson opened him roughly, stretching him without mercy—not that he thought

Ryder wanted any. He kept pushing back on Branson's fingers, eager for more. The lube was still on the nightstand, and two pumps were enough to slick up his cock. Ryder rolled onto his stomach, spreading his legs. He liked that position, and so did Branson. He could sink so deep inside him, then use all his power to fuck him into the mattress. Mmm, yes, he would.

He pressed the slippery head of his cock against Ryder's hole, then halted, allowing the tension and anticipation to build. "You want this, chéri?"

Ryder wiggled against him. "Please. Need your cock, Bran. Need it so bad."

How could he wait any longer after that? He sank into him, inch by inch, until he was halfway, then waited for a second to let Ryder catch his breath. "Don't stop. Don't need you to stop. Need you. All of you," Ryder whimpered.

He slammed home, Ryder crying out. "You have me, chéri. You have all of me."

38

All Ryder could do was fist the sheets and hang on. God, would he ever get used to that glorious feeling of eight inches splitting him wide open? It burned, and it stung, and it felt so goddamn good he never wanted it to end. Until Branson moved, battering into him with precise, forceful thrusts that had Ryder's body shaking. Hell, the entire bed shuddered and creaked, and the neighbors were getting another earful again.

He closed his eyes, focusing on his ass, the way Branson's cock hit his happy spot every time he surged in, sending sparks throughout Ryder's body. If he kept that up, Ryder would come in under a minute. The tension built in his body already, his balls clenching against his body, and his belly tickling on the inside with the need to come. But he wasn't ready yet emotionally. He needed it to last this time. He needed...

"Stop," he said, and Branson froze. Ryder's heart warmed at the man's immediate response to that word.

Branson slowly pulled out. "Everything okay?"

"Yeah. I want to ride you..."

As soon as Branson was out, Ryder crawled to his knees, then pushed the man onto his back, smiling at the baffled expression on Branson's face. He straddled him, reached back, and held Branson's cock with one hand. "I want to fuck myself on your cock...come all over your chest and face...show you how good you make me feel."

"Fuck, yeah," Branson growled.

Ryder sank down, careful at first, then with more confidence until he was fully seated. Jesus, Branson's cock was so fucking big, so deep inside him. He felt every inch, his channel stretching so wide it made his skin too tight for his body. It *ached*, stinging and twitching and building. He couldn't hold still any longer, and he raised his hips, then lowered himself again.

"Oh, fuck, chéri... You're beautiful like this."

In the back of Ryder's mind, an alarm bell went off. Branson sounded different. Emotional. Sappy, almost. But he pushed it down. He had to be imagining it, and even if he wasn't, it didn't matter right now. Not now when he was riding that perfect cock, giving himself the sweetest torture.

He leaned back, letting Branson sink into him until he couldn't go deeper, until all Ryder felt was Branson. A daze came over him, a floating sensation as if he detached from his body, his mind separating itself. His body chased the pleasure while his mind roamed free on a high of ecstasy, climbing and climbing until he rose above the clouds. His muscles burned and ached, but then Branson's hands grabbed his hips, helping him lift and lower himself again and again.

His cock throbbed, begging to be touched, but he wouldn't. It required self-discipline, forcing his body through the buildup toward a hands-free orgasm, but it would be worth it. If he came like that, his orgasms were ten times more intense.

"Chéri..." Branson grunted between clenched teeth, as much a plea as a warning. His body trembled underneath Ryder's, sending all the telltale signs he was hanging on by his fingernails.

"Help me," Ryder begged him. "I need you to help me."

His body was about to give out, and he was so close. So fucking close his balls were tingling already.

Branson let out a growl, then snapped his hips and drove upward into Ryder, filling him with a force that made their flesh slap together. Ryder's body shook, bringing him to the precipice. One more, maybe two.

He didn't have to beg this time. With another grunt, Branson thrust upward again, then again, and Ryder fell. He soared, his skin itching, the breath whooshing from his lungs as his balls unloaded. His cock sprayed its load, and he couldn't even lift his hand to direct it anywhere, so it hit Branson's chest and chin, the sheets, and even Ryder himself. He didn't care, couldn't muster the brainpower to think, let alone act. His body went rigid, then slack, and he dropped down on Branson's chest like a sack of potatoes.

Still floating from his high, he reveled in how deeply sated he felt. Not even a spark of energy left. Mmm, and how perfect was that sensation of cum dripping out of his ass. It had been—

Wait. Cum dripping?

He froze. "You forgot the condom."

Underneath him, Branson's body jerked, and a gasp flew from his lips. "Shit!"

Ryder rolled off him, panic clawing at his insides. "D-do I need to get tested? When was your last test?"

Branson sat up straight, his face edged with the same

despair Ryder felt inside. "I didn't do it on purpose. I swear, Ryder. I would never—

How could he think Ryder would ever accuse him of that? "I know you didn't. The thought never even crossed my mind."

"I'm so sorry, so sorry. I wasn't thinking... I've never forgotten it. Ever. But I was... You were... I have no excuse. I'm sorry."

Ryder had never seen Branson like this, so raw and vulnerable, stripped of all his usual swagger and confidence. He clutched his hand. "Hey, take a deep breath. It's okay. I didn't think of it either, and I damn well should've noticed you weren't wearing a condom."

"My last test was three months ago, and it was all negative...but I haven't slept with anyone else but you."

Ryder blew out a long breath. "Okay. Then we're good. I was tested after I found out about Paul screwing around. I was fucking terrified he'd infected me with an STD, but it all came back negative. Apparently, he'd been good about using condoms with others... Something to be grateful for under the circumstances, I suppose. And I haven't been with anyone else since either."

Branson's face slowly regained color. "Oh, I'm glad to hear that. I'm sorry for the scare. I should've—"

"Stop apologizing. We both forgot in the heat of the moment. This is not on you alone."

"Thank you. Jesus, what a way to come down from a spectacular round of sex..."

Ryder rolled his eyes. "Yeah, let's not do this again."

The mood to cuddle was ruined, and the drying cum on his body was starting to itch. "Wanna grab a shower?" he asked.

Branson raised his eyebrows. "Together?"

"Well, yeah. To make up for scaring each other shitless?"

"I'm down with that."

It wasn't until they were both in the bathroom, waiting for the water to heat up, that Ryder realized they'd only showered together once before...the very first time they'd had sex. He'd suggested it spontaneously, more because he figured Branson would like it, and he wanted to make up for making him feel guilty. But he'd forgotten—again—how intimate showering was.

"If you'd rather I waited until you're done..." Branson said softly, and Ryder looked up. Branson was studying him.

He sighed. "I don't think I've ever met anyone who's as good at reading body language as you are. It's a little scary."

"I don't want you to feel uncomfortable."

"I always forget how...intimate showering is. More so than sex."

"It is. It's much harder to hide. Do you want to hide from me, chéri?"

"I don't know. Yes, I'm a little uncomfortable, but it's nothing I can't handle. I think it's... I don't know the rules of this, the framework. We're friends but also roommates who have sex on occasion. My goal was to keep things simple and casual, but showering together is anything but simple and casual."

He wasn't even sure how it had happened, but he was in the shower now, the perfectly hot water raining down on him. Branson patiently waited for his turn, and Ryder stepped aside to soap his hair and let Branson have the water.

"Do you want us to come up with some rules?" Branson asked. "Would that help you? Or would you rather let it run its course?"

Ryder pondered it as he rinsed his hair while Branson washed his. "What kind of rules?"

"For example, whether you'd want us to be exclusive or not."

Exclusive… That was something that fit boyfriends more than their arrangement, and yet Ryder liked it. It would mean ditching condoms, which might not be a big thing but did make things sexier. He only had to focus on the cum still dripping out of his ass and the wonderfully dirty feeling that gave him to realize the benefits.

"I'd never cheat on you if we agreed to being exclusive," Branson said.

"I know." He didn't even hesitate with that response. He trusted Branson, maybe more than he'd ever trusted Paul. "I think I'd like that."

"Yeah?" Branson's happiness made Ryder's insides flutter.

"I like not having to use a condom. It's… It's dirty, somehow, and I like it."

"Good. I like it too."

Ryder took a washcloth and some shower gel and starting washing himself. "What else?"

"Hmm, let me think… I'd be okay with you sleeping in my bed after sex or just in general. I kinda like waking up with you."

Sleeping in Branson's bed? Like, as a routine? "You mean, like, every night?"

Branson shrugged. "Not necessarily. Just if and when you're in the mood. All I'm saying is that I'm okay with that."

Ryder liked the idea, which surprised him at first, but when he thought about it a bit more, it made sense. He was a tactile person, and so was Branson. They both liked to cuddle, so to give explicit permission to do that, to state it was allowed under the rules of their relationship, was smart. It set them free to fulfill their need without having to worry about either getting rejected or facing repercussions because it would lead to misunderstandings about the underlying intention.

"I'm on board with that."

"And other than that, I think we've discovered this week that we're well matched as roommates. I cook..."

"I do the dishes and keep the kitchen tidy..."

"I take out the trash..."

Thank fuck for that because for some weird reason, even the smell of trash made Ryder gag. Paul had always bitched about it, calling him a wimp. Seriously, who the fuck cared? As if taking out the trash was, like, the absolute peak of adulthood.

"And we already agreed to split the costs for groceries, so we've got all that covered."

Ryder rinsed the last bit of soap off his body, feeling much better now that he was clean again. Cum was super sexy, but not when it was dry. "You're right. We do really mesh well as roommates."

"And as friends." Branson turned off the water.

"And as friends." Ryder smiled at him.

"But especially with the benefits."

"Those are pretty spectacular, yes."

"Good." Branson leaned in, then kissed Ryder on his cheek. "I'm glad we're on the same page that we're perfect together."

Wait, *what?*

39

Had he pushed too hard? Branson wasn't sure. After the shower, Ryder had pulled back from him, keeping his distance, though Branson didn't get the impression he was upset or angry. More... baffled. Shocked, maybe? So he'd allow him time to mull everything over. And maybe discuss stuff with Dorian, since Ryder had left to hang out with him.

Branson had been disappointed Ryder hadn't asked him to come with him, but he knew he was expecting way too much, way too soon. Ryder didn't do things on a whim. He had to think this through...and Branson would have to be patient and wait until he'd made up his mind.

In the meantime, it would give him the perfect opportunity to spend some time with his parents. His father had started chemo, and according to Branson's mom, he was tired but in good spirits. Brenda had returned to her post in Turkey, and Branson had promised her he'd check in and tell her the truth about how their dad was doing. Not that he hadn't planned on visiting anyway, but it offered him an extra push.

His parents had bought an apartment in Bethesda years before so they'd have a "home" whenever they were in the US. That had turned out to be a smart decision now, as they were remaining stateside until his father needed no more treatment. It wasn't too bad a drive for Branson, especially on a Sunday when the traffic was half of what it was on weekdays.

"Hey, honey," his mom said as she opened the door, then pulled him in for a fierce hug. "I'm so happy you're here. Your father has been looking forward to this."

Branson raised an eyebrow as he let go. "That sounds rather desperate."

His mom chuckled. "He is. He's going stir crazy, being forced to sit still."

That, Branson could imagine. His father had always been physically active. "I'm glad to offer some distraction."

His father lay propped up on the chaise longue part of the couch, a blanket covering his legs. He looked a little better than the last time Branson had seen him but still so much frailer than usual.

"Hey, Dad." He kneeled next to the couch and hugged his father, taking care to be gentle. "How are you feeling?"

"Like crap," his father said, direct as always. He could be diplomatic if he wanted to, but he was known to be a straight shooter.

"I'll make you some coffee," Branson's mom said.

Branson cringed. His mom preferred her coffee as weak as she could get it. "Thanks, Mom."

"No worries, she bought me a Keurig," his father whispered, then winked at him. "It's still not the best, but it's a lot better than the dishwater she made before."

Thank fuck for small favors. He'd be spared from forcing down the crap she usually made. Branson smiled as he settled on a reading chair. "How was the first round of chemo?"

His father sighed. "Hell. I've never been this tired in my life except for when I had mono in high school. It reminds me of that, with nausea as an added factor."

"Sounds like fun. Will that remain the case throughout all treatments?"

"They don't know. Some people get used to it. Others are sick as a dog every time. My hair isn't affected yet, so there's that, though honestly, that's the least of my concerns. I'd happily trade my hair for more energy... But talk to me about what's been going on in your life. I need some distraction."

Branson could understand that completely. "I'm good. Truly good. Better than I've been in a long time."

His father's scrutinizing eyes missed little. "Would that have something to do with that conversation you had with your mother and sister in the hospital?"

"Mom told you about that?"

His father's expression softened. "Not to gossip, Bran. She was worried about you."

Branson sighed. "I've been forced to look in a mirror, so to speak, and I didn't like what I saw. It's inspired me to make some changes in my life."

"Like what?"

"Did Mom talk to you about the extreme adaptability?" His father nodded. "Then you understand what's been on my mind. I did some research, and I recognized a lot about that. It's contributed to my analytical skills because I learned to read people, to take a group's temperature, and then adapt my response. So I'm not saying it's all been bad. But I had to face that I've done the same in my friendships and other relationships...and that wasn't so easy to accept. I think I missed out on a lot because I've never been myself..."

"I'm sorry. I hope you'll believe that if we had known about this sooner, we would've told you. This wasn't on our radar when you guys were growing up."

"I know, Dad. I don't blame you or Mom at all. I just wished I'd been aware sooner. If Ryder hadn't pointed it out..."

"Ryder?"

"He's..."

How did he explain this? His first instinct was to hide how much Ryder meant to him. What if they never got together? His parents would realize he'd gotten rejected. On the other hand, so what? Wasn't it about time he showed all of himself and not just the good parts?

"He's my new coworker, a forensic accountant...who's also a new friend and my new roommate."

"Roommate? Honey, why didn't you tell us you were struggling financially?" his mom asked as she put down a cup of coffee in front of him, then served his father. "I know we've been focused on your dad, but we would've helped."

"Lisa." His father's tone was mild, but the gentle rebuke was unmistakable. "Let's not jump to conclusions. I can think of more than one reason why Branson would take a roommate. But even if he was, it's his choice if he wants to share that with us. He's a grown man, sweetheart."

Branson wanted to kiss his dad. The irony was that mere months ago, Branson would've felt that comment superfluous. He wouldn't have taken offense at his mother's words. But Ryder opening his eyes to the concept of consent in its broadest definition had changed everything. Branson was so much more aware of all the small instances where people didn't respect someone else's boundaries.

"I didn't mean to belittle you," his mom said.

"I know, Mom, but Dad is right. I'm not doing it for financial reasons. He's..." He took a deep breath. "He's my person, Mom. He's it. I want to spend the rest of my life with him...but he doesn't know yet."

His mom's eyes grew misty. "Oh, honey, that's wonderful. Do you think he reciprocates your feelings?"

"I do, but I can't push him. Ryder is a rational thinker, and I need to give him time to reach the conclusions on his own."

His father grinned. "Considering that you already got him to move in with you, I'd say your chances of success are such that I'd put my money on you."

Branson laughed. "You guys will love him. He's super smart, and his skills with numbers are unparalleled. Plus, he's super cute, and he has a dry sense of humor, and he's just..." Both his parents stared at him with amazement. "I really like him," he finished lamely.

"Honey, you're besotted. That little speech just now? Those were the words of a man in love," his mom said. "I'm so happy for you. I hope we'll get to meet him soon."

"I hope so too," Branson said, his insides warm at his parents' full acceptance.

"I'll make us some lunch," his mom said, still smiling. "Why don't you talk shop with your dad? You know he loves that stuff."

Branson and his dad both chuckled as she walked to the kitchen.

"Did you see the news about the case against some companies for illegal campaign contributions?" his dad then asked. "I'm curious what the deeper story is there. That seemed to come out of nowhere. I didn't even know the FBI was investigating that."

Out of all the things to talk about, his father had to pick something Branson couldn't share more about than had already been revealed in the press. Luckily, the media had dug up quite a bit already, and while no one had made the connection between the campaign fraud and the Pride Bombing and the assassination, Henley had told Coulson multiple investigative reporters were on the trail, smelling something fishy. It would only be a matter of time before they connected the dots, and the story would break. Coulson was determined to beat the press to it and arrest the suspects before it all became public. Obviously, Branson couldn't share any of that with his father.

"Grand juries are secret for a reason. You don't want to give people like that a heads-up that they're being looked into. That would only provide them with the opportunity to make evidence disappear."

"True, true, but it's been almost six years. One would think they'd caught on to that fraud sooner if it happened on that scale."

"Some people excel at hiding their tracks, Dad."

His father must've picked up on something in Branson's voice or expression because he froze for a moment. He didn't ask, and Branson knew he wouldn't. His father realized all too well Branson couldn't talk about it, and he'd never put him in that difficult position. Instead, his eyes grew warm and loving.

"Bran, I'm so proud of you. I need you to know that. What you do is all behind the scenes, and few people may be aware of it, but you're serving your country just as much as those in the front lines. True to the CIA's motto, you really are our country's first line of defense."

Branson had to swallow before he could answer. "Thank you, Dad. That means a lot to me. I love my job, you know that. It's frustrating and discouraging at times, but when we get it right, we save lives...or we bring people to justice."

He didn't need to say more. His father would read between the lines.

"Justice matters, especially to the victims and their loved ones."

"Yes, it does."

His father repositioned himself, wincing as he moved.

"You okay, Dad?" Branson frowned. His father wasn't a man who ever complained about pain. He'd been a Marine, for fuck's sake. He was intimately familiar with pain, as he'd once told Branson. So for him to react to moving his body was worrisome.

"It's the incision site from the colectomy. It keeps bothering me."

"Is it inflamed? Did the surgeon have a look at it?"

"It's not. She said it wasn't uncommon for it to stay painful for a while, but she'll keep an eye on it."

"When's your next checkup?"

"With her? Two weeks from now. They'll run new scans to see if the chemo is working."

It had to work. The idea of losing his dad wasn't something he'd even waste a thought on because it was too terrifying. He wasn't ready yet. One day, he'd have to say goodbye, but please not yet.

"Bran," his father said softly and reached out his hand.

Branson sunk on his knees next to him, clinging to his hand as tears filled his eyes. "I'm scared, Dad... I'm so scared."

His father squeezed his hand, then put his other hand on top of Branson's head. "I will fight this with every cell in my body, and I'm determined to beat this. But if I don't... No, Bran, listen to me," he said when Branson wanted to say something. "If I don't, I'm counting on you to take care of your mom. With your sister abroad, she needs you. Promise me."

Then the tears came, Branson's throat so tight he could barely breathe. "Always, Dad. I promise," he said between sobs.

"Good. Then I can focus on the battle and not have to worry about the home front."

40

They'd been called to the White House, a first for Ryder, who felt like he was dreaming as he followed the Secret Service agent down the hallway of the West Wing, Branson on his heels. The place was humming with activity, and they passed multiple staffers hurrying to whatever it was they were on their way to. A meeting, most likely. Most of the jobs here consisted of endless meetings, Ryder had been told.

"Here we are." The agent gestured to her left. "The Roosevelt Room."

Already? Damn. Ryder had hoped they'd be able to walk around a bit more. Not that he would express anything of the kind. "Thank you," he said instead because manners and all.

They weren't the first to arrive. Coulson was talking to Calix in hushed tones, and Seth was already seated at the table, as were all the bigwigs from their previous emergency meeting. Only this time, the president would join them. Ryder hadn't been told why the meeting had been convened, but he had a suspicion, considering what he'd uncovered the day before.

"Want to sit here?" Branson pointed at two chairs in the back, farthest away from where the president would presumably be sitting. Branson knew him well.

"Yes, please."

The room quickly filled, and then the president walked in, and everyone hushed. Amazing how one man—or maybe one position—could have that effect.

"Let's get started," the president said, checking his watch as he sat down at the head of the table. "Not to be rude, but technically, I have two more meetings I'm supposed to attend right now."

"Trust me, Mr. President, you'll want to be here for this one," Coulson said. Everyone hushed. "But first, I'd like to introduce you to Branson Grove and Ryder Treese. Branson has been the key analyst for Hamza Bashir for the last five years, and Ryder joined the team recently as a forensic accountant. Both have been instrumental in the progress we've made."

Ryder's cheeks were on fire with all eyes on him, but the president sent him a friendly smile. "Thank you both for your service to your country and the sacrifices you and your families have made. This nation owes you much."

"Thank you, Mr. President," Branson said. "It's our honor, sir."

Thank fuck Branson knew what to say because Ryder had been tongue-tied there for a minute. Under the table, Branson bumped his knee as if to say he knew. Such a sweet gesture and Ryder relaxed.

"Mr. President and everyone else, we've reached a crucial point in the investigation," Coulson announced. "We are confident we have sufficient evidence to indict the key suspects for their roles in the Pride Bombing, the assassination of President Markinson, and the murders of Annabeth Markinson and Sarah Bradbury Shafer."

A wave of gasps traveled through the room, and Ryder's heart skipped a beat. This was it. This was the moment they had all waited for, that they had worked so hard for. This was the culmination of years of effort to find the culprits... and now they had them.

"Wesley Quirk was released on bail last week, and while he's on suspension from the Baltimore PD pending trial, he's still welcome at the shooting club. Our undercover agent there overheard a conversation between Quirk and Steve Duron yesterday. In it, Quirk and Duron mentioned orders from George Washington to *take care* of the weak links. George Washington is the code name Kingmakers used on the PPN forum, most likely Basil King. We suspect that the weak links they referred to are Naomi Beckingham and her boyfriend, Ralph Durrick."

"I assume *taking care of* is a euphemism for killing them?" the president asked.

"That's a reasonable assumption, Mr. President. It's a clear sign they're feeling the heat, and they're getting scared, trying to get rid of potential witnesses against them. For obvious reasons, we want to avoid that. But there's more. Ryder, can you summarize what you discovered yesterday?"

He had to present it himself? In front of the president? Holy shit, couldn't Coulson have given him a heads-up? Under the table, Branson's hand found his thigh, squeezing as if to say he believed in him. At least, that was what Ryder told himself. He could do this.

"Yes. Of course." He closed his eyes for a moment and inhaled, forcing himself to focus on the facts, the numbers. "The first financial transaction between Kingmakers and the Alhuriya Group, the company El Sewedy's father owns, was in 2013. They purchased arms and munition. Ever since there have been regular transactions for various military supplies. That means there's a well-established connection between Kingmakers and El Sewedy senior."

He did a quick check around the room to make sure everyone was still with him, relaxing when no one seems confused.

"Those transactions provided me with various bank accounts associated with Kingmakers and with father and son El Sewedy. On one of these, we hit the jackpot. Corey and I were able to trace the transactions back to a US bank account Kingmakers owned, and when we subpoenaed the transactions from that account, we found more accounts associated with Kingmakers. Between November 2015 and November 2016, a total of fifteen million dollars was wired from Kingmakers to El Sewedy. Between June 2020 and September 2020, another five million was sent. These periods correspond with the time frame of the Pride Bombing and the assassination of President Markinson, respectively. We have irrefutable financial evidence Kingmakers paid El Sewedy large sums of money that can serve no other purpose than to pay for services rendered."

"Jesus Christ." Calix leaned back in his chair, his eyes bulging. "Fifteen million dollars. That's the price they paid for the Pride Bombing. That's how much the lives of 153 people were worth, including my Matthew..."

His voice broke at the end, and much to Ryder's surprise, the president took Calix's hand in his and held it as they all waited until Calix had composed himself again.

"I know how you feel," Seth said quietly. "I had the same sentiments when I heard."

Calix took a deep breath. "I apologize for letting my emotions get the best of me."

The president shook his head as he let go of Calix's hand. "No, Cal. This is personal. We can be professional about this while still acknowledging the losses we've experienced."

"You're right." Calix took another deep breath. "Thank you. Mr. President."

"Thank you, Ryder. Fantastic work from you and Corey. There's more," Coulson said, and everyone focused on him. "With the information we found on that forum, we were able to trace everyone who was a part of that PPN group. As far as we can tell, none of them were involved in executing any of the plans, but they sure as hell encouraged them. And considering they knew about a presidential assassination ahead of time and didn't do anything to stop it, we can prosecute them for that."

"Coulson, can I ask something?" the president said. Coulson nodded. "The one aspect that's still a tad fuzzy to me is the relationship between PPN and Kingmakers. Is Basil King truly a right extremist? If not, how did he end up with this group?"

"That's an excellent question, Mr. President, and one that had us scratching our heads as well. As far as we can tell, Basil King isn't right-wing. Yes, he's a conservative, but not that extreme. He's an opportunist, though, and we suspect he used his existing connection with Jon Brooks to court PPN. Or maybe even founded it, making everyone believe he supported that ideology."

"But why?" Calix asked. "Why throw up that whole smoke screen?"

"So he could blame them when things went wrong. He needed foot soldiers, a scapegoat, in case the domestic connection was ever discovered. He never expected us to find him, but he'd counted on the possibility of Quirk being traced back to PPN. If we did, he'd throw them under the bus. In all likelihood, they don't know about Kingmakers. To them, *George Washington* is someone in the DC area who has the clout to make things happen. The guys who work for Kingmakers know. Steve Duron, Laurence Paskewitch, they know. Quirk, we're not certain of, but we're leaning toward no. Time will tell."

"So the bottom line is that it really was all about the money," President Shafer said softly. "All of it. The Pride Bombing, the assassination, even Annabeth and my Sarah… just for money so they could make a profit in the future."

"Yes." Coulson sounded apologetic. "Yes, it was, Mr. President."

"We knew this…" Shafer gestured with his hands. "We've known this for a while, but now that we have all the facts, it's somehow still a shock."

"It is," Seth said. "Even when we know what humans are capable of, we're still hurt and disappointed when our worst fears are confirmed."

"We have two more facts we want to share with you all," Coulson took over again. "The first is that we have a positive ID on Steve Duron from people who worked on the other floats in the same building in May and June 2015. They recognized him from his picture and identified him as Ryan Wallace, which matches the name Milan Bradbury was given for the man who spent a few weeks in the South Bronx. Steve Duron placed the two big bombs, no doubt about it. Their misdirection worked for a long time, but in the end, we still found the real culprits."

"That's great work, Coulson," Calix said. "You and your team should be extremely proud."

"It was a team effort," Sheehan said, and even Ryder picked up on the underlying butt hurt. "I don't think it's fair to single out Coulson and his team when more people have worked on this...and he wasn't the agent in charge of the investigation."

"Considering you were all too happy to let Coulson be the public face of the investigation toward me and everyone else to potentially save your own hide should things go wrong, I think it's only fair he now gets the praise as well," Shafer said, his voice unusually sharp. "After all, this is the first time you and I meet, Special Agent Sheehan, whereas I've seen Coulson at least weekly for the last year."

Sheehan's cheeks grew red, and he cast his eyes down, probably embarrassed to death by the public reprimand. Understandable, but he had kind of asked for it by trying to take the credit. Judging by the deadly look the FBI director sent Sheehan, Ryder wasn't the only one who felt that way.

Coulson cleared his throat. "Thank you, Mr. President. I appreciate your kind words. Let me close off with the last bit of information, and this has been a shocking development. We have evidence that General John Doty, the former secretary of defense, not only knew about Kingmakers' role in the Pride Bombing and the assassination but was also involved in the planning and execution of both. Moreover, he may have been considering a sort of coup, declaring himself president after they'd taken both President Markinson and you out, Mr. President."

Deadly silence filled the room, everyone too stunned to even gasp. Ryder couldn't wrap his head around it. A general who had plotted to assassinate the president and vice president? To make himself president?

"We suspect he's been feeding Kingmakers information, Mr. President," Seth said. "Classified intel, perhaps. That's still something we're looking into, but he may be the mole we suspected having."

"Thank god we kept him out of the loop on the investigation, then," Calix said. "At least he didn't know how close we were to cracking the case."

"If we hadn't, I doubt we would've gotten this far without a much higher body count," Coulson agreed. "But this is the case, Mr. President. We all agree we're ready to make the arrests...but we don't have eyes on El Sewedy at this moment. Branson?"

Branson sat up straight, letting go of Ryder's thigh. Huh, had he held his hand there the whole time? Ryder hadn't even noticed. "He's fled the UAE, Mr. President, probably alerted we were on his trail, and we suspect he returned to Yemen. It will take us a while to find him again. My guess is he will go to ground."

"Is there reason to suspect he's planning anything else?" Director Heeder asked.

"No, sir. None at all. We assume he still has sleepers in the US, and Ryder has already found some payments that will help us track them, but nothing concrete."

President Shafer leaned back in his chair, taking off his glasses and scratching his beard. Branson didn't envy him the responsibility of making this call. "Suzy, you on board with this?"

The attorney general nodded. "Fully, Mr. President. I'm confident we'll be able to get a conviction based on what we have now and even more with the extra information their arrests, warrants, and subpoenas will bring. We'll employ all legal strategies and put the full weight of the Justice Department behind it."

"Ella?" the president asked. "Where do you stand?"

"I say we arrest them, Mr. President. We'll get El Sewedy

later. Besides, I don't know how much of a threat he still is. If he's doing it for the money, who will hire him after we go public with this?"

Ryder agreed with her line of reasoning. Sure, El Sewedy might still be contacted by real terrorist groups, but even that didn't seem likely. Crazy as it sounded, those groups would probably look down on El Sewedy and condemn him for the wrong motives. Who would want to be associated with someone like him, someone who had carried out attacks for money rather than out of a true belief, however wrong and distorted that belief might be?

"Calix?" the president checked in with his chief of staff.

"I agree. We have to prioritize catching domestic terrorists over foreign ones under these circumstances. Kingmakers and everyone in their network pose a much higher risk than El Sewedy, and we can't afford to lose potential witnesses."

The president nodded, putting his glasses back on, then looked around the room. "Does anyone disagree? If you do, or if you have any concerns that haven't been addressed yet, please speak up. I need to know I've heard all sides and opinions."

No one spoke, and when Branson did a quick check around the room, he didn't spot any hesitation or even a hint of disagreement.

President Shafer leaned forward and placed his hands on the table. "Then that's what we'll do. Let's get the bastards. Coulson and Suzy, make sure to have someone from both your departments brief Levar so he knows what and what not to share with the press. The poor guy is about to get trampled."

41

For the first time in his career, Levar was scared to step into the press room. Scared to the point where his hands were shaking and his stomach was queasy. He'd prepared his press statement with Calix, Coulson, Seth, and a representative from the AG's office, and he'd received a lengthy briefing on which details he could and couldn't release to the press. But still, he felt like a deer about to run a course through a forest filled with hunters intent on taking him out.

"Levar." Calix put a hand on his shoulder. "You've got this."

Levar nodded, swallowing in a futile attempt to get rid of the dryness in his throat. "Thank you. I don't feel like it. I'm scared I'll make a mistake."

"Even if you do, that's okay. We all understand...and let's face it, none of us could do it."

True, but that didn't make it any easier that Levar had no choice. Facing the press was his job, even on days like this when he wanted to be anywhere else but here. He pinched his eyes shut. "I need a moment."

"Take your time. They'll wait."

Oh yes, they would. They'd only become hungrier, more eager to hear this mysterious press release that had been announced earlier that morning. And once he was done, they'd pounce.

He smelled him before a pair of strong arms wrapped around him. "I'm here, baby."

A sob of relief escaped him as he leaned into Henley's embrace. "Thank god. I'm so scared."

Henley held him closer. "I know."

No words of wisdom, no advice. Just a simple affirmation that he understood. Levar inhaled deeply, letting the faint fragrance of Henley's aftershave comfort him. "Will you be in the room?"

Henley never attended press briefings anymore, if only because they all wanted to avoid even a hint of impropriety or a conflict of interest.

"If you want me there. I have Calix's permission."

He had the best boss in the world. Calix must've foreseen how hard this would be for Levar and had already arranged for Henley to be there. "I do."

"Then I'll be there. Look at me when it gets too much, okay? Lean on me."

Levar nodded, and then Henley kissed him. Not a brief peck on his lips but a full-out kiss, tongue and all. Levar stopped shaking, and his heart rate slowed down. Funny, Henley's kisses usually had the opposite effect.

Henley released him. "Go get 'em, baby."

Levar straightened his shoulders, took another deep breath, then walked into the press room. The buzz of voices faded, and every face, mic, and camera in the room turned to him. God help him. He waited until Henley had taken a spot all the way in the back of the room, right next to Calix.

"Good afternoon. An hour ago, the FBI arrested eight American individuals in connection with the Pride Bombing and the assassination of President Markinson."

He stopped, having expected the wave of shock that golfed through the room. He let it ride out until silence had returned.

"Their names are Wesley Quirk, 34, of Baltimore, Maryland. Jonathan Brooks, 48, of Oklahoma City. Steve Duron, 43, of Rockville, Maryland. Laurence Paskewich, 44, of Tysons Corner, Virginia. Naomi Beckingham, 26, of Derby, Kansas. Ralph Durrick, 29, of Derby, Kansas..."

He waited, wanting everyone's full attention for the last two names.

"...Kurt Barrow, 49, of Bethesda, Maryland, and Basil King, 38, of Washington DC. Barrow and King are the owners of Kingmakers, a private military contractor. The latter two have also been charged with the conspiracy to the murders of First Lady Annabeth Markinson and First Lady Sarah Shafer."

Seeing genuine shock on the faces of the press was rare, but he had the whole room deadly quiet. Pale faces, open mouths, everyone clearly trying to process what it all meant.

"All individuals are in federal custody and will be prosecuted for multiple federal charges related to an act of domestic terrorism. Their properties have been seized by the FBI, and relevant material and digital belongings have been taken into custody for further investigation. The FBI has raided the offices of Kingmakers, located here in DC, as well as served subpoenas to several connected individuals and companies suspected of involvement. At this time, we will not release any information on the roles of each of these individuals and companies in the Pride Bombing and the assassination, as this is an ongoing investigation. The FBI does ask anyone with relevant information about these individuals and companies that could relate to the Pride Bombing or the assassination to come forward. The FBI can be reached through an anonymous tip line, the number of which is showed on your screen right now. You can also submit information through the FBI's website, FBI.gov/tips."

He checked his notes. One more thing and then he was done. "At this time, we are not sharing information on the relationship between the suspects and Hamza Bashir or Al Saalihin. Please keep in mind that this is an ongoing investigation and that a lot of the details are classified information that will not yet be released to the press. I will now try to answer the questions I'm at liberty to answer."

He braced himself and rightfully so because he'd barely gotten the last syllable out before every hand in the room shot up and every reporter was shouting his name. Good god, this was pandemonium. For a second, his eyes darted to Henley, who sent him an encouraging smile, and then Levar picked a random reporter. "Alan, go ahead."

Alan from the Chicago Tribune shouted his question, and even then, Levar caught only fragments of it as the other reporters wouldn't stop calling out their own questions. Oh, for fuck's sake. This would never work. He had to get some kind of control back. He put his fingers in his mouth and gave a shrill whistle that restored order to the room. "People! One at a time or no one will get anything usable from this. Alan."

"How long has the FBI known these two attacks were acts of domestic terrorism?"

"It's important to note that while the FBI believes Americans were involved in the attacks, they were carried out by a foreign terrorist group, so it would be considered a mix of domestic and foreign terrorism."

Alan smiled. "That doesn't answer my question."

Of course he didn't, and Levar hadn't expected to get away with it, but he'd had to try. "Almost from the beginning, there were aspects to the Pride Bombing that suggested domestic involvement."

"What kind of aspects?"

"I can't answer that." He looked around the room. "Donna."

"Does the suspected involvement of Kingmakers suggest a motive?"

He'd known that question would be asked. "I'm not going to speculate about motive at this point."

"But considering they're a defense contractor, that seems rather obvious."

"Affirming or denying that would mean speculating about motive, which isn't something I'll engage in." He pointed at the NBC reporter. "Carol."

"Can you say anything about the type of evidence the FBI has for the domestic involvement in the Pride Bombing and the assassination as well as the murders of the two First Ladies?"

Levar nodded. "In general terms, yes. Let me make it clear that while the FBI has taken the lead on this entire investigation, this has been a joint effort by the entire intelligence community. Almost all federal intelligence agencies have been involved, including the ATF, the NSA, and the CIA as well as several foreign intelligence agencies. This investigation started after the Pride Bombing, and it's still ongoing. The evidence against these suspects is overwhelming and consists of phone calls, emails, CCTV footage, surveillance, physical evidence, tips from others, and much more."

He gestured at the next reporter. "Is there a connection

with the case against Kingmakers and the four defense contractors who were indicted for illegal campaign contributions?"

They had hoped for this question. On one hand, Coulson had warned Levar not to speculate about motive, mostly so the suspects wouldn't be aware of how much information the authorities had on the whole scheme. But on the other hand, they wanted the press to dig deeper, hoping they'd be able to find people who might be unwilling to talk to the government but would feel more comfortable as an anonymous source for a reporter. This question was the perfect setup.

"The FBI is not willing to provide clarity about the possible connection, but it does seem too much of a coincidence not to look into."

He answered question after question, his brain in a constant stage of strange hyperawareness, registering every little detail, every nonverbal communication. Every few minutes, he let his gaze drift to Henley, who stood unmoving, watching Levar. He drew strength from his presence, even though Henley did nothing but stand there, meet his eyes, and smile at him. It was enough.

"Will the president address the nation about this?" James, the FNW News reporter, asked.

"Not at this point."

"Why not? Doesn't the president feel that catching the real culprits behind the Pride Bombing he spent so much time lamenting about as well as the death of his own wife warrants a personal response from him?"

Journalism 101: always check the premise of the question. "I'd hope that *any* American would lament the 153 lives that were lost at the Pride Bombing, as well mourn the loss of President Markinson, Mrs. Markinson, and Mrs. Shafer,"

Levar snapped at him, then took a deep breath. "Their deaths were not a loss for the president alone, but for all their loved ones and the country as a whole. I also object to your classification of the suspects that were arrested today as the *real* culprits. When you've found a more appropriate way to ask a question, you can try again."

Henley had his hand in front of his mouth, covering a laugh, and Levar had to work hard to keep himself from reacting. He answered questions until the press ran out of fresh things to ask that he was willing to answer, and he called it quits. When he walked back into the West Wing, Henley stood there waiting for him, and he fell straight into his arms.

His man. His anchor in this storm. His home.

42

Ryder watched in horror as Levar dodged question after question, calmly answering those he could. "How the fuck does he do that?" he mumbled, then shoved a handful of popcorn into his mouth.

They were sitting on the couch in their living room, watching a recording of the press conference. They already knew the highlights, of course, but they'd both wanted to see the whole thing.

"I especially admire his patience. I swear I would've knocked some heads together by now," Branson said, sitting right next to him, dressed in a pair of shorts and nothing else.

Ryder had swallowed when he'd spotted him sitting there, all kinds of sexy and hot. Branson had just showered too, the smell of his shower gel drifting over to Ryder whenever he moved. The man oozed sexiness somehow. How had Ryder never noticed that before? Well, he had, but not to this degree, where he had trouble even concentrating, Branson distracting him too much.

Branson took the popcorn from Ryder's hands. "Don't hog the salty yumminess, chéri. Not nice."

Ryder grinned with his mouth full. "'m hungry."

"So am I."

Branson grabbed a massive hand of popcorn and showed he could fit even more into his mouth, making Ryder laugh harder. He'd better be careful he didn't choke on it. That would be a sad death. He could picture his epitaph. "Here lies Ryder Treese. He choked on popcorn when celebrating the unleashing of hell." Unleashing? Ryder frowned. Or was it unleashment? What did it matter? The result was the same.

They watched as Levar finally wrapped things up. "That was brutal." Branson turned the volume low. "Levar deserves a danger bonus for doing that. You couldn't pay me enough to volunteer."

"I'd be way too scared of revealing classified information. Or saying something stupid."

"Yeah, you gotta think on your feet for that job...and not have any kind of temper because if you do, if the press can somehow trigger you, you're in trouble."

As much as he'd felt pity for Levar, watching that press conference had been epic. Though he'd really, really wished he could've been there when Basil King had been arrested. That would've been even better. "They're all in jail now, right?"

"Yes. The main suspects have been charged with domestic terrorism, which means they won't be released on bail. They're not going anywhere."

"Good."

"Coulson said they're starting the interrogations tomorrow. All suspects have been assigned a lawyer in as far as they didn't hire one themselves, which Basil King did, obviously."

Ryder shuddered. "Can you imagine defending someone like that?"

"Yes and no. Yes, because I believe in a fair legal system, which means everyone needs a lawyer to make sure they're getting a fair trial. Not that that always works out, especially with underpaid and overworked public defenders, but still. It's the principle. But to be one of those thousand-dollars-an-hour lawyers who voluntarily defend scum like Basil King? No. I can't imagine anyone feeling proud of themselves for that. I could never do it."

"God, no."

Branson laughed as he bumped his shoulder. "You're way too honest, chéri. You'd probably tell the DA to ask the right questions during questioning."

Ryder giggled. "I can totally see myself do that. I can't lie. I hate it."

"It's one of the many things I love about you..."

Love. Ryder had noticed how easily Branson used that word. He tended to use superlatives anyway. Or at least to speak in terms that felt a little over the top. Cheesy, even.

Like what he'd said after they had showered, about how perfect they were together. At first, Ryder had thought Branson was serious, that he'd hinted at the two of them being more than friends with benefits, but then he'd thought about it and had reasoned Branson had just been using it as an expression. He probably wanted to make Ryder feel good about their friendship...and the benefits that came with it.

Ryder appreciated it, but Branson didn't need to butter him up or affirm him. Maybe the man was still trying to compensate for crossing Ryder's boundaries in the beginning? Funny how Ryder barely even recalled those incidents. They were in the past, and he didn't waste any energy on them anymore. Branson had changed, and Ryder trusted him blindly now.

Who would've ever predicted that when they had just met? He'd considered Branson annoying, but that was a thing of the past as well. No, when he thought of Branson now, irritation was about the last thing he felt. It was more like...

He frowned. What *did* he feel?

"Chéri?" Branson shot him a worried look sideways as he placed the popcorn on the coffee table.

"Hang on, please. Give me a moment. I'm trying to... Just wait, please."

A weird storm of feelings brewed inside him, too complex to disentangle. All he knew was that he wanted Branson, *needed* him. He ached to touch him and to be touched, but it wasn't sex he wanted. Not the rough fuck he usually craved, the way Branson could make him feel alive with every thrust, every touch. No, he wanted something much softer, something tender and surprising.

He needed Branson's comfort. His companionship, his cuddles. Ryder gave in to that urge and scooted over, begging Branson with a wordless plea to accept him. Branson's smile was sweet as he lifted his arm and pulled Ryder close. Ryder rested his cheek on Branson's naked chest, his heart beating steadily underneath his ear.

Branson stroked his hair. "You okay?"

"Mmm."

Branson brushed his thumb over Ryder's bottom lip. "You don't look okay."

"I feel...weird."

"Weird how?"

He shouldn't tell him. This was where his filter, malfunctioning as it was, needed to kick in and prevent him from blurting out things he'd regret later. The rules had been clear: sex only. Except Branson had hinted he wanted more as well—hints Ryder had dismissed until now as figments of his imagination—and now Ryder was feeling...feelings. Whatever that softness inside him was.

"My head is tired," he finally said. "And I don't want sex."

He'd added the last part for the sake of clarity.

"We're on the same page, then, because I'm not in the mood either."

"No?"

Branson swiped a lock of hair off Ryder's forehead. "No, not in the least. I just wanna hold you, if that's okay."

"Mmm."

Branson wrapped his arms around him tighter, and the warmth and strength of his grip made Ryder feel safe and protected. He blew out a long breath, his mind finding a quiet peace.

"That's better," Branson said after a while.

"Huh?"

"You're relaxing. You were super tense before."

"Oh." He hadn't even noticed, but now that Branson mentioned it, he was feeling relaxed now. His cheek was parked against Branson's chest, the calm rhythm of his heartbeat soothing.

God, he loved being held like this, Branson's body so strong and comforting. Like a rock he could lean on. Branson would never cheat on him, would never ridicule him, would never make him feel like he wasn't good enough. He...

Oh, shit. How the fuck had he been this blind? Why hadn't he recognized it after being with Paul? Maybe because this felt so much bigger and scarier and at the same time so much more grounded and deeper.

"You're tensing up again." Branson blew softly over his head. "What's going on, chéri? Talk to me."

He should face him for this conversation, he really should, but Ryder couldn't make himself move. Not when he felt safe and protected. He'd found his knight in shining armor, and it had been the last person he'd expected it to be.

"I just had a realization. A profound one, you could say," he whispered.

Branson's hand stilled for a moment, then continued its gentle caress of Ryder's hair. "Do you want to talk about it?"

Did he? He should. He couldn't hide this from Branson, if only because he sucked at pretending anyway, and besides, why should he? If he was right—and now that he thought about it a bit more, he couldn't believe he'd missed all the signs and had misinterpreted the ones he had picked up on—Branson wouldn't get upset with him...or reject him. If he was right, this could be his happily ever after.

And so he took a deep breath. "I realized I've fallen in love with you." He swallowed. "I'm in love with you."

"Oh, chéri..." Branson's voice broke, and then Ryder was rolled onto his side, and Branson did the same, facing him. "Are you serious?"

"I'd never joke about something like this." Ryder was almost indignant until he noticed Branson's wary eyes. "Yes, I'm serious." He lifted his hand and stroked Branson's cheek. "I love you."

The full force of his feelings hit him as if saying it out loud had set them free, and he gasped. How had he been blind to the depth of his emotions?

"I'm *so* in love with you," Branson said, choked up. "Je t'aime, mon chéri. Je t'aime beaucoup."

Ryder beamed, recognizing those words even with his meager knowledge of the French language. "I guess you were right about us being perfect for each other." Then something occurred to him. "Did you know you loved me when you asked me to be your roommate?"

Branson pressed a kiss on the tip of Ryder's nose in a casual, intimate gesture that sent Ryder's heart in a gallop. "Consciously, no. But in hindsight, I fell for you a while ago, chéri."

"Well, I suppose us already living together only make things easy now that we're...whatever complicated level we've reached now."

Branson grinned. "Boyfriends, chéri. We're boyfriends. Nothing complicated about it."

Ryder stilled his hand on Branson's cheek. "Dorian knew it."

"What?"

"Dorian. He said something about... I don't remember what he said exactly, but I'm pretty sure he'd picked up on my feelings for you. Not that that's hard. I can't act worth shit, as we've already established..."

Branson chuckled. "Now that I've been promoted to boyfriend, what are my chances of seeing that tape of you in Macbeth?"

Ryder groaned. "Can't really refuse anymore, can I?"

"Nope. I'll exercise my rights as your boyfriend to the fullest. But no worries, it comes with perks as well."

"It does?"

Branson nodded. "Like being allowed to kiss me whenever you feel the urge."

"Oh, that's good to know. So if I'd feel a desire to kiss you, like, right now, I could act on it?"

"You totally can. Fully within your rights as my boyfriend."

Ryder kissed him. How could he not after that exchange? The kiss felt different. Oh, Branson's lips were as soft as always, and they tasted just as perfect. But the kiss was so much softer, sweet and tender, with none of the franticness they usually experienced. Ryder slipped his tongue into Branson's mouth, where it encountered Branson's. Their tempo was lazy and unhurried as they roamed each other's mouths, licking and sliding, nibbling and sucking. Ryder wanted to kiss him forever.

"Chéri..." Branson whispered against his lips.

"Mmm?"

"I'd like to make love to you..."

Branson's eyes were so full of love warmth spread through Ryder. How had he missed that before? And where before, he hadn't been in the mood for sex—or at least, not for their usual rough fuck—this proposal made his heart sing and his body heat up already. Making love for the first time...

"Yes, please. In the bedroom."

Branson smiled. "Yes. No sex on the couch."

See? They were totally on the same page.

Hand in hand, they made their way to the bedroom, where they both stripped and found each other again on Branson's bed. *Their* bed. "I'm moving into your bedroom," Ryder said. "Your bed is much more comfortable than mine."

"And that's the only reason?"

Ryder rolled his eyes. "If I have to explain that to you, we may need to explore the meaning of the words 'I love you.' Not sure you've fully grasped the concept."

He'd barely finished when Branson had covered his

mouth with his own and was kissing him again. "I understood just fine, chéri. You're mine now, and I want you in my bed every night."

Possessiveness was hot. Really hot.

"For now, just let me show you how much I love you..." Branson started a trail of kisses downward. He nuzzled Ryder's neck, following the path with his lips and tongue.

He smoothed his hand down Ryder's chest, his mouth agape with a look of awe that meant more to Ryder than any words would have, though he doubted he'd grow tired of hearing Branson tell him he loved him anytime soon. When Branson reached his left nipple, he flicked it, then rubbed and pinched until it was all red and swollen. The other one got the same treatment.

Branson leaned in and lapped on a nipple, making it all wet and shiny. Ryder, propped up on some pillows, couldn't look away. Branson kept licking, then sucked his nipple, and shoots of electricity coursed through Ryder's body. Fuck, Branson was *killing* him.

Featherlight kisses traveled down his chest until he hit his belly button, which he sucked and kissed, then flat out tongued. Who the fuck knew a belly button could be an erogenous zone? Branson Grove, that was who. Ryder almost felt like a virgin, discovering things about himself he'd never known.

More kisses, a whole shower of them down his happy trail, straight to his cock. He couldn't help but think of Paul, who had so rarely taken the time to appreciate Ryder's body, to show him he loved him...but then again, he hadn't. Not really. No, Ryder didn't want to waste any more energy on Paul. He'd taken enough from Ryder. Ryder had found his forever man, and he was going to enjoy every second with him.

43

He was so goddamn beautiful, the way he lay there, all spread out for Branson. His skin creamy white, his cock red with desire, his eyes dark with want. Perfection. And best of all? Ryder loved him. How had Branson gotten this lucky?

"Bran..." Ryder all but whined, clearly trying to get Branson to move on to his cock. But Branson had something else in mind first. He grabbed Ryder's hips, then yanked him down so he lay flat on his back. Ryder, smart as he was, pulled up his legs and spread them wide, offering Branson full access. Oh, yes.

He dropped on his belly, his mouth so close he breathed over Ryder's leaking cock, making it jump. Ryder had kept waxing himself, and how Branson loved that. He'd never minded some hair down there, but fuck, the sensation of those smooth balls and that perfect little pink hole were out of this world.

He sucked his balls first, the nuts perfectly proportioned to fit in his mouth. Not enough men understood how amazing that felt, both for the giver and the taker. Branson rolled one around in his mouth, then sucked gently, using his tongue for more pressure. They tightened even further in his mouth.

When he let them go, they were glistening, and Ryder had resorted to begging in an endless stream of moans and whimpers. Branson couldn't understand half of it, but the gist was clear. More. Well, he'd get his wish. Branson intended to drive him crazy.

He looked up at him, but Ryder had his eyes closed, his hands clutching the sheets. Branson returned his attention to the job at hand: Ryder's cock, all flushed with a trail of precum dripping from the tip to his stomach. Oh, the urge to take him into his mouth was overwhelming, but he wanted something else first. He so rarely did this because he'd never felt comfortable enough with hookups, but with Ryder, everything was different.

And so Branson put his hands on Ryder's thighs, spread them even wider, then bent his head and lapped a stripe right across Ryder's hole.

"Fuck!" Ryder cried out. "Ohfuckohfuck... Do that again? Please?"

Branson grinned. As if he was going to stop now. Hell no. He was just getting started. He licked again, loving the way Ryder gasped and twitched beneath him. And fuck, he tasted good. Branson dug in, piercing that pink hole with his tongue, nibbling on the surrounding flesh until it was all soft and flushed, and then he entered him with the tip of his tongue.

Every breathy whimper, every unintelligible plea spurred him on until he was straight up making love to that pretty star, kissing and licking and sucking and fucking it until Ryder's hands laced through Branson's hair and his grip became painful. "I can't..." Ryder all but sobbed. "I can't hold back anymore."

"You don't have to. Let it go." Branson was a little surprised Ryder would even try to restrain himself.

"No. No, I want you to be inside me... Want to feel you stretching me. Don't wanna come without you. Together. It needs to be together."

A deep satisfaction filled Branson. Ryder's need to be connected to him was more arousing than any porn had ever been. He snatched the lube off the nightstand, then pumped some onto his fingers. Prep should be a breeze after his thorough rimming, and indeed it was. Within a minute, Ryder was ready.

Branson coated his own cock. No condom. They'd gotten rid of those even before they'd made their relationship official, but Branson hadn't fully gotten used to it. He loved how much more intimate it felt...and god, the sight of his cum dripping out of Ryder's ass? Hottest. Thing. Ever.

Ryder drew his knees to his chest and tucked his arms beneath them, spreading himself wide open. Branson stretched out on top of him, his weight on his knees as he sank inside him. He tried to go slow, he really did, but oh, that ass sucked him in. Ryder was needy and greedy, and Branson fucking loved it.

Ryder bit on his lip as he took Branson in inch by inch, the expression on his face alternating between pleasure and discomfort. "Too fast?" Branson checked.

"No, no... Just... Fuck, you stretch me so wide."

Branson slowly sank in all the way, and when he bottomed out, Ryder let go of his legs and clamped them around Branson, clinging to him as if he never wanted to let him go. Ryder blindly sought Branson's mouth, and he caught his lips in an unending kiss, staying buried deep inside him, not even moving. Just being with him was enough, Ryder's body clenching around his cock, his breath dancing over Branson's skin, his moans music to his ears.

He pulled out only an inch, then slid back in, gentle and deep. His lips never left Ryder's as he set a soothing pace. At times, they only rested against Ryder's, their breaths intermingling, their quiet moans meeting each other, their hearts as close as their bodies, beating in the same rhythm.

"I love you," Branson mumbled. "I love you so much."

"Mmm. Love you too."

Branson didn't grow tired of the slow pace, of the graceful way his hips moved as he filled Ryder's body again and again. He wanted it to last forever, this feeling of being one. Ryder had slung his hands around Branson, his fingers digging into his neck, then his shoulders. His legs hitched higher around Branson's waist, allowing him to pull out a little more before thrusting back in.

Time passed, but they were above it. Nothing else existed but them, their bodies as close as humanly possible. He'd remember this forever, the first time they'd made love. They rocked together, moving completely in sync, and Branson's orgasm built up so slowly he thought he'd be able to last for hours. Every time he closed in on it, he slowed down again, not wanting it to end yet.

Until he reached the point where he had to come, the tension in his body uncomfortable, and his muscles were screaming. He was exhausted, every part of his body aching, but that was a small price to pay for this magical experience.

"I gotta come, chéri," he said. "Can't hold it anymore."

"Same. Together, babe."

Ryder had called him babe. Power surged through Branson, giving him a boost that made him feel like he could fly. Ryder slipped his hand between them, circling his own cock. Branson propped himself up on his trembling forearms, gathering his last bit of strength for the finish. One, two trusts, then one more...and his orgasm rolled over him as gentle and long as their lovemaking had been. Ryder's heated channel pulsed around him as he, too, came, spurting his load between them.

Branson flipped onto his back, bringing Ryder with him as they both lay panting, Ryder's cheek resting on Branson's shoulder. "I love you." Branson kissed the back of his head, since he couldn't reach anywhere else.

"Mmm."

Branson smiled. Wouldn't be the first time he'd fucked Ryder into oblivion...and, hopefully, not the last time either. What a thought that was, that he'd get to spend the rest of his life with this amazing man. On a whim, he kissed the top of his head again, then lifted him onto the mattress. "I'll be right back, chéri."

Ryder moaned in response, the tired grunt of someone too exhausted to lift a finger.

Branson's smile grew only wider as he walked into the bathroom and started running a bath, adding some salts Brenda had given him ages ago. They were supposed to be relaxing. Not that he cared. All he wanted was to take care of his man.

When he came back, Ryder had rolled onto his back, blinking sleepily at Branson. "That was amazing."

"It was. Time to clean you up."

"Can I stay here just a little longer? I promise I'll wash the sheets right after."

"I've got something better for you, chéri."

He bent and lifted Ryder out of bed. He flailed his arms and squealed as he clung to Branson. "What are you doing?"

Branson made sure he had a good grip on him, then

carried him to the bathroom. "We're taking a bath together, my love."

Ryder's smile blossomed into a big, beaming one. "Look at you being all romantic."

Branson kissed his nose. "You deserve all the romance, chéri. I'd give you the moon if I could."

Damn, he'd never known he was capable of saying things like that, let alone *feel* them into the very depths of his soul. Love was amazing, wasn't it?

Maneuvering the two of them into the bathtub was a tight fit, but they made it work, Ryder settling on Branson's lap. Branson let the tub run as full as he dared, then turned off the faucet. Ryder let out a sigh, then sagged against him, his body relaxed. "Thank you."

"My pleasure, chéri."

"Bran?" Ryder asked after a long pause.

"Hmm?"

"What's the next step for us? I don't want to presume, but we're not twenty anymore, and I know you've been serious about wanting a relationship."

"We'll go as slow as you need to. I understand if you need some time to adjust to—"

"I don't."

Hope blossomed in Branson's heart. "No?"

"No. Once I make a decision, I'm all in."

"In that case, I'd love for you to meet my parents. I told them about you, and they're dying to meet you."

Ryder let out a soft gasp. "You talked to them about me?"

"Mmm. I said I'd found my person."

"I didn't tell my parents about you." Ryder sounded guilty. "Well, that's not entirely true. I informed them I was becoming your roommate, but not about the rest of our... arrangement. Which has now expanded even more."

Branson chuckled at Ryder's choice of words. "We'll call it the platinum upgrade."

Ryder laughed, then grew serious again. "I want to introduce you to them. And to Dorian, though he's already met you. He's going to be so happy for me...even if he'll say 'I told you so' a million times first."

"He's earned that right, I'd say. Would you be okay with being open about it at work?"

Ryder groaned. "Oh god, now I have to tell Weston we're boyfriends after all. I'm never going to live that one down, am I?"

"Probably not, but it'll be worth it, right?"

"I suppose so..."

"You suppose?" Branson squeezed Ryder's ass underwater.

"Ow! Okay, okay... Of course it'll be worth it. But it's still humiliating."

"I'll be right there with you, chéri. We'll blame me. How's that? I can take it."

"I can take it as well."

"I know, but let me take care of you, please? We'll throw me under the bus so all teasing will be directed at me."

Ryder looped his hand backward around Branson's neck. "I already like having a boyfriend."

"Me too." The warmth in Branson's heart spread a thousandfold. "Me too, chéri."

44

Four weeks later, in the middle of the night, Branson's phone rang, and they were both awake instantly. Ryder looked at his watch. Three a.m. Nothing good would ever come from phone calls at this time.

"Mom?" Branson said as he picked up the phone, sitting on the edge of the bed. Ryder rolled out of bed so he could stand right next to him. He grabbed the hand Branson offered him, threading their fingers together.

"Oh, god... Will he be okay?" Branson's voice broke at the end, and Ryder squeezed his hand as Branson's mom answered him, too soft for Ryder to hear.

"Does Brenda know?"

All Ryder could pick up was the word *mission*.

"We're on our way."

Branson ended the call, and his eyes were tearing up as he looked up at Ryder. "My dad was rushed to the hospital with sky-high fever and abdominal pain. They suspect the tumor has broken through the walls of his remaining bit of colon, and they're doing emergency surgery."

That didn't sound good. "Let's head over."

"I...I'm scared," Branson whispered, not moving.

Ryder pulled his head against his stomach and held him tight. "I know."

He didn't know what else to say. Platitudes were useless and could even be a lie. He wasn't going to tell him everything would be fine or some shit. If it turned out he was wrong, he'd never forgive himself, and worse, Branson might not either.

"Thank you for being there," Branson said, his eyes closed as he leaned into Ryder, hugging him with all his might. "I don't know how I'd do this without you."

"I love you. That means I'm here for all of it, the good and the bad stuff, including moments like this. Don't thank me for that. It's what you do when you love someone."

"Oh, chéri..." Branson inhaled deeply. "I love you too. You're the best thing that ever happened to me."

Ryder kissed the top of his head. "We need to go, babe."

"Yeah."

Branson let go, then rose, stumbling as if he'd snapped out of a haze. Good. He could take this time to process his emotions later, but right now, they needed to get their asses to the hospital. If things went wrong, he'd need to be there for his mom.

They got dressed quickly, and Ryder grabbed some meal bars, which would come in handy if they had to spend the day there. They rushed out the door, and Branson slid into the passenger seat without asking. Ryder was happy he didn't have to convince him that driving himself wasn't a good idea. At least it should be a quick trip in the dead of night.

"I heard you ask about your sister," he said a few minutes later. "What did your mom say?"

"She's on a mission, so she can't be reached right now."

"When will she be able to communicate again?"

"In twenty-four hours, Mom said."

That could be too late. Ryder didn't say it. Why would he? Branson knew that as well as he did, and voicing it out loud wouldn't change anything.

"We knew when she was commissioned there would be moments like this when her job takes priority over everything else. Dad wouldn't want her to abort a mission for him. In fact, he'd kick her ass if she did." Branson smiled softly. "He's always been incredibly proud of her, and he'd understand if she can't come right now."

"I think he's very proud of both of you."

"He is...and so is my mom."

They were silent after that, but Branson had put his hand on Ryder's thigh, and that small gesture of intimacy made him feel connected to him, even when Ryder couldn't touch him back.

When they arrived at the hospital, they found Branson's mom in a waiting room, slouching in a seat and looking pale and stressed. No wonder.

"Mom," Branson said. She jumped up and stepped into his embrace. Ryder's heart clenched as he watched them, their pain and worry so palpable.

When they let go, tears were dripping down her cheeks. "Thanks for coming, honey."

Branson looked at Ryder. "Don't thank me, Mom. That's what you do when you love someone."

She smiled through her tears as she held out her arms to Ryder. "Thanks for coming with him, sweetie."

Ryder had met Branson's parents the day after they'd gotten together, and he'd loved them instantly. That feeling appeared to be mutual, just like Ryder's parents had welcomed Branson enthusiastically.

"My pleasure, Mrs. Grove."

She released Ryder, then cupped his cheek. "Please, call me Lisa. You're family now."

And just like that, he belonged. Warmth filled Ryder's heart. "Thank you...Lisa."

"Have you heard any updates yet?" Branson asked.

"No, but they warned it could be a while. They weren't sure what they'd find during surgery. But even then, the high fever is worrisome. It could indicate sepsis."

Sepsis. Ryder didn't have any medical training, but he'd lived with a doctor long enough to know that one. It meant the infection had spread to the blood and could now travel throughout the entire body, possibly resulting in multi-organ failure. Paul had lost plenty of patients to sepsis over the years, and the ones that survived could have lasting effects, like damaged kidneys. If Branson's dad contracted sepsis on top of everything else, his already weakened immune system might not be able to fight it off.

Judging by the shock on Branson's face, he knew that too. Words were useless here. Nothing he said would make Branson feel better, so he'd better try to do something practical for him. "Why don't I get us some coffee?" he said. "Would you like coffee too, Lisa?"

She nodded with a grateful smile. "Thank you, sweetie. Milk and sugar, please."

"Sure thing."

He left them by themselves as he set course for a coffee machine. Good thing he knew his way around a bit, having spent plenty of time waiting here for Paul to be done with work. The coffee was horrible, but it was warm and had caffeine, and right now, that trumped everything else. He'd just gotten the second cup and was placing a third when someone gasped behind him.

"Ryder?"

Shit. Paul. He recognized his voice without even turning around. He should've known he'd run into him here at some point.

"What's up, Paul?" he said, pushing the buttons for coffee with milk and sugar. He already had two black coffees for him and Branson, and he grabbed lids and put them on.

"What are you doing here?" Paul walked up to him and stopped so close to his right he couldn't ignore him anymore. With a mental sigh, Ryder faced him.

"My boyfriend's father is in surgery, so I'm here to support him."

Paul appeared stunned for a moment, but then he scoffed. "Boyfriend? That's a bit of a sad lie, don't you think?"

A lie? Paul thought he was making it up? Ryder looked at him, the man he'd once loved. He'd thought him so hot, especially in the scrubs he was wearing now as well. That whole arrogant I'm-a-hotshot-doctor vibe had done it for him, though now he wondered why.

Yes, objectively speaking, Paul was good looking—six foot two, with a pair of startling blue eyes, and in great shape—but his beauty was only on the surface. His eyes didn't have the warmth and the joy that Branson's had. His smile was calculating, never spontaneous and sweet. If he even smiled at all. He was perfect on the outside but so cold and shallow inside. Everything he did was to make him look good, never for someone else. The man didn't have a selfless cell in his body, and if he did, he'd shoved it deep down where no one would ever see it.

"Why the hell would I feel the need to lie to you about having a boyfriend?" he asked.

"'Cause you don't want to look like a loser in front of me?"

Seriously, he thought that? It only showed Paul didn't know him at all. "I'd think that after having been together for five years, you'd know I've never given two fucks about what anyone else thinks. That was always you, Paul, not me."

Paul's eyes narrowed. "We broke up five months ago. Are you really trying to convince me you found someone else in such a short time?"

How had he always ignored how mean Paul could be with these thinly veiled barbs and insults? He'd been so fucking blind. Dorian had always seen it. Maybe that was why Paul had never liked him. Before, he would've ignored it or tried to apologize or do something else to fix it, but he was so done with that. "First of all, I'm not trying to convince you of anything. You asked why I was here, and I answered your question. Second, at the risk of repeating myself, I'm not bothered even in the least by what you think or don't think of me. And third, the implied insult that I would never be able to find another boyfriend is, quite frankly, low and mean, even for you."

Paul looked stunned for a moment. "What else am I supposed to think when you lied to me before?"

"Lied to you? About what?"

"Look, I know you must've felt...inferior, considering I'm a doctor and you're an accountant, but I didn't understand why you had to make up some job working for the CIA."

What the actual fuck? Paul thought he'd been lying about that? He'd been in the application process when they'd still been together, but he hadn't started working there until after they'd broken up. And Paul thought he'd made that up? "Not that I need to defend or explain myself to you, but I *do* work for the CIA as a forensic accountant. And for your information, I've never felt inferior because of your job. I felt small because you made me feel that way, because you constantly criticized and belittled me, making me think everything was my fault...while all that time, you were screwing around behind my back, violating the promise of monogamy we had made to each other."

Paul stood frozen to the spot, his eyes wide. "You work for the CIA?"

"Holy shit, was I speaking a foreign language? Yes, Paul, I do. Why the fuck would you think I'd lie about that? I don't lie, and I don't pretend. If nothing else, you should've known that about me by now."

"I thought you were bragging, making things up to look more important, to compete with me."

Ryder rolled his eyes as he took Lisa's coffee and put a lid on it. "It's not a competition. It never was, at least for me. I loved you, and I gave you everything I had...almost literally. We both know you fucking cleaned me out, and I deserved so much better."

For the first time, Paul looked guilty. "I feel bad about that in hindsight. I should've paid you back. I can give you—"

"I don't want your money. I want nothing from you except to leave me alone. Nothing you can say or do will ever make up for what you did to me, how you betrayed me and my feelings for you. But it's all in the past now. Believe it or don't believe it, the choice is yours, but I know the truth. I do have a boyfriend, and he's amazing. He loves me just the way I am without wanting to change me, and I love him more than I ever thought I was capable of. I'm happy, happier than I've ever been...and I don't give a flying fuck whether you believe it or what your opinions are on that. Have a great life, Paul. Just leave me out of it."

He stared at the coffees. How would he be able to take all three? Maybe clamp one between his arm and his chest? Branson popped up next to him, and he startled. "I'll take two, chéri. You just grab that last one."

"Thanks, babe."

Ryder smiled at him, relieved that this whole conversation with Paul was over. He was done with him, he had been for a long time, and all he wanted now was to walk away and not look back. "Let's go back to your mom."

Paul stepped aside. When they were at the door, Branson turned around. "Ryder forgot to mention that we're not only perfect together but that the sex is spectacular as well. Best sex either of us has ever had, right, chéri?"

Ryder managed to keep it together long enough to answer. "Damn right."

As soon as they were in the hallway, Ryder stopped Branson, curled his free hand around the man's neck, and pulled his head in for a fierce kiss. "Thank you. I love you."

Branson winked at him. "My pleasure. Though you didn't need my help. You were doing a pretty good job of demolishing him all on your own."

"Yeah?"

They set off again, and Branson bumped his shoulder. "It was surprisingly hot to watch."

Ryder laughed. "Thank you once again. I'll remember that if I ever want to get you in the mood."

Branson grinned. "As if you ever have to work hard for that."

"True."

Branson lifted their joined hands and pressed a kiss on Ryder's. "I love you, chéri. You're my everything."

They were okay. No matter what the future would bring, they'd be okay...because they'd be together. Forever.

∽

We have one more book to go...Del's story. Coming in October!

FREEBIES

If you love FREE novellas and bonus chapters, head on over to my website where I offer bonus scenes for several of my books, as well as as two free novellas. Grab them here: https://www.noraphoenix.com/free-stuff/

BOOKS BY NORA PHOENIX

🎧 indicates book is also available as audio book

White House Men

A romantic suspense series set in the White House that combines romance with suspense, a dash of kink, and all the feels.

- **Press** (rivals fall in love in an impossible love) 🎧
- **Friends** (friends to lovers between an FBI and a Secret Service agent) 🎧
- **Click** (a sexy first-time romance with an age gap and an awkward virgin) 🎧
- **Serve** (a high heat MMM romance with age gap and D/s play) 🎧
- **Care** (the president's son falls for his tutor; age gap and daddy kink) 🎧
- **Puzzle** (a CIA analyst meets his match in a nerdy forensic accountant)
- **Heal** (can the president find love again with a sunshine man half his age?)

No Regrets Series

Sexy, kinky, emotional, with a touch of suspense, the No Regrets series is a spin off from the No Shame series that can be read on its own.

- **No Surrender** (bisexual awakening, first time gay, D/s play) 🎧

Perfect Hands Series

Raw, emotional, both sweet and sexy, with a solid dash of kink, that's the Perfect Hands series. All books can be read as standalones.

- **Firm Hand** (daddy care with a younger daddy and an older boy) 🎧
- **Gentle Hand** (sweet daddy care with age play) 🎧
- **Naughty Hand** (a holiday novella to read after Firm Hand and Gentle Hand) 🎧
- **Slow Hand** (a Dom who never wanted to be a Daddy takes in two abused boys) 🎧
- **Healing Hand** (a broken boy finds the perfect Daddy) 🎧

No Shame Series

If you love steamy MM romance with a little twist, you'll love the No Shame series. Sexy, emotional, with a bit of suspense and all the feels. Make sure to read in order, as this is a series with a continuing storyline.

- **No Filter** 🎧
- **No Limits** 🎧
- **No Fear** 🎧
- **No Shame** 🎧

- **No Angel** 🎧

And for all the fun, grab the **No Shame box set** 🎧 which includes all five books plus exclusive bonus chapters and deleted scenes.

Irresistible Omegas Series

An mpreg series with all the heat, epic world building, poly romances (the first two books are MMMM and the rest of the series is MMM), a bit of suspense, and characters that will stay with you for a long time. This is a continuing series, so read in order.

- **Alpha's Sacrifice** 🎧
- **Alpha's Submission** 🎧
- **Beta's Surrender** 🎧
- **Alpha's Pride** 🎧
- **Beta's Strength** 🎧
- **Omega's Protector** 🎧
- **Alpha's Obedience** 🎧
- **Omega's Power** 🎧
- **Beta's Love** 🎧
- **Omega's Truth** 🎧

Or grab *the first box set*, which contains books 1-3 plus exclusive bonus material and *the second box set*, which has books 4-6 and exclusive extras.

Ballsy Boys Series

Sexy porn stars looking for real love! Expect plenty of steam, but all the feels as well. They can be read as stand-alones, but are more fun when read in order.

- **Ballsy** (free prequel)
- **Rebel** 🎧
- **Tank** 🎧
- **Heart** 🎧
- **Campy** 🎧
- **Pixie** 🎧

Or grab *the box set*, which contains all five books plus an exclusive bonus novella!

Kinky Boys Series

Super sexy, slightly kinky, with all the feels.

- **Daddy** 🎧
- **Ziggy** 🎧

Ignite Series

An epic dystopian sci-fi trilogy (one book out, two more to follow) where three men have to not only escape a government that wants to jail them for being gay but aliens as well. Slow burn MMM romance.

- **Ignite** 🎧
- **Smolder** 🎧
- **Burn** 🎧

Now also available in a ***box set*** 🎧, which includes all three books, bonus chapters, and a bonus novella.

Stand Alones

I also have a few stand alones, so check these out!

- **Professor Daddy** (sexy daddy kink between a

college prof and his student. Age gap, no ABDL) 🎧
- **Out to Win** (two men meet at a TV singing contest) 🎧
- **Captain Silver Fox** (falling for the boss on a cruise ship) 🎧
- **Coming Out on Top** (snowed in, age gap, size difference, and a bossy twink) 🎧
- **Ranger** (struggling Army vet meets a sunshiney animal trainer - cowritten with K.M. Neuhold) 🎧

Books in German

Quite a few of my books have been translated into German, with more to come!

Indys Männer

- **Indys Flucht** No Filter)
- **Josh Wunsch** (No Limits)
- **Aarons Handler** (No Fear)
- **Brads Bedürfnisse** (No Shame)
- **Indys Weihnachten** (No Angel)

Mein Daddy Dom

- **Daddy Rhys** (Firm Hand)
- **Daddy Brendan** (Gentle Hand)
- **Weihnachten mit den Daddys** (Naughty Hand)
- **Daddy Ford** (Slow Hand)
- **Daddy Gale** (Healing Hand)

Das Hayes Rudel

- **Lidons Angebot** (Alpha's Sacrifice)

- **Enars Unterordnung** (Alpha's Submission)
- **Lars' Hingabe** (Beta's Surrender)
- **Brays Stolz** (Alpha's Pride)
- **Keans Stärke** (Beta's Strength)
- **Gias Beschützer** (Omega's Protector)
- **Levs Gehorsam** (Alpha's Obedience)
- **Sivneys Macht** (Omega's Power)
- **Lucans Liebe** (Beta's Love)
- **Sandos** Wahrheit (Omega's Truth)

Standalones

- **Mein Professor Daddy** (Professor Daddy)
- **Eingeschneit mit dem Bären** (Coming Out on Top)
- **Eine Nacht mit dem Kapitän** (Captain Silver Fox)
- **Ranger** (Ranger, cowritten with K.M. Neuhold)

Books in Other Languages

- **L'Occasione Della Vita** - Italian - The Time of my Life / Out to Win
- **Posizioni Inaspettate** - Italian - Coming Out on Top
- **L'offerta di Lidon** - Italian - Alpha's Sacrifice
- **La Sottomissione di Enar** - Italian - Alpha's Submission
- **Le Garçon du Professeur** - French - Professor Daddy
- **Une Main de Fer** - French - Firm Hand
- **Une Main de Velours** - French - Gentle Hand
- **Con Mano Firme** - Spanish - Firm Hand

MORE ABOUT NORA PHOENIX

Would you like the long or the short version of my bio?

The short? You got it.

I write steamy gay romance books and I love it. I also love reading books. Books are everything.

How was that?

A little more detail? Gotcha.

I started writing my first stories when I was a teen...on a freaking typewriter. I still have these, and they're adorably romantic. And bad, haha. Fear of failing kept me from following my dream to become a romance author, so you can imagine how proud and ecstatic I am that I finally overcame my fears and self doubt and did it. I adore my genre because I love writing and reading about flawed, strong men who are just a tad broken..but find their happy ever after anyway.

My favorite books to read are pretty much all MM/gay romances as long as it has a happy end. Kink is a plus... Aside from that, I also read a lot of nonfiction and not just books on writing. Popular psychology is a favorite topic of mine and so are self help and sociology.

Hobbies? Ain't nobody got time for that. Just kidding. I love traveling, spending time near the ocean, and hiking. But I love books more.

Come hang out with me in my Facebook Group Nora's Nook where I share previews, sneak peeks, freebies, fun stuff, and much more: https://www.facebook.com/groups/norasnook/

My weekly newsletter not only gives you updates, exclusive content, and all the inside news on what I'm working on, but also lists the best new releases, 99c deals, and freebies in gay romance for that weekend. Load up your Kindle for less money! Sign up here: http://www.noraphoenix.com/newsletter/

You can also stalk me on Twitter: @NoraFromBHR

On Instagram:

https://www.instagram.com/nora.phoenix/

On Bookbub:

https://www.bookbub.com/profile/nora-phoenix

Or become my patron on Patreon: https://www.patreon.com/noraphoenix

Printed in Great Britain
by Amazon